image comics presents

THE WALKING DEAD™

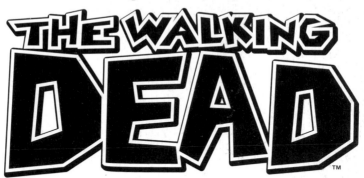

ROBERT KIRKMAN
CREATOR, WRITER

CHARLIE ADLARD
PENCILER

STEFANO GAUDIANO
INKER

CLIFF RATHBURN
GRAY TONES

RUS WOOTON
LETTERER

CHARLIE ADLARD
&
DAVE STEWART
COVER

SEAN MACKIEWICZ
EDITOR

SKYBOUND

For SKYBOUND ENTERTAINMENT

Robert Kirkman - CEO
J.J. Didde - President
Sean Mackiewicz - Editorial Director
Shawn Kirkham - Director of Business Development
Brian Huntington - Online Editorial Director
Helen Leigh - Office Manager
Lizzy Iverson - Administrative Assistant

For international rights inquiries,
please contact: foreign@skybound.com

WWW.SKYBOUND.COM

IMAGE COMICS, INC.
Robert Kirkman - Chief Operating Officer
Erik Larsen - Chief Financial Officer
Todd McFarlane - President
Marc Silvestri - Chief Executive Officer
Jim Valentino - Vice-President

Eric Stephenson - Publisher
Ron Richards - Director of Business Development
Jennifer de Guzman - Director of Trade Book Sales
Kat Salazar - Director of PR & Marketing
Jeremy Sullivan - Director of Digital Sales
Emilio Bautista - Sales Assistant
Branwyn Bigglestone - Senior Accounts Manager
Emily Miller - Accounts Manager
Jessica Ambriz - Administrative Assistant
Tyler Shainline - Events Coordinator
David Brothers - Content Manager
Jonathan Chan - Production Manager
Drew Gill - Art Director
Meredith Wallace - Print Manager
Monica Garcia - Senior Production Artist
Jenna Savage - Production Artist
Addison Duke - Production Artist
IMAGECOMICS.COM

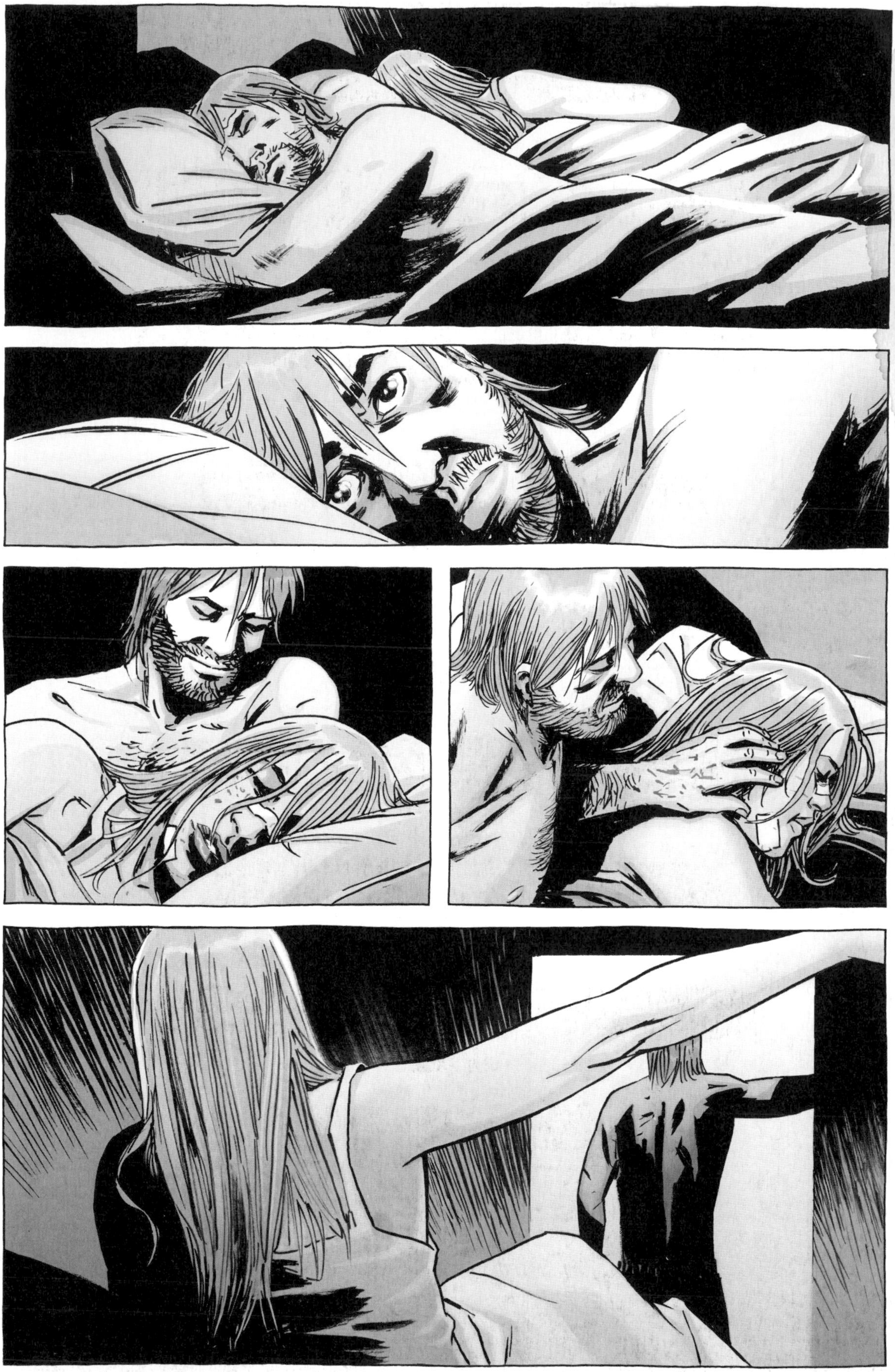

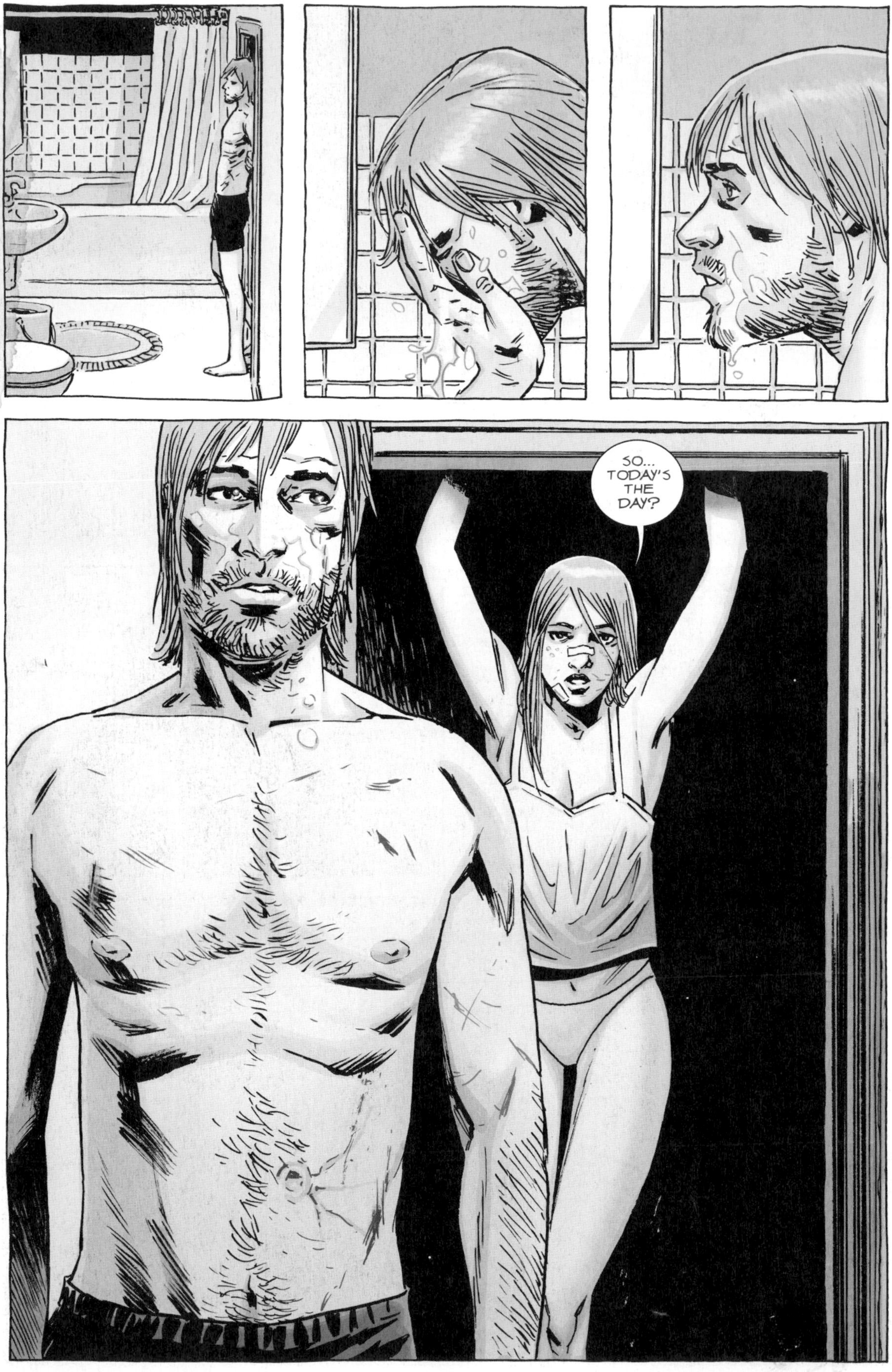
SO... TODAY'S THE DAY?

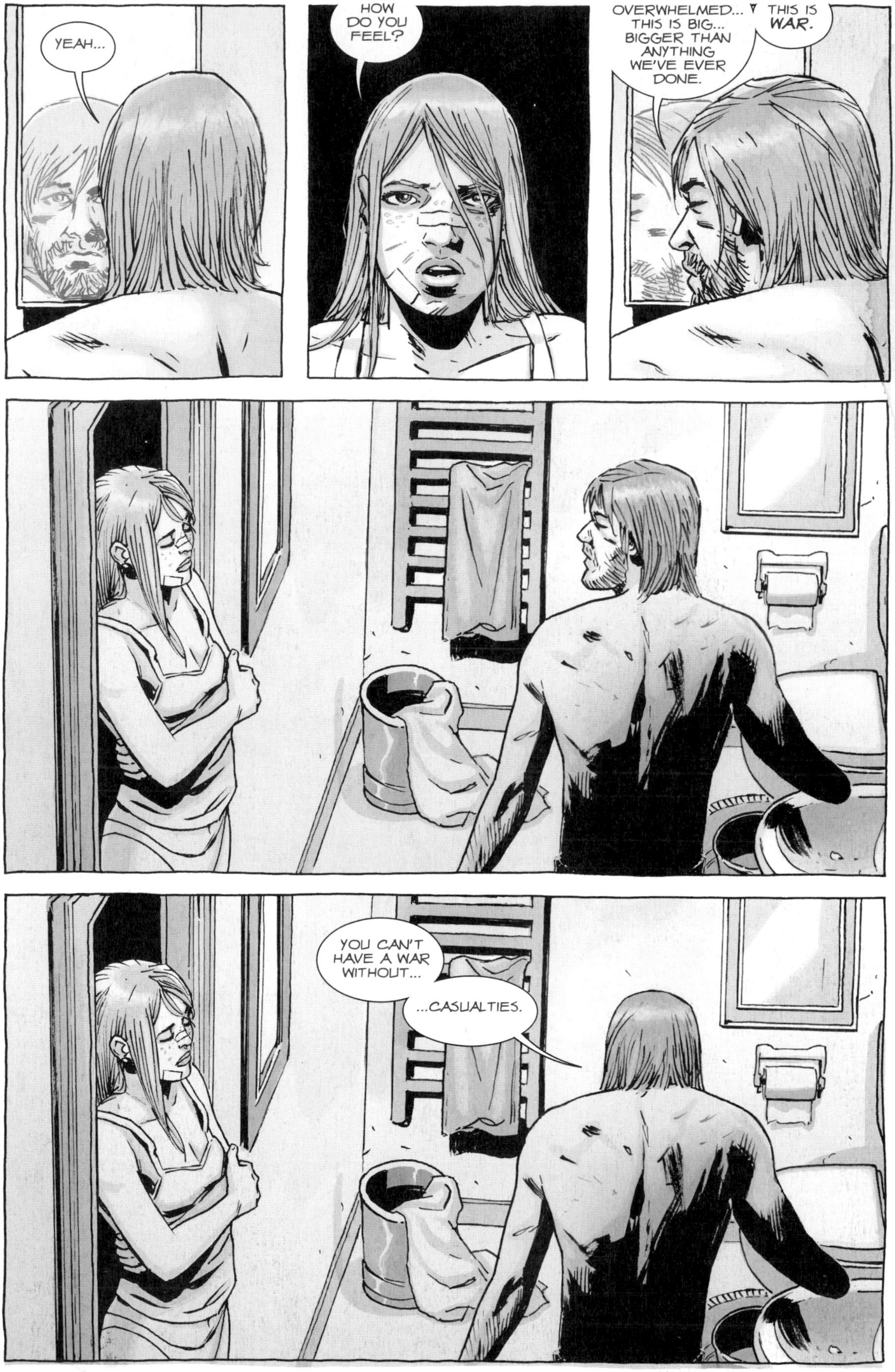
YEAH...
HOW DO YOU FEEL?
OVERWHELMED... THIS IS BIG... BIGGER THAN ANYTHING WE'VE EVER DONE.
THIS IS WAR.
YOU CAN'T HAVE A WAR WITHOUT...
...CASUALTIES.

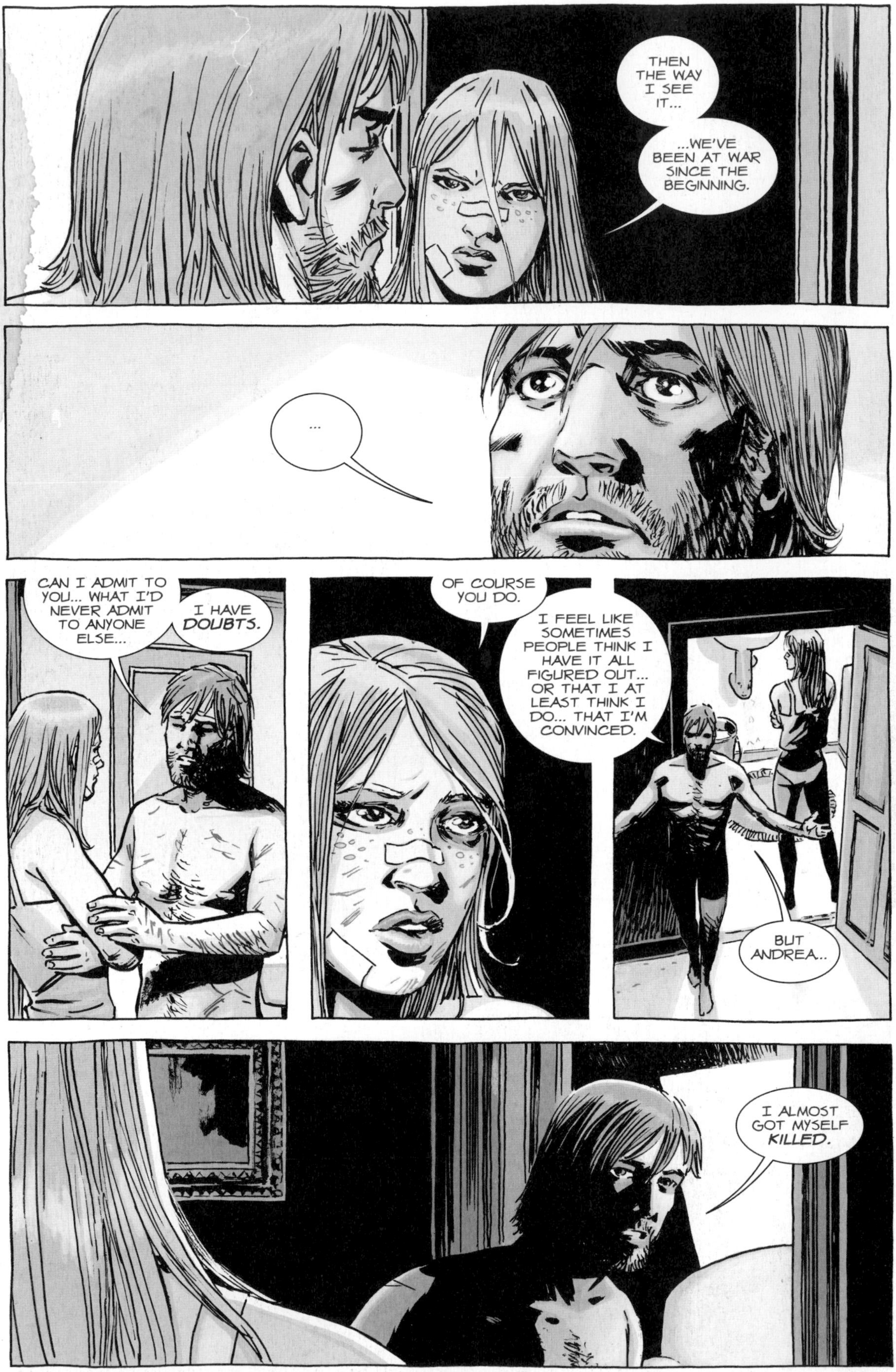
THEN THE WAY I SEE IT...
...WE'VE BEEN AT WAR SINCE THE BEGINNING.
...
CAN I ADMIT TO YOU... WHAT I'D NEVER ADMIT TO ANYONE ELSE...
I HAVE DOUBTS.
OF COURSE YOU DO.
I FEEL LIKE SOMETIMES PEOPLE THINK I HAVE IT ALL FIGURED OUT... OR THAT I AT LEAST THINK I DO... THAT I'M CONVINCED.
BUT ANDREA...
I ALMOST GOT MYSELF KILLED.

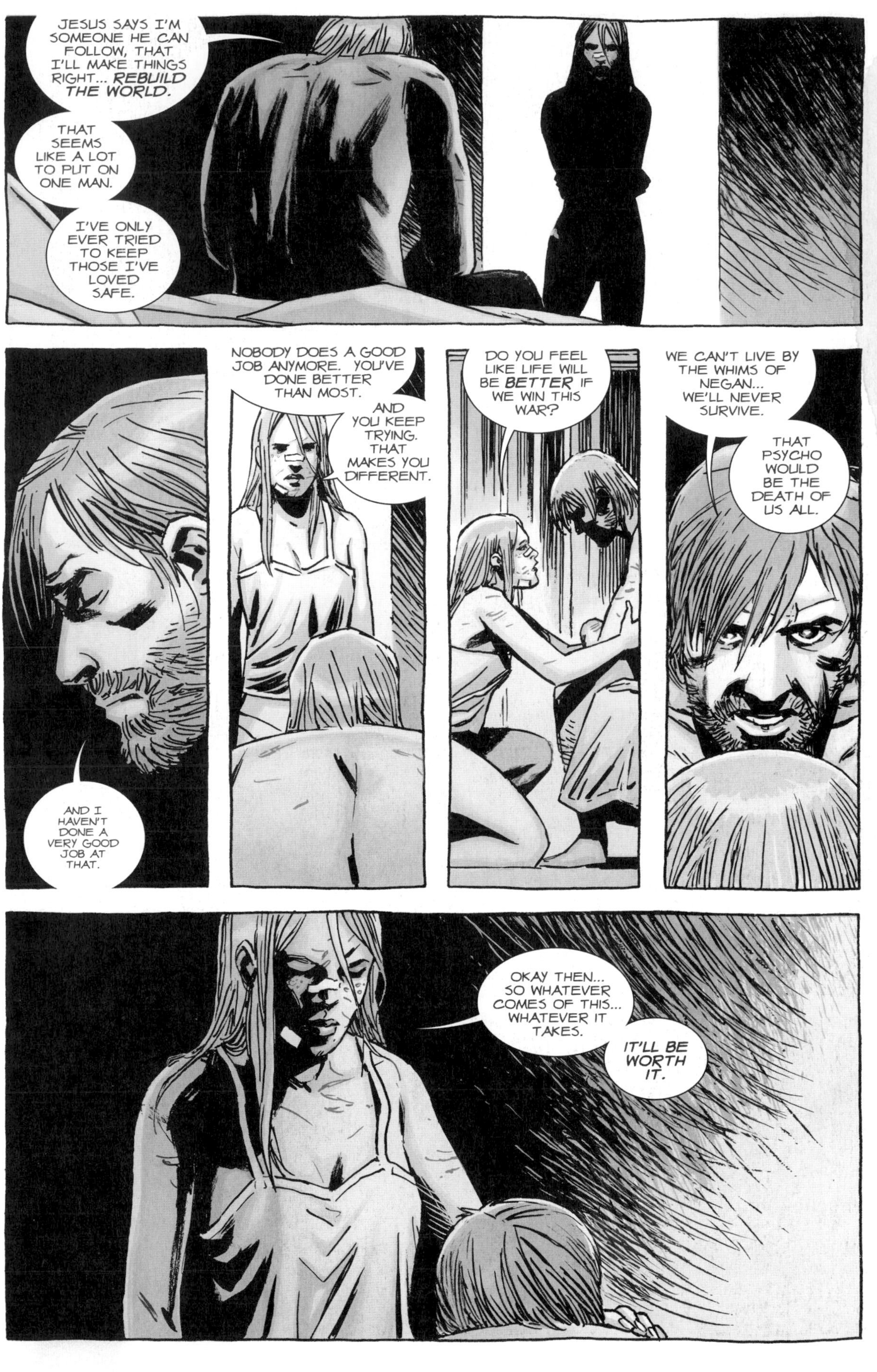
JESUS SAYS I'M SOMEONE HE CAN FOLLOW, THAT I'LL MAKE THINGS RIGHT... REBUILD THE WORLD.
THAT SEEMS LIKE A LOT TO PUT ON ONE MAN.
I'VE ONLY EVER TRIED TO KEEP THOSE I'VE LOVED SAFE.
AND I HAVEN'T DONE A VERY GOOD JOB AT THAT.
NOBODY DOES A GOOD JOB ANYMORE. YOU'VE DONE BETTER THAN MOST.
AND YOU KEEP TRYING. THAT MAKES YOU DIFFERENT.
DO YOU FEEL LIKE LIFE WILL BE BETTER IF WE WIN THIS WAR?
WE CAN'T LIVE BY THE WHIMS OF NEGAN... WE'LL NEVER SURVIVE.
THAT PSYCHO WOULD BE THE DEATH OF US ALL.
OKAY THEN... SO WHATEVER COMES OF THIS... WHATEVER IT TAKES.
IT'LL BE WORTH IT.

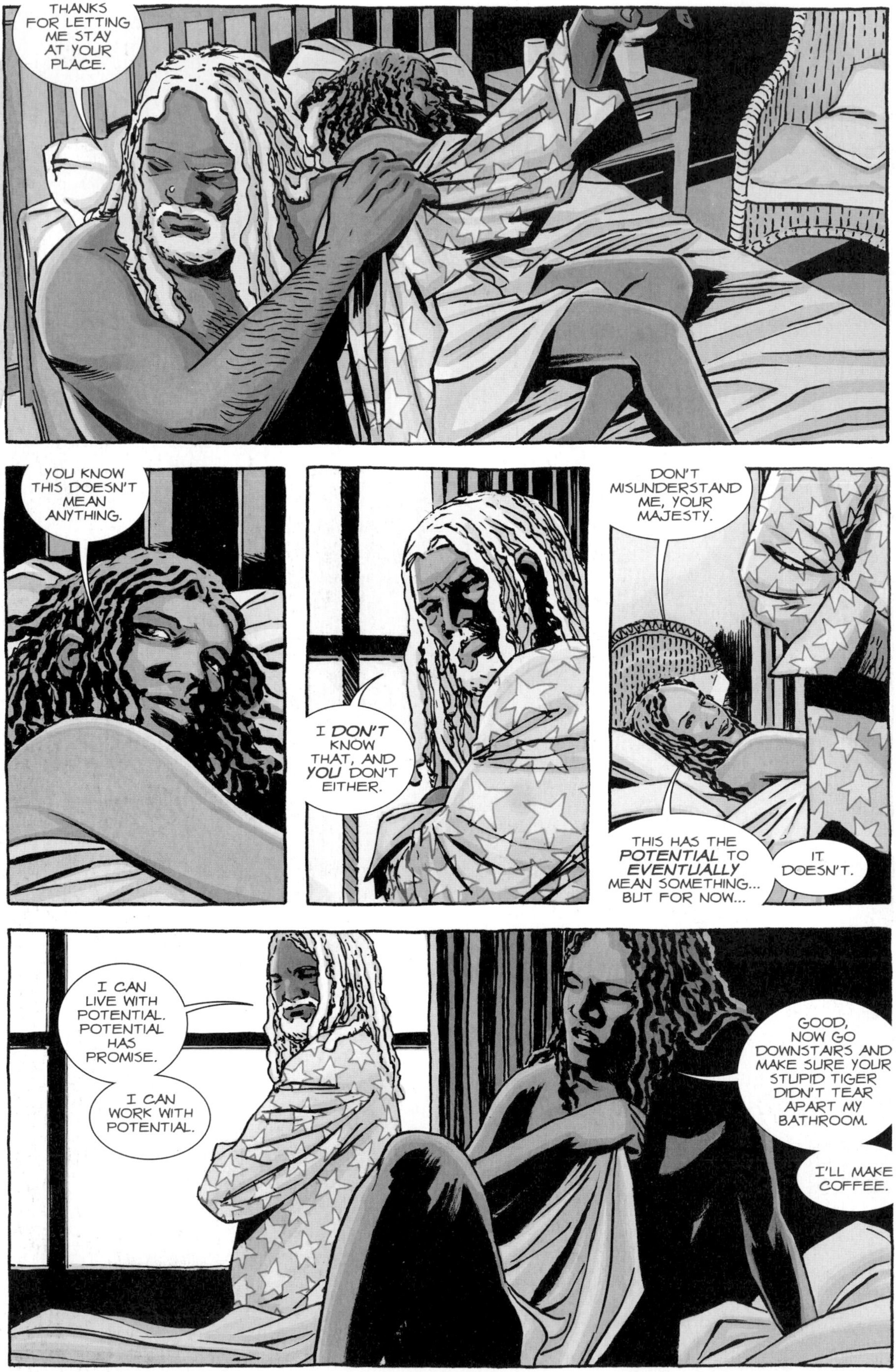
THANKS FOR LETTING ME STAY AT YOUR PLACE.
YOU KNOW THIS DOESN'T MEAN ANYTHING.
I DON'T KNOW THAT, AND YOU DON'T EITHER.
DON'T MISUNDERSTAND ME, YOUR MAJESTY.
THIS HAS THE POTENTIAL TO EVENTUALLY MEAN SOMETHING... BUT FOR NOW...
IT DOESN'T.
I CAN LIVE WITH POTENTIAL. POTENTIAL HAS PROMISE.
I CAN WORK WITH POTENTIAL.
GOOD, NOW GO DOWNSTAIRS AND MAKE SURE YOUR STUPID TIGER DIDN'T TEAR APART MY BATHROOM.
I'LL MAKE COFFEE.

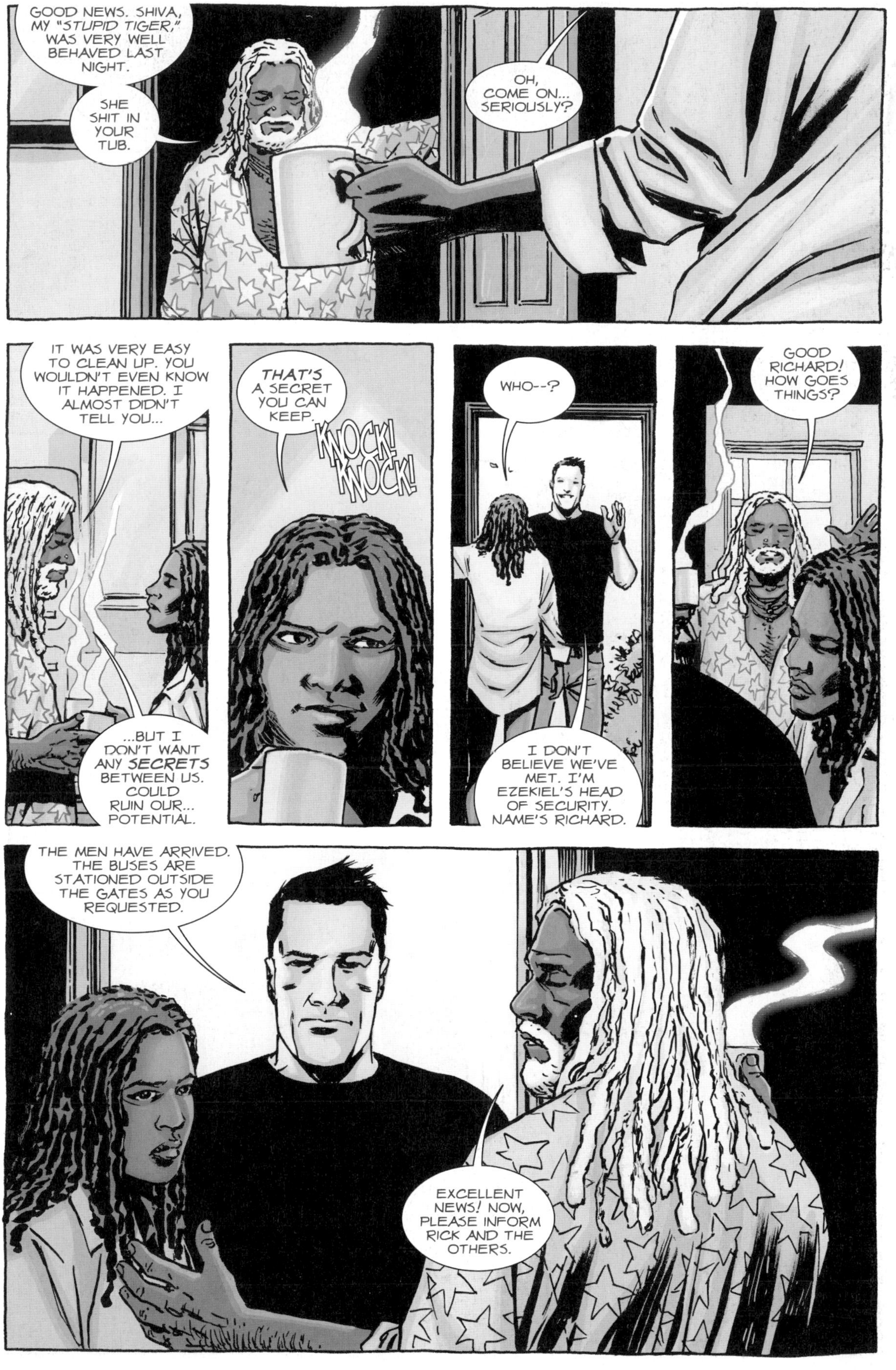

GOOD NEWS. SHIVA, MY "STUPID TIGER," WAS VERY WELL BEHAVED LAST NIGHT.
SHE SHIT IN YOUR TUB.
OH, COME ON... SERIOUSLY?
IT WAS VERY EASY TO CLEAN UP. YOU WOULDN'T EVEN KNOW IT HAPPENED. I ALMOST DIDN'T TELL YOU...
...BUT I DON'T WANT ANY SECRETS BETWEEN US. COULD RUIN OUR... POTENTIAL.
THAT'S A SECRET YOU CAN KEEP.
KNOCK! KNOCK!
WHO--?
I DON'T BELIEVE WE'VE MET. I'M EZEKIEL'S HEAD OF SECURITY. NAME'S RICHARD.
GOOD RICHARD! HOW GOES THINGS?
THE MEN HAVE ARRIVED. THE BUSES ARE STATIONED OUTSIDE THE GATES AS YOU REQUESTED.
EXCELLENT NEWS! NOW, PLEASE INFORM RICK AND THE OTHERS.

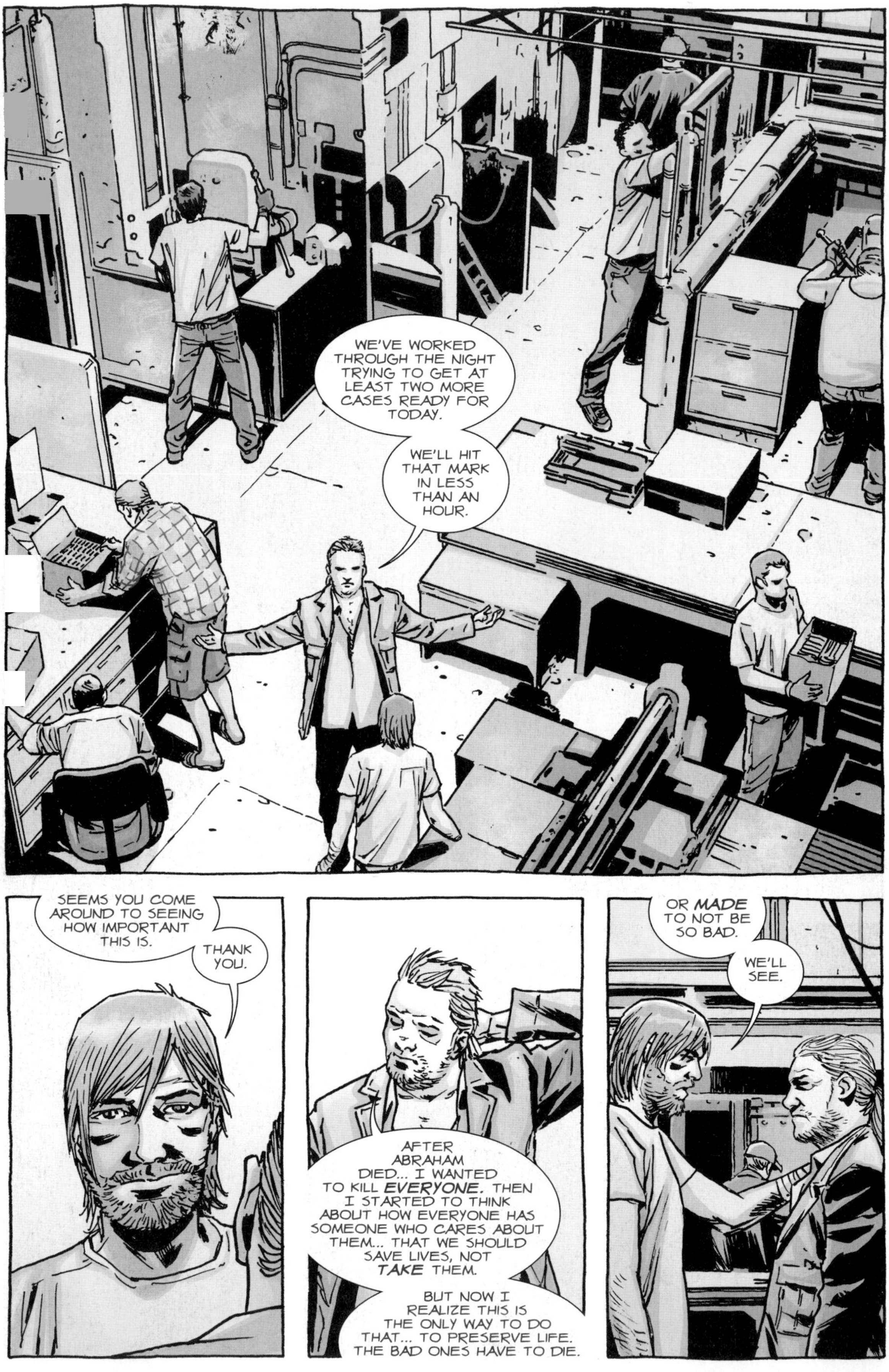
WE'VE WORKED THROUGH THE NIGHT TRYING TO GET AT LEAST TWO MORE CASES READY FOR TODAY.
WE'LL HIT THAT MARK IN LESS THAN AN HOUR.
SEEMS YOU COME AROUND TO SEEING HOW IMPORTANT THIS IS.
THANK YOU.
AFTER ABRAHAM DIED... I WANTED TO KILL *EVERYONE.* THEN I STARTED TO THINK ABOUT HOW EVERYONE HAS SOMEONE WHO CARES ABOUT THEM... THAT WE SHOULD SAVE LIVES, NOT *TAKE* THEM.
BUT NOW I REALIZE THIS IS THE ONLY WAY TO DO THAT... TO PRESERVE LIFE. THE BAD ONES HAVE TO DIE.
OR *MADE* TO NOT BE SO BAD.
WE'LL SEE.

TAKE AS MUCH TIME AS YOU NEED.

THANK YOU, FATHER.

I WANTED TO CALL THIS MEETING TO MAKE SURE THERE WEREN'T ANY LAST MINUTE DETAILS WE WERE OVERLOOKING BEFORE WE DO THIS.

ALL OUR PEOPLE ARE GATHERED, THE SUPPLIES ARE LOADED... WE'RE PREPARED TO MOVE.

MY PEOPLE ARE HERE... WE'RE READY TO GO.

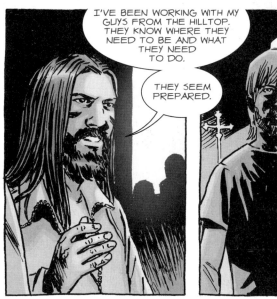

I'VE BEEN WORKING WITH MY GUYS FROM THE HILLTOP. THEY KNOW WHERE THEY NEED TO BE AND WHAT THEY NEED TO DO.

THEY SEEM PREPARED.

GOOD... LET'S GO OVER THE PLAN ONE MORE TIME...

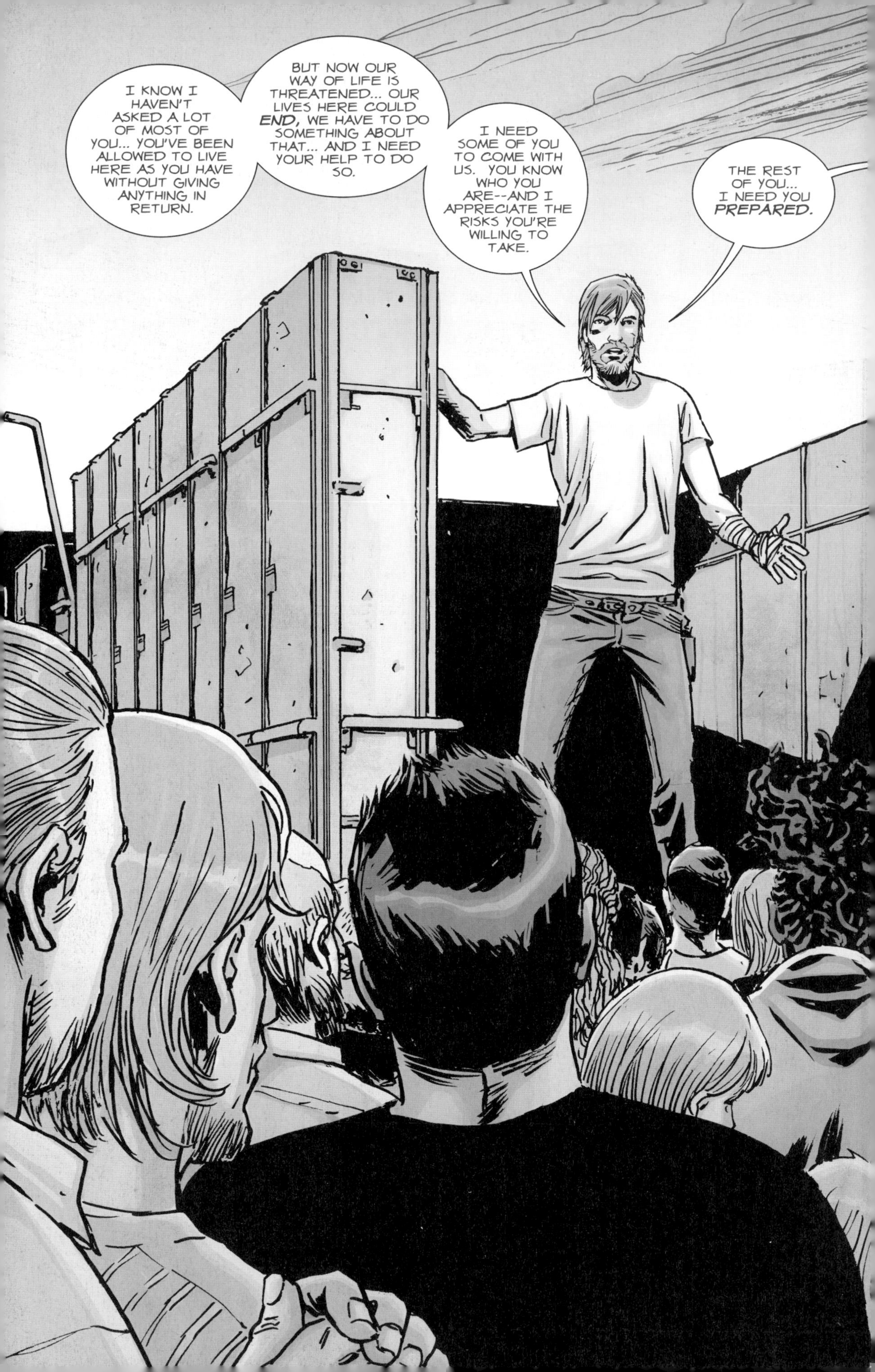
I KNOW I HAVEN'T ASKED A LOT OF MOST OF YOU... YOU'VE BEEN ALLOWED TO LIVE HERE AS YOU HAVE WITHOUT GIVING ANYTHING IN RETURN.
BUT NOW OUR WAY OF LIFE IS THREATENED... OUR LIVES HERE COULD **END,** WE HAVE TO DO SOMETHING ABOUT THAT... AND I NEED YOUR HELP TO DO SO.
I NEED SOME OF YOU TO COME WITH US. YOU KNOW WHO YOU ARE--AND I APPRECIATE THE RISKS YOU'RE WILLING TO TAKE.
THE REST OF YOU... I NEED YOU ***PREPARED.***

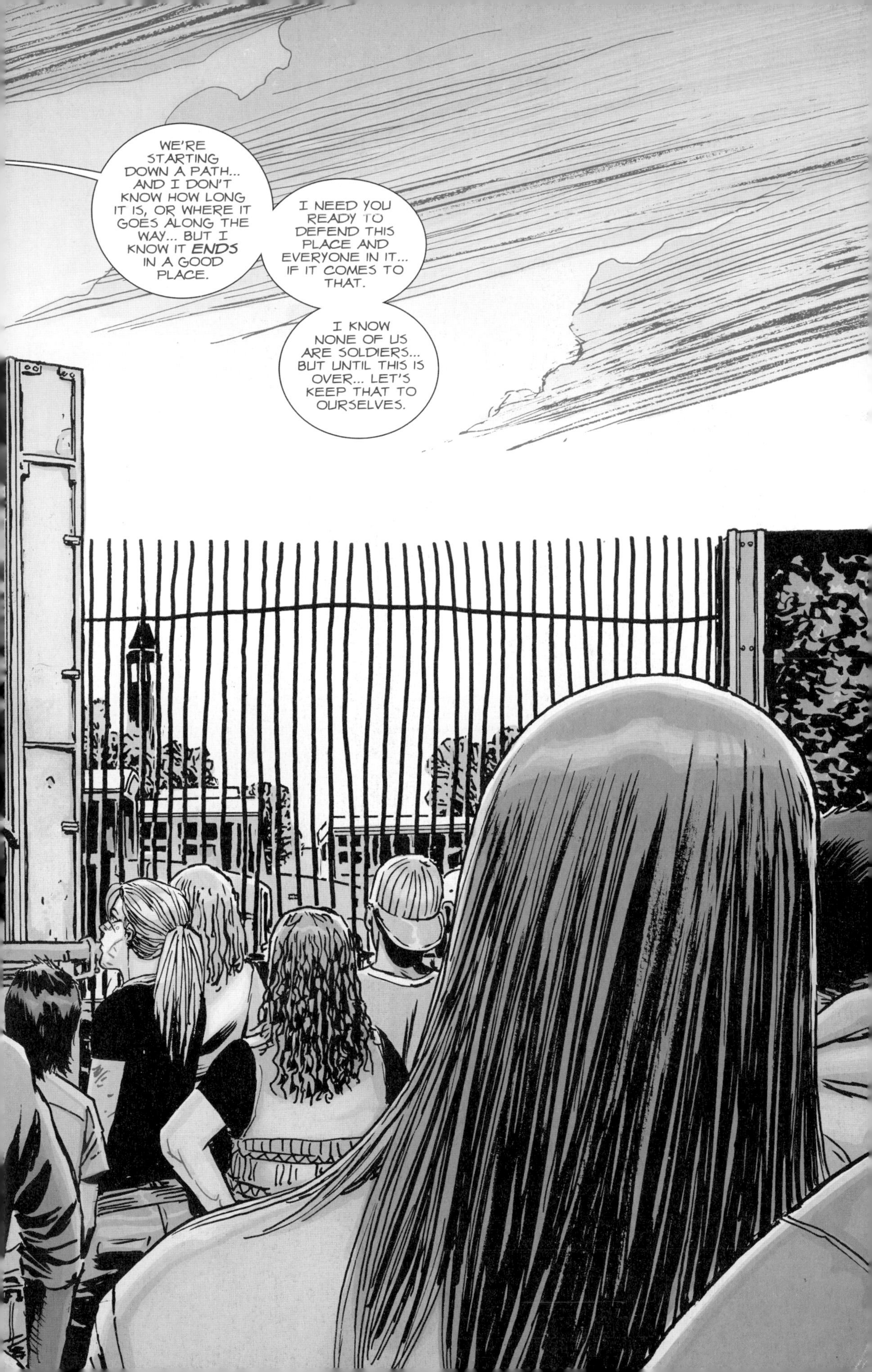
WE'RE STARTING DOWN A PATH... AND I DON'T KNOW HOW LONG IT IS, OR WHERE IT GOES ALONG THE WAY... BUT I KNOW IT *ENDS* IN A GOOD PLACE.
I NEED YOU READY TO DEFEND THIS PLACE AND EVERYONE IN IT... IF IT COMES TO THAT.
I KNOW NONE OF US ARE SOLDIERS... BUT UNTIL THIS IS OVER... LET'S KEEP THAT TO OURSELVES.

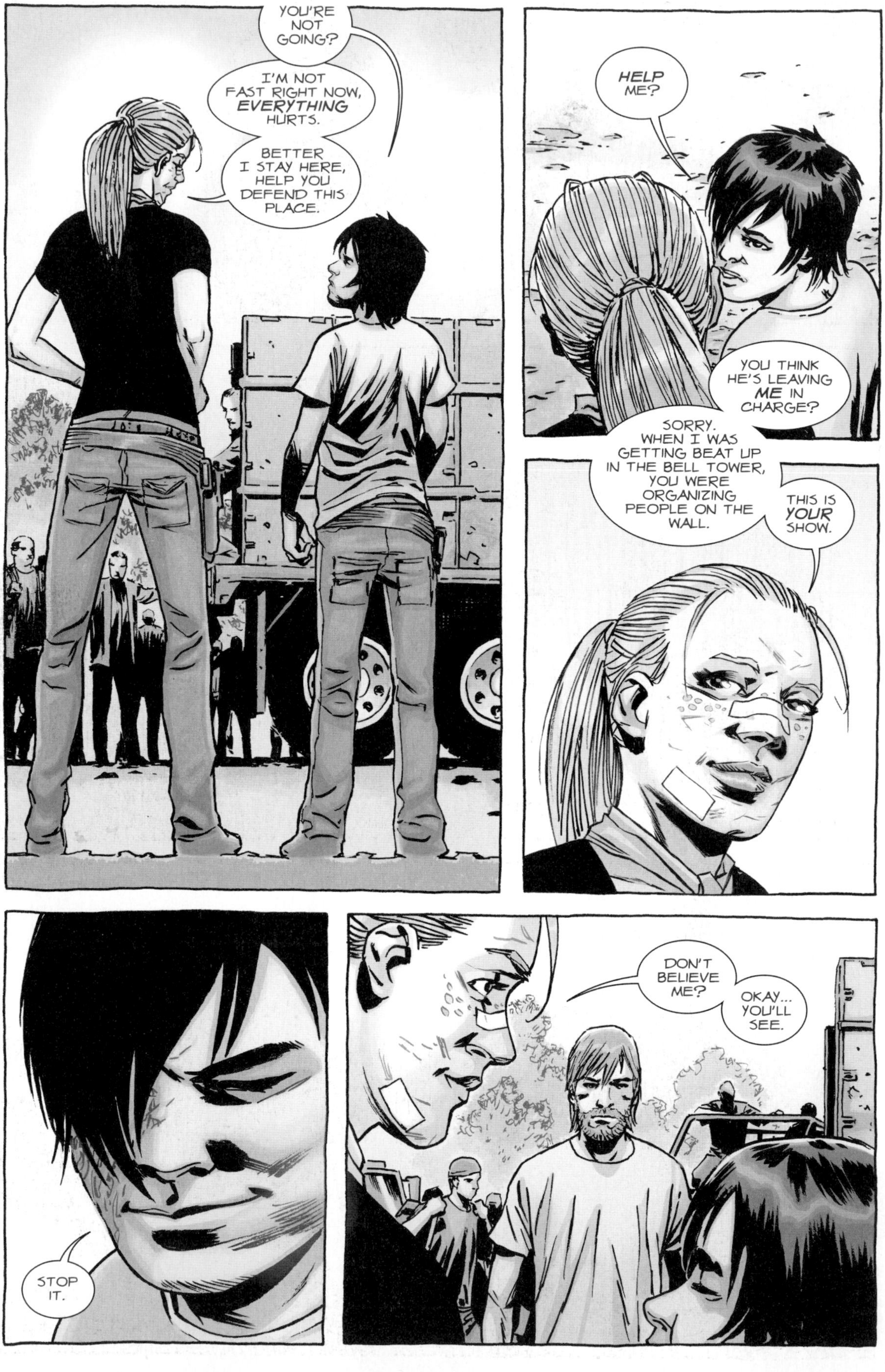
YOU'RE NOT GOING?
I'M NOT FAST RIGHT NOW, EVERYTHING HURTS.
BETTER I STAY HERE, HELP YOU DEFEND THIS PLACE.
HELP ME?
YOU THINK HE'S LEAVING ME IN CHARGE?
SORRY. WHEN I WAS GETTING BEAT UP IN THE BELL TOWER, YOU WERE ORGANIZING PEOPLE ON THE WALL.
THIS IS YOUR SHOW.
STOP IT.
DON'T BELIEVE ME?
OKAY... YOU'LL SEE.

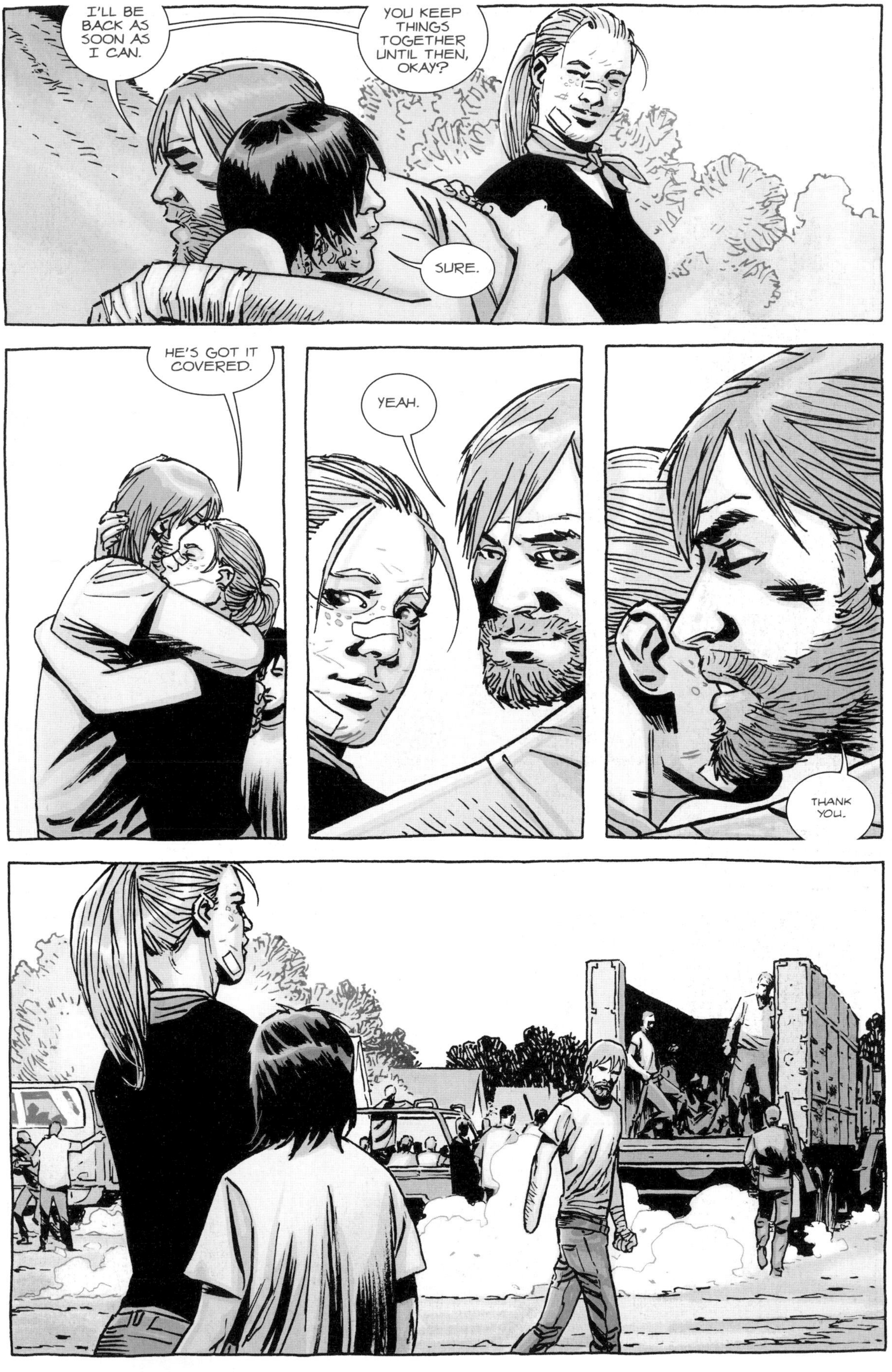
I'LL BE BACK AS SOON AS I CAN.
YOU KEEP THINGS TOGETHER UNTIL THEN, OKAY?
SURE.
HE'S GOT IT COVERED.
YEAH.
THANK YOU.

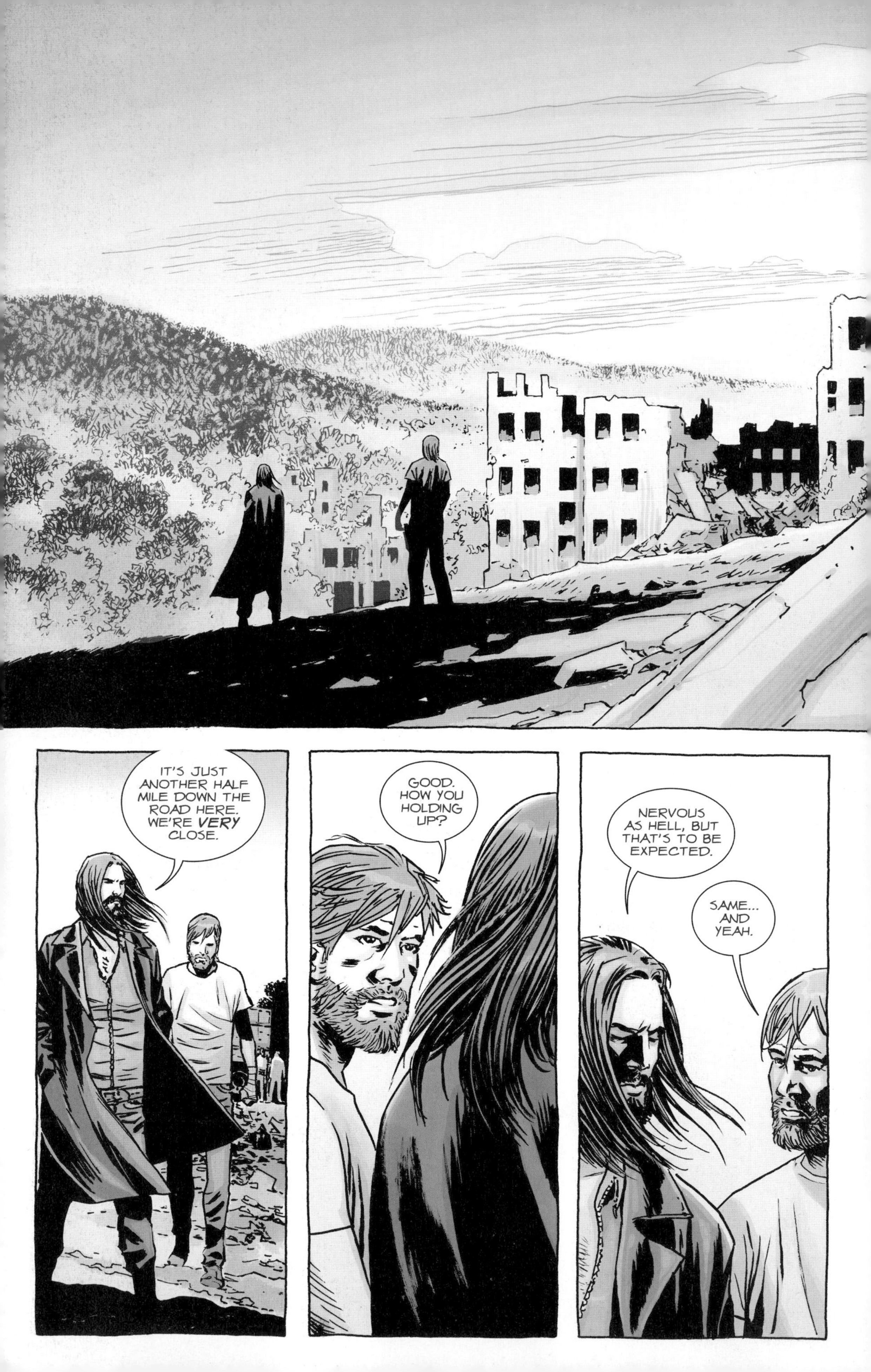
IT'S JUST ANOTHER HALF MILE DOWN THE ROAD HERE. WE'RE *VERY* CLOSE.
GOOD. HOW YOU HOLDING UP?
NERVOUS AS HELL, BUT THAT'S TO BE EXPECTED.
SAME... AND YEAH.

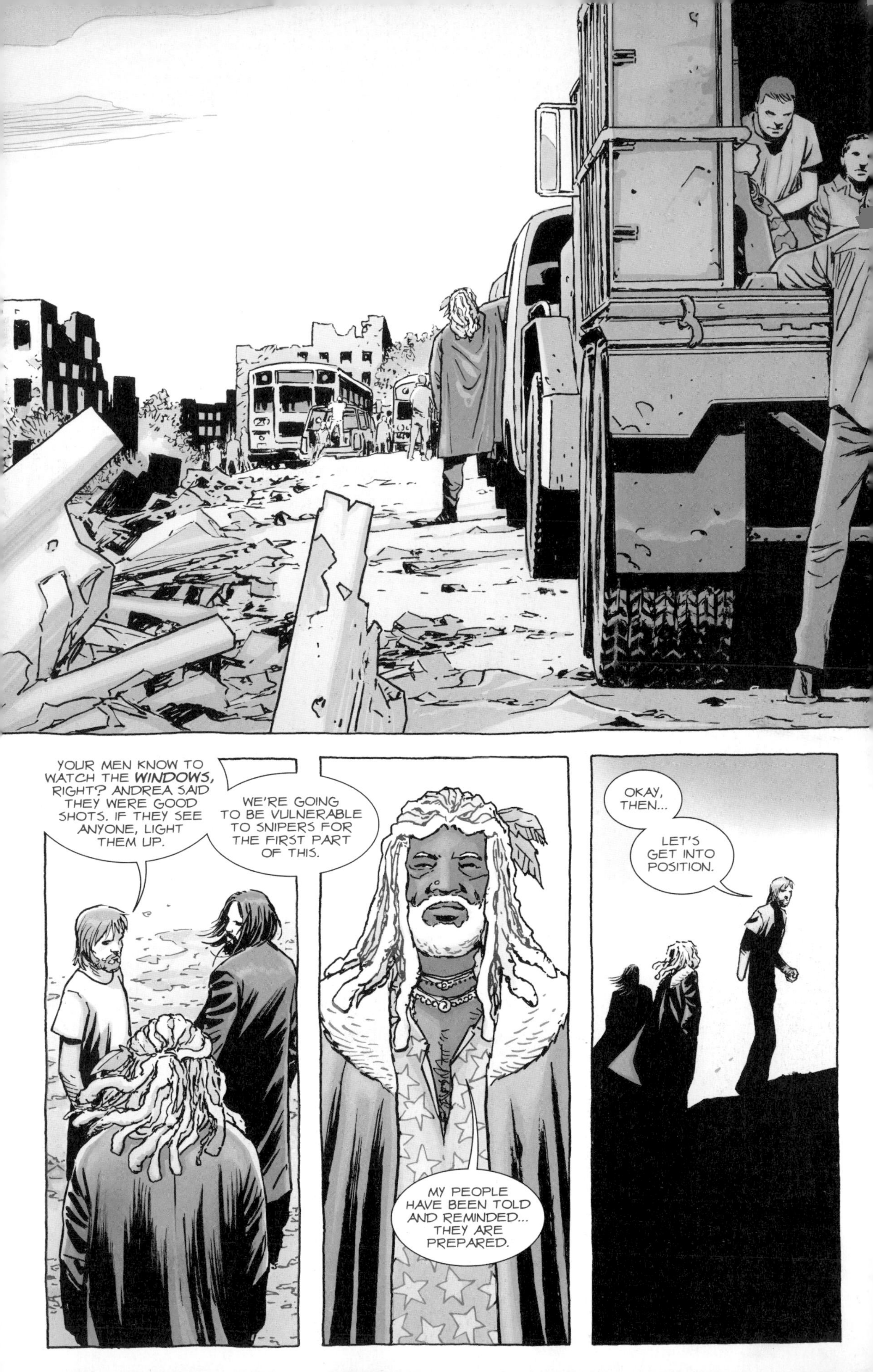
YOUR MEN KNOW TO WATCH THE WINDOWS, RIGHT? ANDREA SAID THEY WERE GOOD SHOTS. IF THEY SEE ANYONE, LIGHT THEM UP.
WE'RE GOING TO BE VULNERABLE TO SNIPERS FOR THE FIRST PART OF THIS.
MY PEOPLE HAVE BEEN TOLD AND REMINDED... THEY ARE PREPARED.
OKAY, THEN...
LET'S GET INTO POSITION.

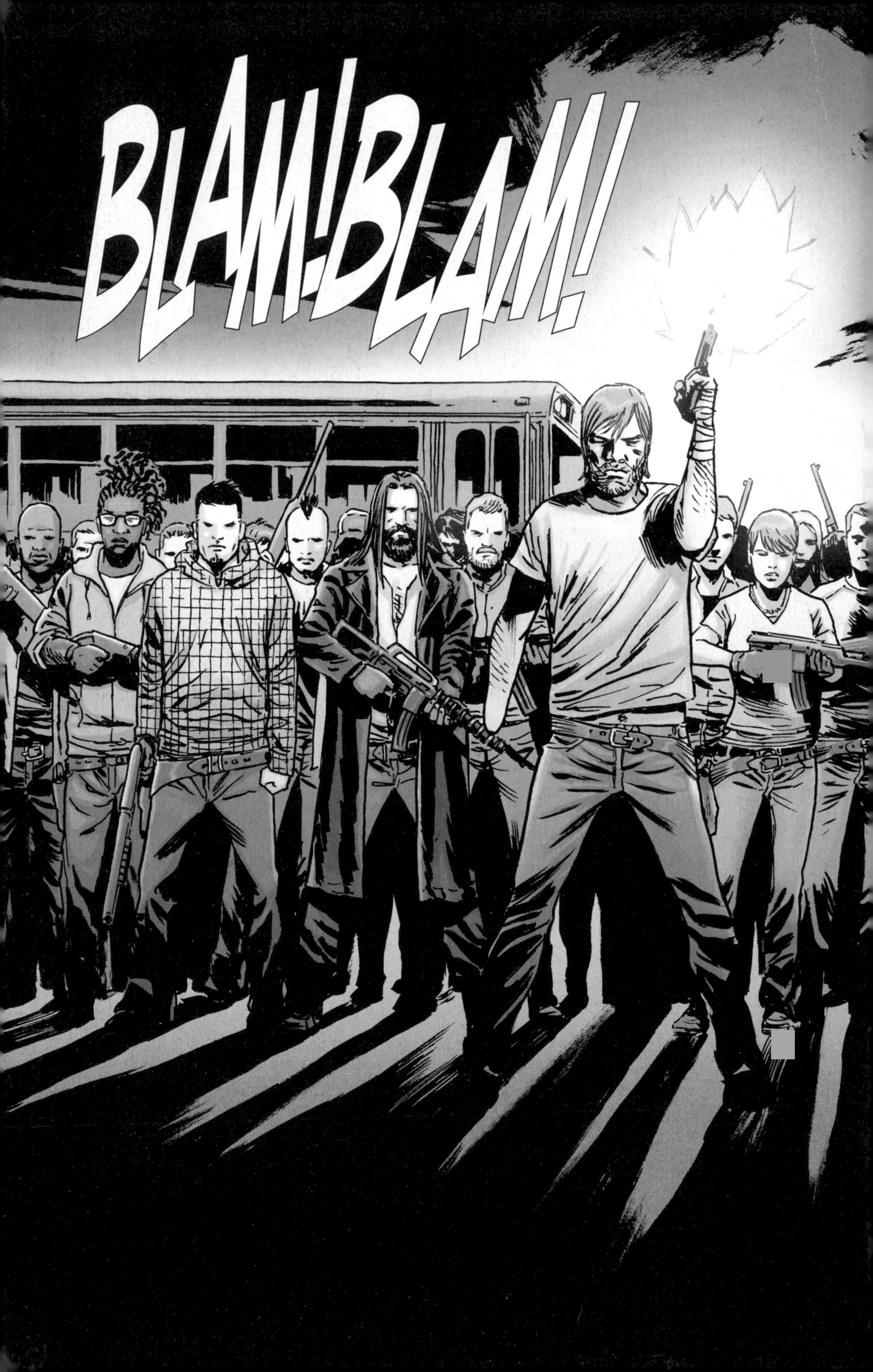
BLAM! BLAM!

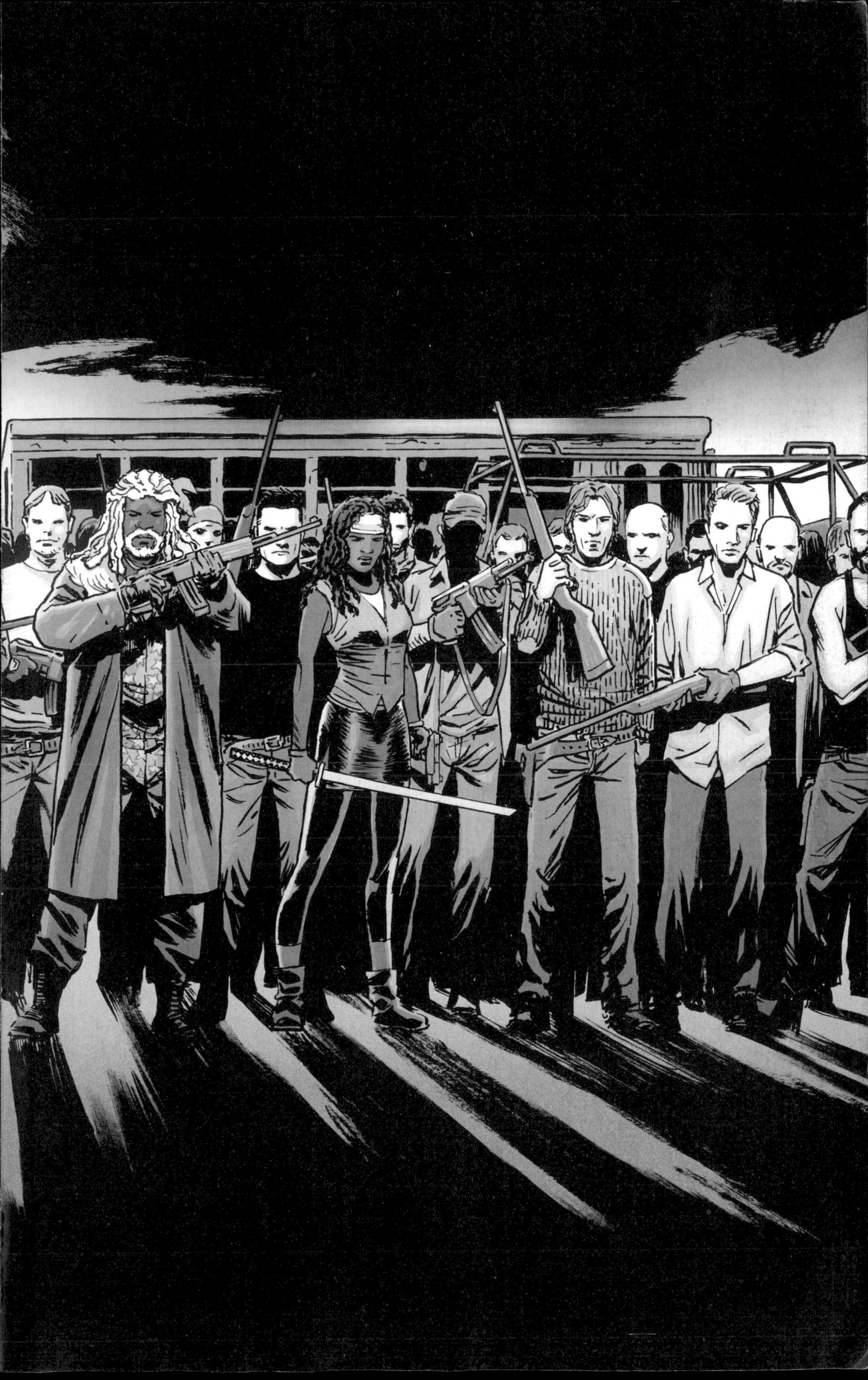

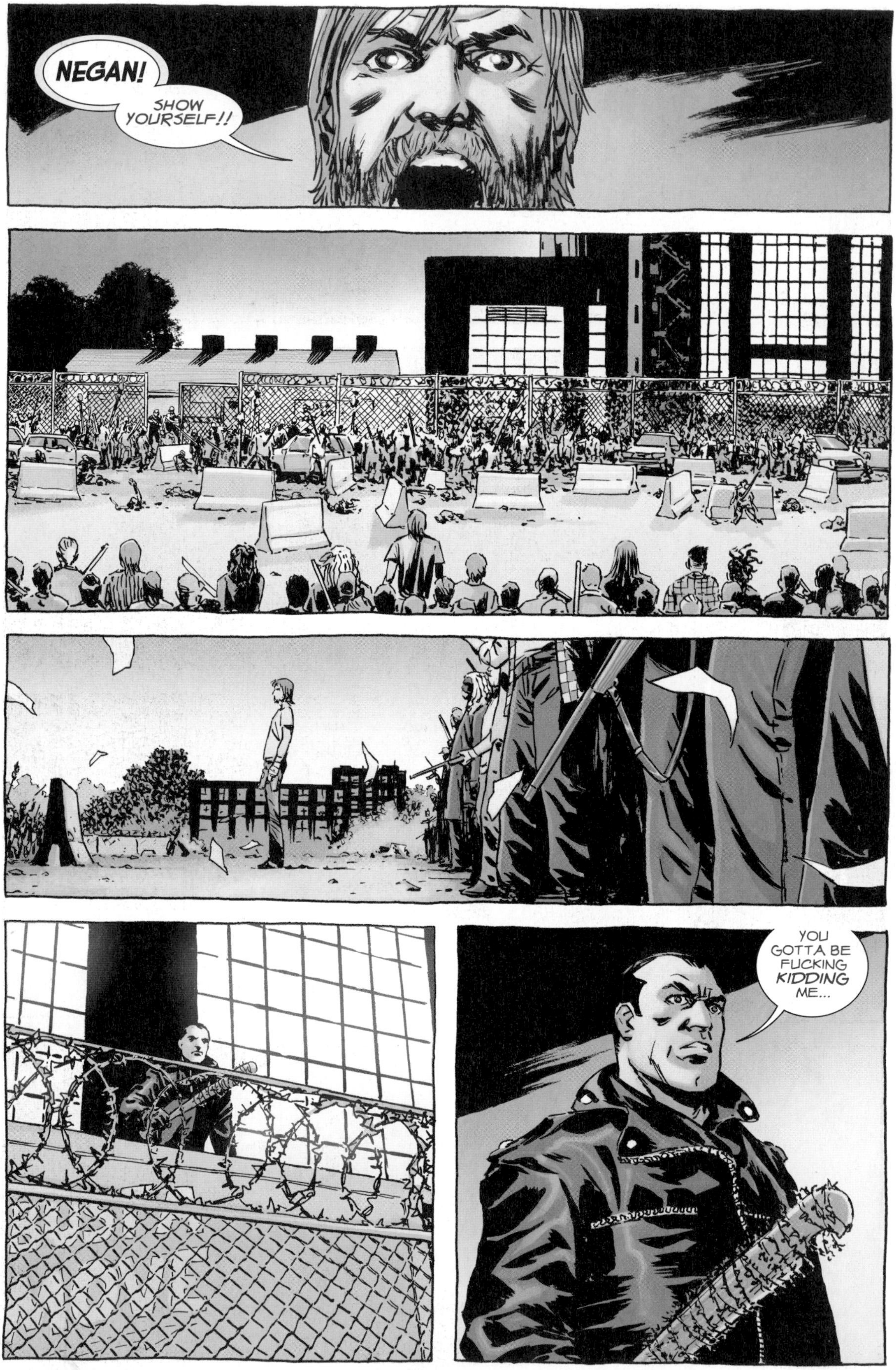
NEGAN!
SHOW YOURSELF!!
YOU GOTTA BE FUCKING KIDDING ME...

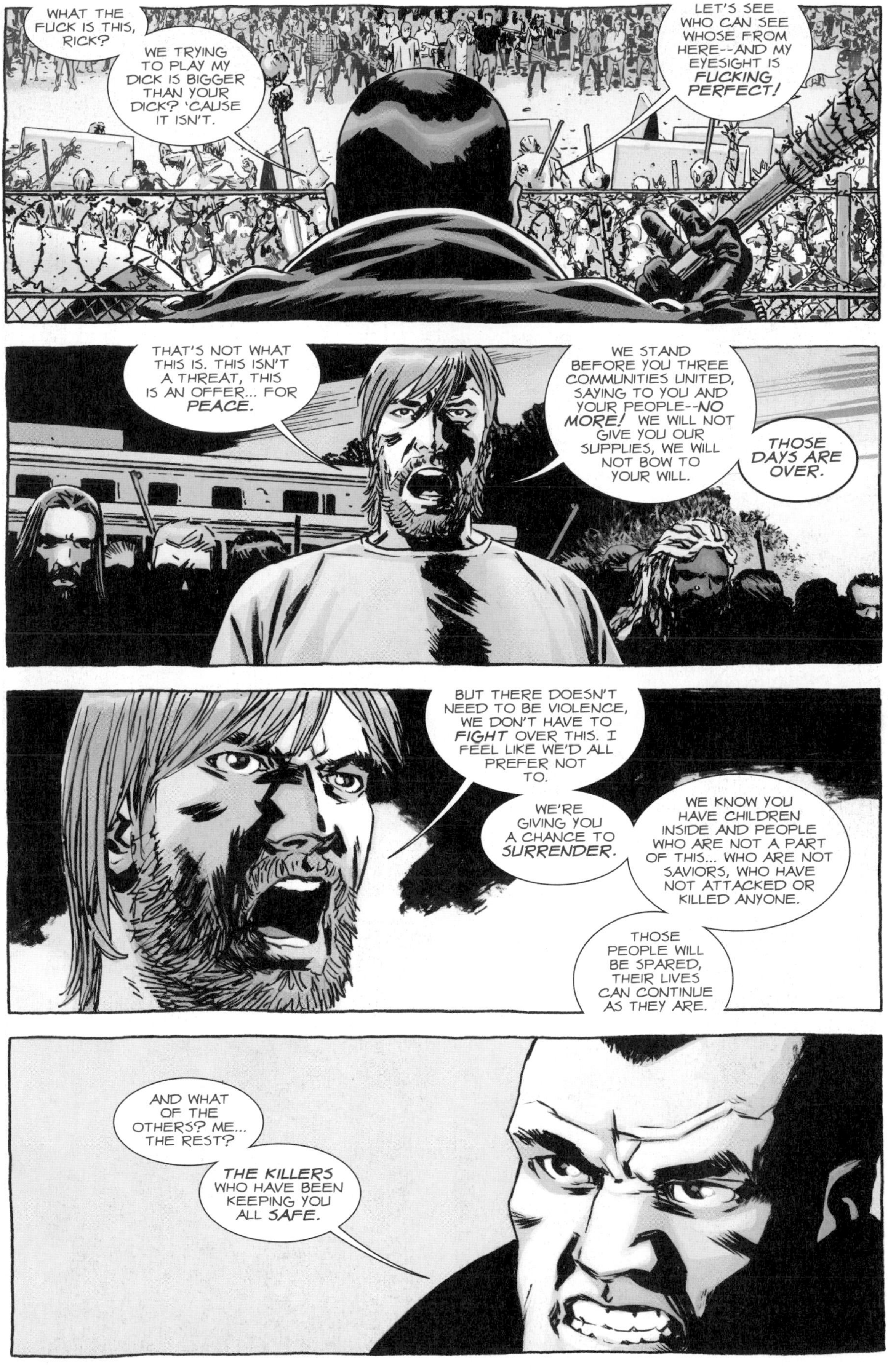
WHAT THE FUCK IS THIS, RICK?
WE TRYING TO PLAY MY DICK IS BIGGER THAN YOUR DICK? 'CAUSE IT ISN'T.
LET'S SEE WHO CAN SEE WHOSE FROM HERE--AND MY EYESIGHT IS *FUCKING PERFECT!*
THAT'S NOT WHAT THIS IS. THIS ISN'T A THREAT, THIS IS AN OFFER... FOR *PEACE.*
WE STAND BEFORE YOU THREE COMMUNITIES UNITED, SAYING TO YOU AND YOUR PEOPLE--*NO MORE!* WE WILL NOT GIVE YOU OUR SUPPLIES, WE WILL NOT BOW TO YOUR WILL.
THOSE DAYS ARE OVER.
BUT THERE DOESN'T NEED TO BE VIOLENCE, WE DON'T HAVE TO *FIGHT* OVER THIS. I FEEL LIKE WE'D ALL PREFER NOT TO.
WE'RE GIVING YOU A CHANCE TO *SURRENDER.*
WE KNOW YOU HAVE CHILDREN INSIDE AND PEOPLE WHO ARE NOT A PART OF THIS... WHO ARE NOT SAVIORS, WHO HAVE NOT ATTACKED OR KILLED ANYONE.
THOSE PEOPLE WILL BE SPARED, THEIR LIVES CAN CONTINUE AS THEY ARE.
AND WHAT OF THE OTHERS? ME... THE REST?
THE KILLERS WHO HAVE BEEN KEEPING YOU ALL *SAFE.*

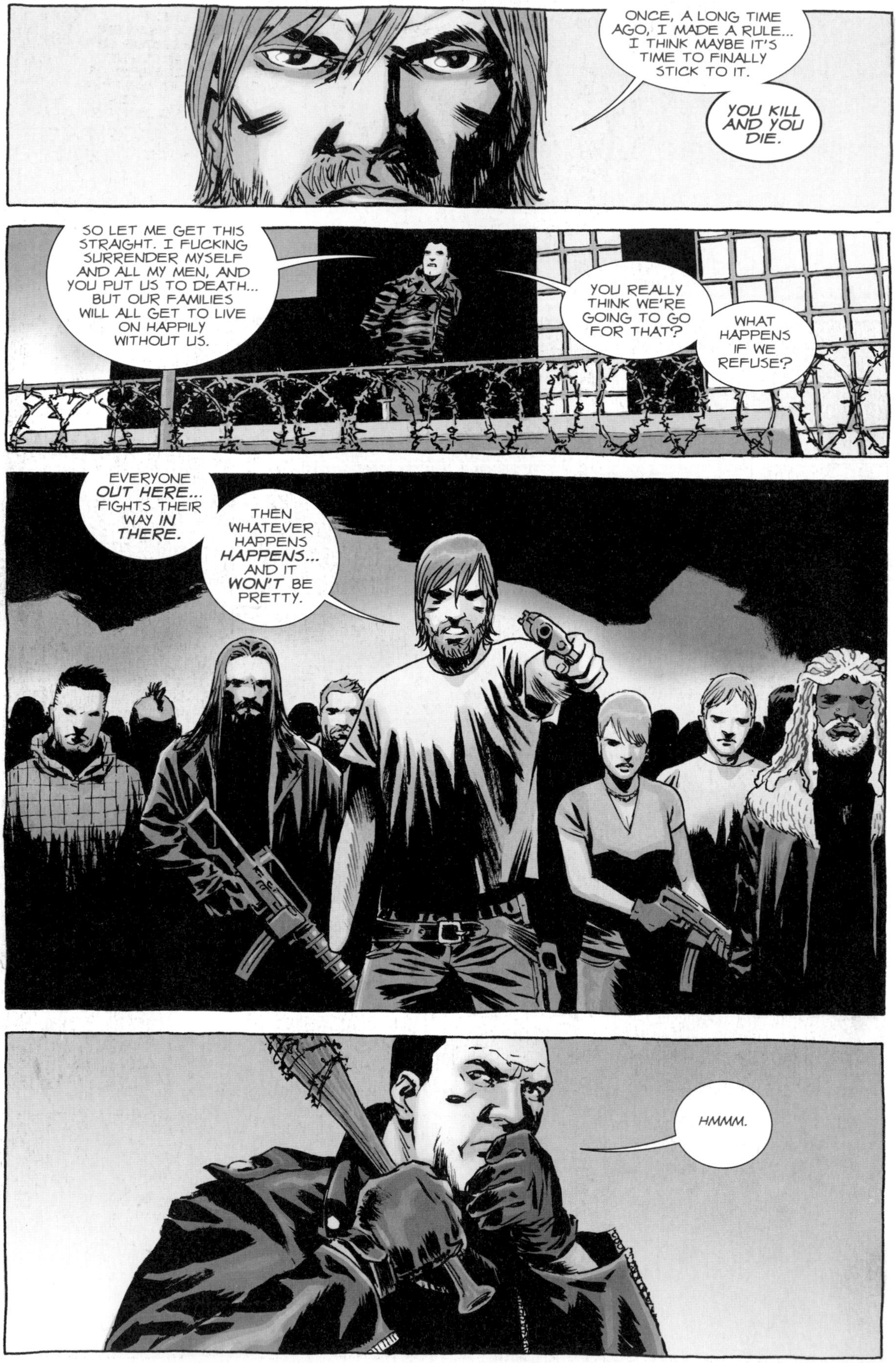
ONCE, A LONG TIME AGO, I MADE A RULE... I THINK MAYBE IT'S TIME TO FINALLY STICK TO IT.
YOU KILL AND YOU DIE.
SO LET ME GET THIS STRAIGHT. I FUCKING SURRENDER MYSELF AND ALL MY MEN, AND YOU PUT US TO DEATH... BUT OUR FAMILIES WILL ALL GET TO LIVE ON HAPPILY WITHOUT US.
YOU REALLY THINK WE'RE GOING TO GO FOR THAT?
WHAT HAPPENS IF WE REFUSE?
EVERYONE OUT HERE... FIGHTS THEIR WAY IN THERE.
THEN WHATEVER HAPPENS HAPPENS... AND IT WON'T BE PRETTY.
HMMM.

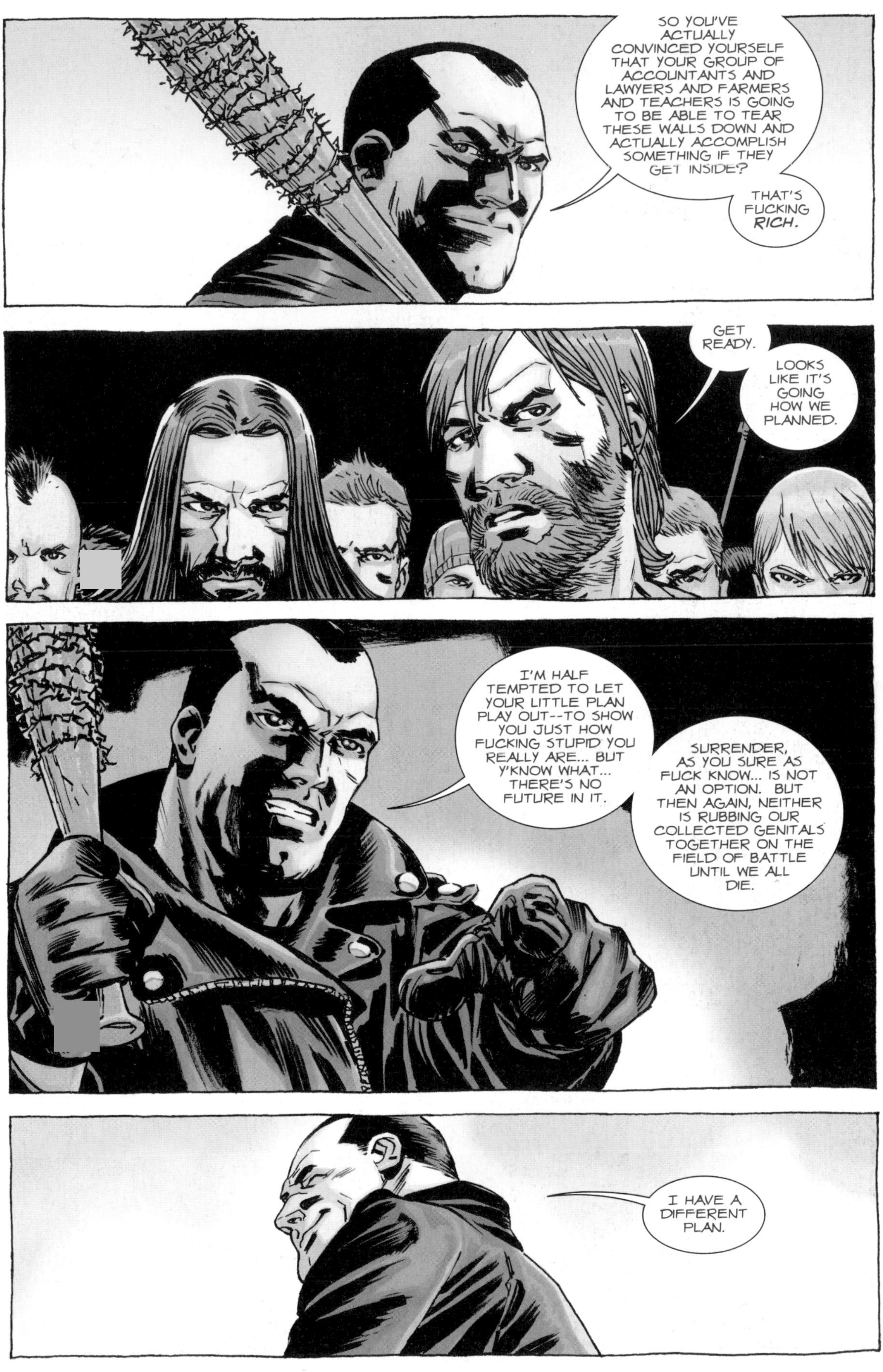
SO YOU'VE ACTUALLY CONVINCED YOURSELF THAT YOUR GROUP OF ACCOUNTANTS AND LAWYERS AND FARMERS AND TEACHERS IS GOING TO BE ABLE TO TEAR THESE WALLS DOWN AND ACTUALLY ACCOMPLISH SOMETHING IF THEY GET INSIDE?
THAT'S FUCKING *RICH.*
GET READY.
LOOKS LIKE IT'S GOING HOW WE PLANNED.
I'M HALF TEMPTED TO LET YOUR LITTLE PLAN PLAY OUT--TO SHOW YOU JUST HOW FUCKING STUPID YOU REALLY ARE... BUT Y'KNOW WHAT... THERE'S NO FUTURE IN IT.
SURRENDER, AS YOU SURE AS FUCK KNOW... IS NOT AN OPTION. BUT THEN AGAIN, NEITHER IS RUBBING OUR COLLECTED GENITALS TOGETHER ON THE FIELD OF BATTLE UNTIL WE ALL DIE.
I HAVE A DIFFERENT PLAN.

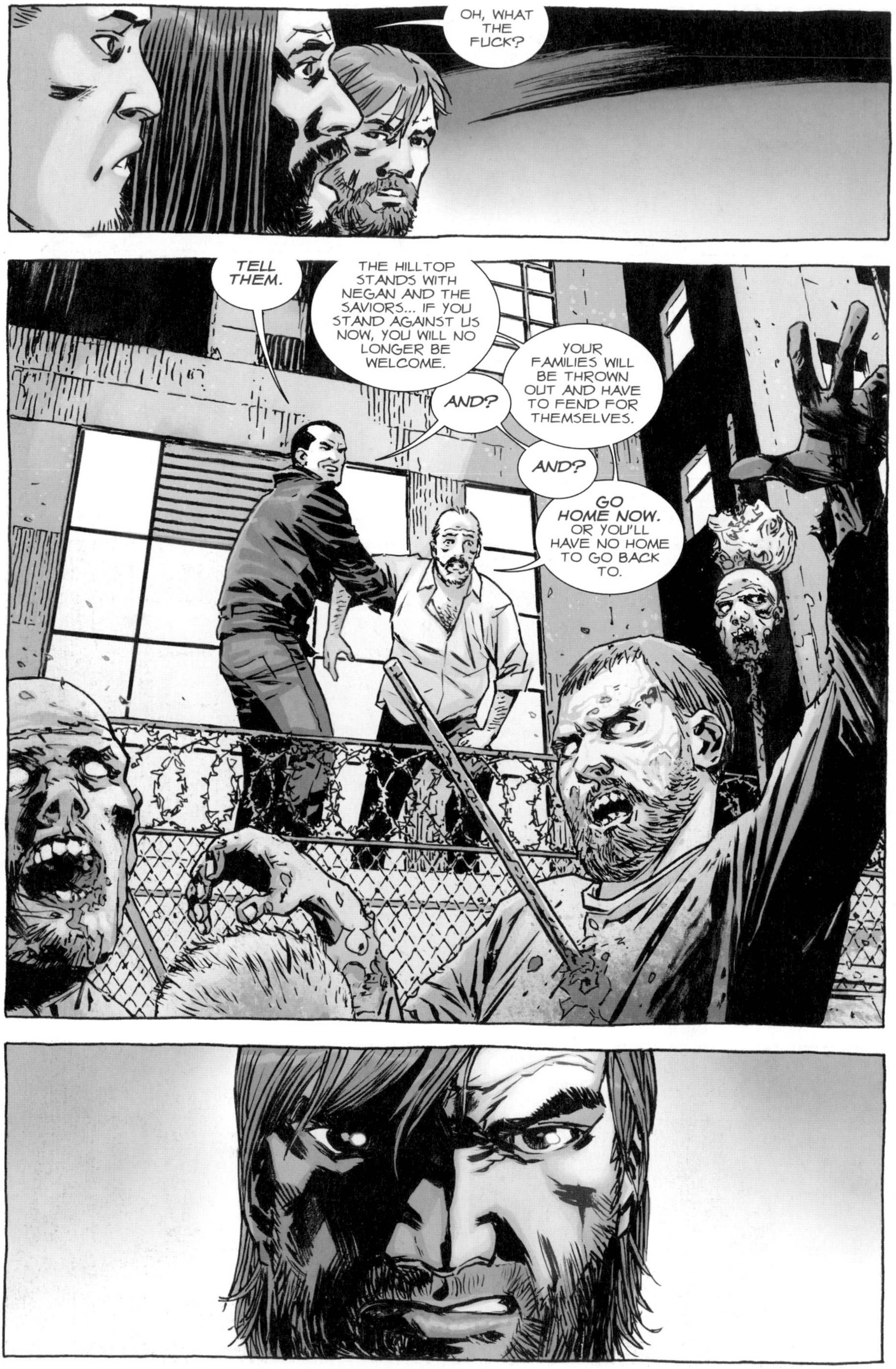
OH, WHAT THE FUCK?
TELL THEM.
THE HILLTOP STANDS WITH NEGAN AND THE SAVIORS... IF YOU STAND AGAINST US NOW, YOU WILL NO LONGER BE WELCOME.
AND?
YOUR FAMILIES WILL BE THROWN OUT AND HAVE TO FEND FOR THEMSELVES.
AND?
GO HOME NOW. OR YOU'LL HAVE NO HOME TO GO BACK TO.

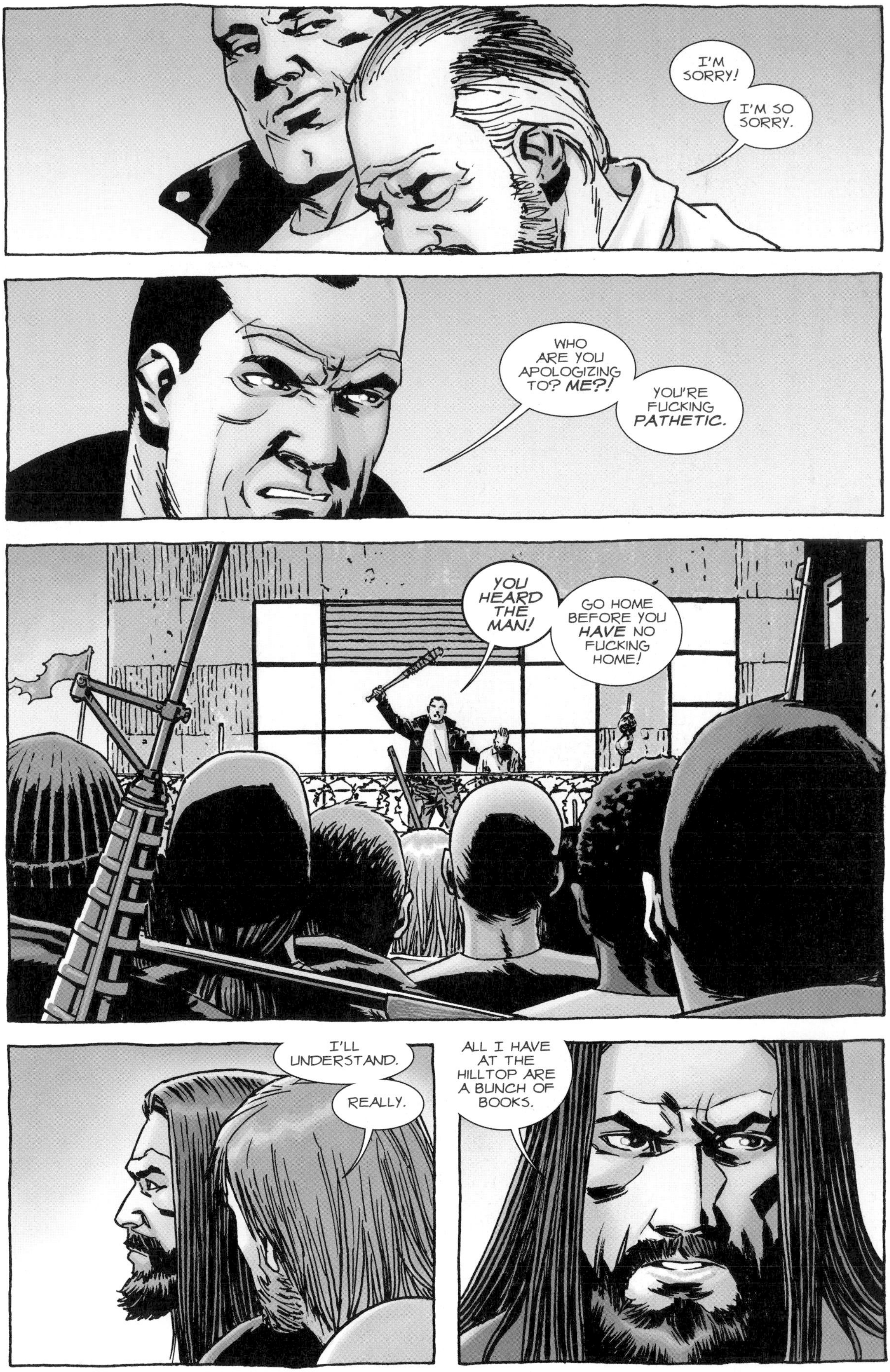
I'M SORRY!
I'M SO SORRY.
WHO ARE YOU APOLOGIZING TO? ME?!
YOU'RE FUCKING PATHETIC.
YOU HEARD THE MAN!
GO HOME BEFORE YOU HAVE NO FUCKING HOME!
I'LL UNDERSTAND.
REALLY.
ALL I HAVE AT THE HILLTOP ARE A BUNCH OF BOOKS.

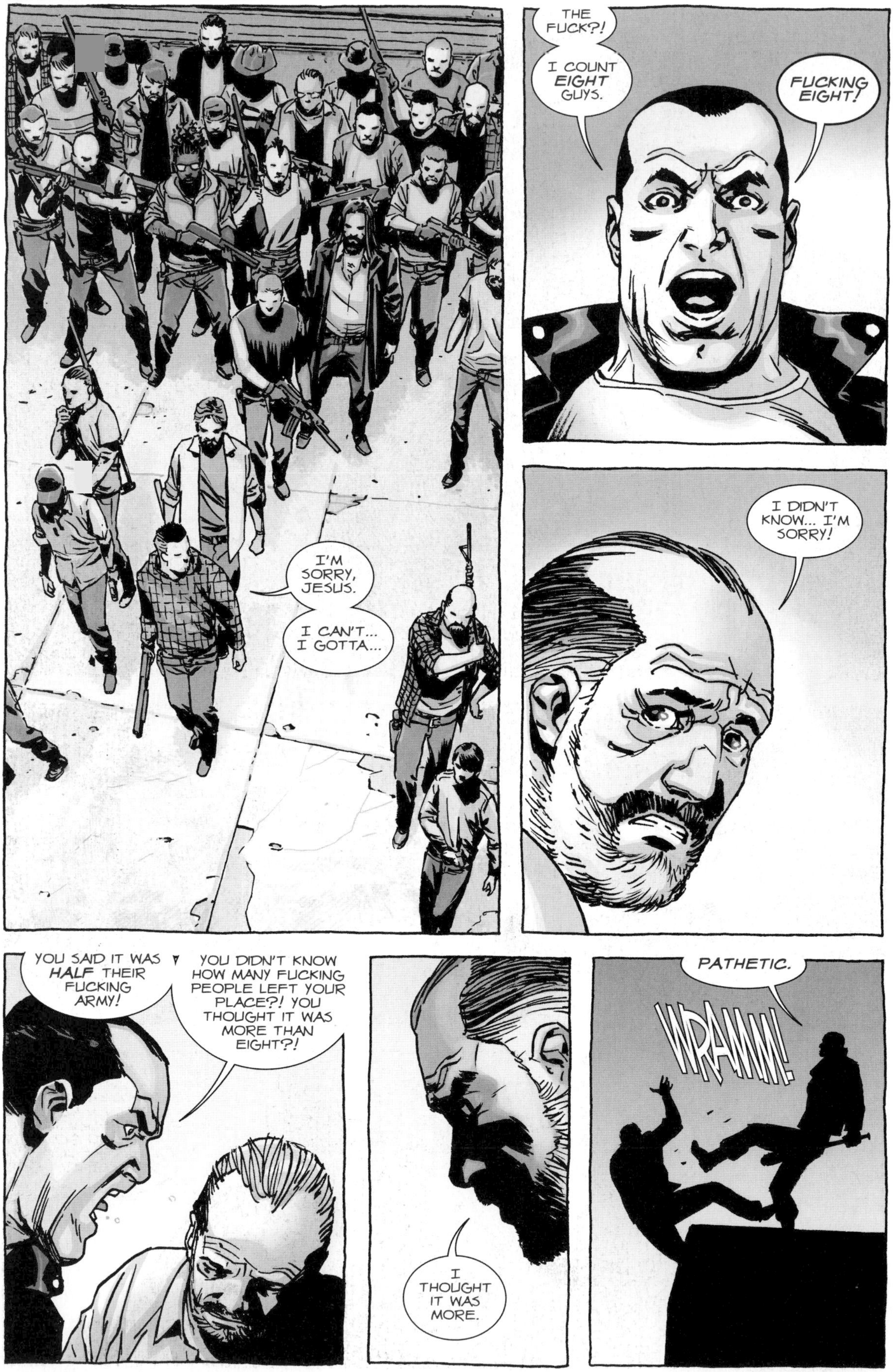
I'M SORRY, JESUS.
I CAN'T... I GOTTA...
THE FUCK?!
I COUNT EIGHT GUYS.
FUCKING EIGHT!
I DIDN'T KNOW... I'M SORRY!
YOU SAID IT WAS HALF THEIR FUCKING ARMY!
YOU DIDN'T KNOW HOW MANY FUCKING PEOPLE LEFT YOUR PLACE?! YOU THOUGHT IT WAS MORE THAN EIGHT?!
I THOUGHT IT WAS MORE.
PATHETIC.
WRAMM!

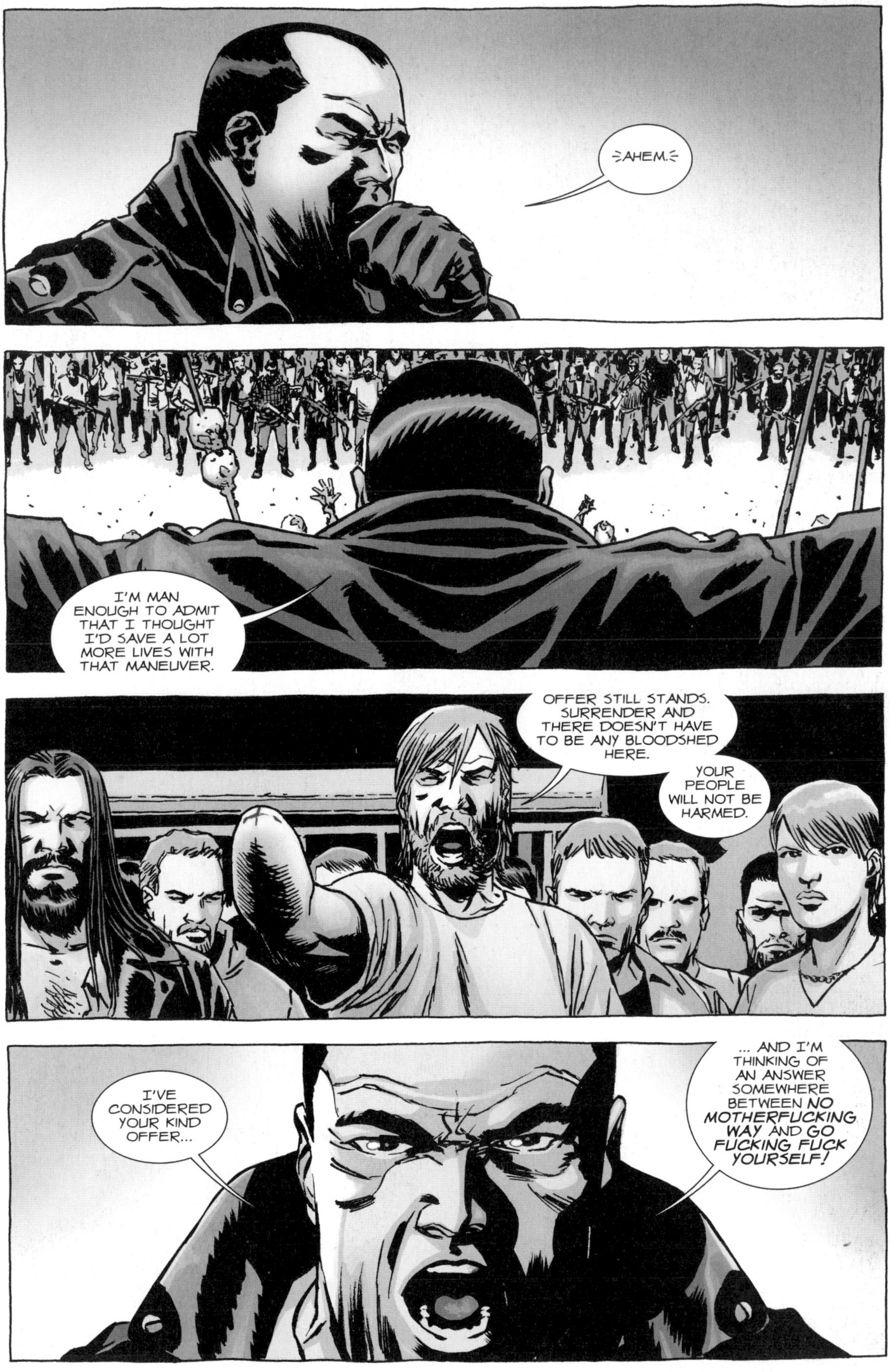
AHEM.
I'M MAN ENOUGH TO ADMIT THAT I THOUGHT I'D SAVE A LOT MORE LIVES WITH THAT MANEUVER.
OFFER STILL STANDS. SURRENDER AND THERE DOESN'T HAVE TO BE ANY BLOODSHED HERE.
YOUR PEOPLE WILL NOT BE HARMED.
I'VE CONSIDERED YOUR KIND OFFER...
... AND I'M THINKING OF AN ANSWER SOMEWHERE BETWEEN NO MOTHERFUCKING WAY AND GO FUCKING FUCK YOURSELF!

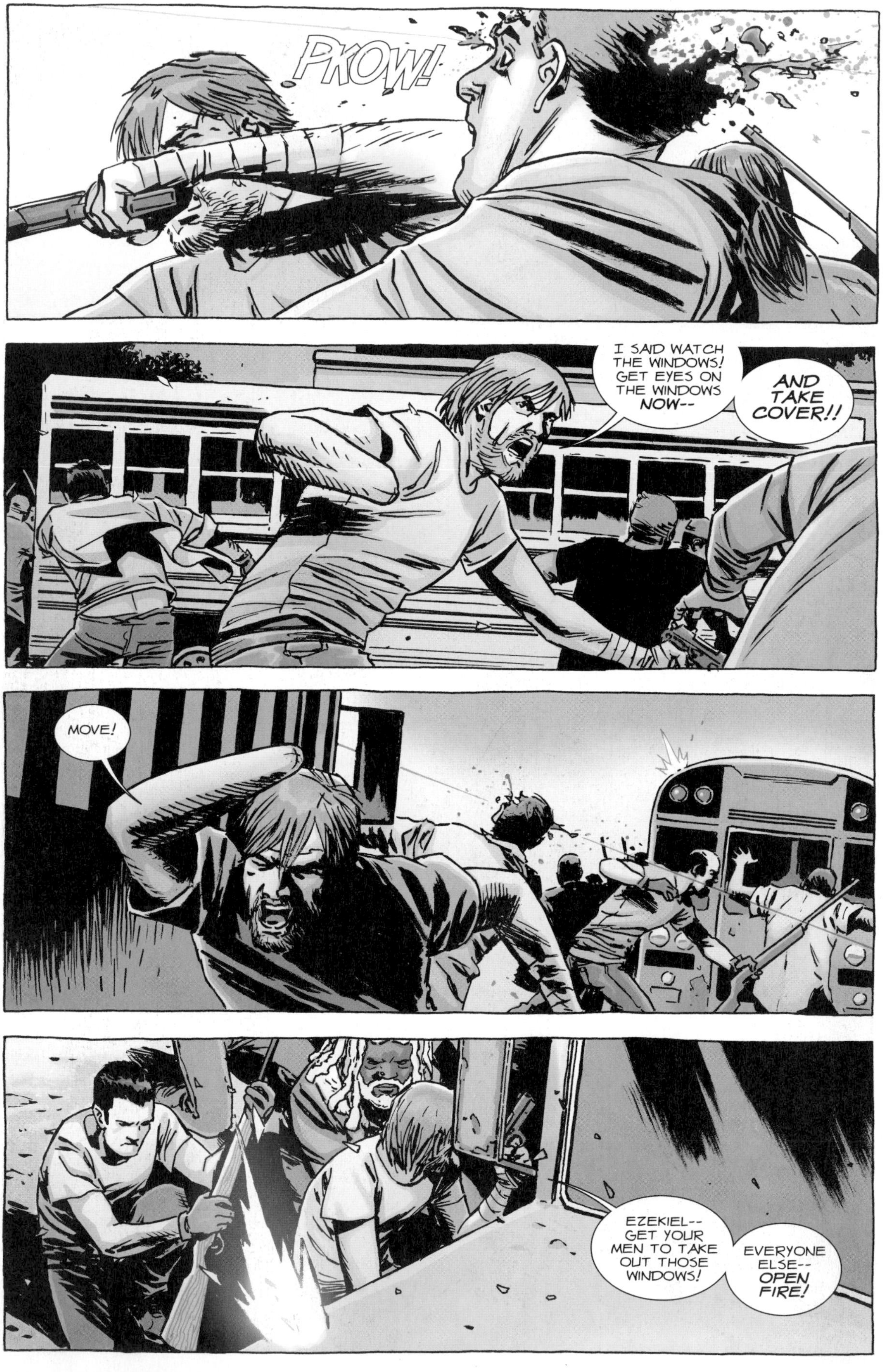
PKOW!
I SAID WATCH THE WINDOWS! GET EYES ON THE WINDOWS NOW--
AND TAKE COVER!!
MOVE!
EZEKIEL-- GET YOUR MEN TO TAKE OUT THOSE WINDOWS!
EVERYONE ELSE-- OPEN FIRE!

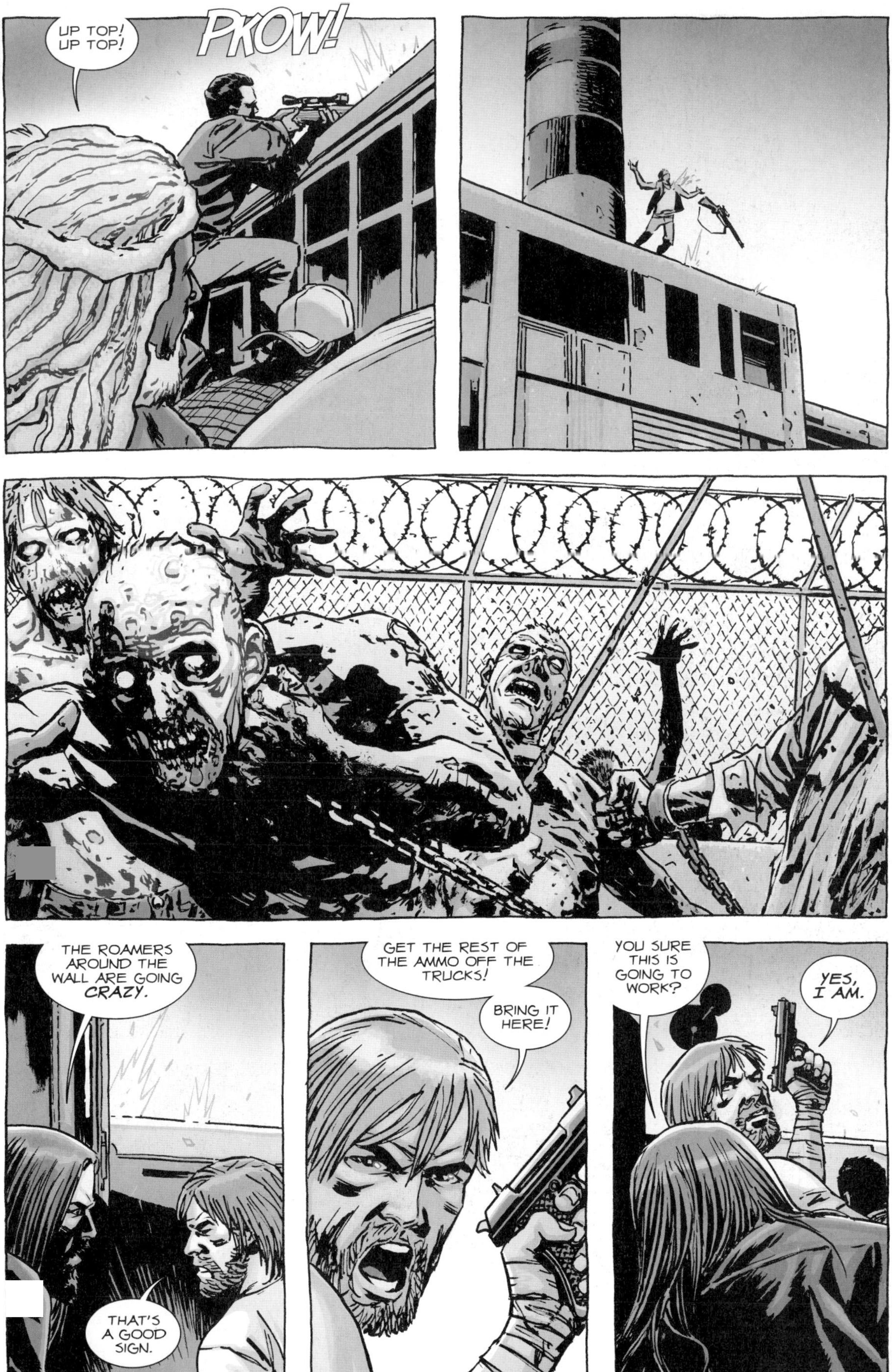
UP TOP! UP TOP!
PKOW!
THE ROAMERS AROUND THE WALL ARE GOING CRAZY.
THAT'S A GOOD SIGN.
GET THE REST OF THE AMMO OFF THE TRUCKS!
BRING IT HERE!
YOU SURE THIS IS GOING TO WORK?
YES, I AM.

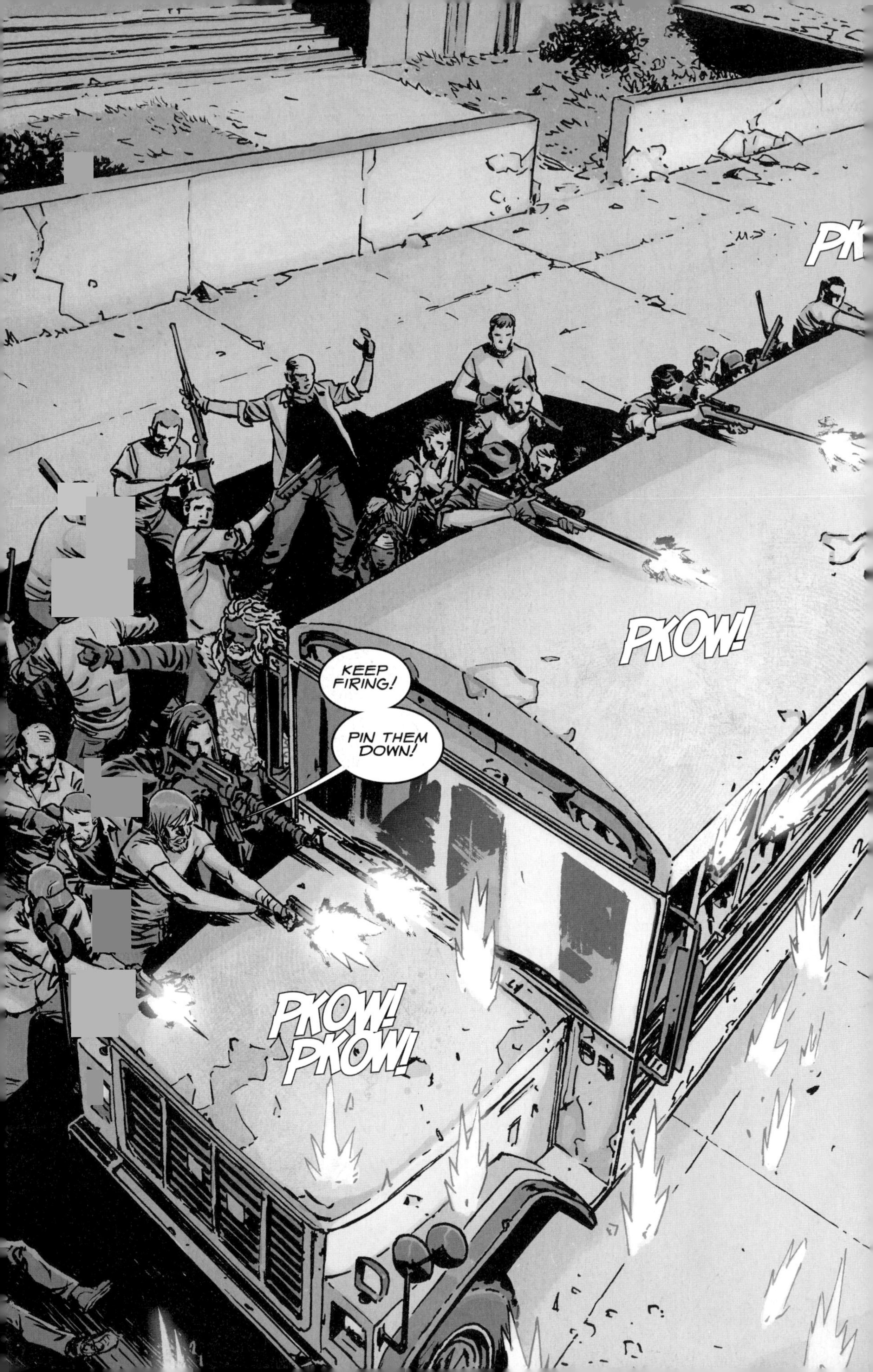
PKOW!
KEEP FIRING!
PIN THEM DOWN!
PKOW!
PKOW!

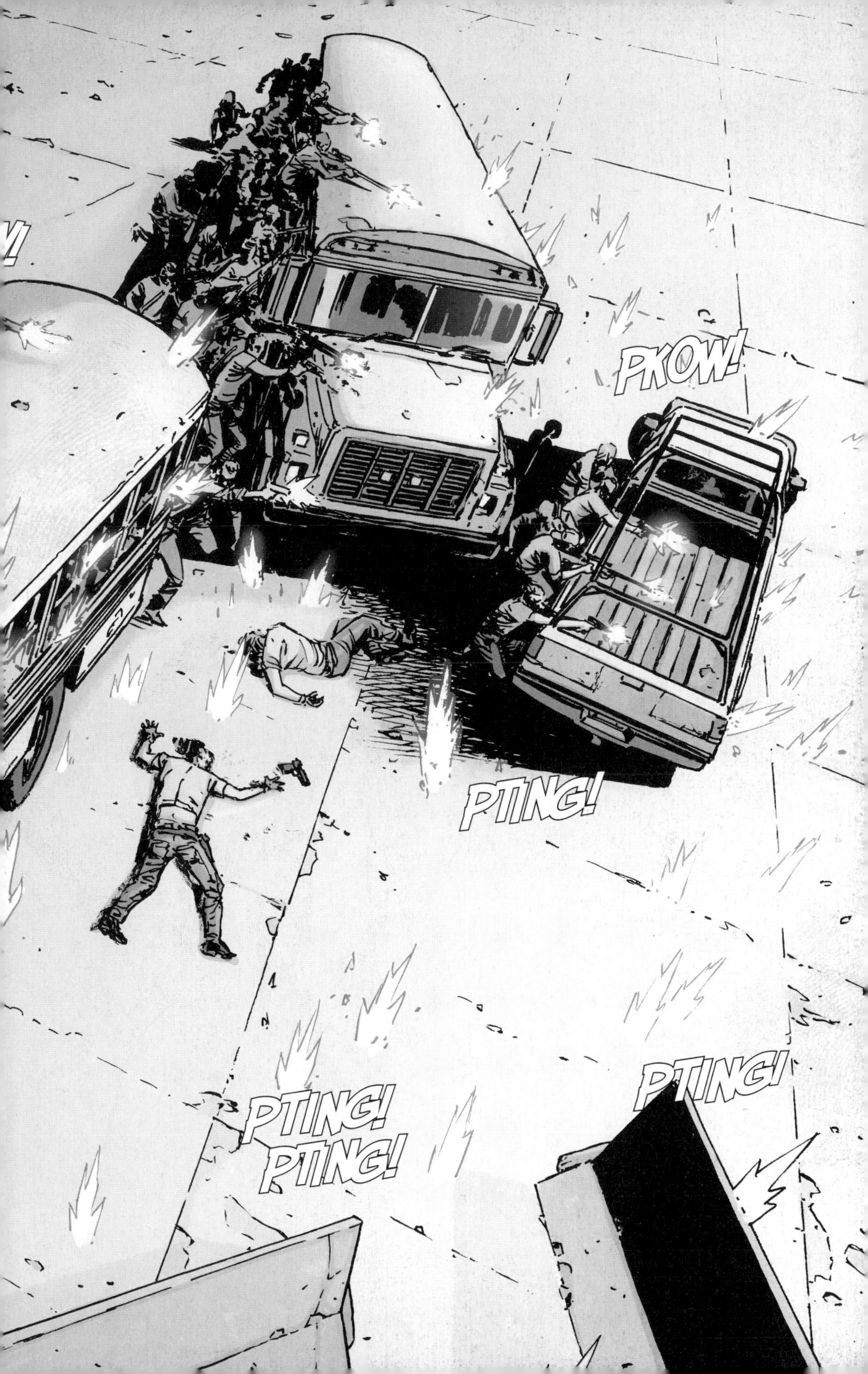

PKOW!
PTING!
PTING!
PTING!
PTING!

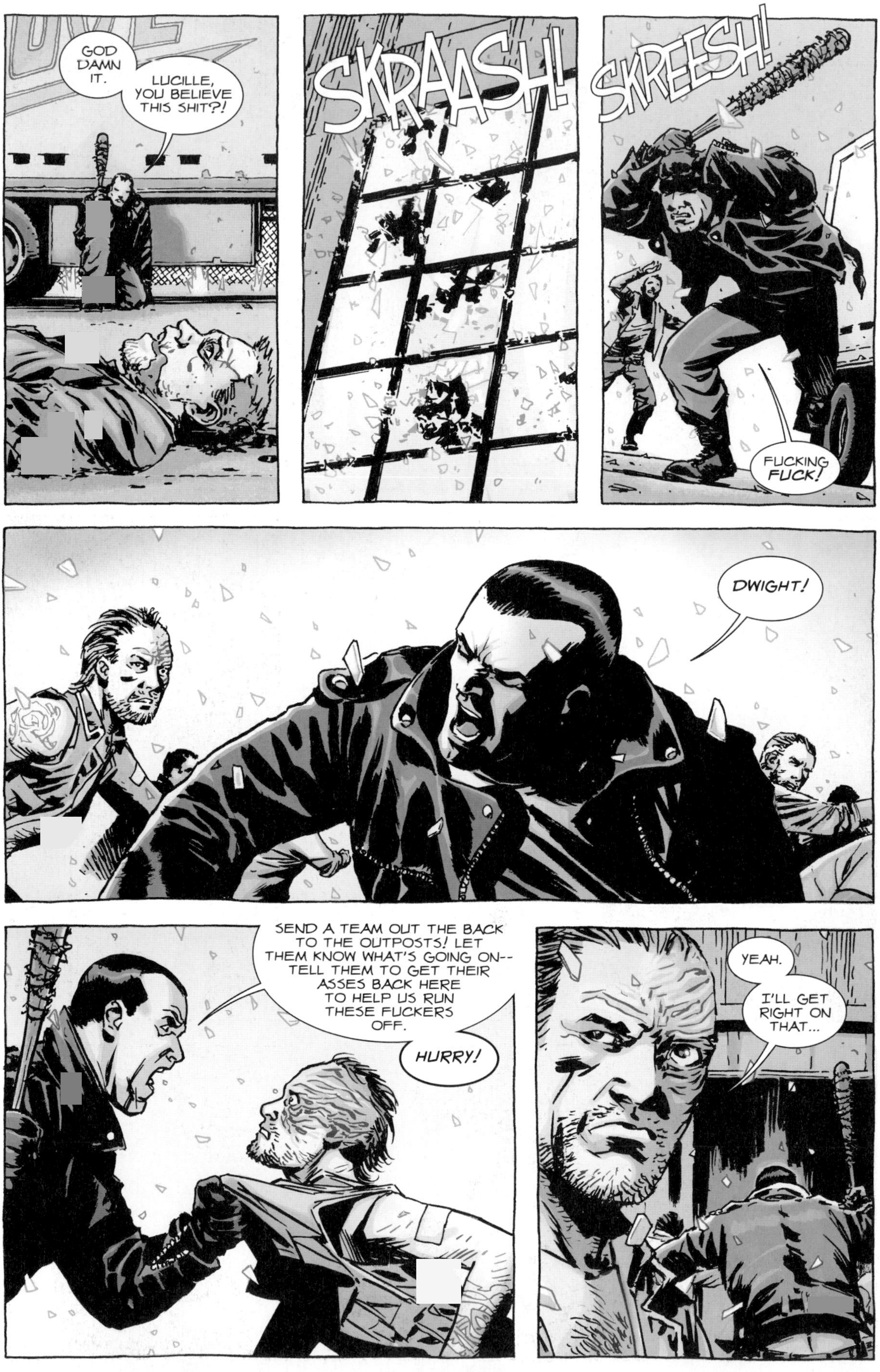
GOD DAMN IT.
LUCILLE, YOU BELIEVE THIS SHIT?!
SKRAASH!
SKREESH!
FUCKING FUCK!
DWIGHT!
SEND A TEAM OUT THE BACK TO THE OUTPOSTS! LET THEM KNOW WHAT'S GOING ON-- TELL THEM TO GET THEIR ASSES BACK HERE TO HELP US RUN THESE FUCKERS OFF.
HURRY!
YEAH.
I'LL GET RIGHT ON THAT...

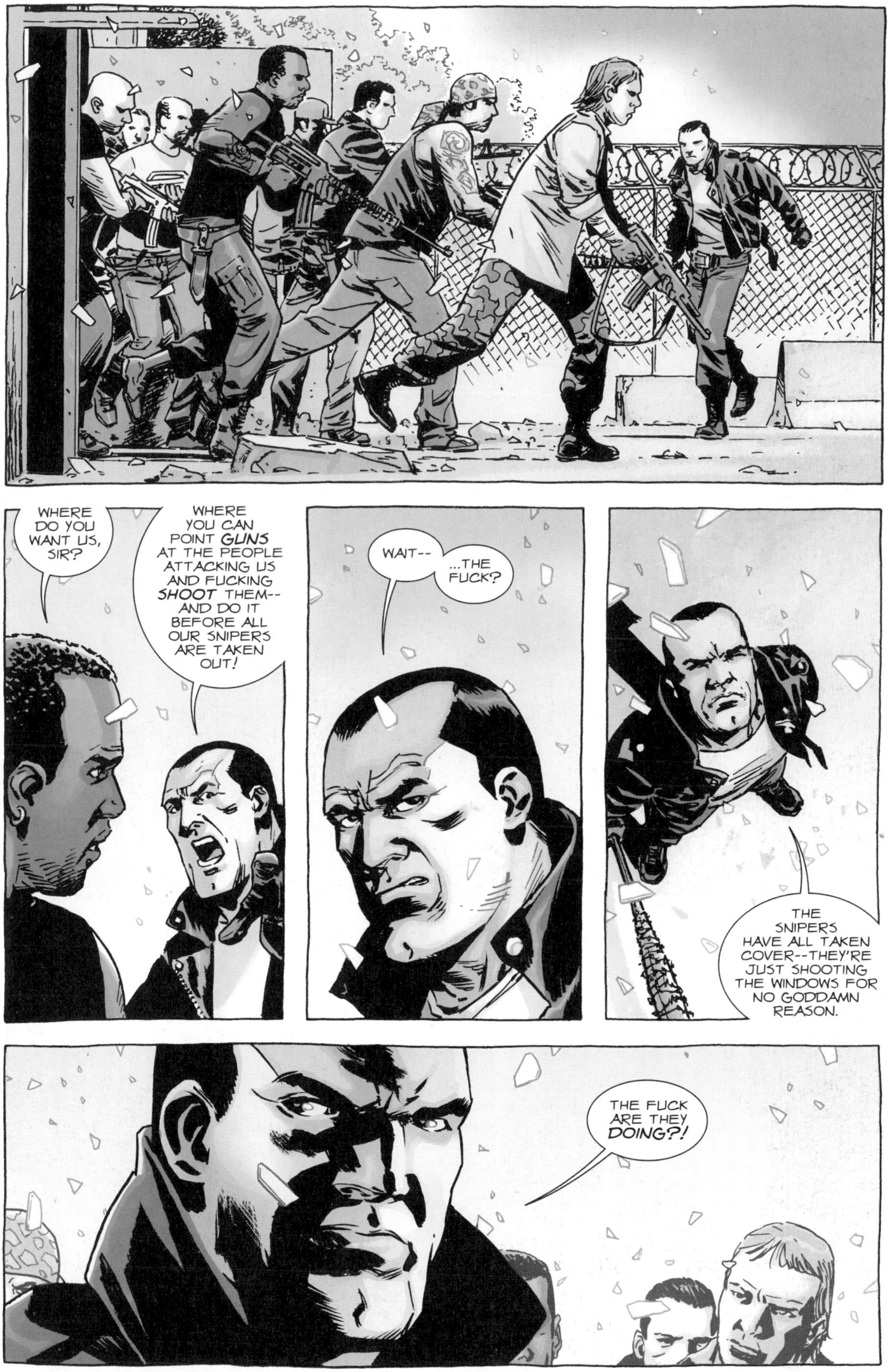

WHERE DO YOU WANT US, SIR?
WHERE YOU CAN POINT GUNS AT THE PEOPLE ATTACKING US AND FUCKING SHOOT THEM-- AND DO IT BEFORE ALL OUR SNIPERS ARE TAKEN OUT!
WAIT--
...THE FUCK?
THE SNIPERS HAVE ALL TAKEN COVER--THEY'RE JUST SHOOTING THE WINDOWS FOR NO GODDAMN REASON.
THE FUCK ARE THEY DOING?!

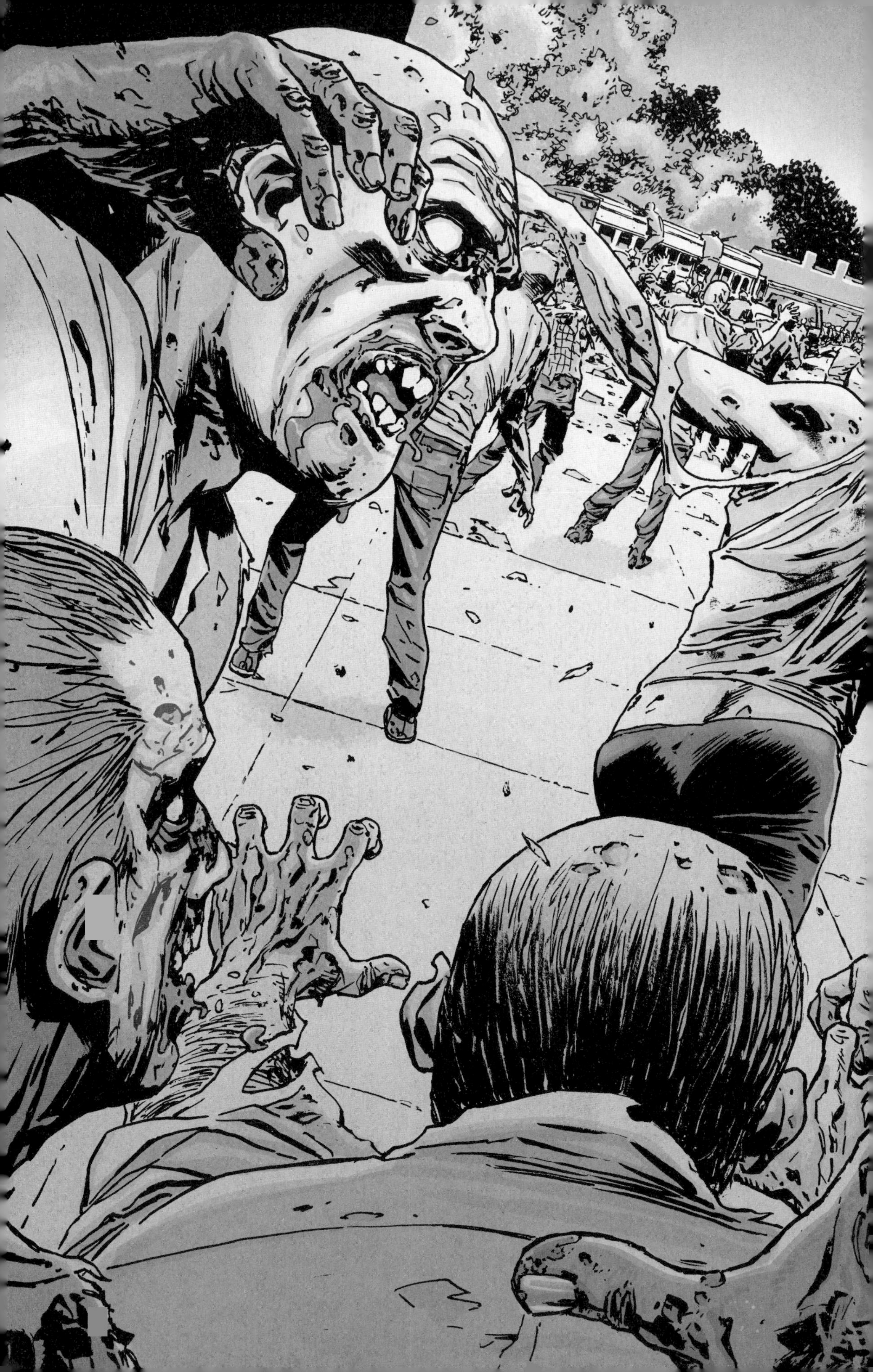

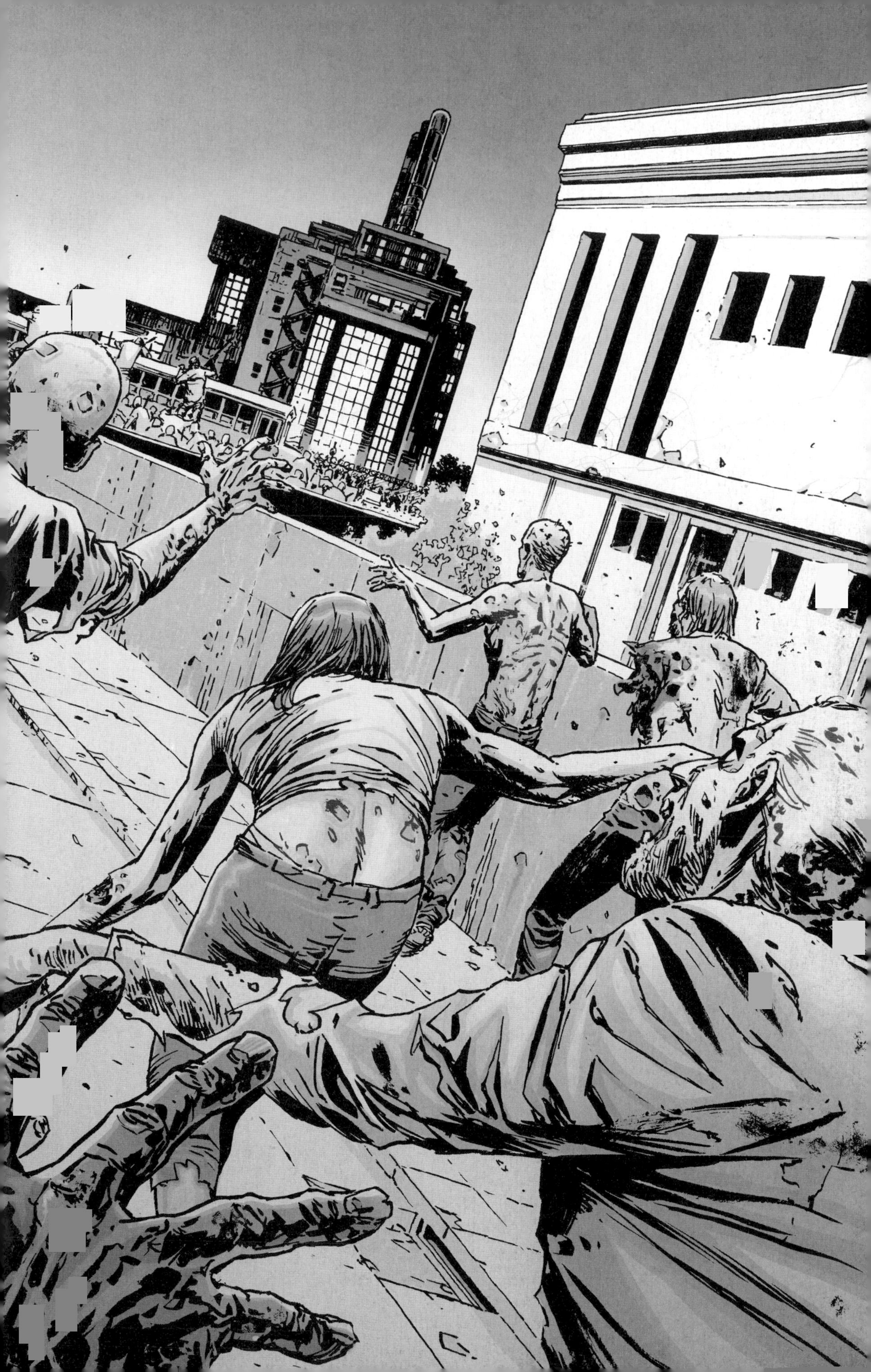

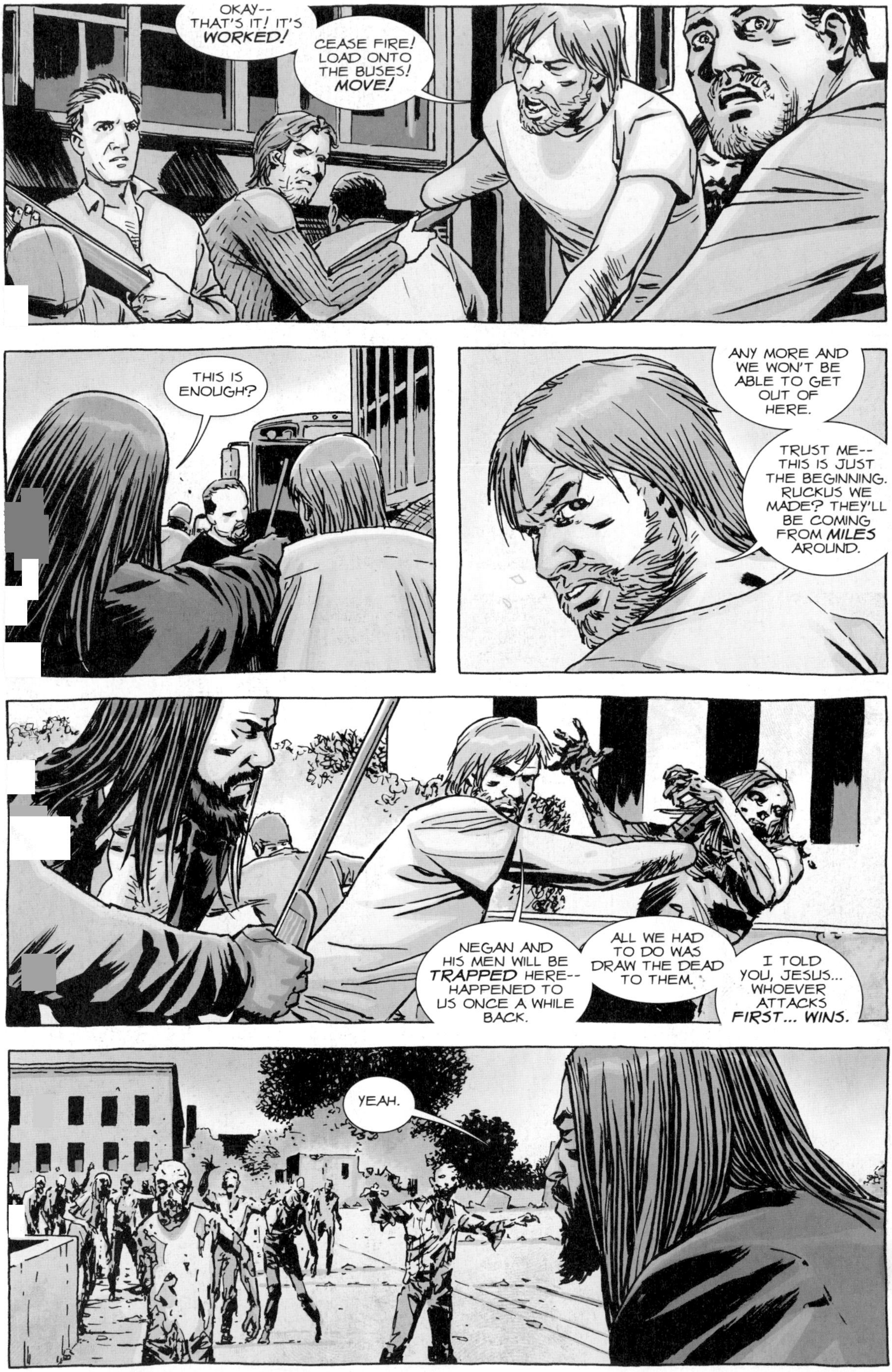
OKAY-- THAT'S IT! IT'S WORKED!
CEASE FIRE! LOAD ONTO THE BUSES! MOVE!
THIS IS ENOUGH?
ANY MORE AND WE WON'T BE ABLE TO GET OUT OF HERE.
TRUST ME-- THIS IS JUST THE BEGINNING. RUCKUS WE MADE? THEY'LL BE COMING FROM MILES AROUND.
NEGAN AND HIS MEN WILL BE TRAPPED HERE-- HAPPENED TO US ONCE A WHILE BACK.
ALL WE HAD TO DO WAS DRAW THE DEAD TO THEM.
I TOLD YOU, JESUS... WHOEVER ATTACKS FIRST... WINS.
YEAH.

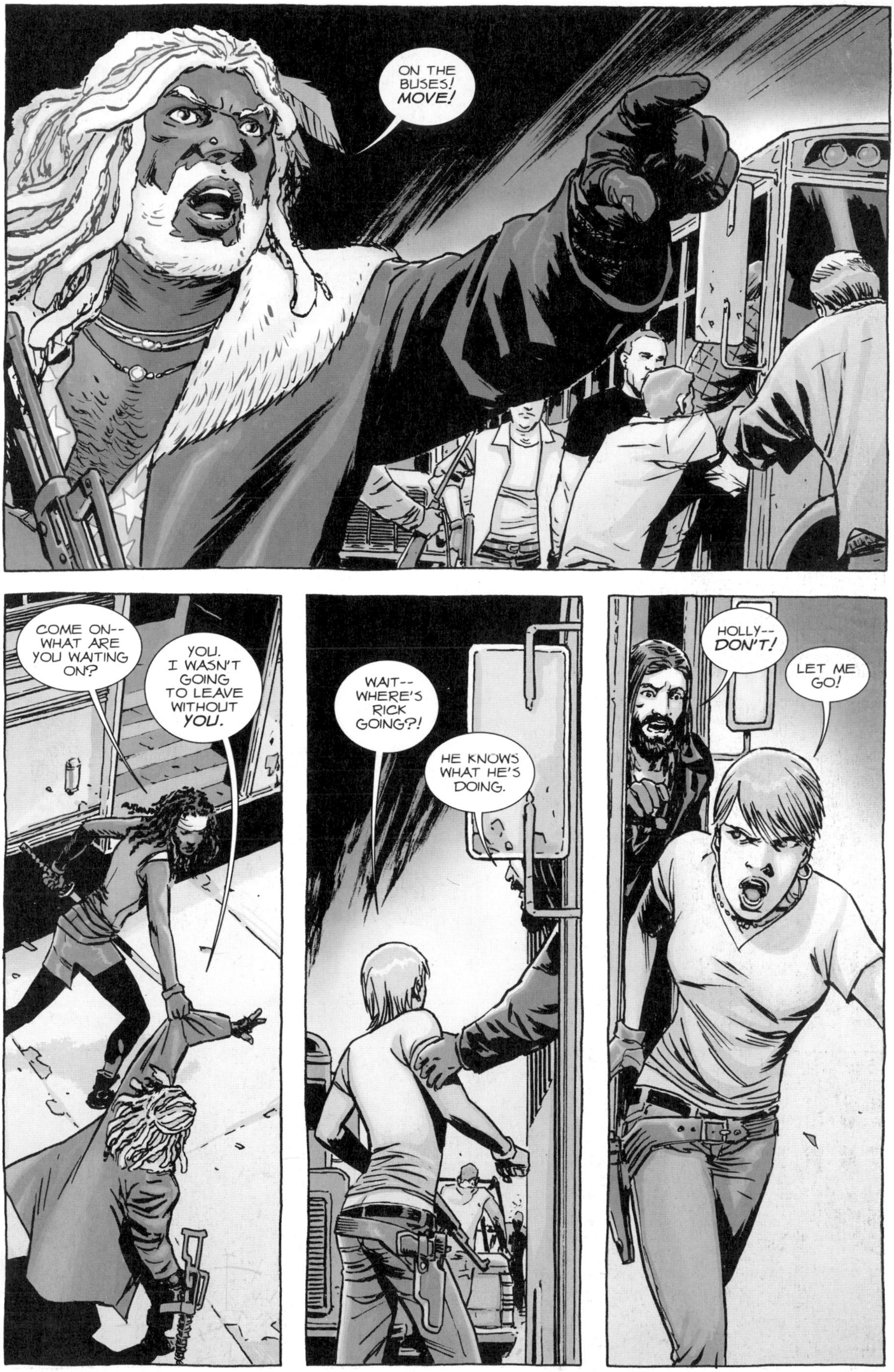
ON THE BUSES! MOVE!
COME ON-- WHAT ARE YOU WAITING ON?
YOU. I WASN'T GOING TO LEAVE WITHOUT YOU.
WAIT-- WHERE'S RICK GOING?!
HE KNOWS WHAT HE'S DOING.
HOLLY-- DON'T!
LET ME GO!

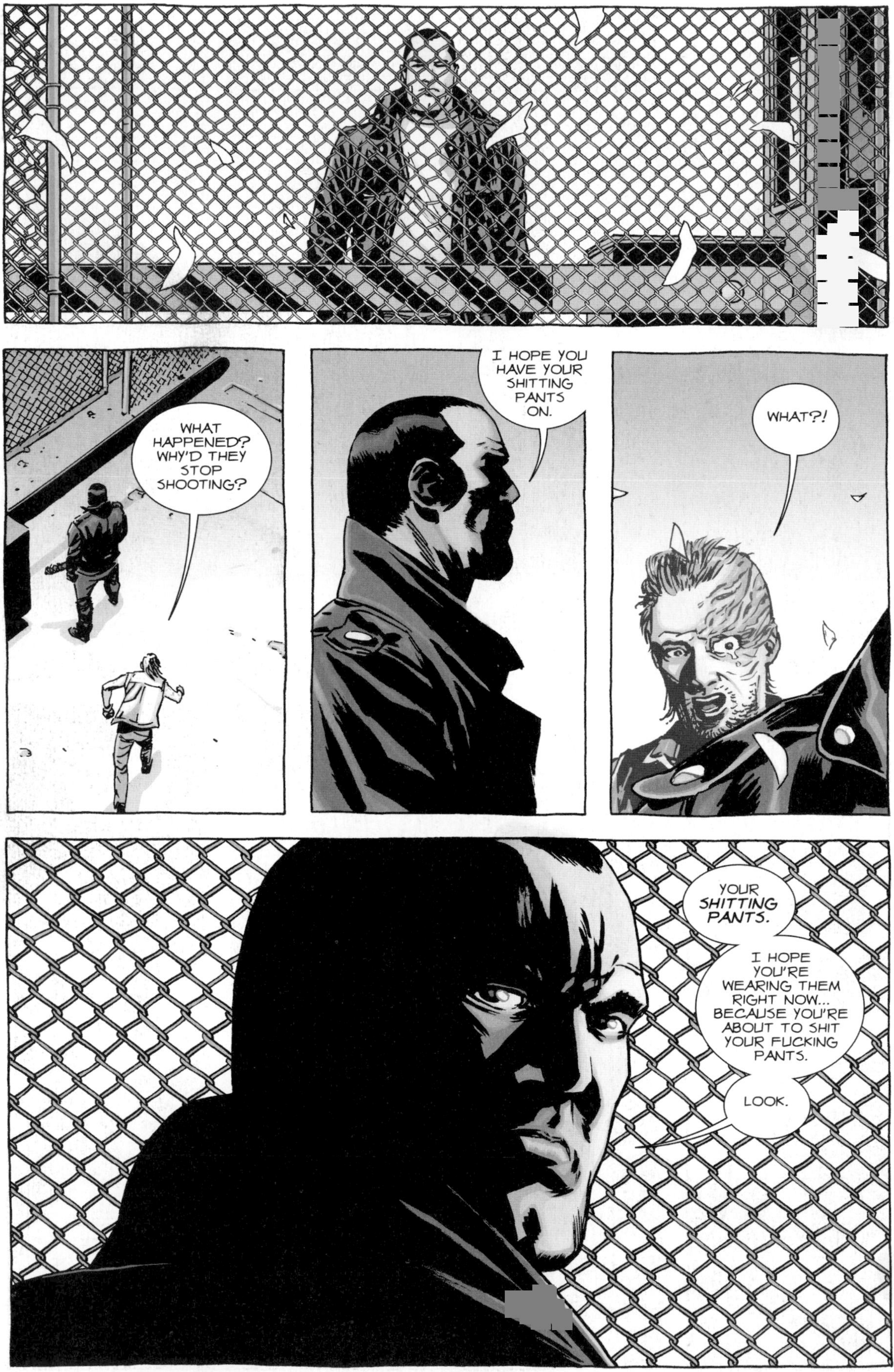
WHAT HAPPENED? WHY'D THEY STOP SHOOTING?
I HOPE YOU HAVE YOUR SHITTING PANTS ON.
WHAT?!
YOUR SHITTING PANTS.
I HOPE YOU'RE WEARING THEM RIGHT NOW... BECAUSE YOU'RE ABOUT TO SHIT YOUR FUCKING PANTS.
LOOK.

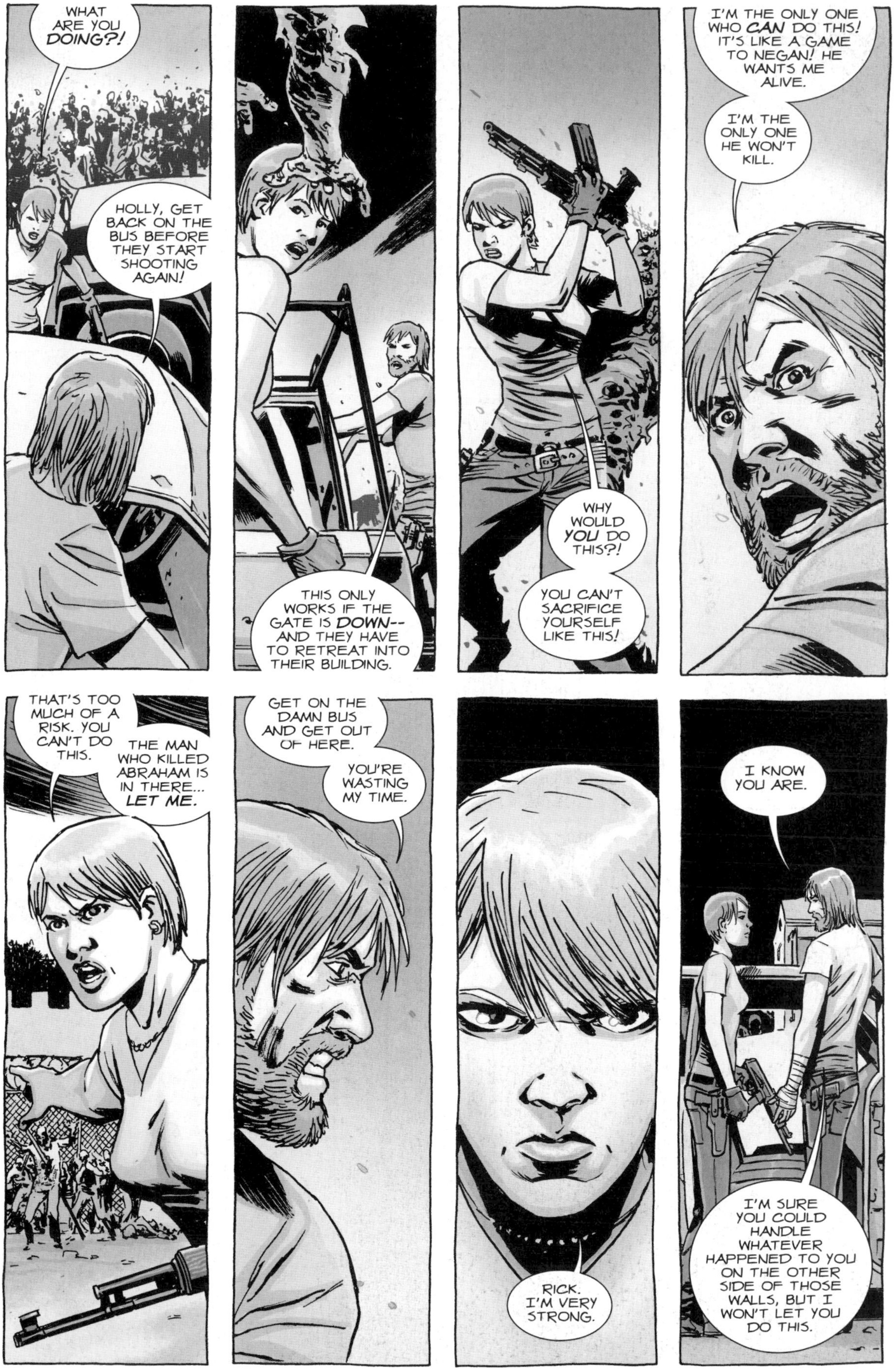
WHAT ARE YOU DOING?!
HOLLY, GET BACK ON THE BUS BEFORE THEY START SHOOTING AGAIN!
THIS ONLY WORKS IF THE GATE IS DOWN-- AND THEY HAVE TO RETREAT INTO THEIR BUILDING.
WHY WOULD YOU DO THIS?!
YOU CAN'T SACRIFICE YOURSELF LIKE THIS!
I'M THE ONLY ONE WHO CAN DO THIS! IT'S LIKE A GAME TO NEGAN! HE WANTS ME ALIVE.
I'M THE ONLY ONE HE WON'T KILL.
THAT'S TOO MUCH OF A RISK. YOU CAN'T DO THIS.
THE MAN WHO KILLED ABRAHAM IS IN THERE... LET ME.
GET ON THE DAMN BUS AND GET OUT OF HERE.
YOU'RE WASTING MY TIME.
RICK. I'M VERY STRONG.
I KNOW YOU ARE.
I'M SURE YOU COULD HANDLE WHATEVER HAPPENED TO YOU ON THE OTHER SIDE OF THOSE WALLS, BUT I WON'T LET YOU DO THIS.

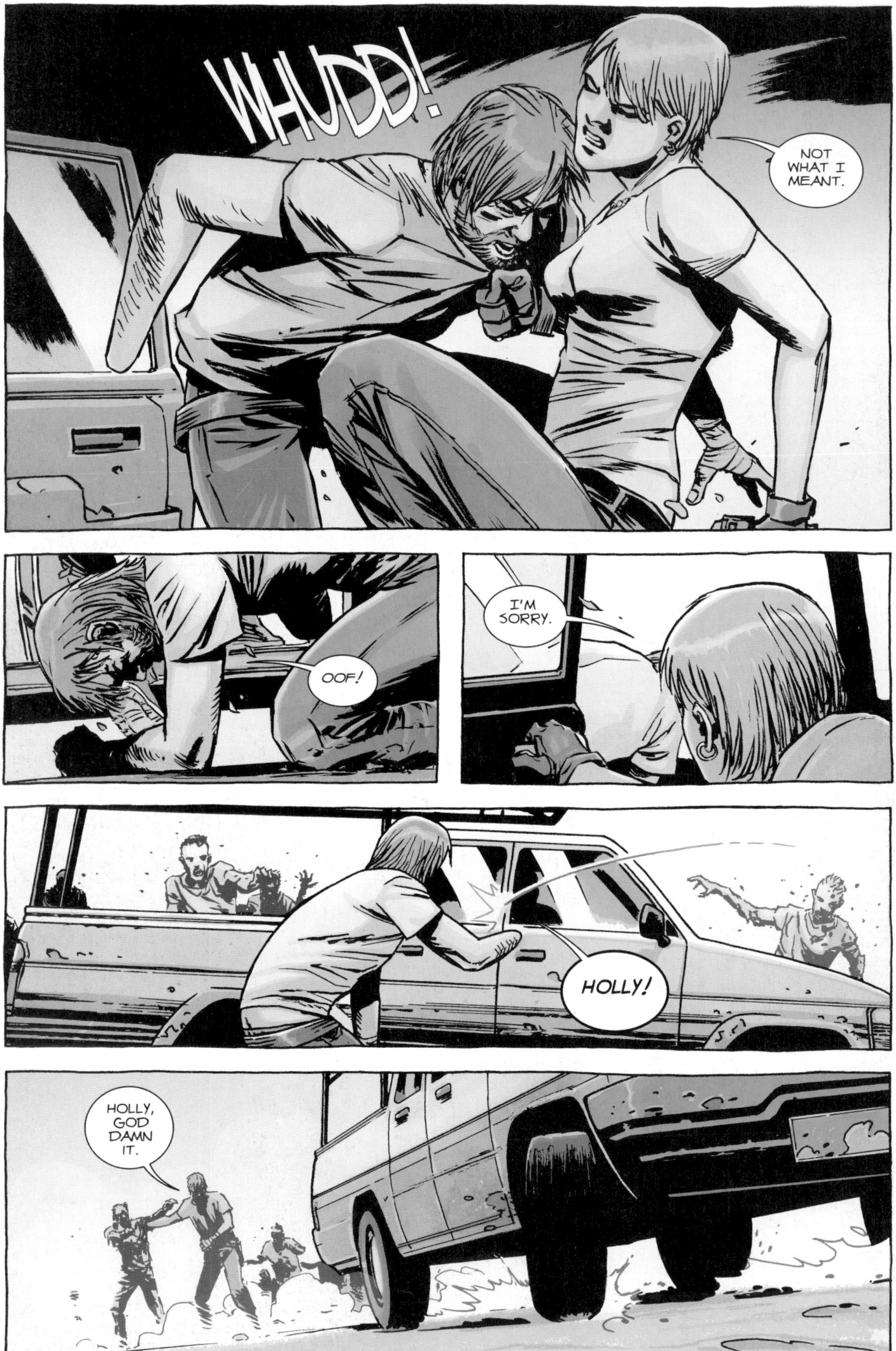
WHUDD!
NOT WHAT I MEANT.
OOF!
I'M SORRY.
HOLLY!
HOLLY, GOD DAMN IT.

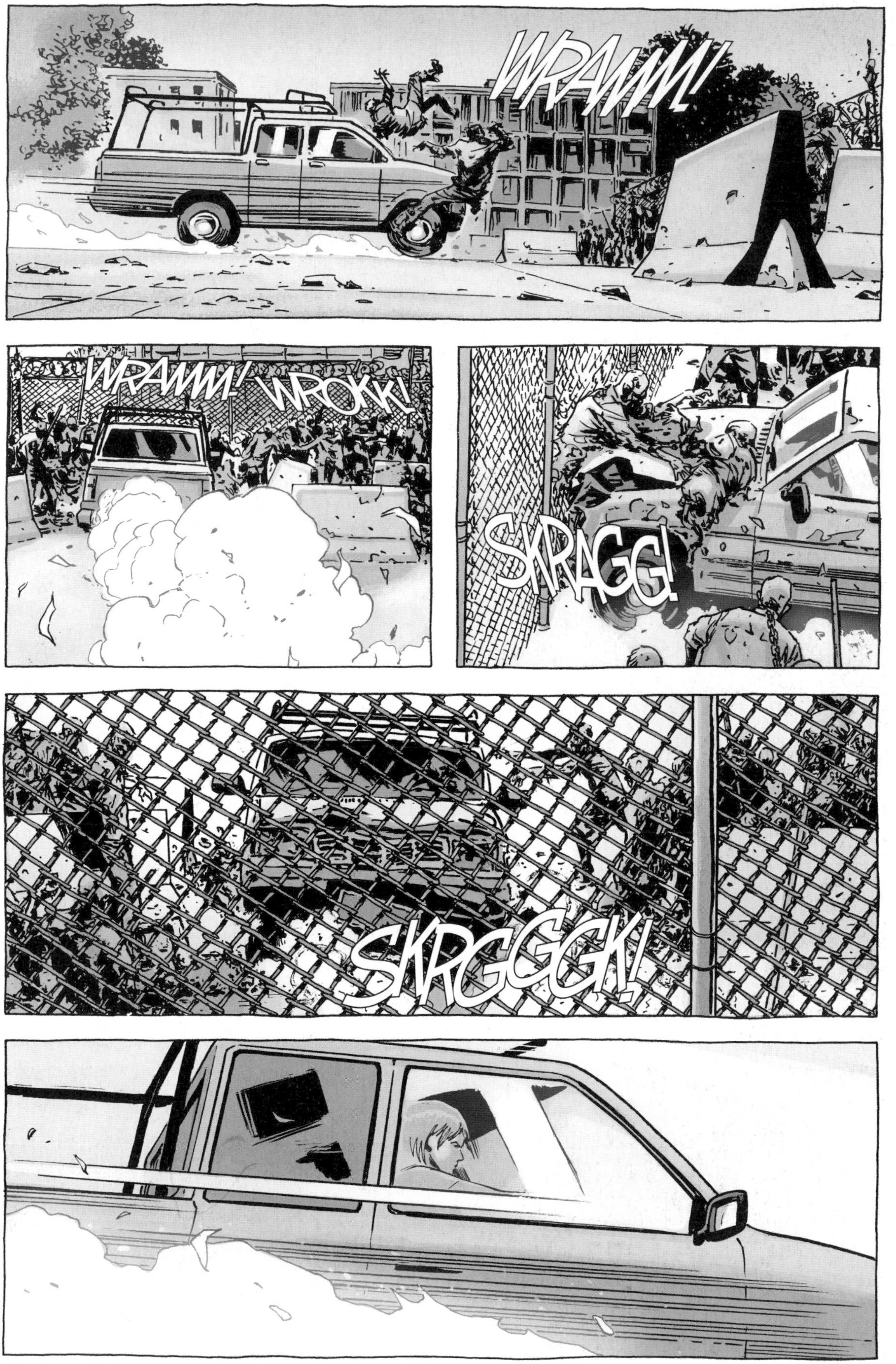
WRAMM!
WRAMM!
WROKK!
SKRAGG!
SKRGGGK!

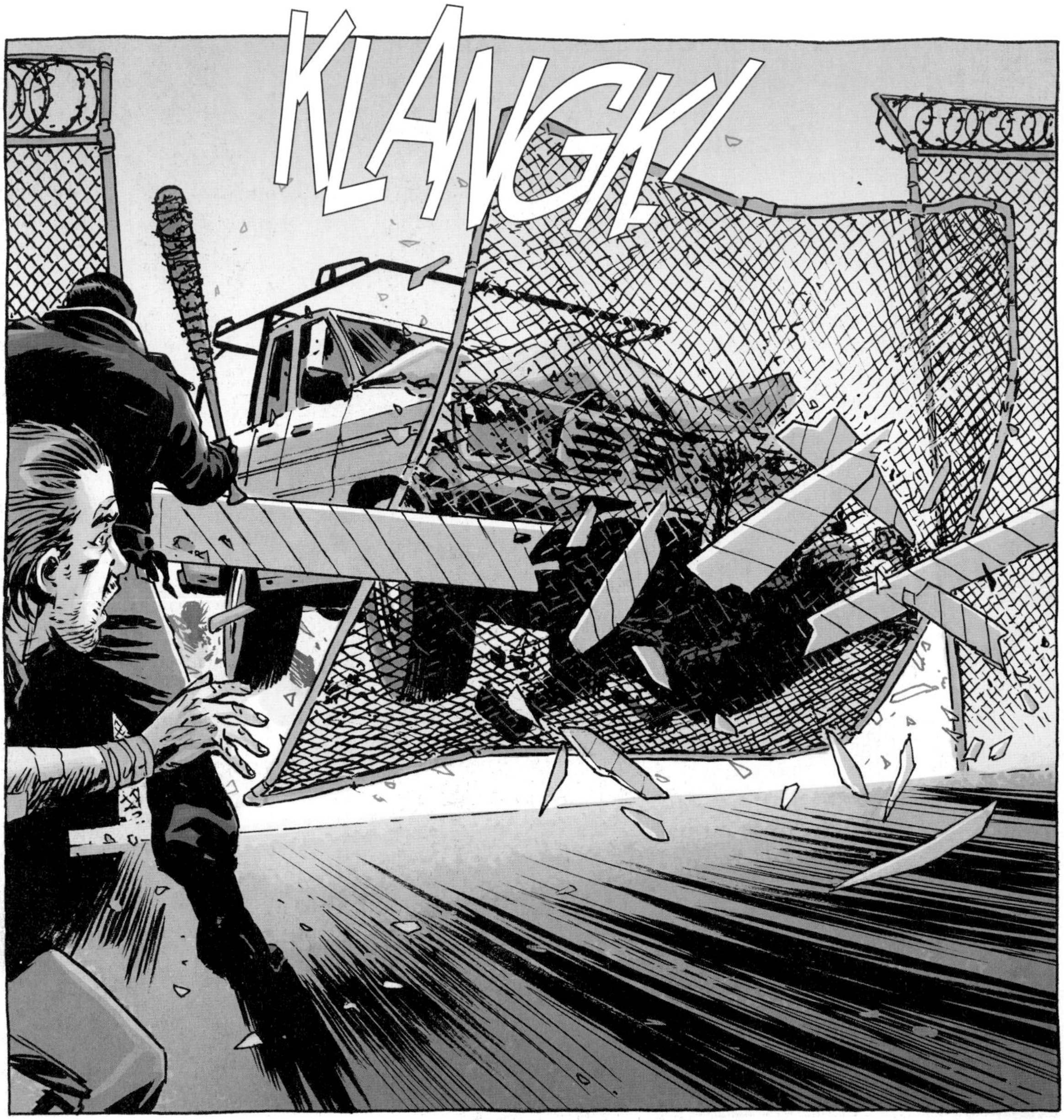
KLANGK!

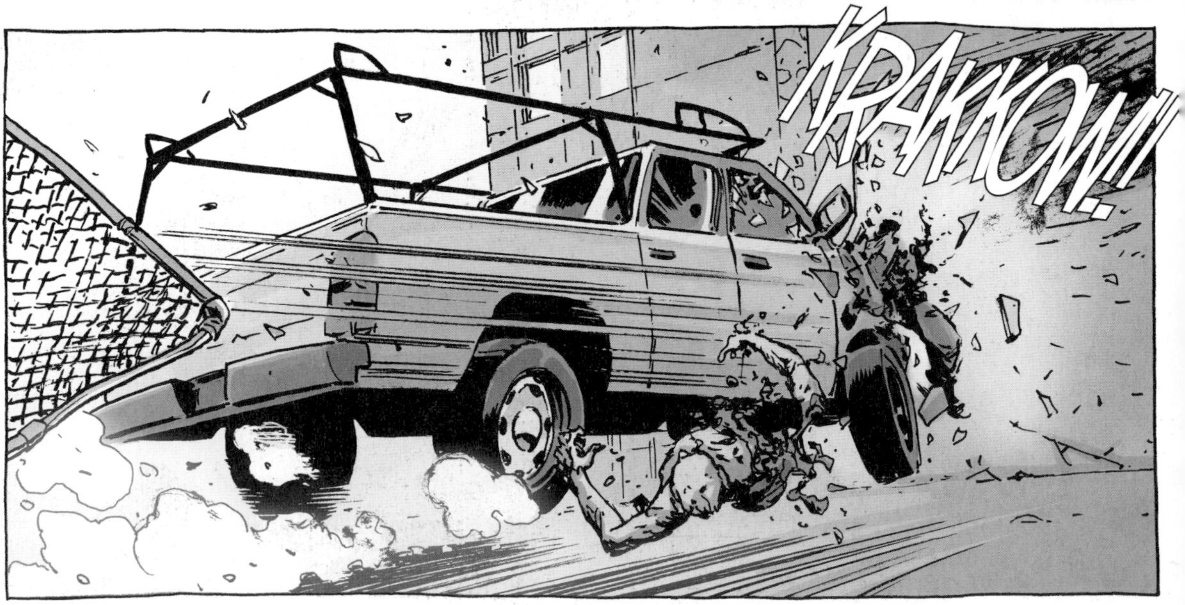
KRAKKOW!!

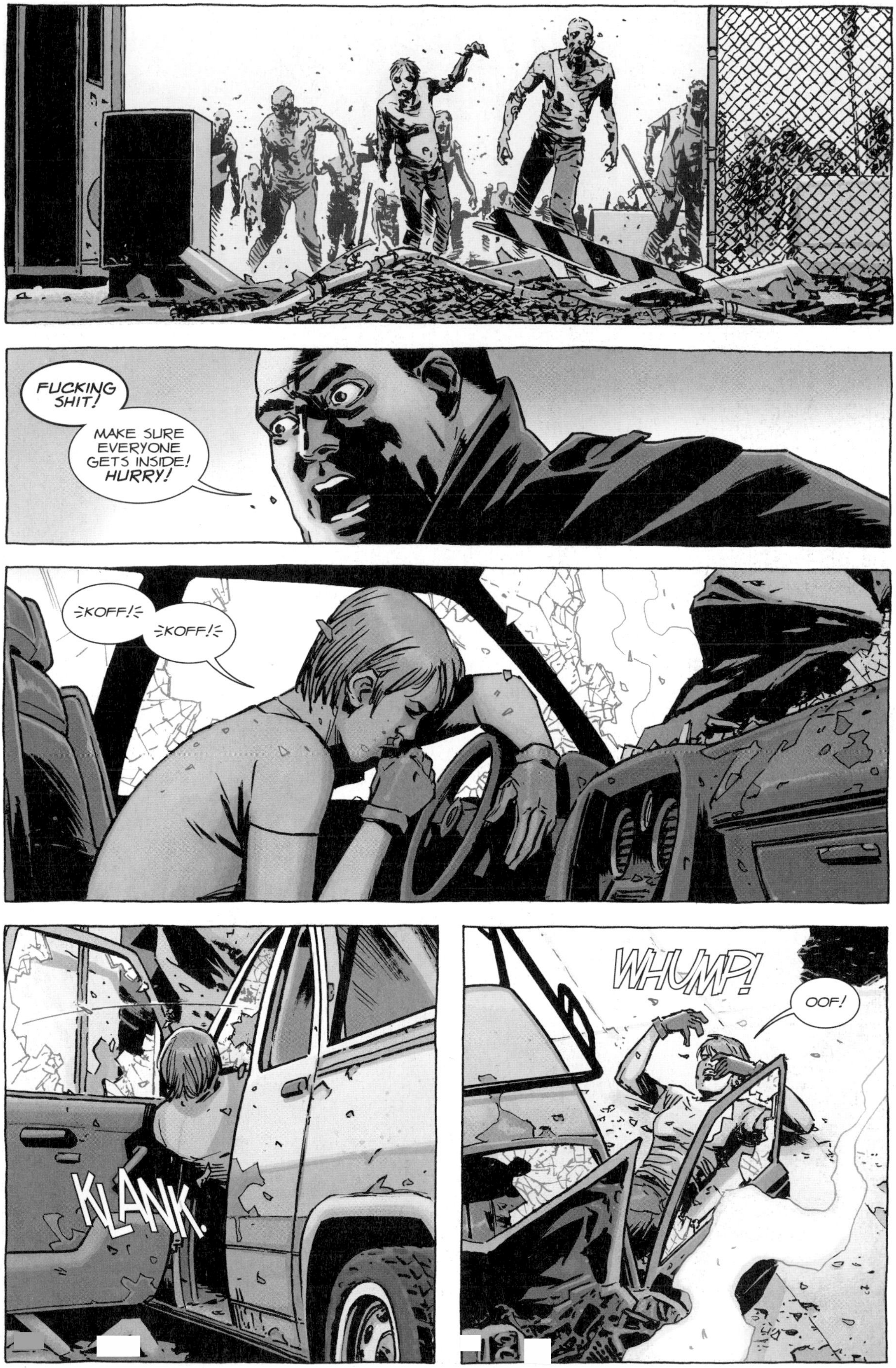
FUCKING SHIT!
MAKE SURE EVERYONE GETS INSIDE! HURRY!
KOFF!
KOFF!
KLANK.
WHUMP!
OOF!

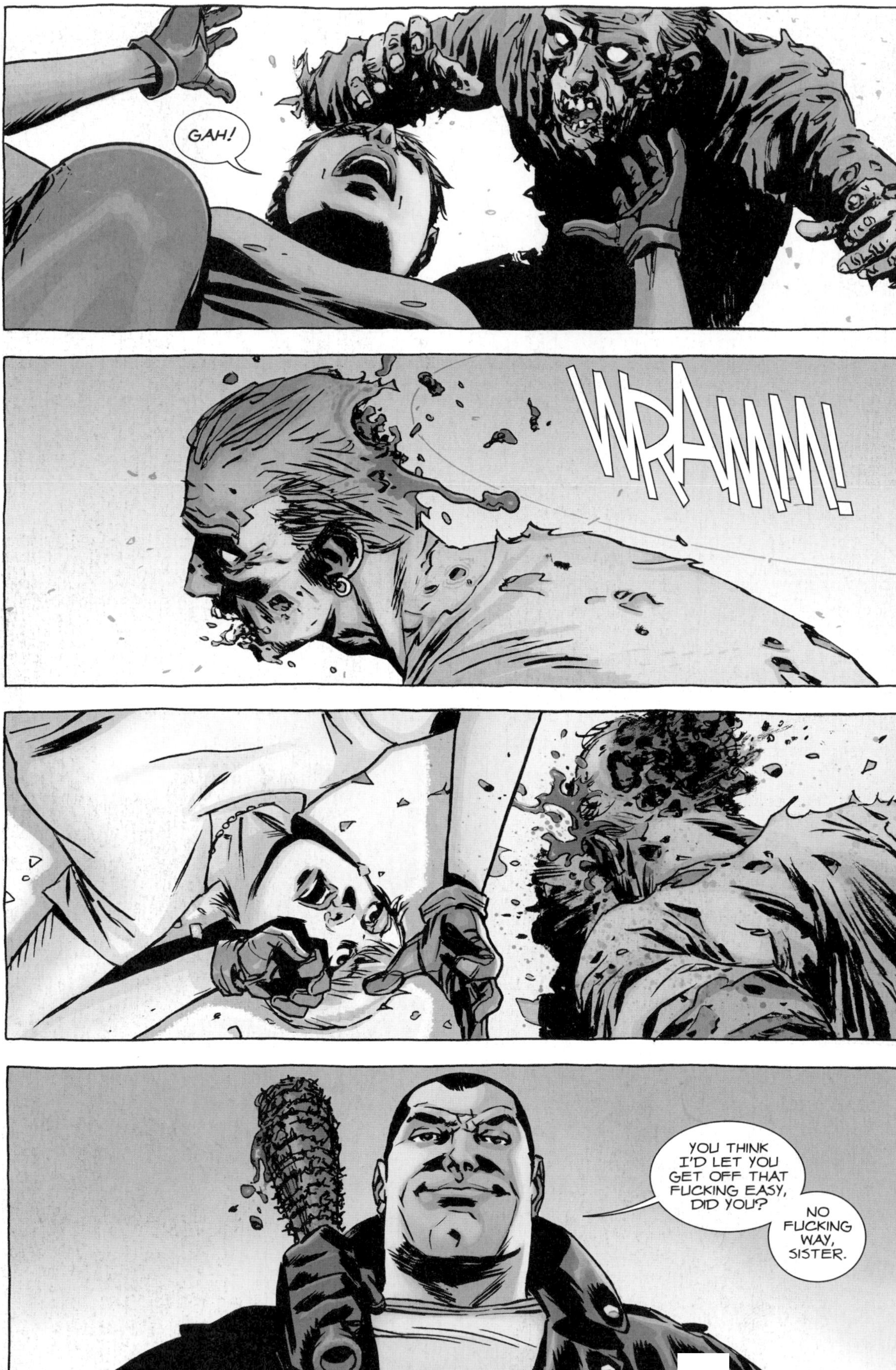
GAH!
WRAMM!
YOU THINK I'D LET YOU GET OFF THAT FUCKING EASY, DID YOU?
NO FUCKING WAY, SISTER.

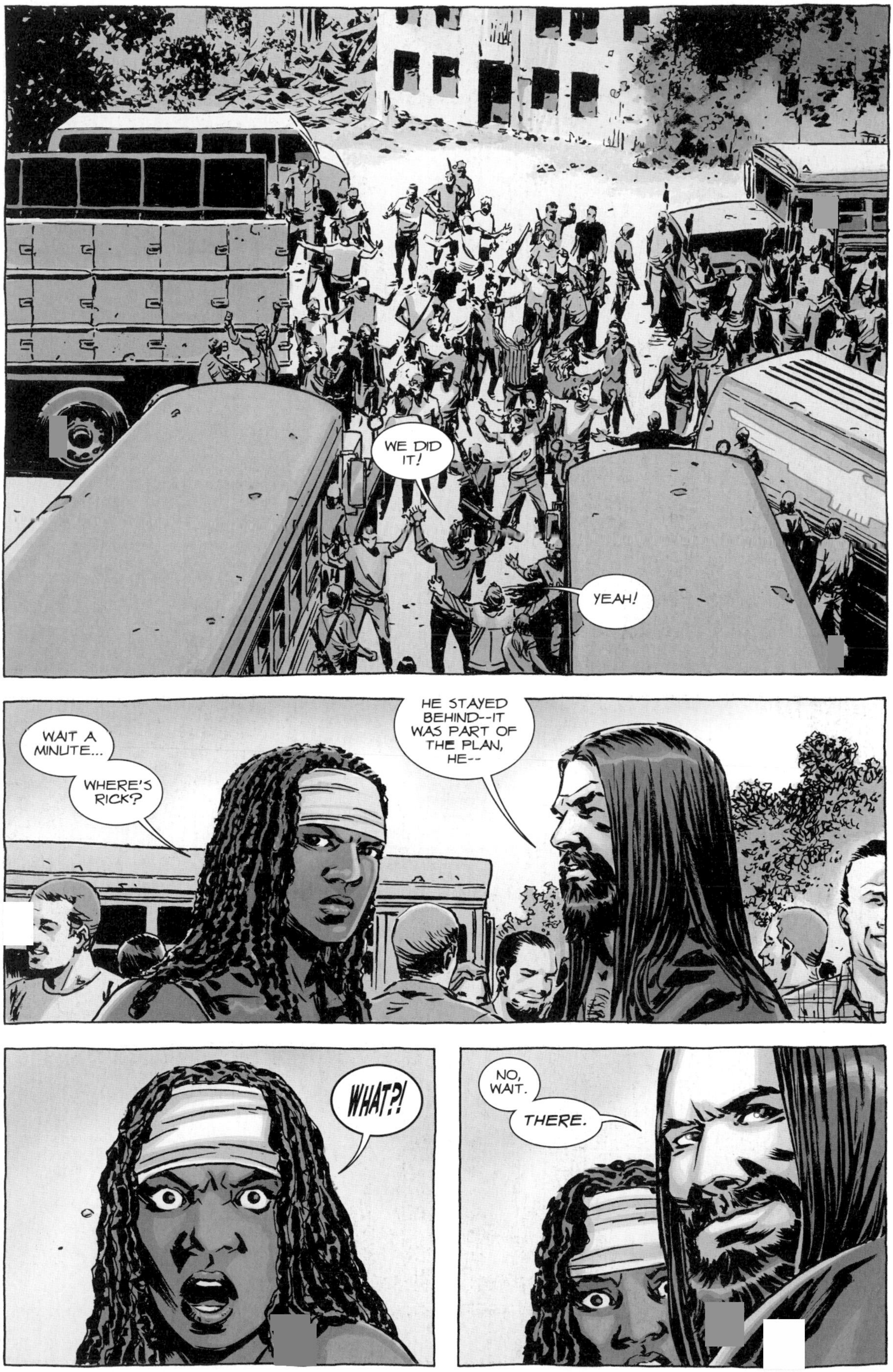
WE DID IT!
YEAH!
WAIT A MINUTE...
WHERE'S RICK?
HE STAYED BEHIND--IT WAS PART OF THE PLAN, HE--
WHAT?!
NO, WAIT.
THERE.

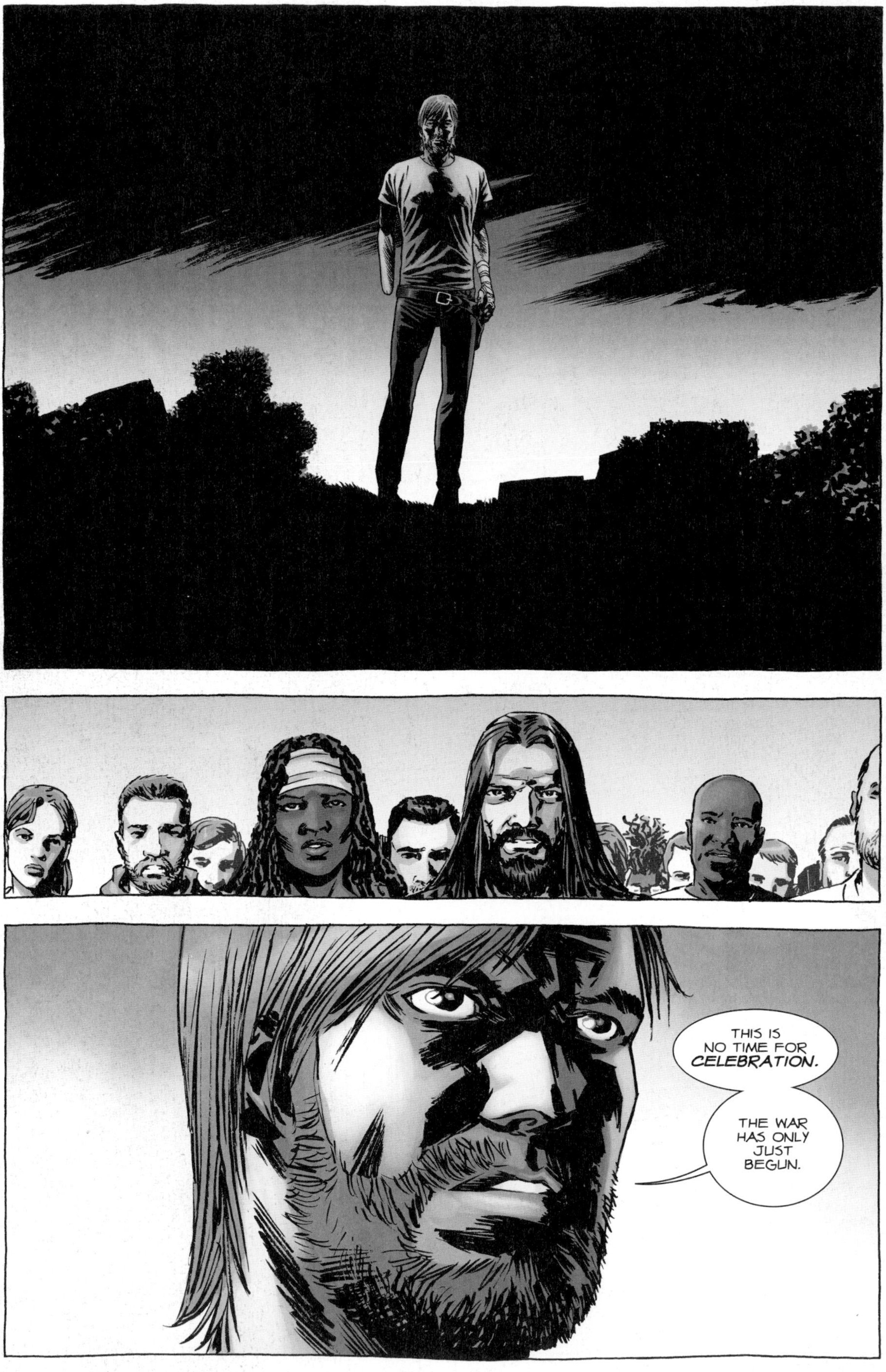
THIS IS NO TIME FOR *CELEBRATION.*
THE WAR HAS ONLY JUST BEGUN.

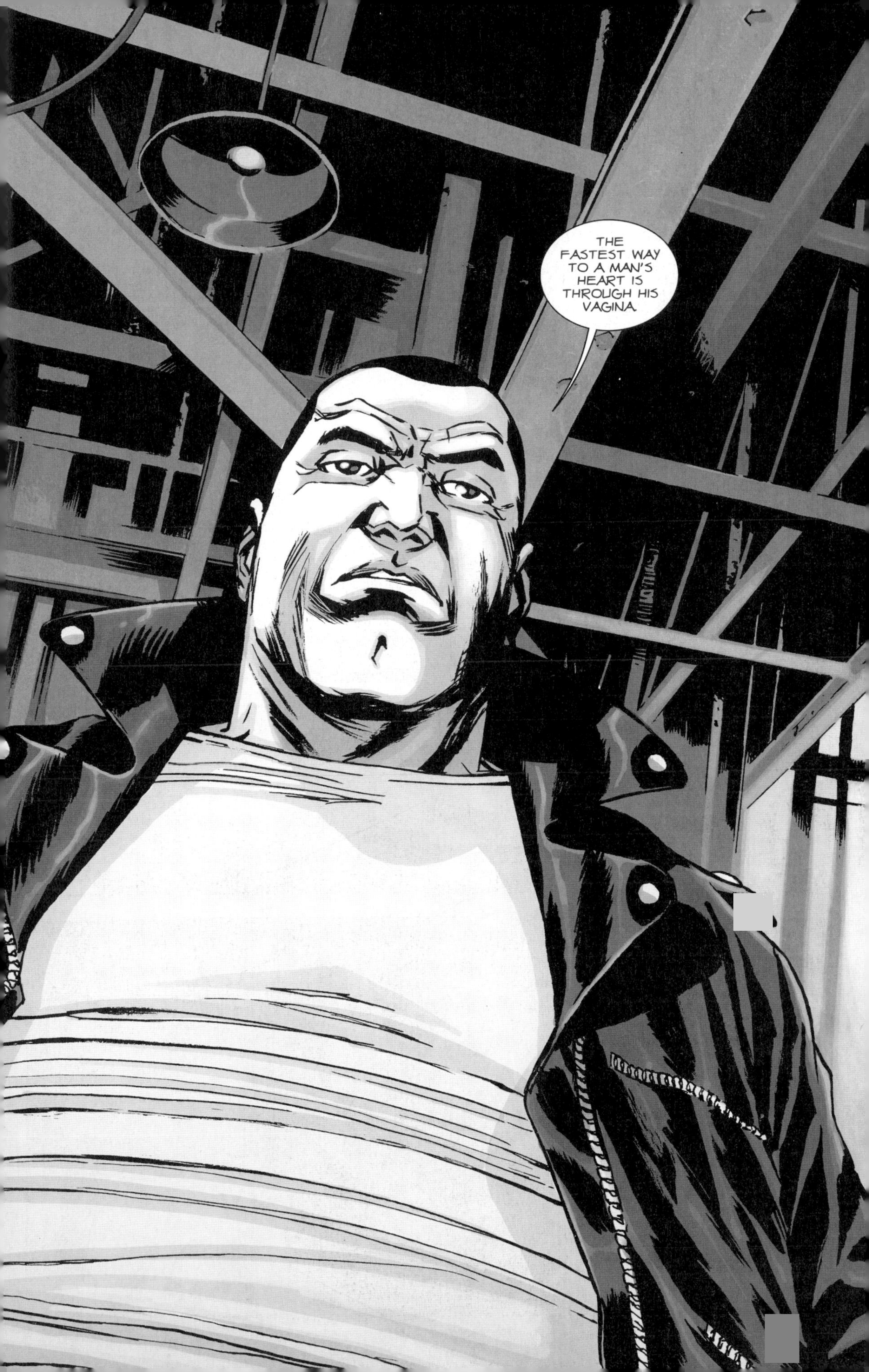
THE FASTEST WAY TO A MAN'S HEART IS THROUGH HIS VAGINA.

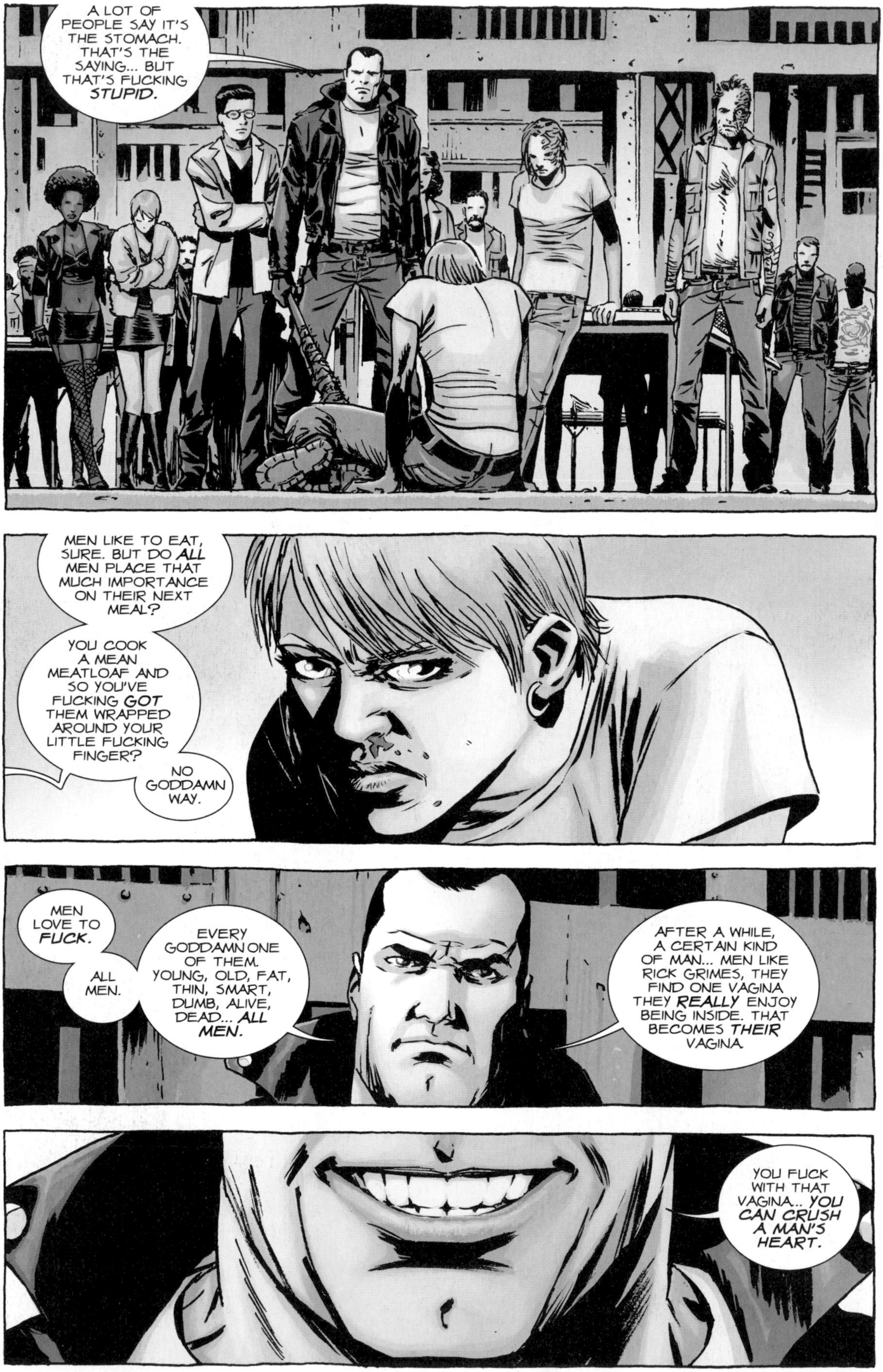
A LOT OF PEOPLE SAY IT'S THE STOMACH. THAT'S THE SAYING... BUT THAT'S FUCKING STUPID.
MEN LIKE TO EAT, SURE. BUT DO ALL MEN PLACE THAT MUCH IMPORTANCE ON THEIR NEXT MEAL?
YOU COOK A MEAN MEATLOAF AND SO YOU'VE FUCKING GOT THEM WRAPPED AROUND YOUR LITTLE FUCKING FINGER?
NO GODDAMN WAY.
MEN LOVE TO FUCK.
ALL MEN.
EVERY GODDAMN ONE OF THEM. YOUNG, OLD, FAT, THIN, SMART, DUMB, ALIVE, DEAD... ALL MEN.
AFTER A WHILE, A CERTAIN KIND OF MAN... MEN LIKE RICK GRIMES, THEY FIND ONE VAGINA THEY REALLY ENJOY BEING INSIDE. THAT BECOMES THEIR VAGINA.
YOU FUCK WITH THAT VAGINA... YOU CAN CRUSH A MAN'S HEART.

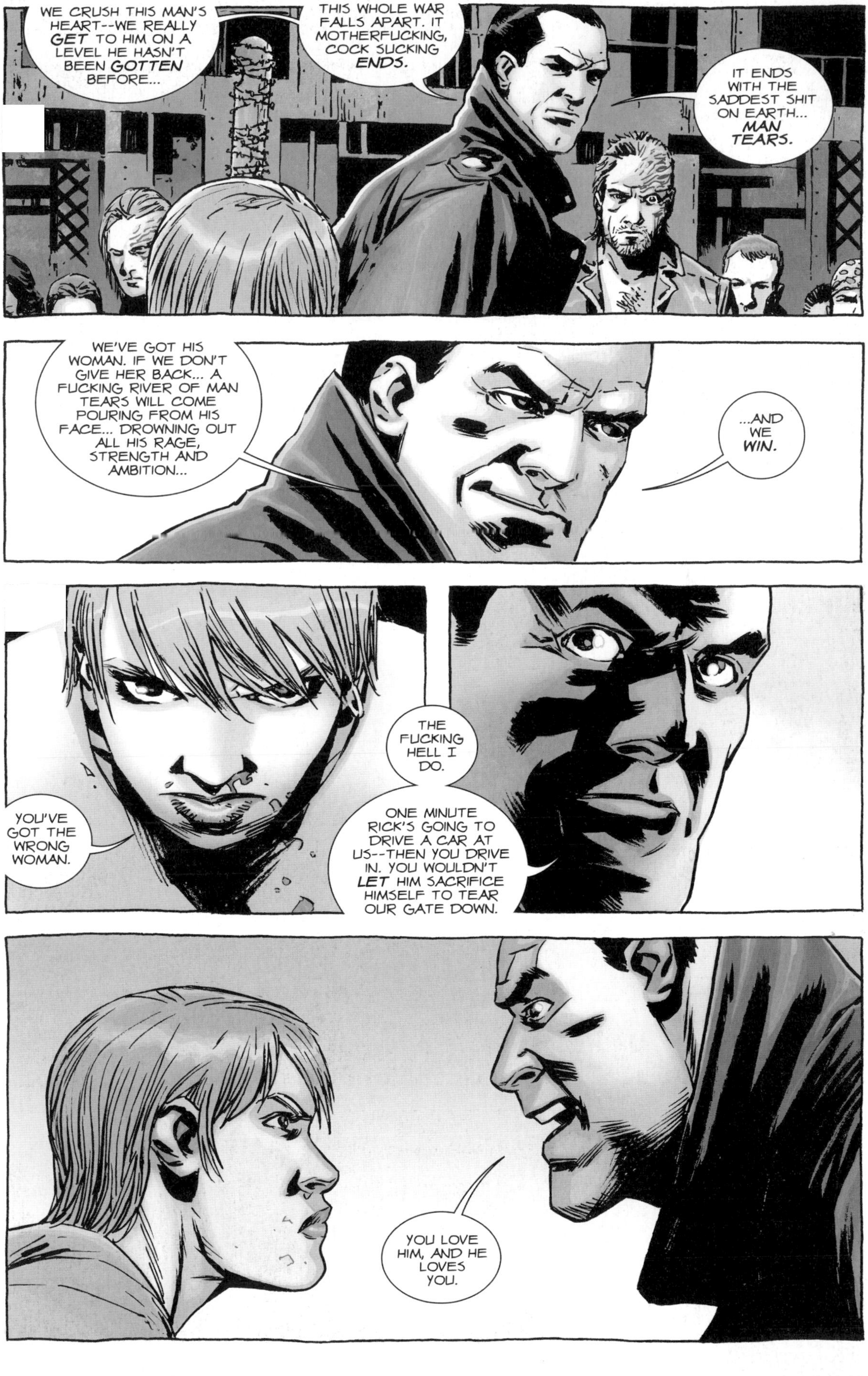
WE CRUSH THIS MAN'S HEART--WE REALLY GET TO HIM ON A LEVEL HE HASN'T BEEN GOTTEN BEFORE...
THIS WHOLE WAR FALLS APART. IT MOTHERFUCKING, COCK SUCKING ENDS.
IT ENDS WITH THE SADDEST SHIT ON EARTH... MAN TEARS.
WE'VE GOT HIS WOMAN. IF WE DON'T GIVE HER BACK... A FUCKING RIVER OF MAN TEARS WILL COME POURING FROM HIS FACE... DROWNING OUT ALL HIS RAGE, STRENGTH AND AMBITION...
...AND WE WIN.
YOU'VE GOT THE WRONG WOMAN.
THE FUCKING HELL I DO.
ONE MINUTE RICK'S GOING TO DRIVE A CAR AT US--THEN YOU DRIVE IN. YOU WOULDN'T LET HIM SACRIFICE HIMSELF TO TEAR OUR GATE DOWN.
YOU LOVE HIM, AND HE LOVES YOU.

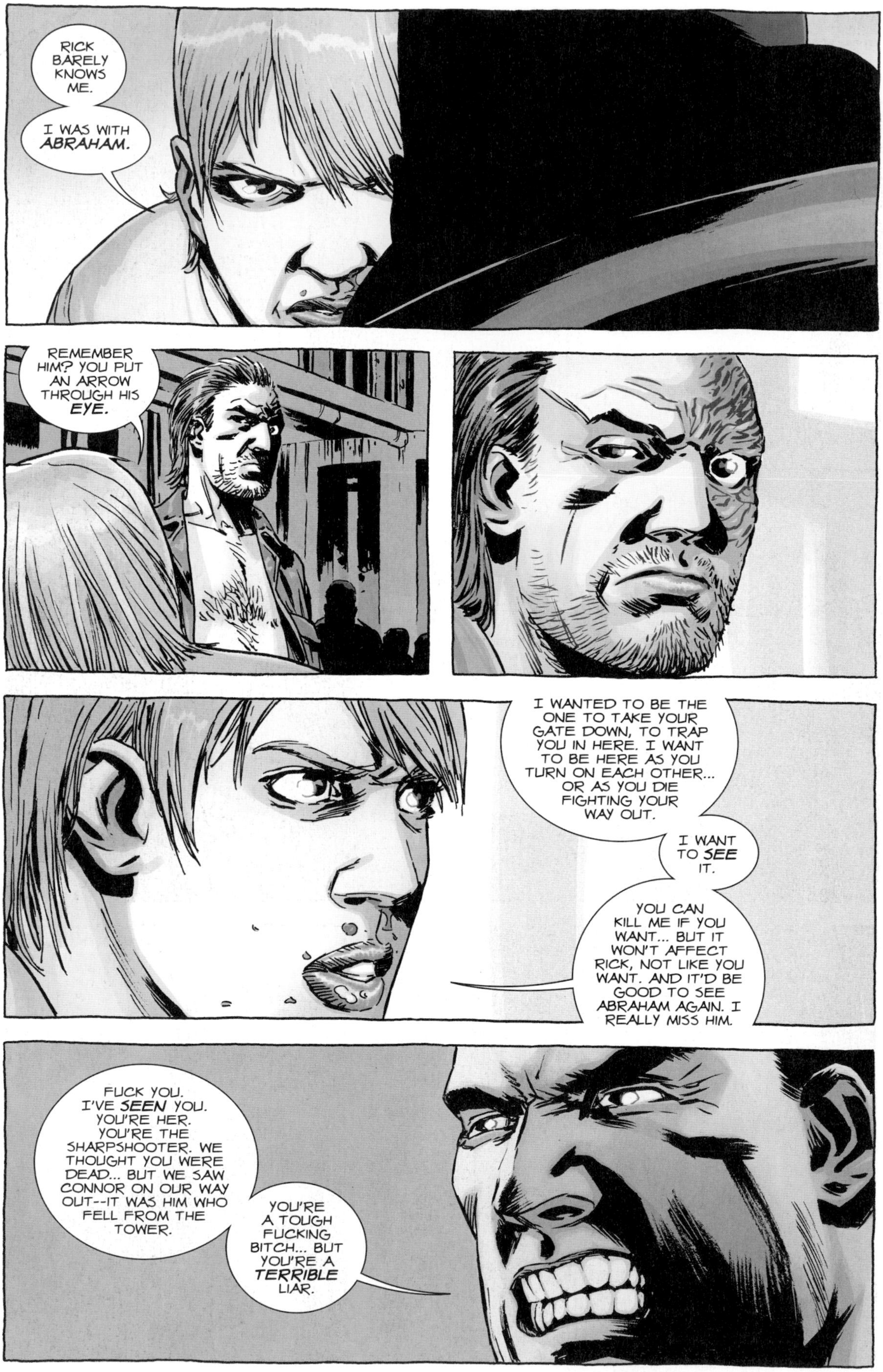
RICK BARELY KNOWS ME.
I WAS WITH ABRAHAM.
REMEMBER HIM? YOU PUT AN ARROW THROUGH HIS EYE.
I WANTED TO BE THE ONE TO TAKE YOUR GATE DOWN, TO TRAP YOU IN HERE. I WANT TO BE HERE AS YOU TURN ON EACH OTHER... OR AS YOU DIE FIGHTING YOUR WAY OUT.
I WANT TO SEE IT.
YOU CAN KILL ME IF YOU WANT... BUT IT WON'T AFFECT RICK, NOT LIKE YOU WANT. AND IT'D BE GOOD TO SEE ABRAHAM AGAIN. I REALLY MISS HIM.
FUCK YOU. I'VE SEEN YOU. YOU'RE HER. YOU'RE THE SHARPSHOOTER. WE THOUGHT YOU WERE DEAD... BUT WE SAW CONNOR ON OUR WAY OUT--IT WAS HIM WHO FELL FROM THE TOWER.
YOU'RE A TOUGH FUCKING BITCH... BUT YOU'RE A TERRIBLE LIAR.

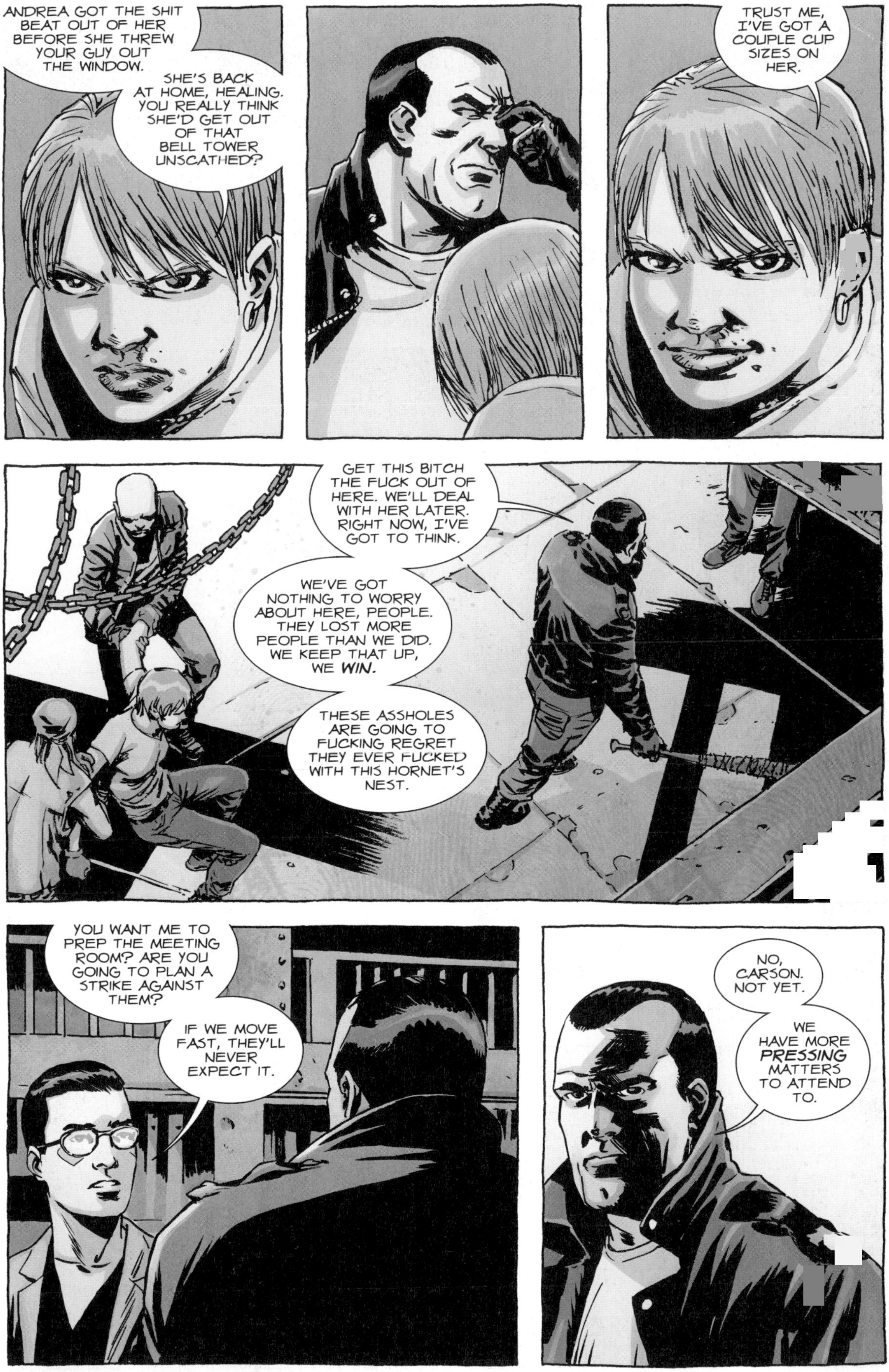
ANDREA GOT THE SHIT BEAT OUT OF HER BEFORE SHE THREW YOUR GUY OUT THE WINDOW.
SHE'S BACK AT HOME, HEALING. YOU REALLY THINK SHE'D GET OUT OF THAT BELL TOWER UNSCATHED?
TRUST ME, I'VE GOT A COUPLE CUP SIZES ON HER.
GET THIS BITCH THE FUCK OUT OF HERE. WE'LL DEAL WITH HER LATER. RIGHT NOW, I'VE GOT TO THINK.
WE'VE GOT NOTHING TO WORRY ABOUT HERE, PEOPLE. THEY LOST MORE PEOPLE THAN WE DID. WE KEEP THAT UP, WE WIN.
THESE ASSHOLES ARE GOING TO FUCKING REGRET THEY EVER FUCKED WITH THIS HORNET'S NEST.
YOU WANT ME TO PREP THE MEETING ROOM? ARE YOU GOING TO PLAN A STRIKE AGAINST THEM?
IF WE MOVE FAST, THEY'LL NEVER EXPECT IT.
NO, CARSON. NOT YET.
WE HAVE MORE PRESSING MATTERS TO ATTEND TO.

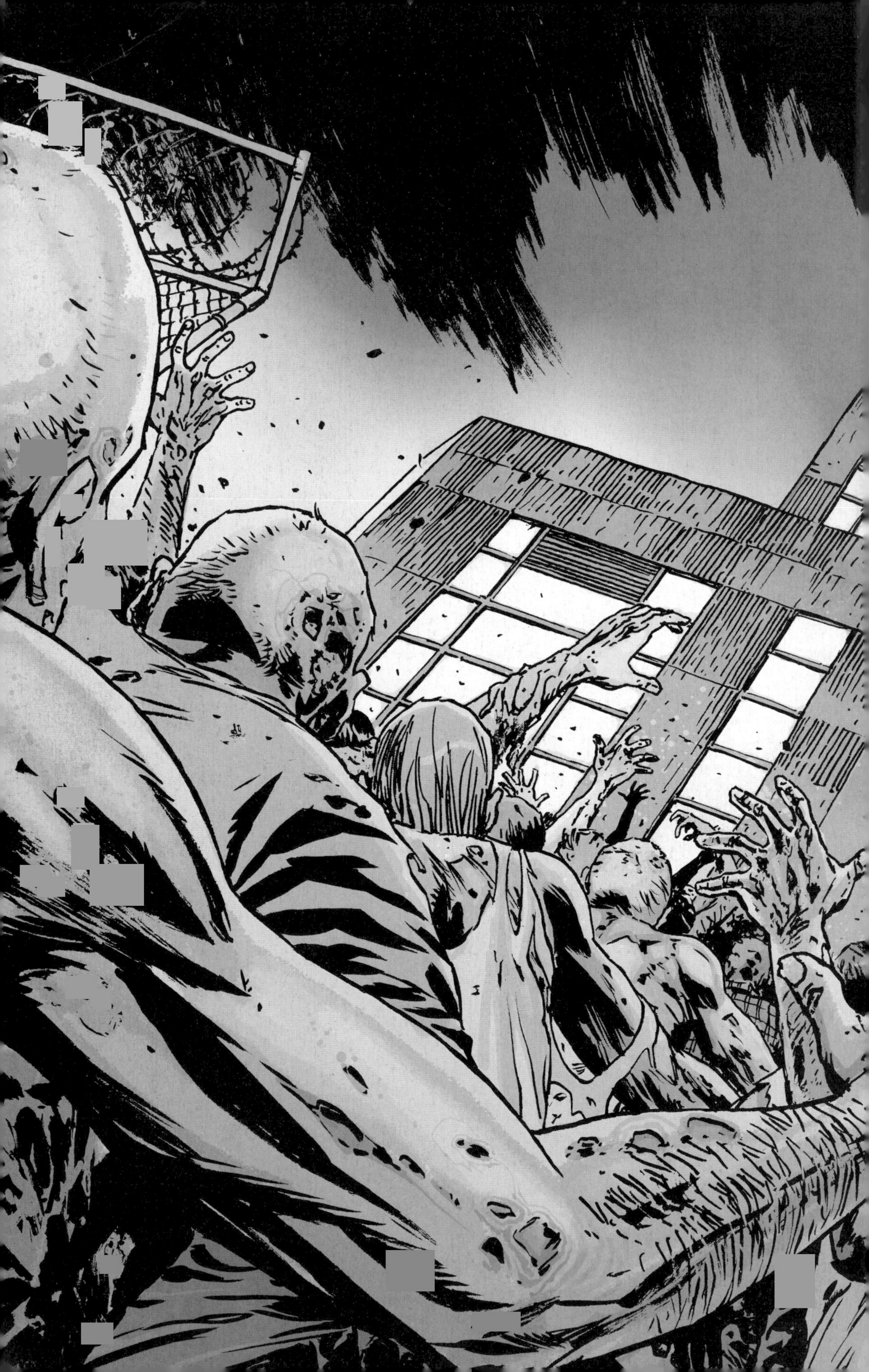

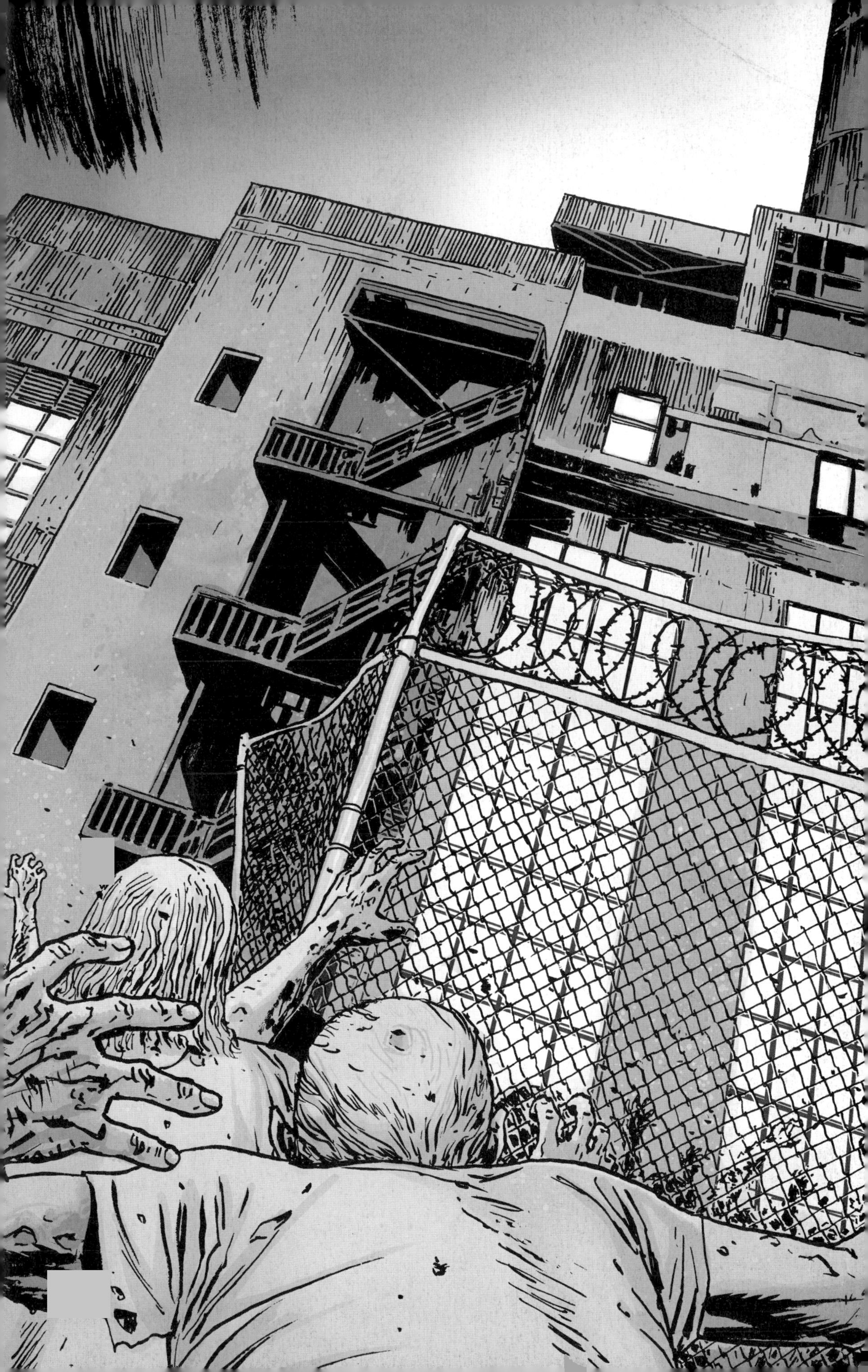

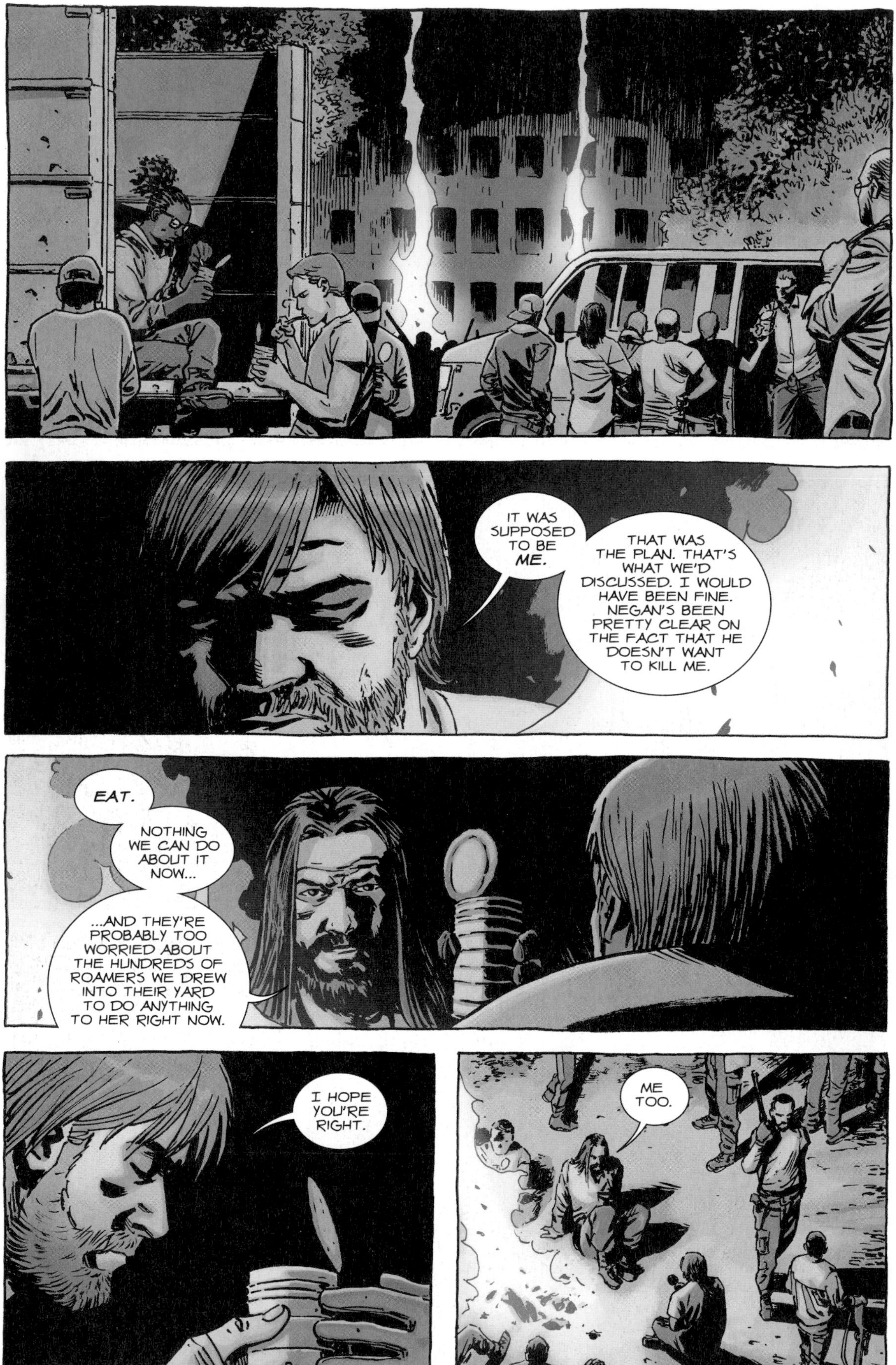

IT WAS SUPPOSED TO BE *ME.*
THAT WAS THE PLAN. THAT'S WHAT WE'D DISCUSSED. I WOULD HAVE BEEN FINE. NEGAN'S BEEN PRETTY CLEAR ON THE FACT THAT HE DOESN'T WANT TO KILL ME.
EAT.
NOTHING WE CAN DO ABOUT IT NOW...
...AND THEY'RE PROBABLY TOO WORRIED ABOUT THE HUNDREDS OF ROAMERS WE DREW INTO THEIR YARD TO DO ANYTHING TO HER RIGHT NOW.
I HOPE YOU'RE RIGHT.
ME TOO.

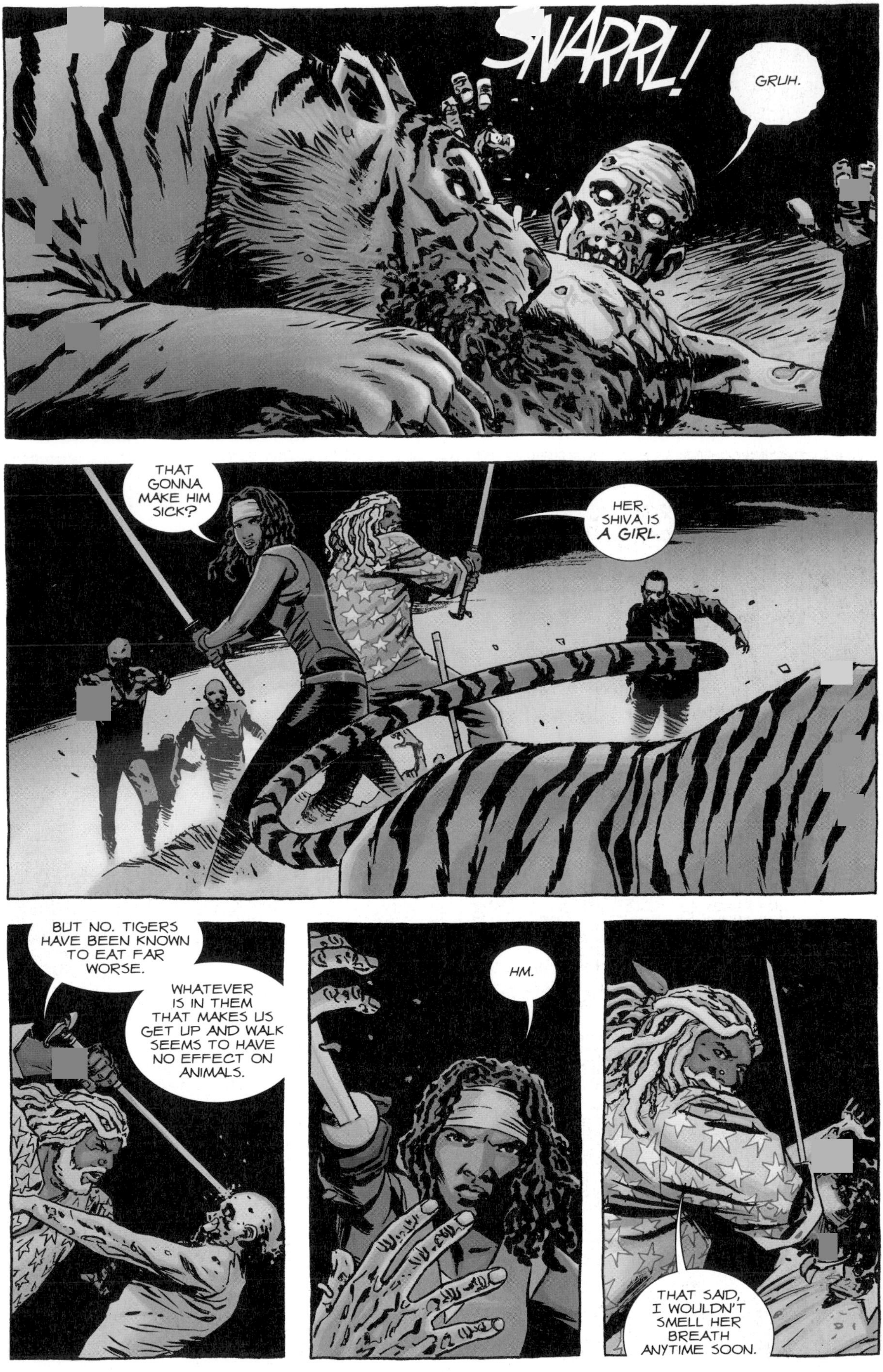
SNARRL!
GRUH.
THAT GONNA MAKE HIM SICK?
HER. SHIVA IS A GIRL.
BUT NO. TIGERS HAVE BEEN KNOWN TO EAT FAR WORSE.
WHATEVER IS IN THEM THAT MAKES US GET UP AND WALK SEEMS TO HAVE NO EFFECT ON ANIMALS.
HM.
THAT SAID, I WOULDN'T SMELL HER BREATH ANYTIME SOON.

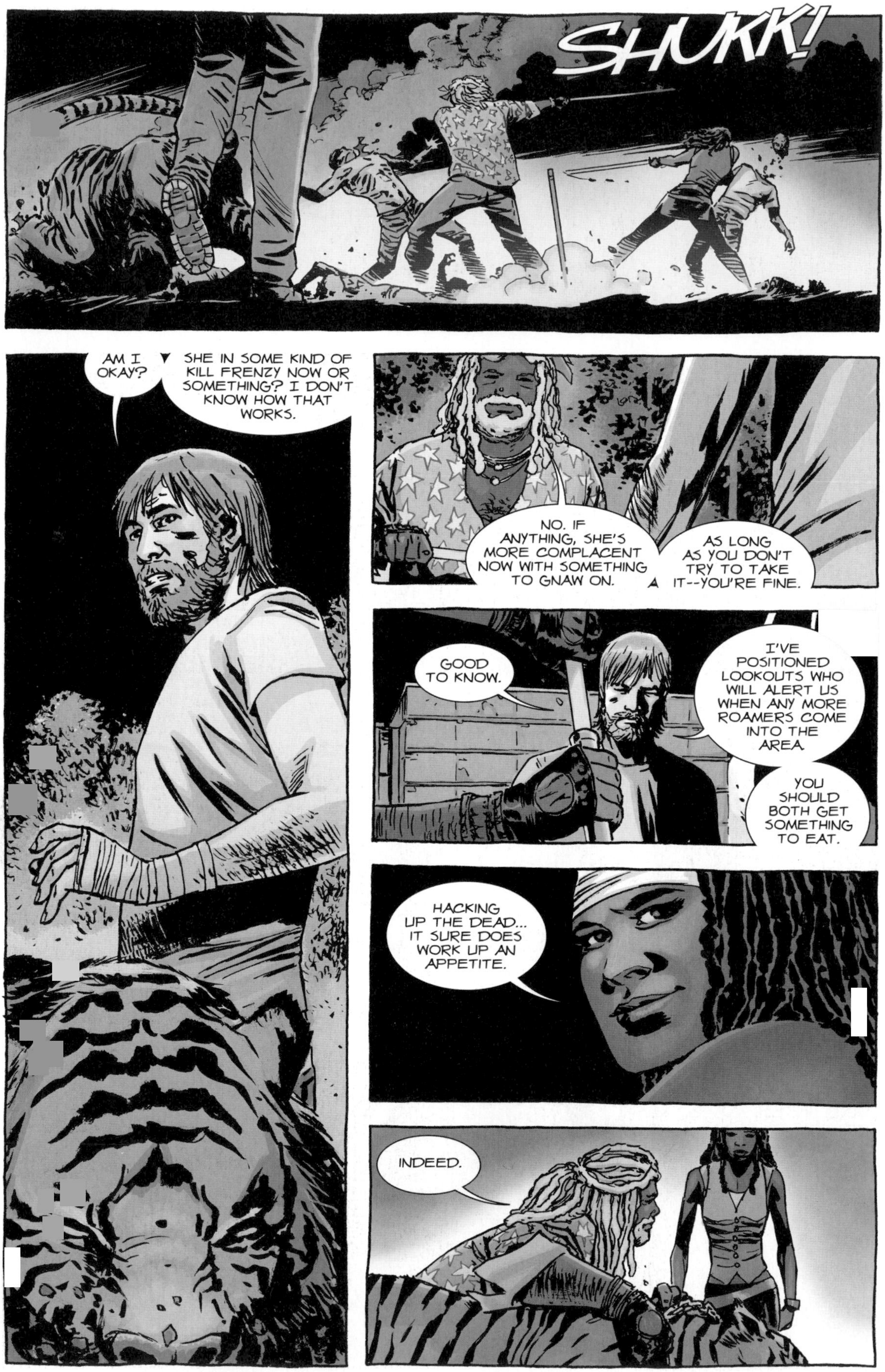
SHUKK!
AM I OKAY?
SHE IN SOME KIND OF KILL FRENZY NOW OR SOMETHING? I DON'T KNOW HOW THAT WORKS.
NO. IF ANYTHING, SHE'S MORE COMPLACENT NOW WITH SOMETHING TO GNAW ON.
AS LONG AS YOU DON'T TRY TO TAKE IT--YOU'RE FINE.
GOOD TO KNOW.
I'VE POSITIONED LOOKOUTS WHO WILL ALERT US WHEN ANY MORE ROAMERS COME INTO THE AREA.
YOU SHOULD BOTH GET SOMETHING TO EAT.
HACKING UP THE DEAD... IT SURE DOES WORK UP AN APPETITE.
INDEED.

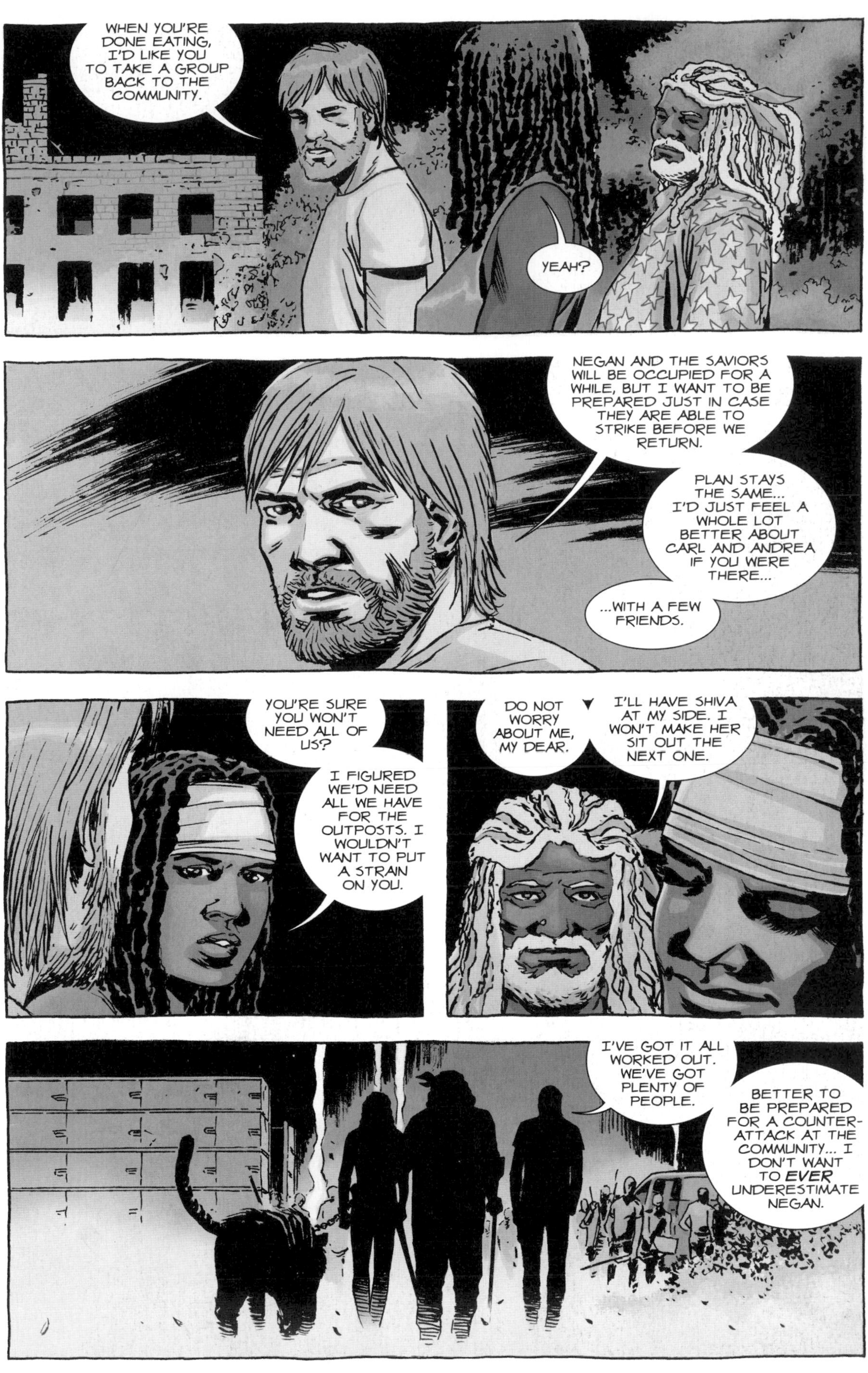
WHEN YOU'RE DONE EATING, I'D LIKE YOU TO TAKE A GROUP BACK TO THE COMMUNITY.
YEAH?
NEGAN AND THE SAVIORS WILL BE OCCUPIED FOR A WHILE, BUT I WANT TO BE PREPARED JUST IN CASE THEY ARE ABLE TO STRIKE BEFORE WE RETURN.
PLAN STAYS THE SAME... I'D JUST FEEL A WHOLE LOT BETTER ABOUT CARL AND ANDREA IF YOU WERE THERE...
...WITH A FEW FRIENDS.
YOU'RE SURE YOU WON'T NEED ALL OF US?
I FIGURED WE'D NEED ALL WE HAVE FOR THE OUTPOSTS. I WOULDN'T WANT TO PUT A STRAIN ON YOU.
DO NOT WORRY ABOUT ME, MY DEAR.
I'LL HAVE SHIVA AT MY SIDE. I WON'T MAKE HER SIT OUT THE NEXT ONE.
I'VE GOT IT ALL WORKED OUT. WE'VE GOT PLENTY OF PEOPLE.
BETTER TO BE PREPARED FOR A COUNTER-ATTACK AT THE COMMUNITY... I DON'T WANT TO *EVER* UNDERESTIMATE NEGAN.

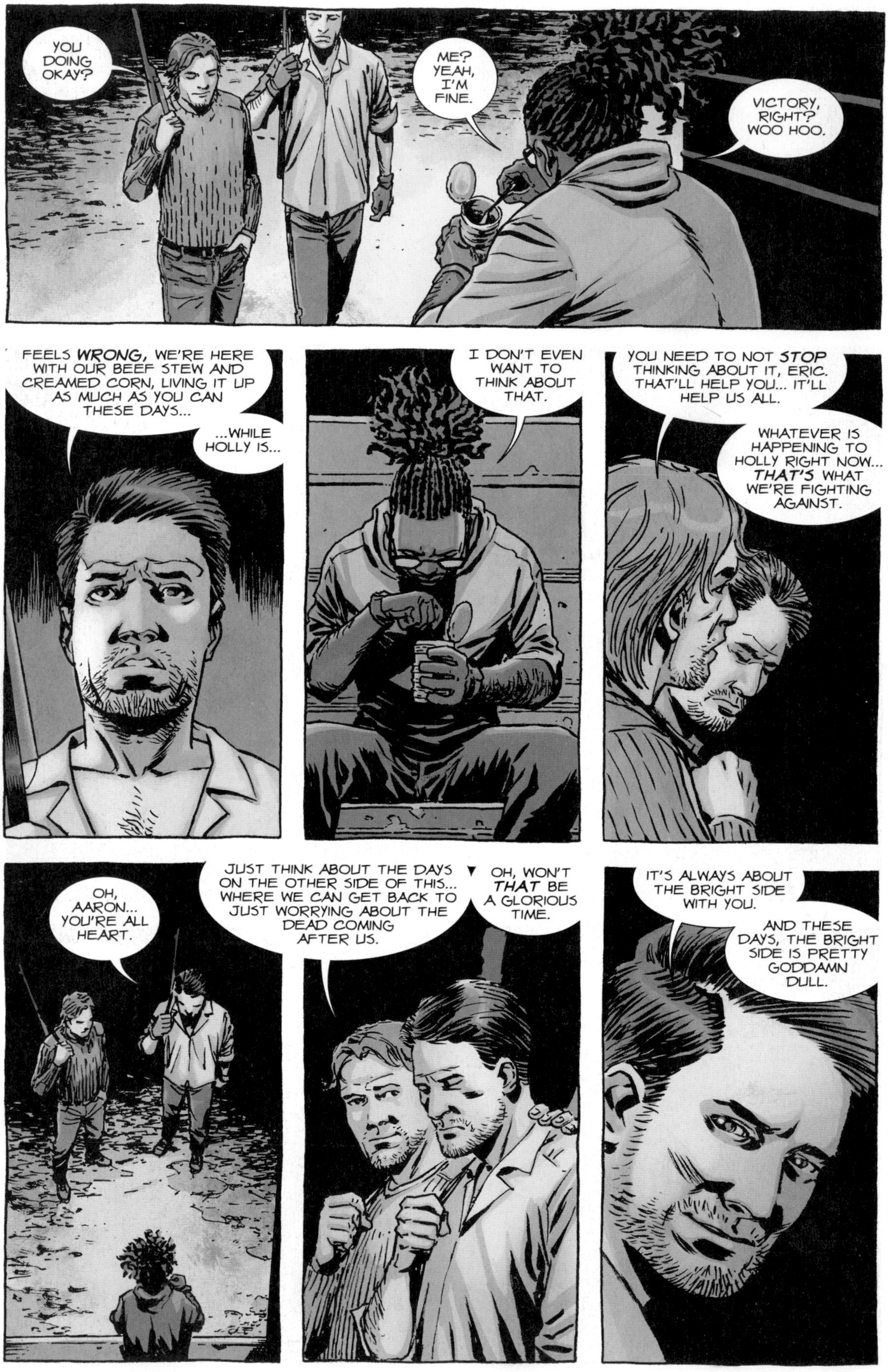
YOU DOING OKAY?
ME? YEAH, I'M FINE.
VICTORY, RIGHT? WOO HOO.
FEELS WRONG, WE'RE HERE WITH OUR BEEF STEW AND CREAMED CORN, LIVING IT UP AS MUCH AS YOU CAN THESE DAYS...
...WHILE HOLLY IS...
I DON'T EVEN WANT TO THINK ABOUT THAT.
YOU NEED TO NOT STOP THINKING ABOUT IT, ERIC. THAT'LL HELP YOU... IT'LL HELP US ALL.
WHATEVER IS HAPPENING TO HOLLY RIGHT NOW... THAT'S WHAT WE'RE FIGHTING AGAINST.
OH, AARON... YOU'RE ALL HEART.
JUST THINK ABOUT THE DAYS ON THE OTHER SIDE OF THIS... WHERE WE CAN GET BACK TO JUST WORRYING ABOUT THE DEAD COMING AFTER US.
OH, WON'T THAT BE A GLORIOUS TIME.
IT'S ALWAYS ABOUT THE BRIGHT SIDE WITH YOU.
AND THESE DAYS, THE BRIGHT SIDE IS PRETTY GODDAMN DULL.

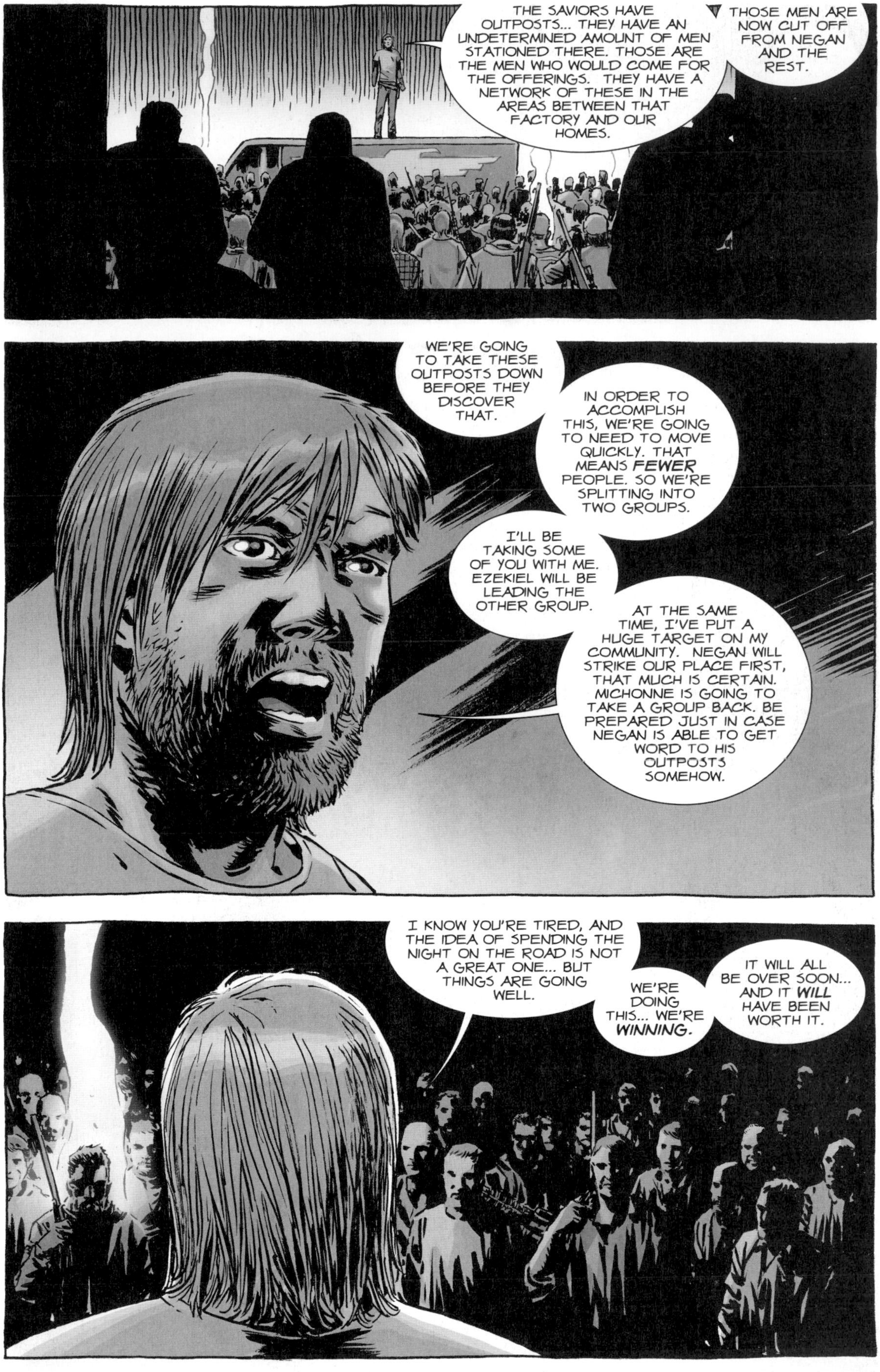
THE SAVIORS HAVE OUTPOSTS... THEY HAVE AN UNDETERMINED AMOUNT OF MEN STATIONED THERE. THOSE ARE THE MEN WHO WOULD COME FOR THE OFFERINGS. THEY HAVE A NETWORK OF THESE IN THE AREAS BETWEEN THAT FACTORY AND OUR HOMES.
THOSE MEN ARE NOW CUT OFF FROM NEGAN AND THE REST.
WE'RE GOING TO TAKE THESE OUTPOSTS DOWN BEFORE THEY DISCOVER THAT.
IN ORDER TO ACCOMPLISH THIS, WE'RE GOING TO NEED TO MOVE QUICKLY. THAT MEANS FEWER PEOPLE. SO WE'RE SPLITTING INTO TWO GROUPS.
I'LL BE TAKING SOME OF YOU WITH ME. EZEKIEL WILL BE LEADING THE OTHER GROUP.
AT THE SAME TIME, I'VE PUT A HUGE TARGET ON MY COMMUNITY. NEGAN WILL STRIKE OUR PLACE FIRST, THAT MUCH IS CERTAIN. MICHONNE IS GOING TO TAKE A GROUP BACK. BE PREPARED JUST IN CASE NEGAN IS ABLE TO GET WORD TO HIS OUTPOSTS SOMEHOW.
I KNOW YOU'RE TIRED, AND THE IDEA OF SPENDING THE NIGHT ON THE ROAD IS NOT A GREAT ONE... BUT THINGS ARE GOING WELL.
WE'RE DOING THIS... WE'RE WINNING.
IT WILL ALL BE OVER SOON... AND IT WILL HAVE BEEN WORTH IT.

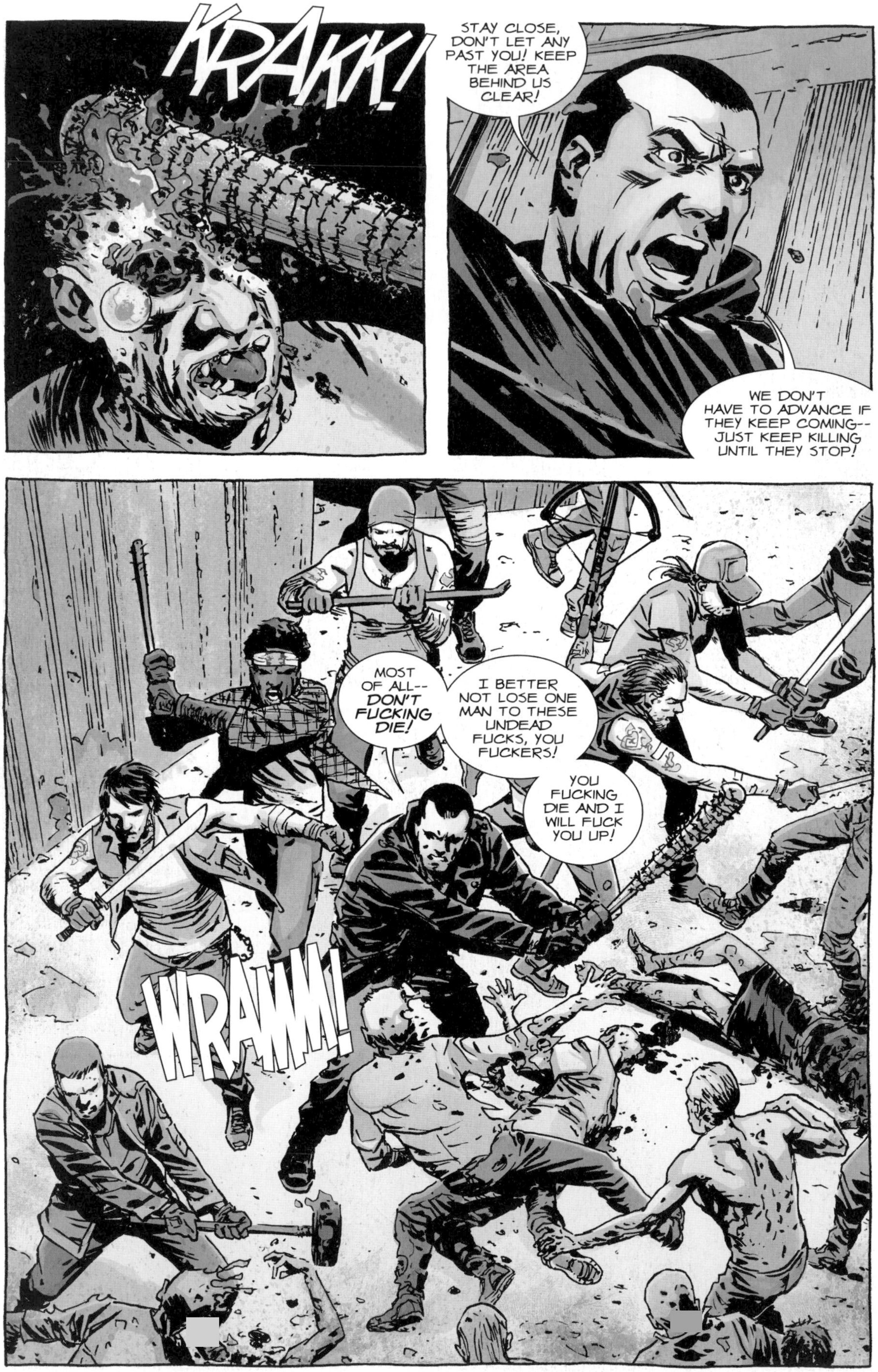
KRAKK!
STAY CLOSE, DON'T LET ANY PAST YOU! KEEP THE AREA BEHIND US CLEAR!
WE DON'T HAVE TO ADVANCE IF THEY KEEP COMING-- JUST KEEP KILLING UNTIL THEY STOP!
MOST OF ALL-- DON'T FUCKING DIE!
I BETTER NOT LOSE ONE MAN TO THESE UNDEAD FUCKS, YOU FUCKERS!
YOU FUCKING DIE AND I WILL FUCK YOU UP!
WRAMM!

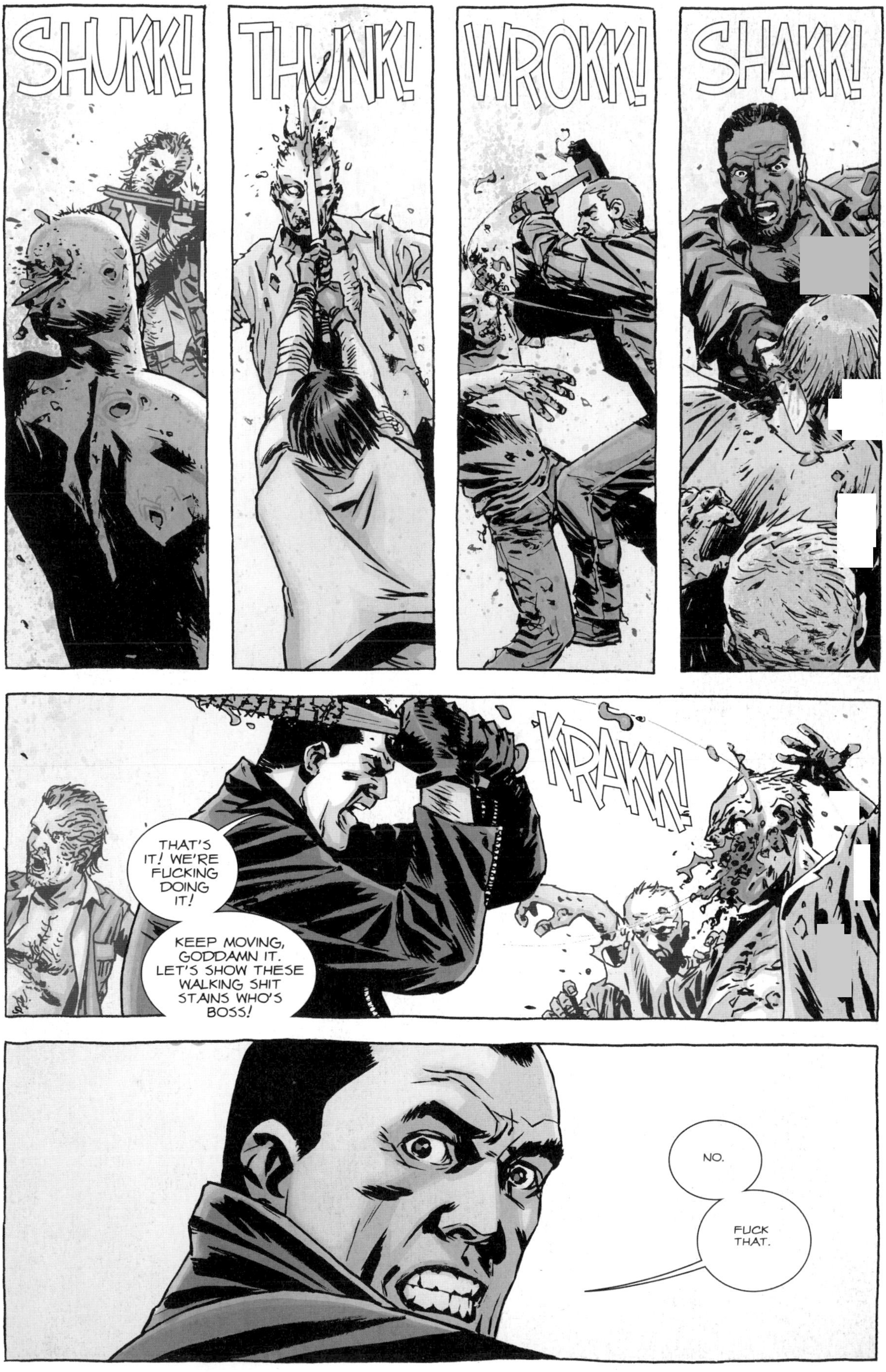
SHUKK!
THUNK!
WROKK!
SHAKK!
KRAKK!
THAT'S IT! WE'RE FUCKING DOING IT!
KEEP MOVING, GODDAMN IT. LET'S SHOW THESE WALKING SHIT STAINS WHO'S BOSS!
NO.
FUCK THAT.

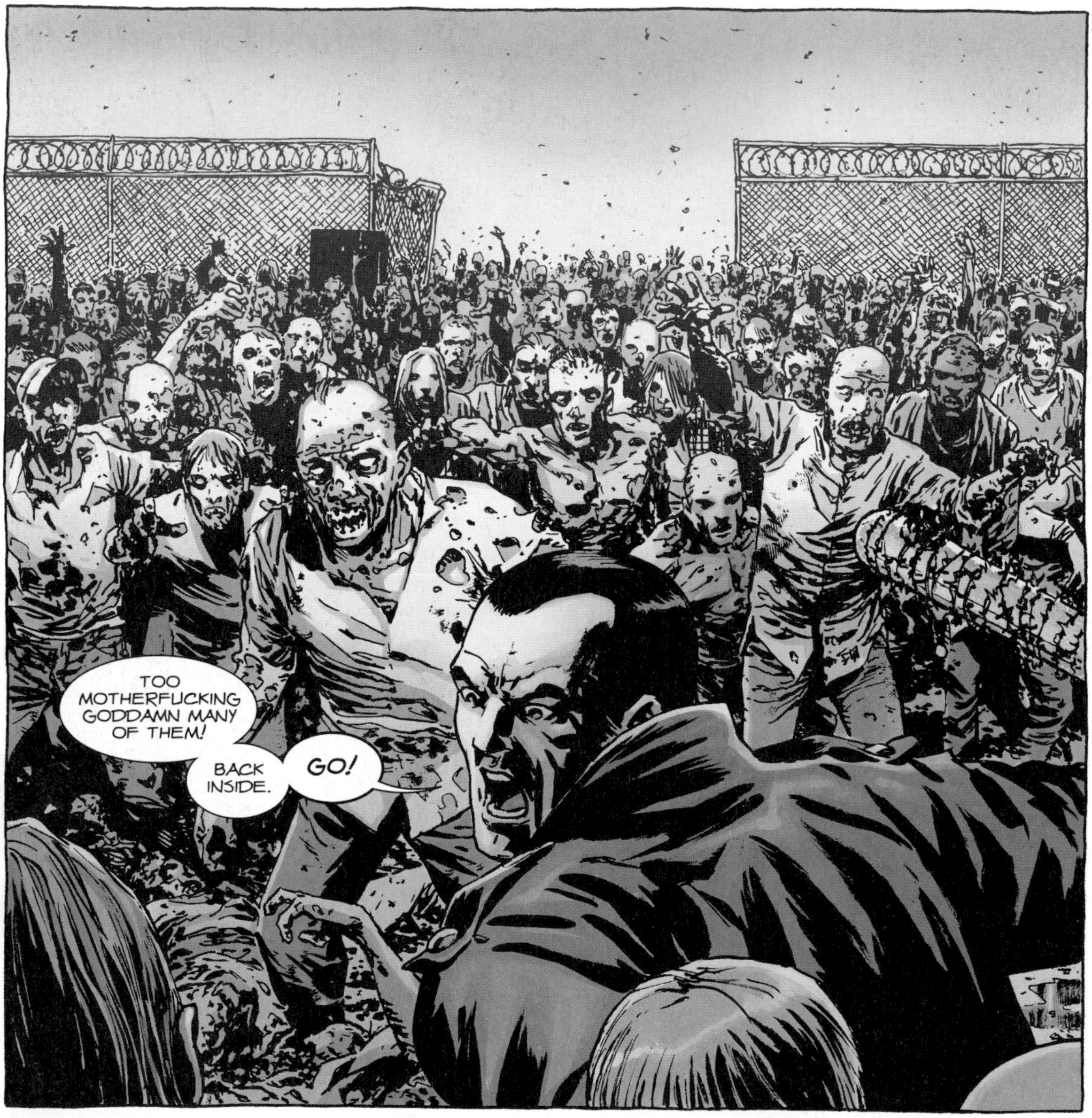
TOO MOTHERFUCKING GODDAMN MANY OF THEM!
BACK INSIDE.
GO!

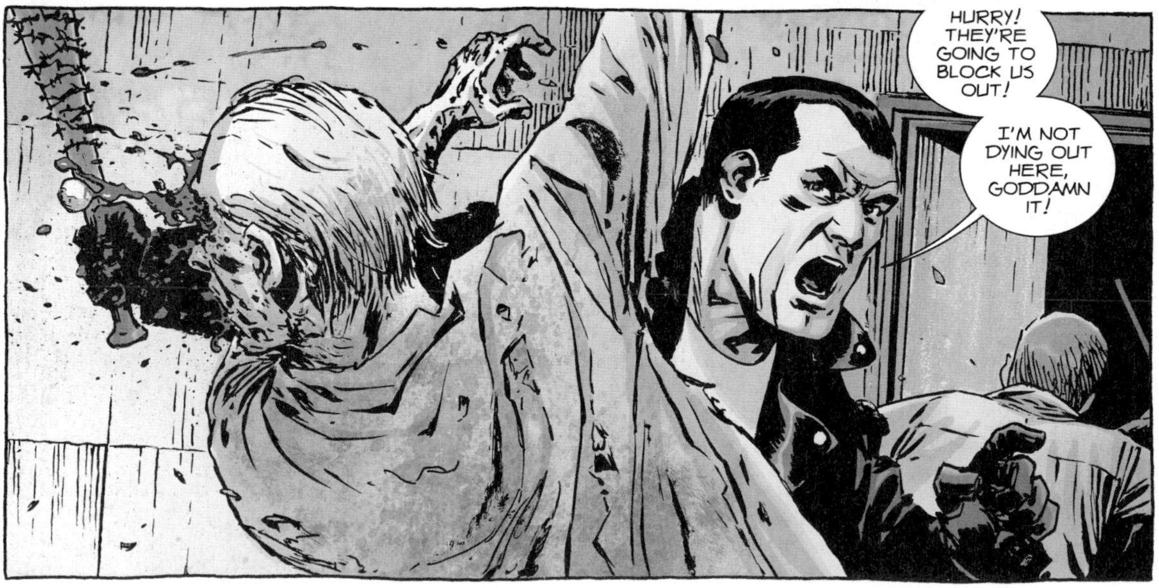
HURRY! THEY'RE GOING TO BLOCK US OUT!
I'M NOT DYING OUT HERE, GODDAMN IT!

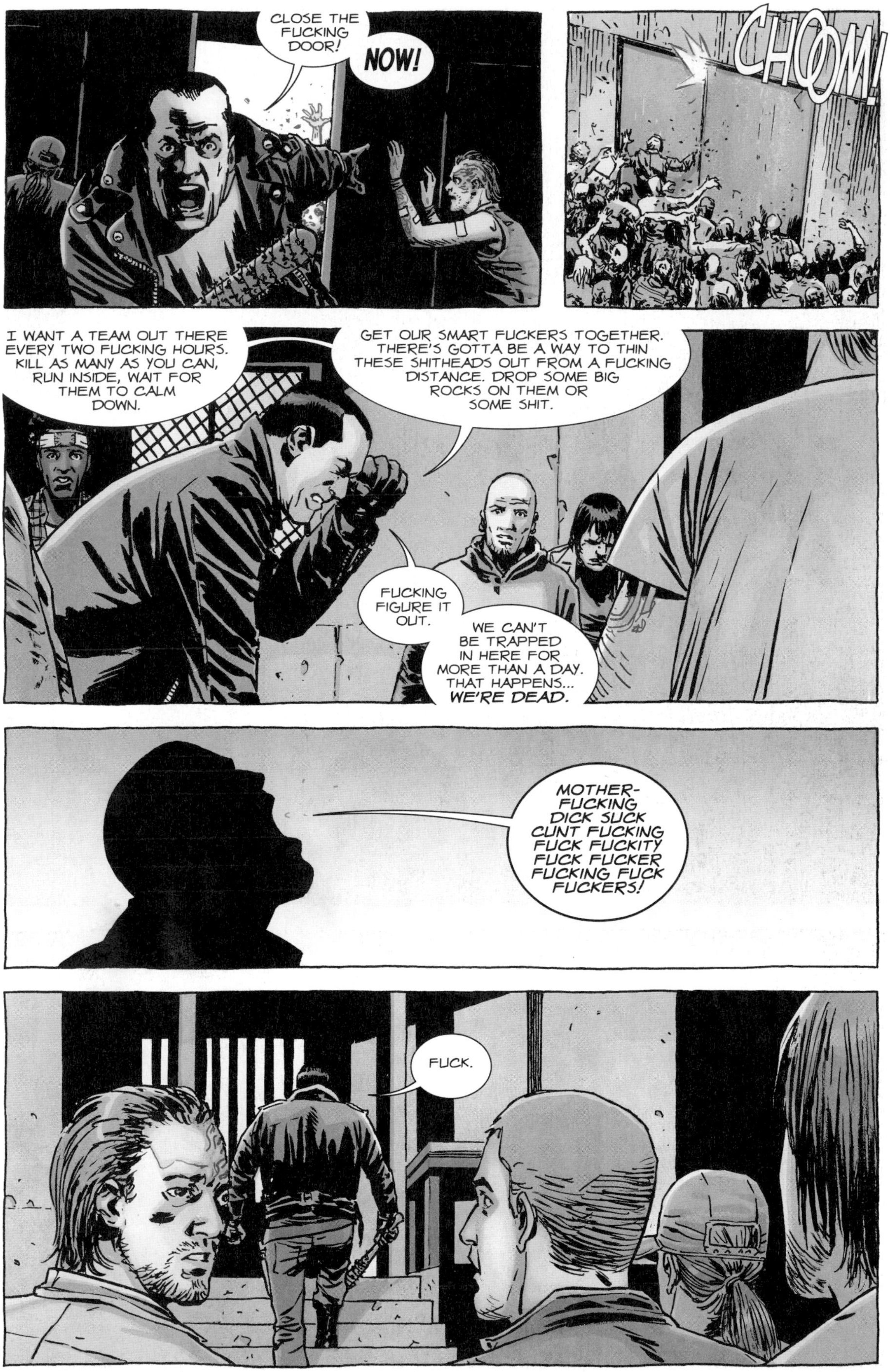
CLOSE THE FUCKING DOOR!
NOW!
CHOOM!
I WANT A TEAM OUT THERE EVERY TWO FUCKING HOURS. KILL AS MANY AS YOU CAN, RUN INSIDE, WAIT FOR THEM TO CALM DOWN.
GET OUR SMART FUCKERS TOGETHER. THERE'S GOTTA BE A WAY TO THIN THESE SHITHEADS OUT FROM A FUCKING DISTANCE. DROP SOME BIG ROCKS ON THEM OR SOME SHIT.
FUCKING FIGURE IT OUT.
WE CAN'T BE TRAPPED IN HERE FOR MORE THAN A DAY. THAT HAPPENS... WE'RE DEAD.
MOTHER-FUCKING DICK SUCK CUNT FUCKING FUCK FUCKITY FUCK FUCKER FUCKING FUCK FUCKERS!
FUCK.

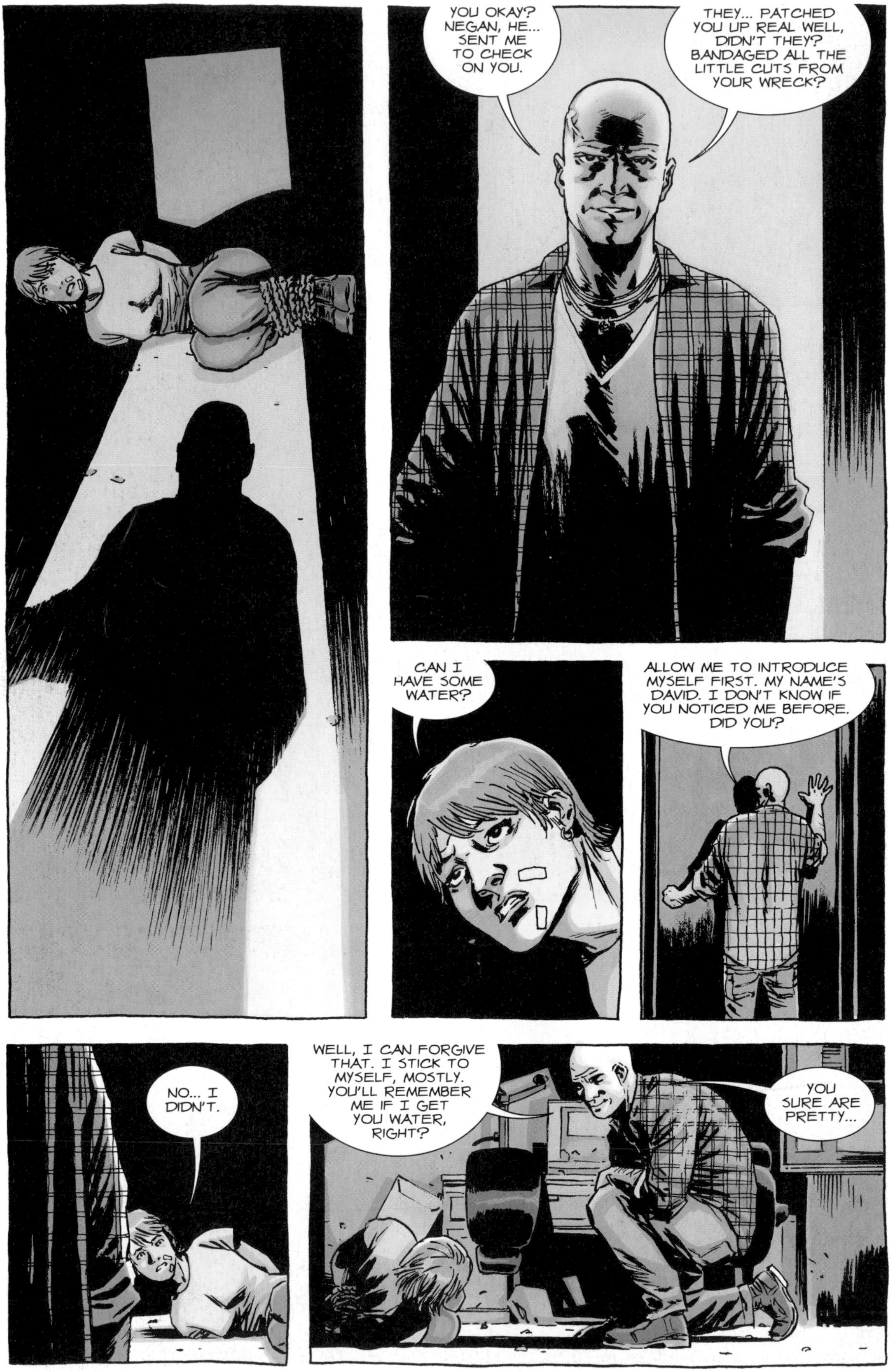
YOU OKAY? NEGAN, HE... SENT ME TO CHECK ON YOU.
THEY... PATCHED YOU UP REAL WELL, DIDN'T THEY? BANDAGED ALL THE LITTLE CUTS FROM YOUR WRECK?
CAN I HAVE SOME WATER?
ALLOW ME TO INTRODUCE MYSELF FIRST. MY NAME'S DAVID. I DON'T KNOW IF YOU NOTICED ME BEFORE. DID YOU?
NO... I DIDN'T.
WELL, I CAN FORGIVE THAT. I STICK TO MYSELF, MOSTLY. YOU'LL REMEMBER ME IF I GET YOU WATER, RIGHT?
YOU SURE ARE PRETTY...

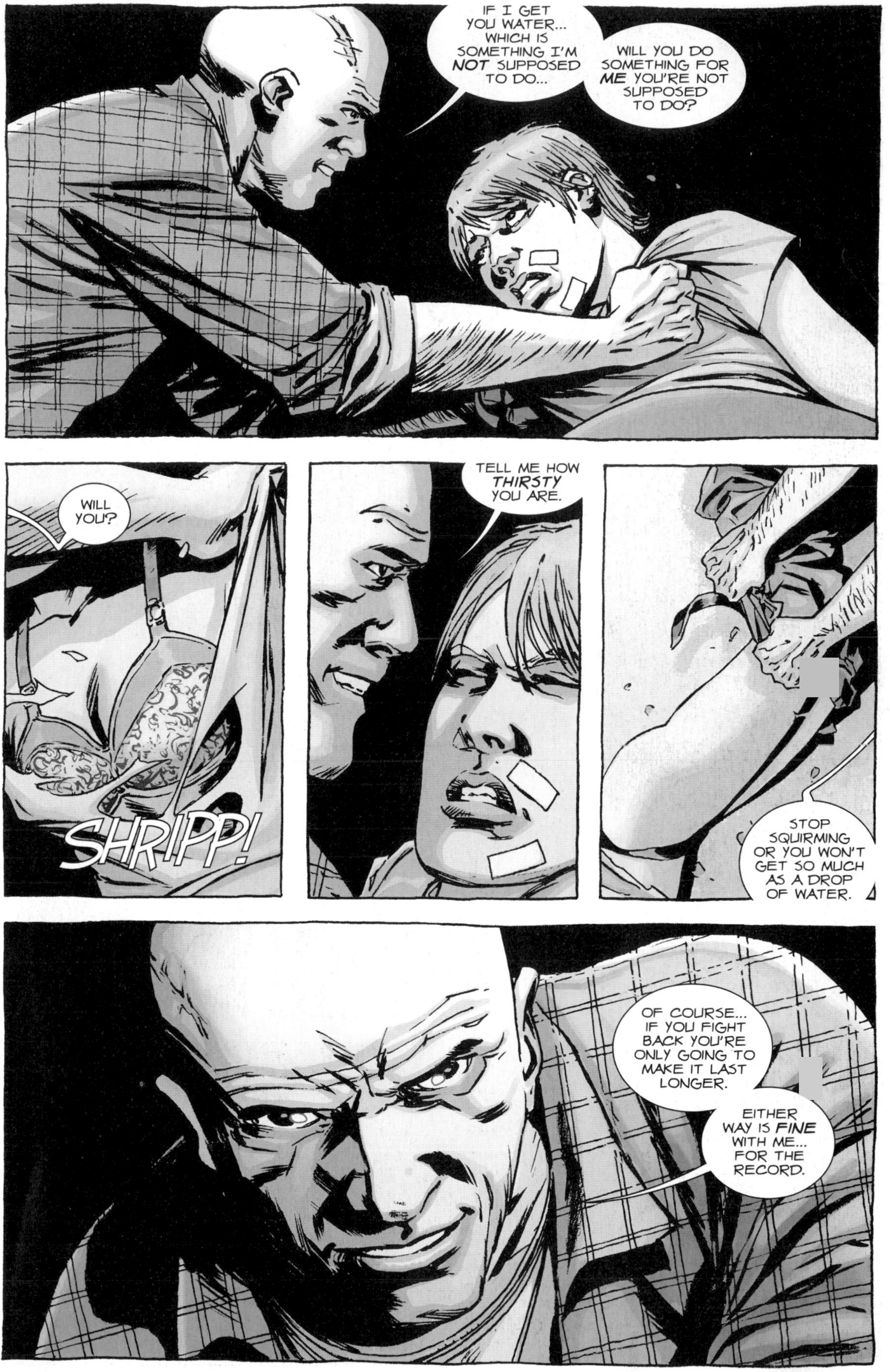
IF I GET YOU WATER... WHICH IS SOMETHING I'M **NOT** SUPPOSED TO DO...
WILL YOU DO SOMETHING FOR **ME** YOU'RE NOT SUPPOSED TO DO?
WILL YOU?
SHRIPP!
TELL ME HOW **THIRSTY** YOU ARE.
STOP SQUIRMING OR YOU WON'T GET SO MUCH AS A DROP OF WATER.
OF COURSE... IF YOU FIGHT BACK YOU'RE ONLY GOING TO MAKE IT LAST LONGER.
EITHER WAY IS **FINE** WITH ME... FOR THE RECORD.

DAVID!

WHAT THE FUCKING FUCK ARE YOU DOING IN HERE?!

NEGAN, SIR--

I--

DO YOU REALLY THINK I NEED YOU TO ANSWER THAT? I CAN FUCKING SEE YOU'RE TRYING TO *RAPE* THIS WOMAN.

YOU WERE GOING TO FUCKING RAPE THIS WOMAN, WEREN'T YOU?!

...

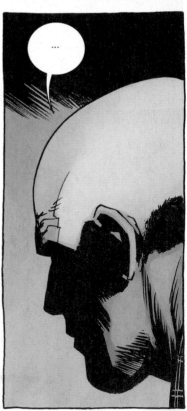

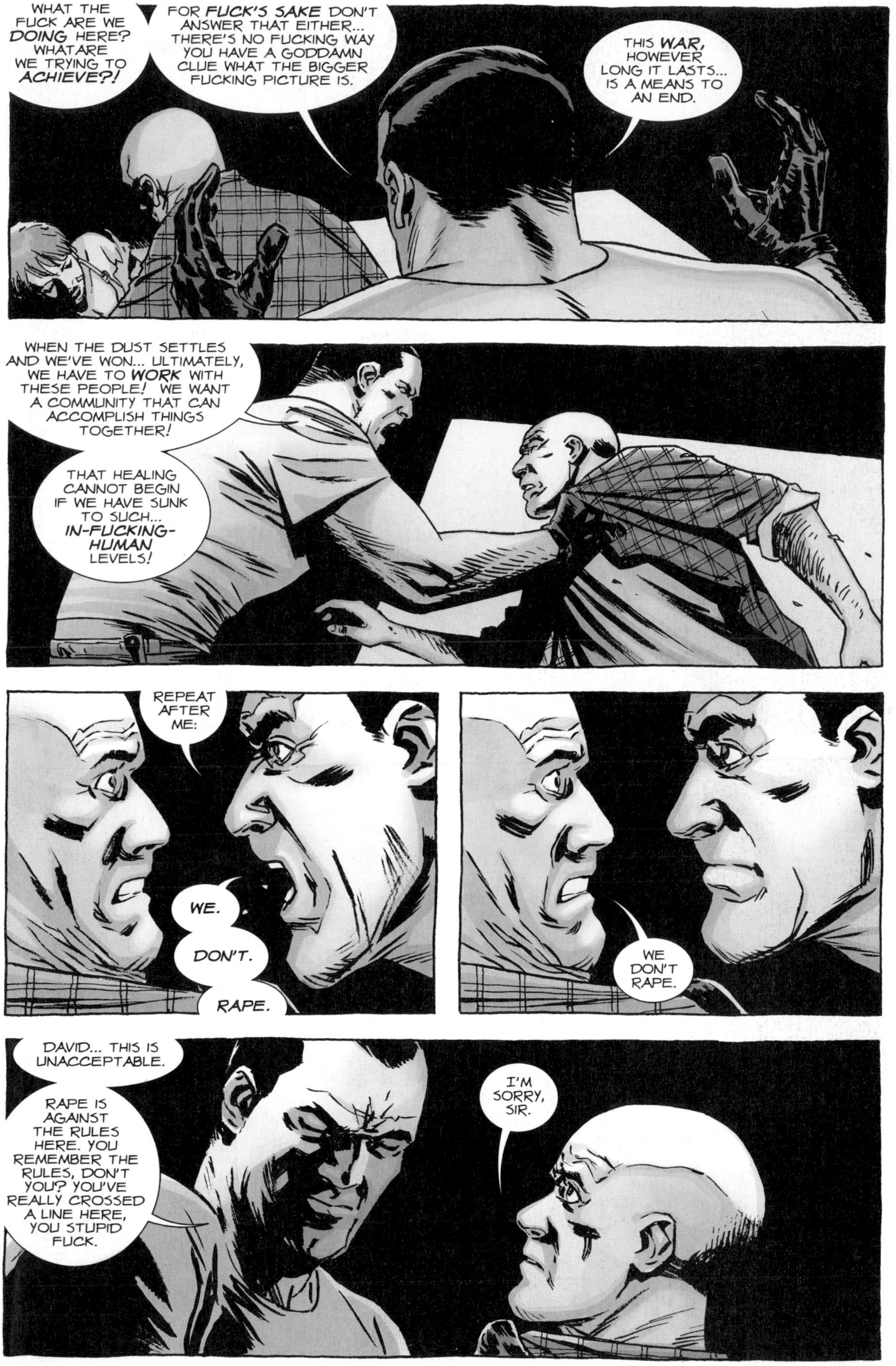
WHAT THE FUCK ARE WE DOING HERE? WHATARE WE TRYING TO ACHIEVE?!
FOR FUCK'S SAKE DON'T ANSWER THAT EITHER... THERE'S NO FUCKING WAY YOU HAVE A GODDAMN CLUE WHAT THE BIGGER FUCKING PICTURE IS.
THIS WAR, HOWEVER LONG IT LASTS... IS A MEANS TO AN END.
WHEN THE DUST SETTLES AND WE'VE WON... ULTIMATELY, WE HAVE TO WORK WITH THESE PEOPLE! WE WANT A COMMUNITY THAT CAN ACCOMPLISH THINGS TOGETHER!
THAT HEALING CANNOT BEGIN IF WE HAVE SUNK TO SUCH... IN-FUCKING-HUMAN LEVELS!
REPEAT AFTER ME:
WE.
DON'T.
RAPE.
WE DON'T RAPE.
DAVID... THIS IS UNACCEPTABLE.
RAPE IS AGAINST THE RULES HERE. YOU REMEMBER THE RULES, DON'T YOU? YOU'VE REALLY CROSSED A LINE HERE, YOU STUPID FUCK.
I'M SORRY, SIR.

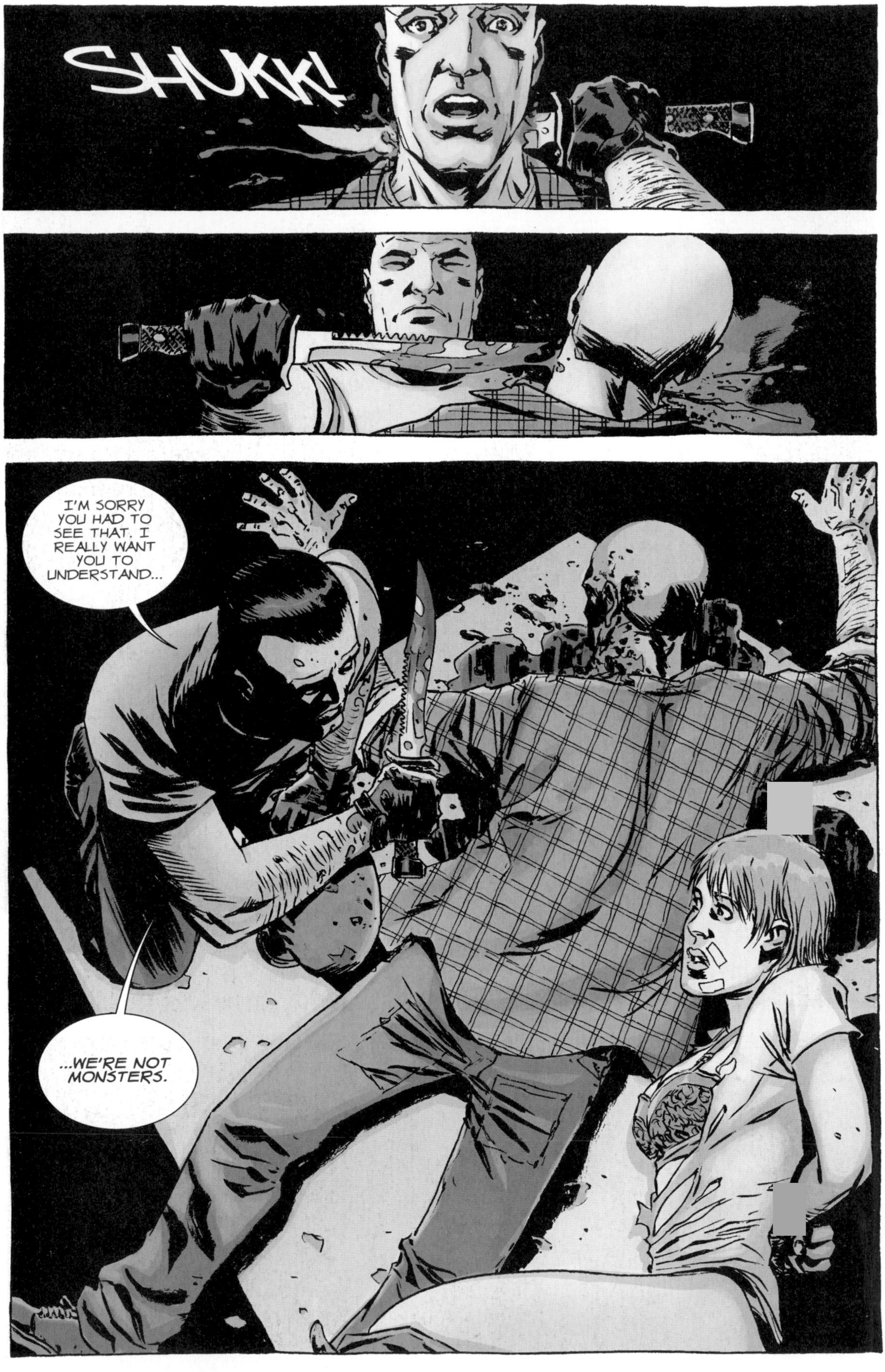
SHUKK!
I'M SORRY YOU HAD TO SEE THAT. I REALLY WANT YOU TO UNDERSTAND...
...WE'RE NOT MONSTERS.

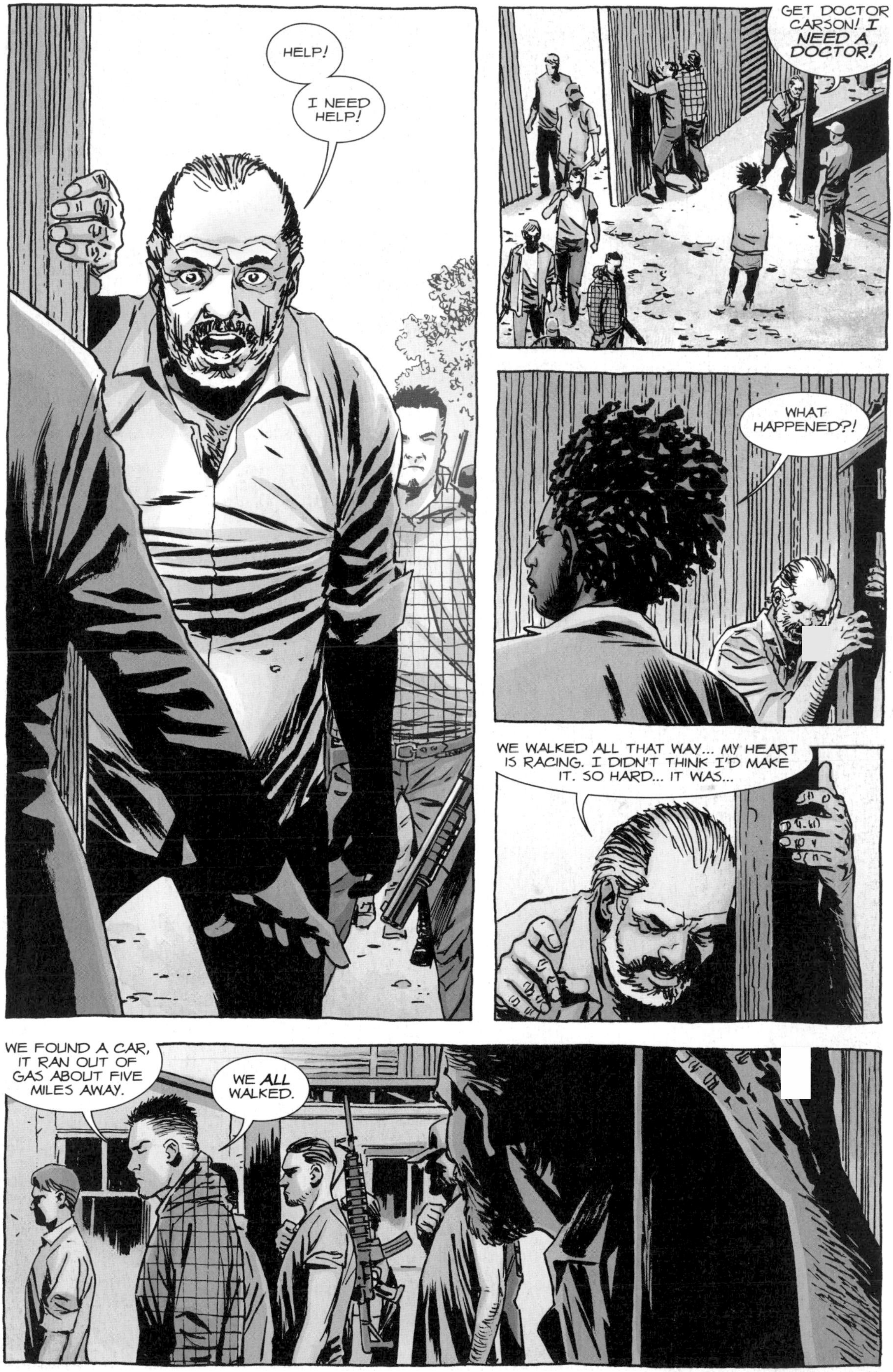
HELP!
I NEED HELP!
GET DOCTOR CARSON! I NEED A DOCTOR!
WHAT HAPPENED?!
WE WALKED ALL THAT WAY... MY HEART IS RACING. I DIDN'T THINK I'D MAKE IT. SO HARD... IT WAS...
WE FOUND A CAR, IT RAN OUT OF GAS ABOUT FIVE MILES AWAY.
WE ALL WALKED.

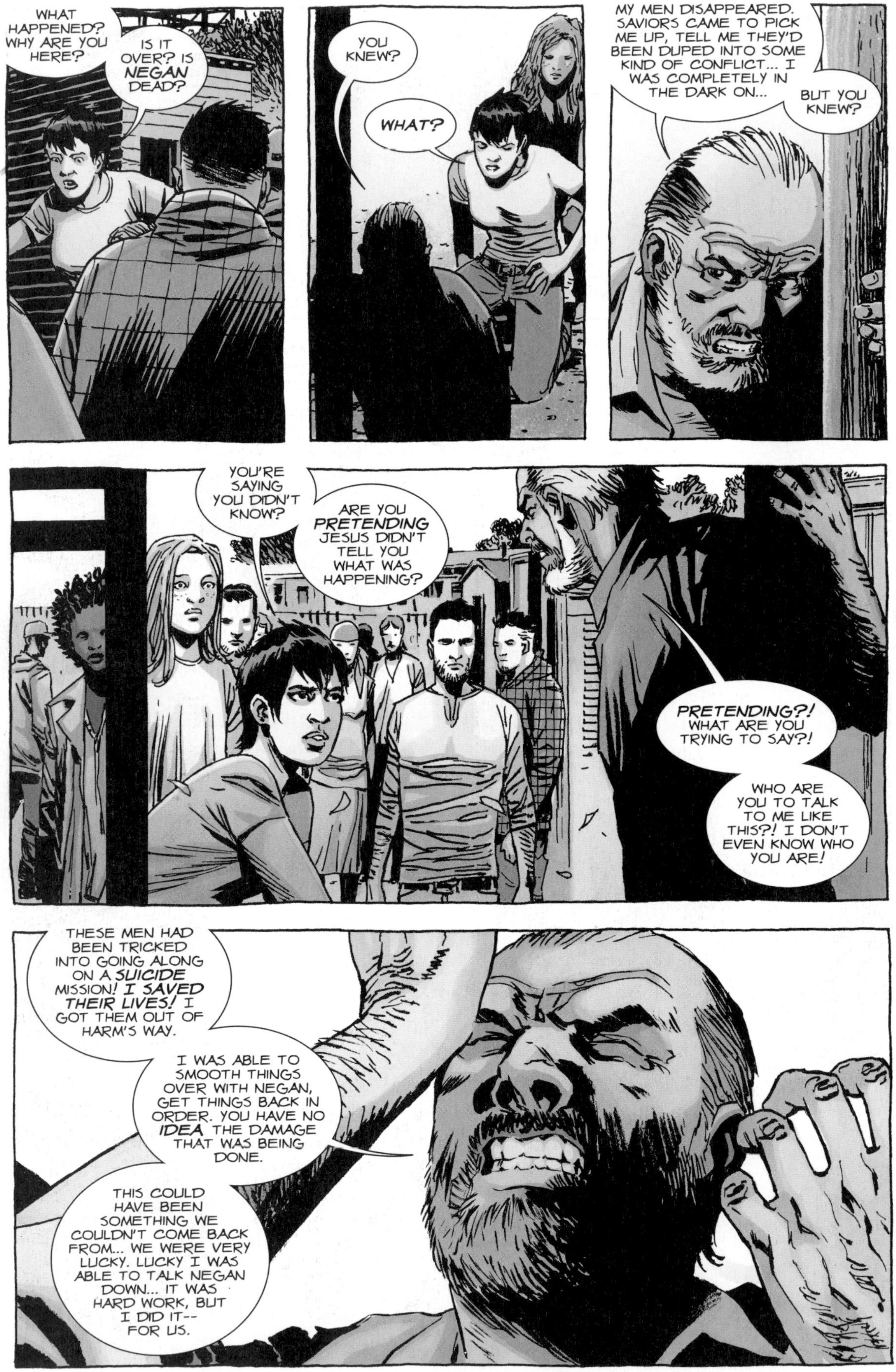
WHAT HAPPENED? WHY ARE YOU HERE?
IS IT OVER? IS NEGAN DEAD?
YOU KNEW?
WHAT?
MY MEN DISAPPEARED. SAVIORS CAME TO PICK ME UP, TELL ME THEY'D BEEN DUPED INTO SOME KIND OF CONFLICT... I WAS COMPLETELY IN THE DARK ON...
BUT YOU KNEW?
YOU'RE SAYING YOU DIDN'T KNOW?
ARE YOU PRETENDING JESUS DIDN'T TELL YOU WHAT WAS HAPPENING?
PRETENDING?! WHAT ARE YOU TRYING TO SAY?!
WHO ARE YOU TO TALK TO ME LIKE THIS?! I DON'T EVEN KNOW WHO YOU ARE!
THESE MEN HAD BEEN TRICKED INTO GOING ALONG ON A SUICIDE MISSION! I SAVED THEIR LIVES! I GOT THEM OUT OF HARM'S WAY.
I WAS ABLE TO SMOOTH THINGS OVER WITH NEGAN, GET THINGS BACK IN ORDER. YOU HAVE NO IDEA THE DAMAGE THAT WAS BEING DONE.
THIS COULD HAVE BEEN SOMETHING WE COULDN'T COME BACK FROM... WE WERE VERY LUCKY. LUCKY I WAS ABLE TO TALK NEGAN DOWN... IT WAS HARD WORK, BUT I DID IT-- FOR US.

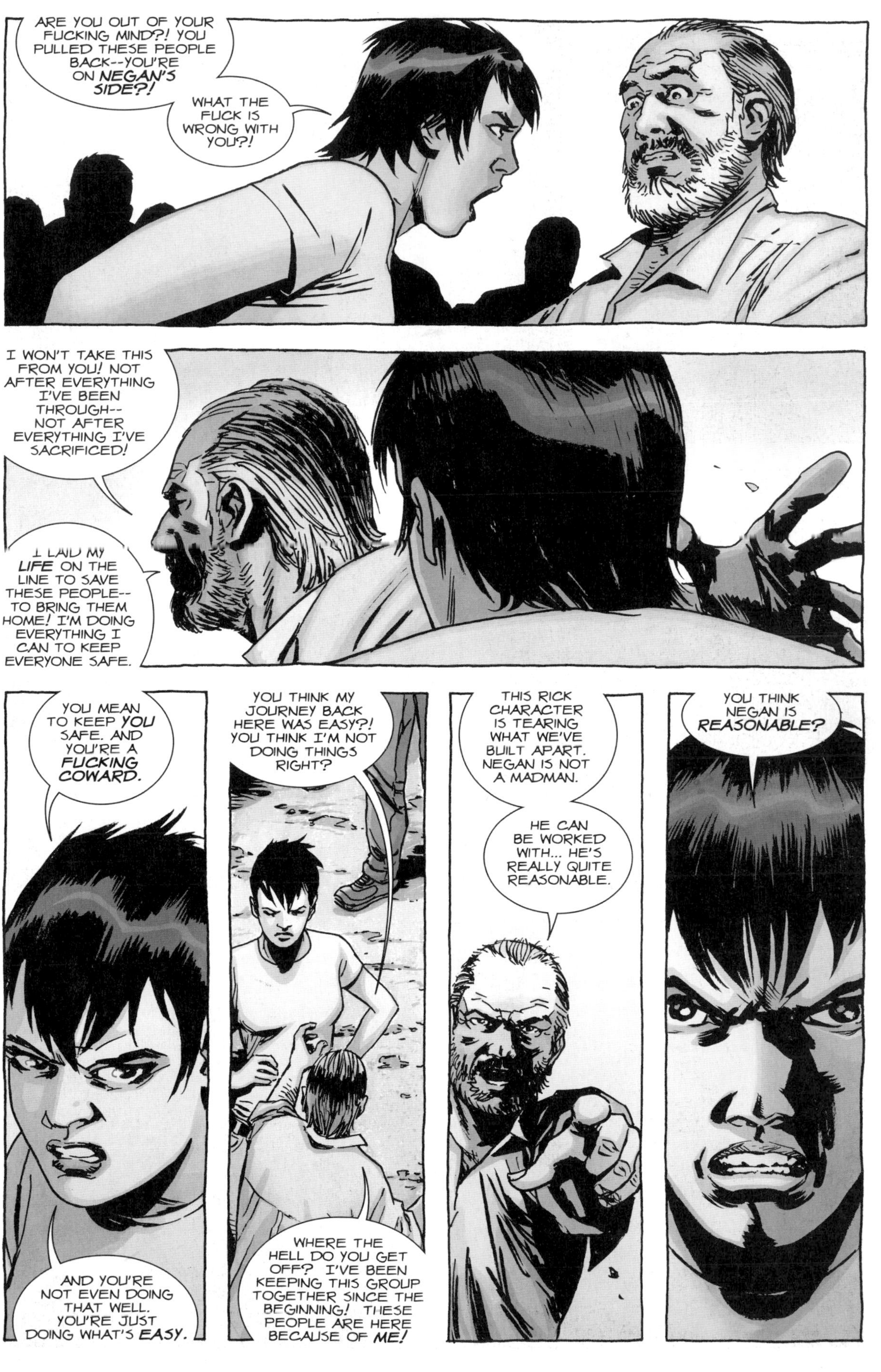
ARE YOU OUT OF YOUR FUCKING MIND?! YOU PULLED THESE PEOPLE BACK--YOU'RE ON NEGAN'S SIDE?!
WHAT THE FUCK IS WRONG WITH YOU?!
I WON'T TAKE THIS FROM YOU! NOT AFTER EVERYTHING I'VE BEEN THROUGH-- NOT AFTER EVERYTHING I'VE SACRIFICED!
I LAID MY LIFE ON THE LINE TO SAVE THESE PEOPLE-- TO BRING THEM HOME! I'M DOING EVERYTHING I CAN TO KEEP EVERYONE SAFE.
YOU MEAN TO KEEP YOU SAFE. AND YOU'RE A FUCKING COWARD.
AND YOU'RE NOT EVEN DOING THAT WELL. YOU'RE JUST DOING WHAT'S EASY.
YOU THINK MY JOURNEY BACK HERE WAS EASY?! YOU THINK I'M NOT DOING THINGS RIGHT?
WHERE THE HELL DO YOU GET OFF? I'VE BEEN KEEPING THIS GROUP TOGETHER SINCE THE BEGINNING! THESE PEOPLE ARE HERE BECAUSE OF ME!
THIS RICK CHARACTER IS TEARING WHAT WE'VE BUILT APART. NEGAN IS NOT A MADMAN.
HE CAN BE WORKED WITH... HE'S REALLY QUITE REASONABLE.
YOU THINK NEGAN IS REASONABLE?

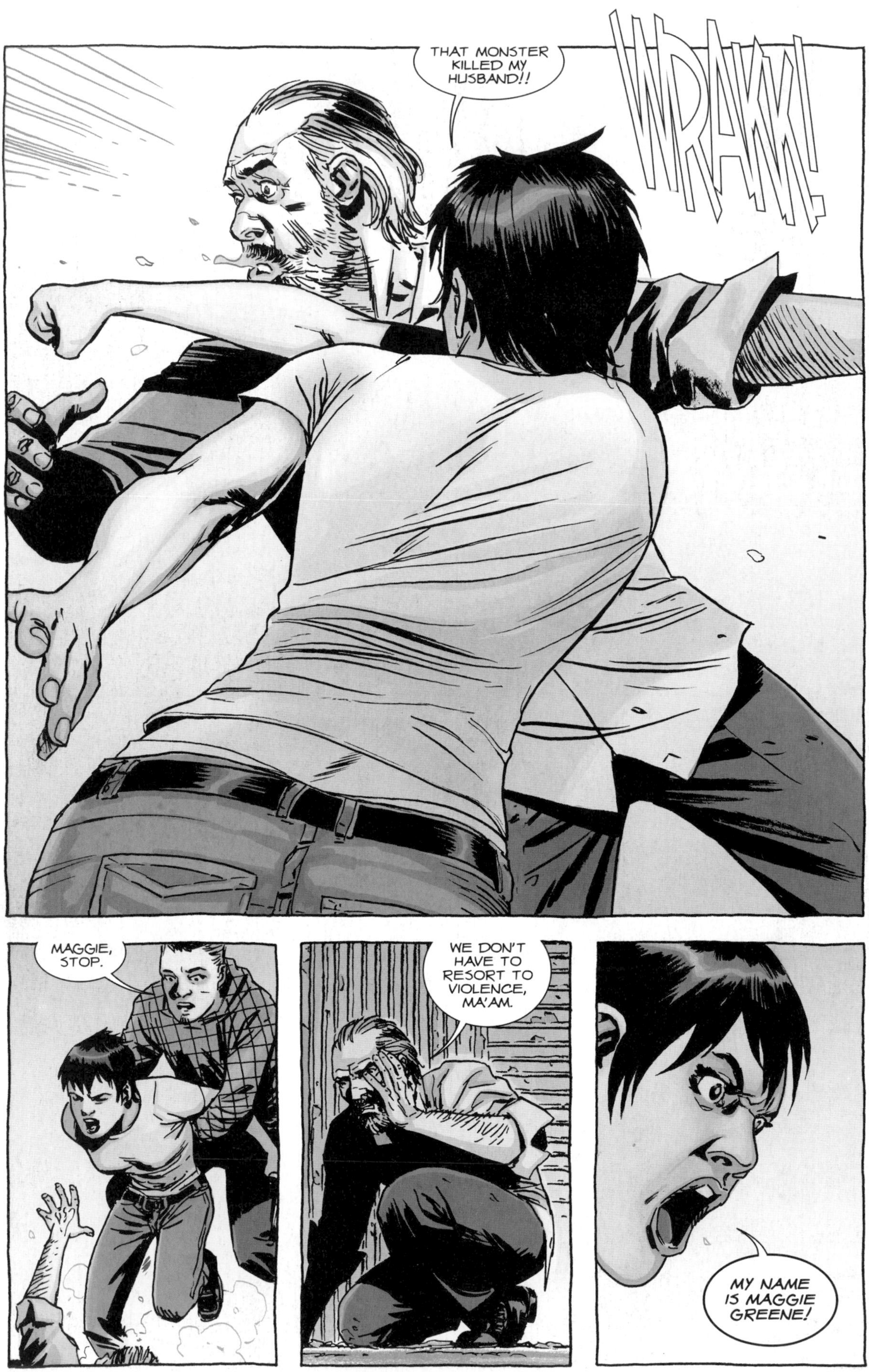
THAT MONSTER KILLED MY HUSBAND!!
WRAKK!
MAGGIE, STOP.
WE DON'T HAVE TO RESORT TO VIOLENCE, MA'AM.
MY NAME IS MAGGIE GREENE!

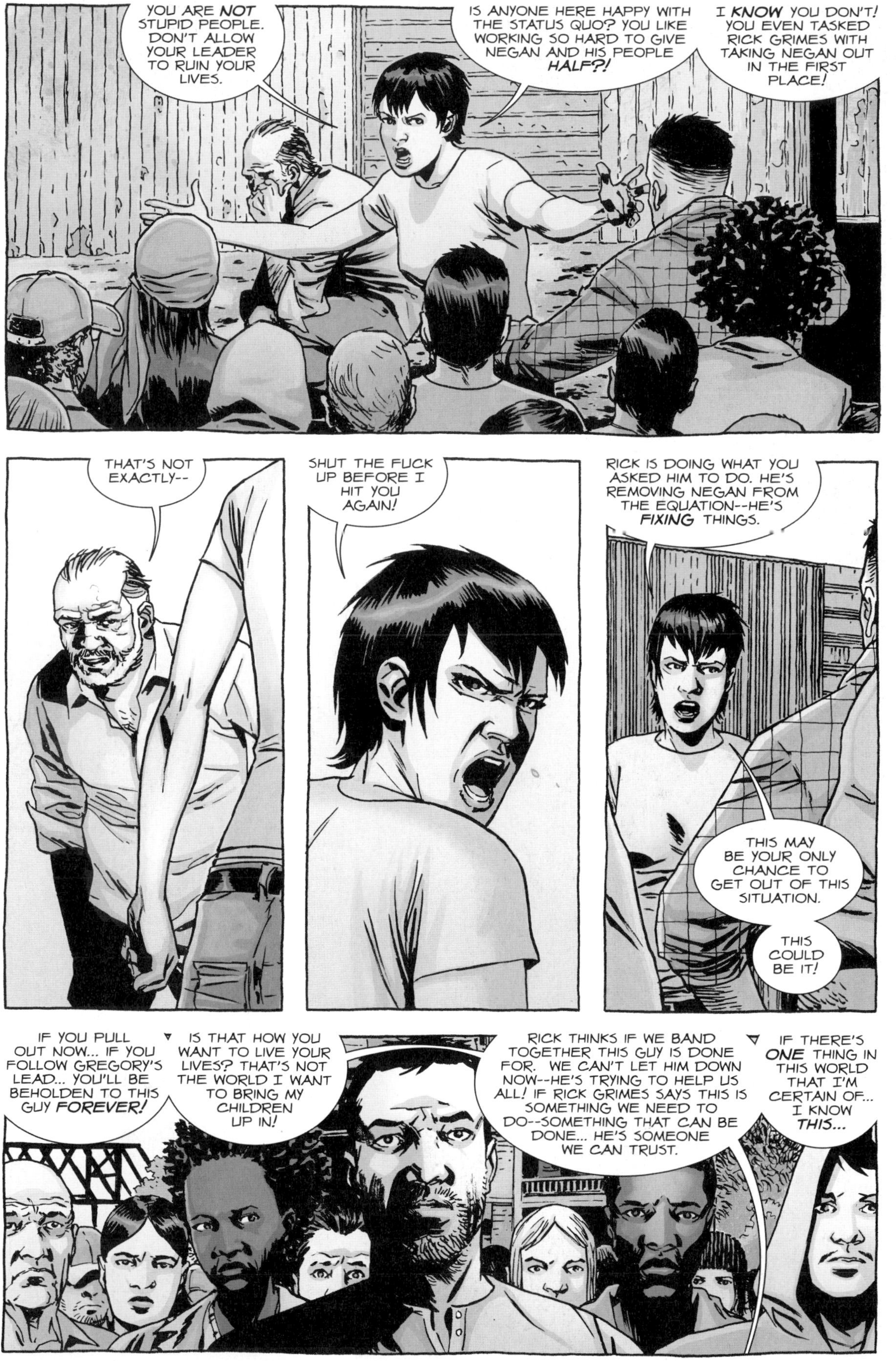
YOU ARE NOT STUPID PEOPLE. DON'T ALLOW YOUR LEADER TO RUIN YOUR LIVES.
IS ANYONE HERE HAPPY WITH THE STATUS QUO? YOU LIKE WORKING SO HARD TO GIVE NEGAN AND HIS PEOPLE HALF?!
I KNOW YOU DON'T! YOU EVEN TASKED RICK GRIMES WITH TAKING NEGAN OUT IN THE FIRST PLACE!
THAT'S NOT EXACTLY--
SHUT THE FUCK UP BEFORE I HIT YOU AGAIN!
RICK IS DOING WHAT YOU ASKED HIM TO DO. HE'S REMOVING NEGAN FROM THE EQUATION--HE'S FIXING THINGS.
THIS MAY BE YOUR ONLY CHANCE TO GET OUT OF THIS SITUATION.
THIS COULD BE IT!
IF YOU PULL OUT NOW... IF YOU FOLLOW GREGORY'S LEAD... YOU'LL BE BEHOLDEN TO THIS GUY FOREVER!
IS THAT HOW YOU WANT TO LIVE YOUR LIVES? THAT'S NOT THE WORLD I WANT TO BRING MY CHILDREN UP IN!
RICK THINKS IF WE BAND TOGETHER THIS GUY IS DONE FOR. WE CAN'T LET HIM DOWN NOW--HE'S TRYING TO HELP US ALL! IF RICK GRIMES SAYS THIS IS SOMETHING WE NEED TO DO--SOMETHING THAT CAN BE DONE... HE'S SOMEONE WE CAN TRUST.
IF THERE'S ONE THING IN THIS WORLD THAT I'M CERTAIN OF... I KNOW THIS...

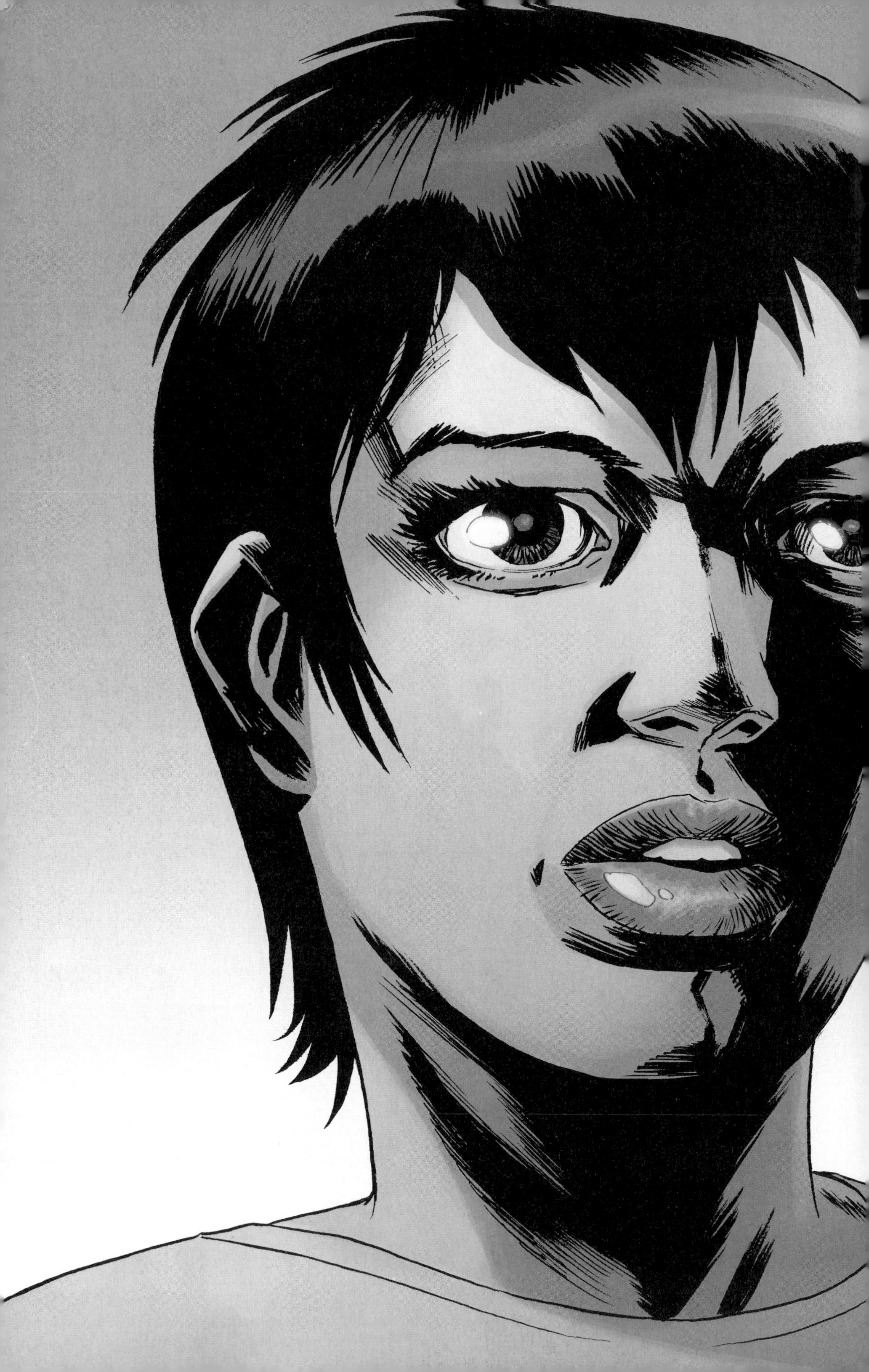

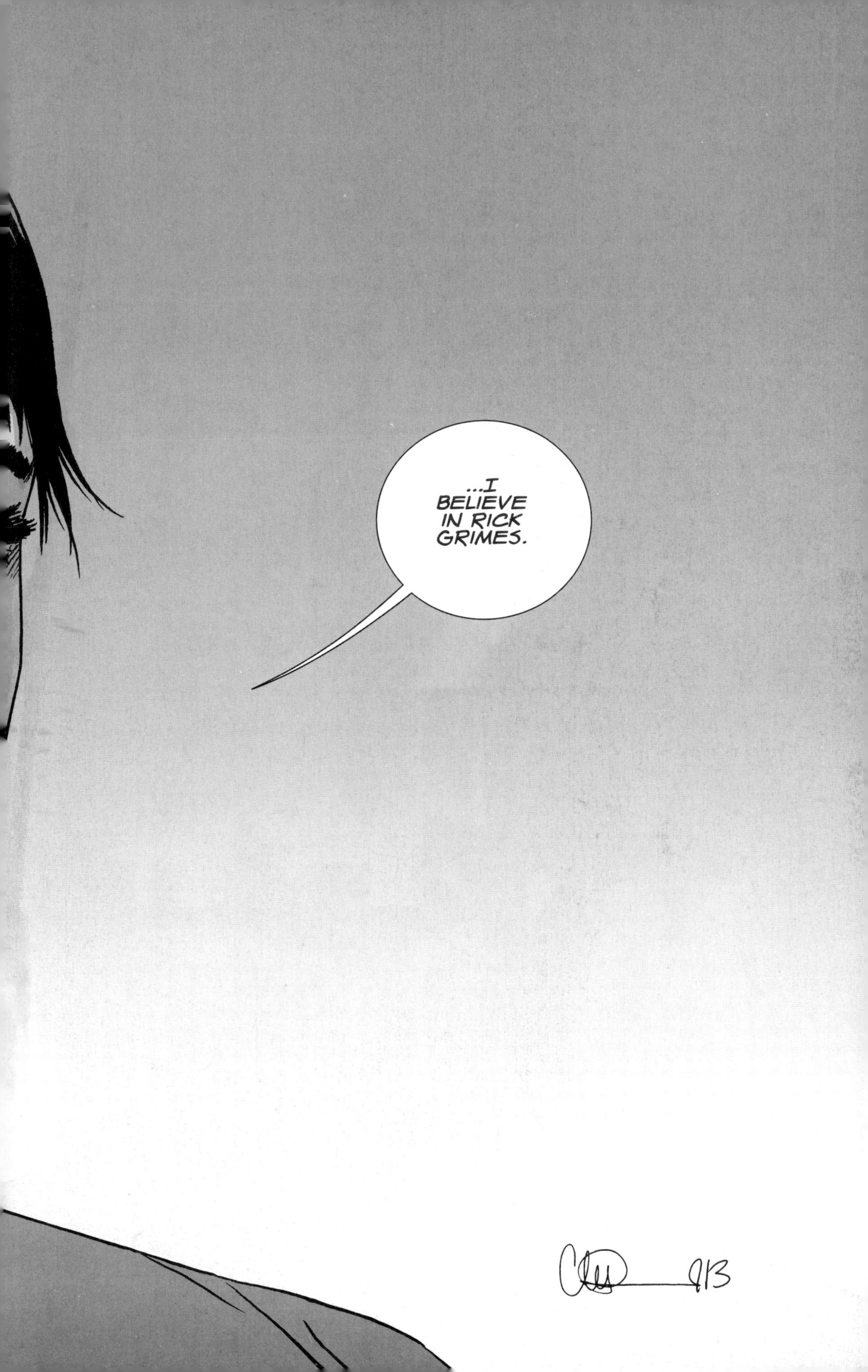
...I BELIEVE IN RICK GRIMES.

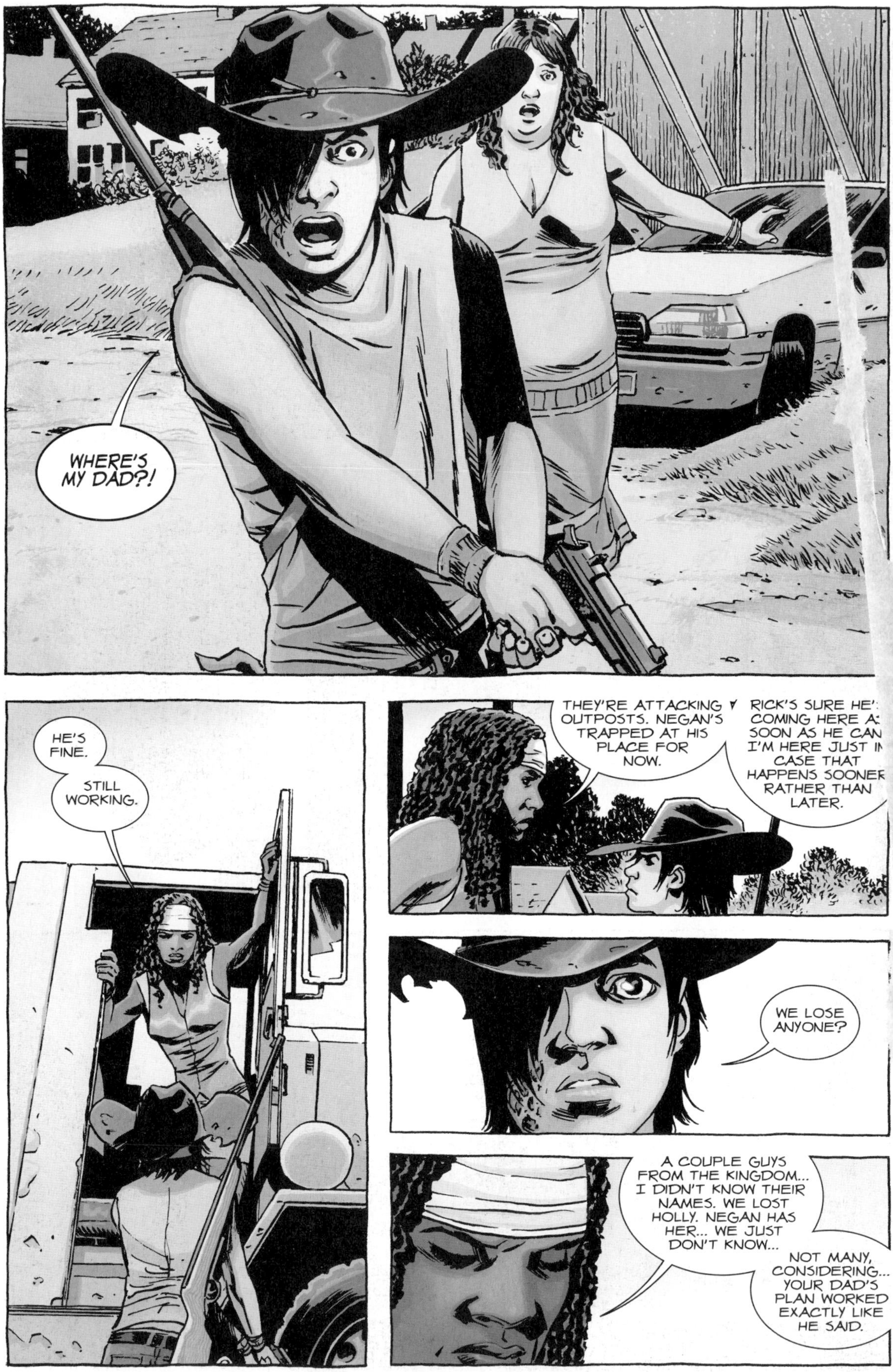
WHERE'S MY DAD?!
HE'S FINE.
STILL WORKING.
THEY'RE ATTACKING OUTPOSTS. NEGAN'S TRAPPED AT HIS PLACE FOR NOW.
RICK'S SURE HE'S COMING HERE AS SOON AS HE CAN. I'M HERE JUST IN CASE THAT HAPPENS SOONER RATHER THAN LATER.
WE LOSE ANYONE?
A COUPLE GUYS FROM THE KINGDOM... I DIDN'T KNOW THEIR NAMES. WE LOST HOLLY. NEGAN HAS HER... WE JUST DON'T KNOW...
NOT MANY, CONSIDERING... YOUR DAD'S PLAN WORKED EXACTLY LIKE HE SAID.

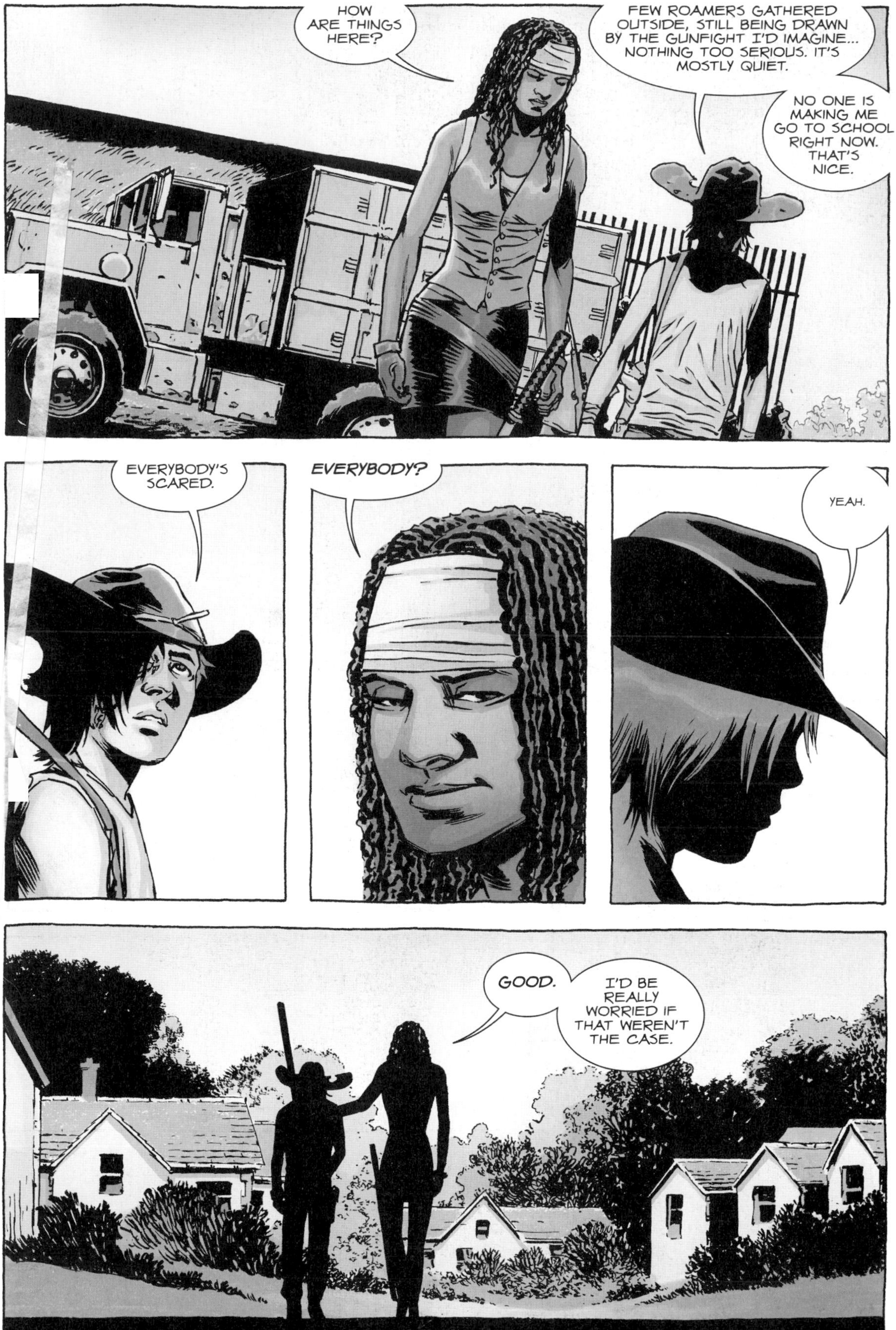
HOW ARE THINGS HERE?
FEW ROAMERS GATHERED OUTSIDE, STILL BEING DRAWN BY THE GUNFIGHT I'D IMAGINE... NOTHING TOO SERIOUS. IT'S MOSTLY QUIET.
NO ONE IS MAKING ME GO TO SCHOOL RIGHT NOW. THAT'S NICE.
EVERYBODY'S SCARED.
EVERYBODY?
YEAH.
GOOD.
I'D BE REALLY WORRIED IF THAT WEREN'T THE CASE.

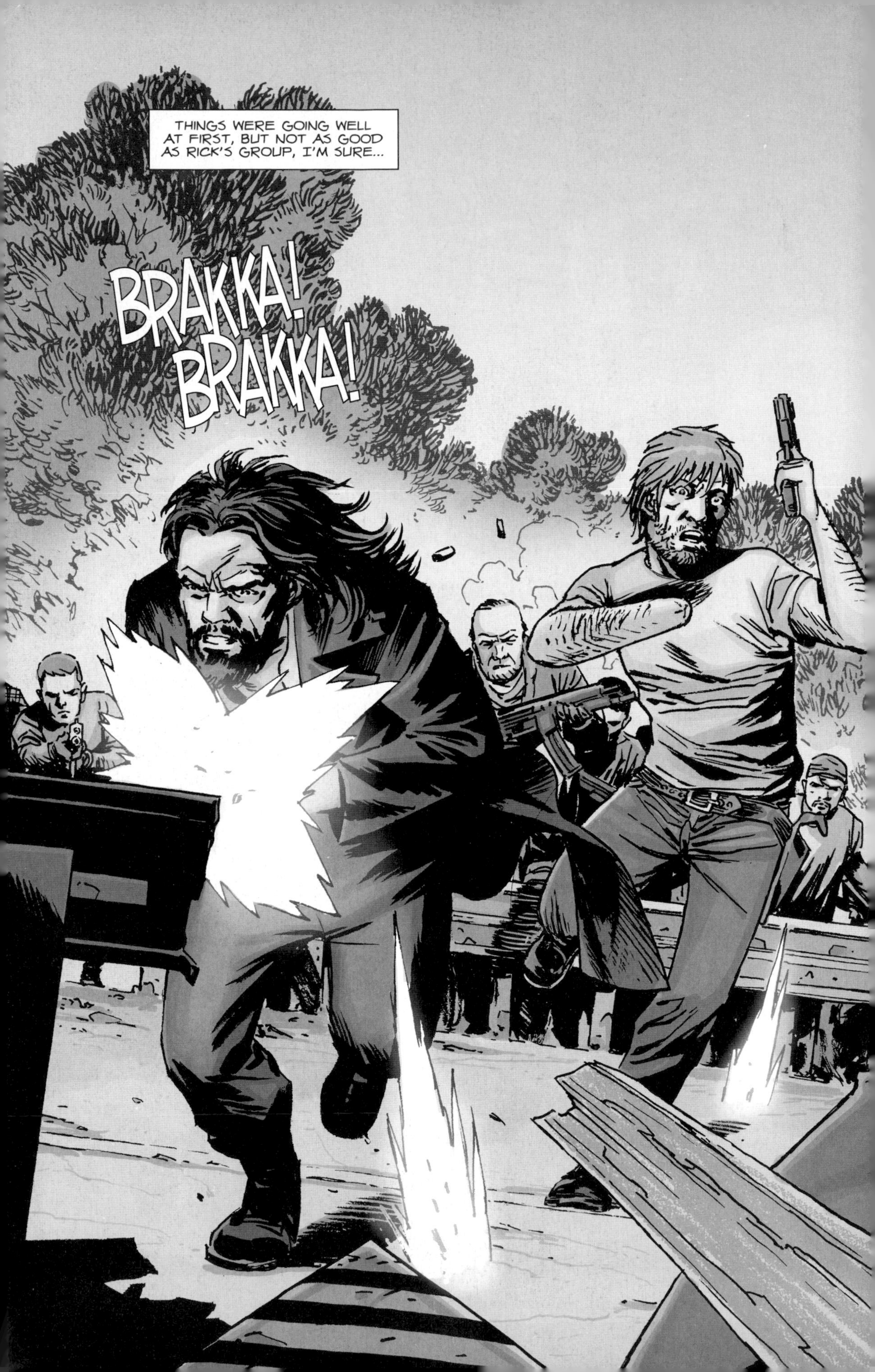
THINGS WERE GOING WELL AT FIRST, BUT NOT AS GOOD AS RICK'S GROUP, I'M SURE...
BRAKKA! BRAKKA!

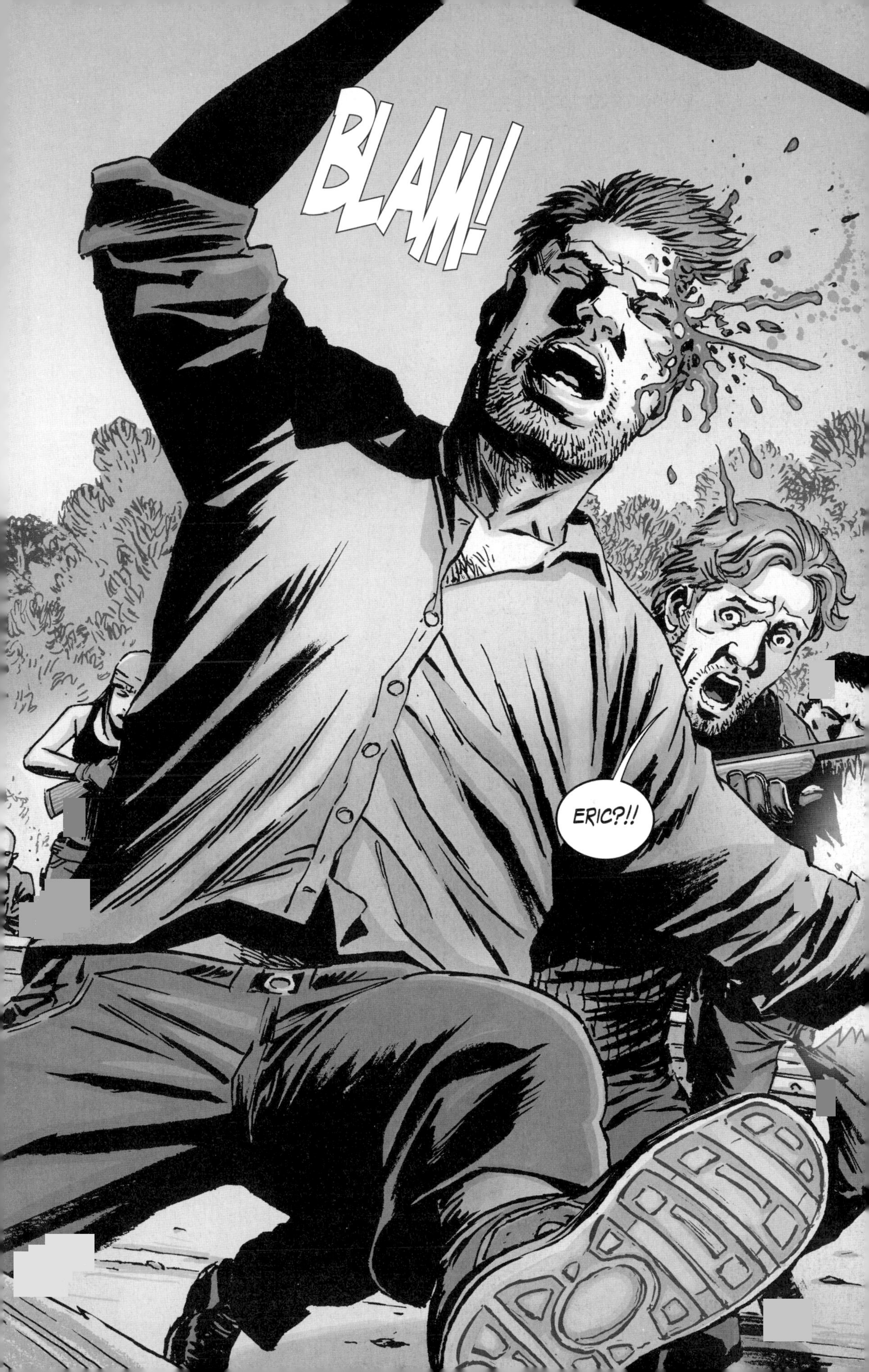
BLAM!
ERIC?!!

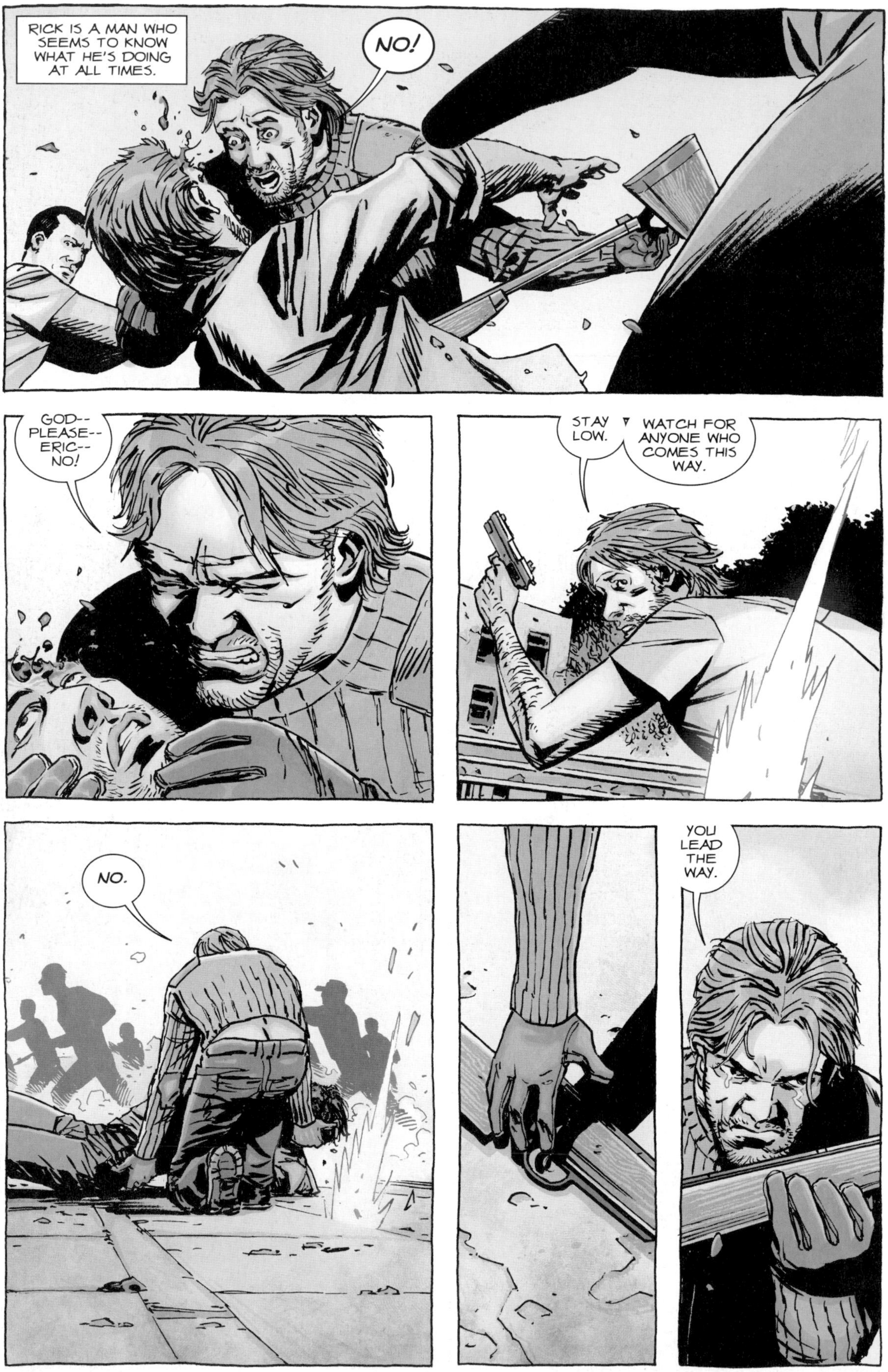
RICK IS A MAN WHO SEEMS TO KNOW WHAT HE'S DOING AT ALL TIMES.
NO!
GOD-- PLEASE-- ERIC-- NO!
STAY LOW.
WATCH FOR ANYONE WHO COMES THIS WAY.
NO.
YOU LEAD THE WAY.

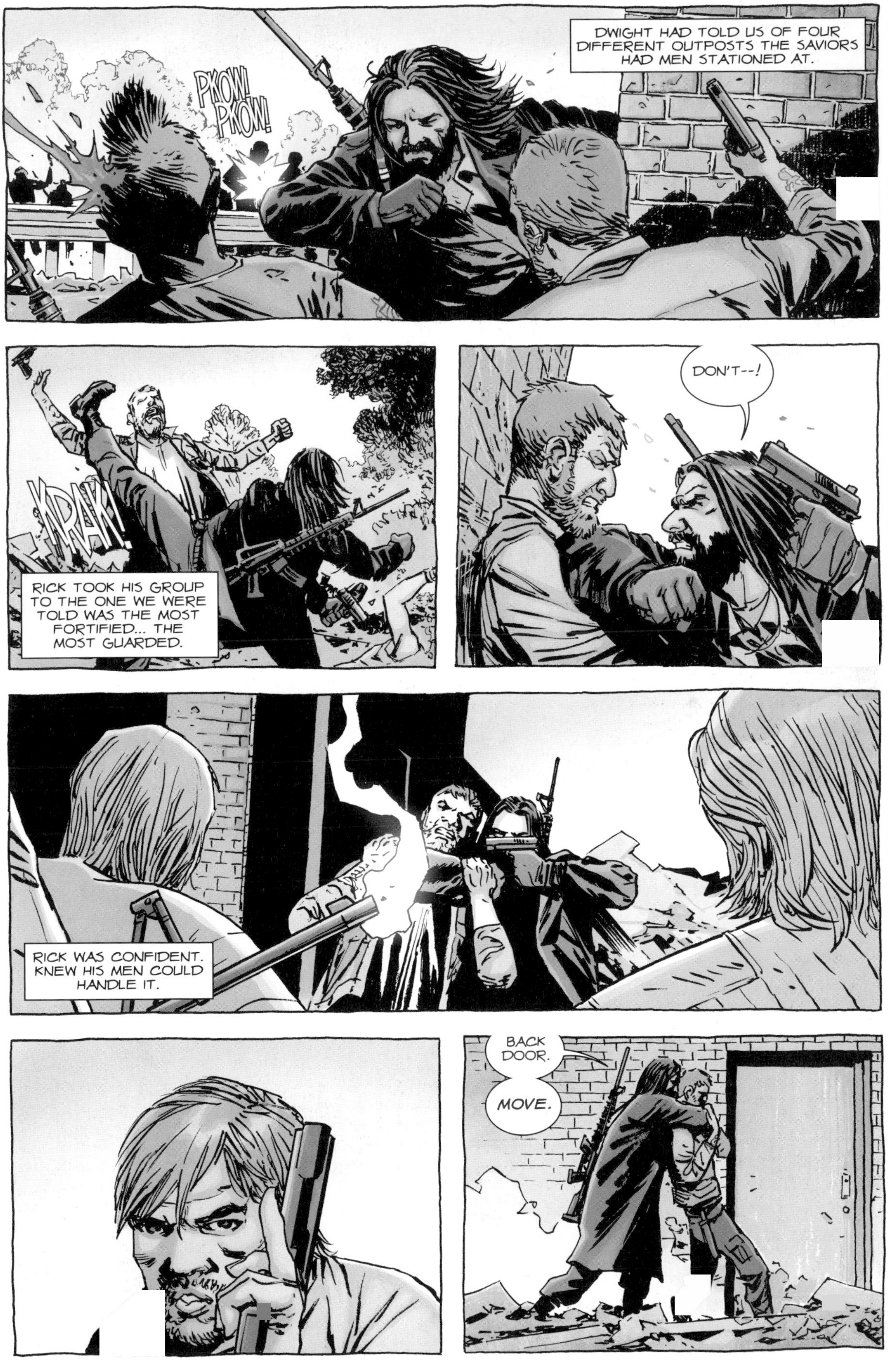
DWIGHT HAD TOLD US OF FOUR DIFFERENT OUTPOSTS THE SAVIORS HAD MEN STATIONED AT.
PKOW! PKOW!
KRAK!
RICK TOOK HIS GROUP TO THE ONE WE WERE TOLD WAS THE MOST FORTIFIED... THE MOST GUARDED.
DON'T--!
RICK WAS CONFIDENT. KNEW HIS MEN COULD HANDLE IT.
BACK DOOR.
MOVE.

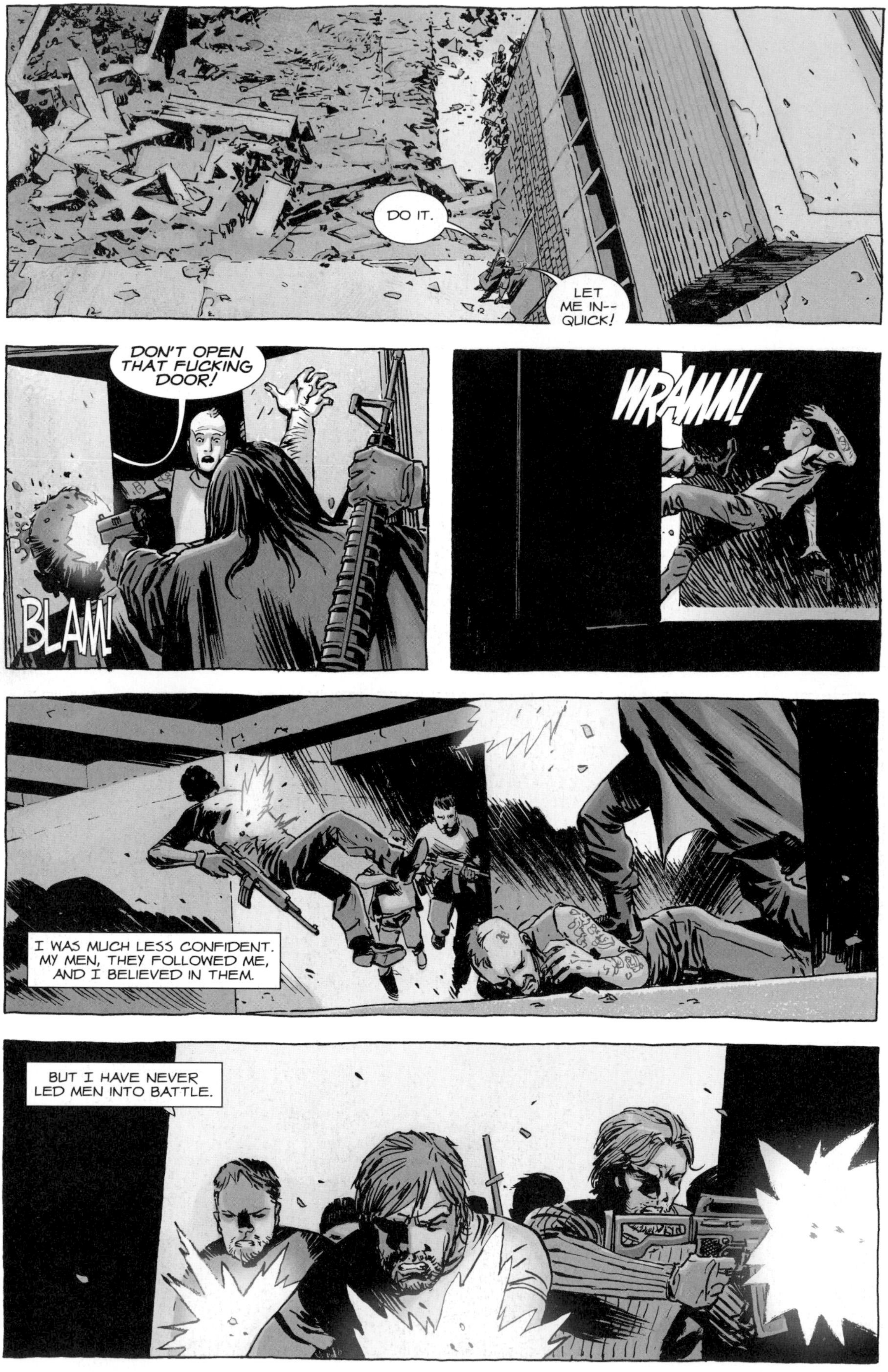
DO IT.
LET ME IN-- QUICK!
DON'T OPEN THAT FUCKING DOOR!
BLAM!
WRAMM!
I WAS MUCH LESS CONFIDENT. MY MEN, THEY FOLLOWED ME, AND I BELIEVED IN THEM.
BUT I HAVE NEVER LED MEN INTO BATTLE.

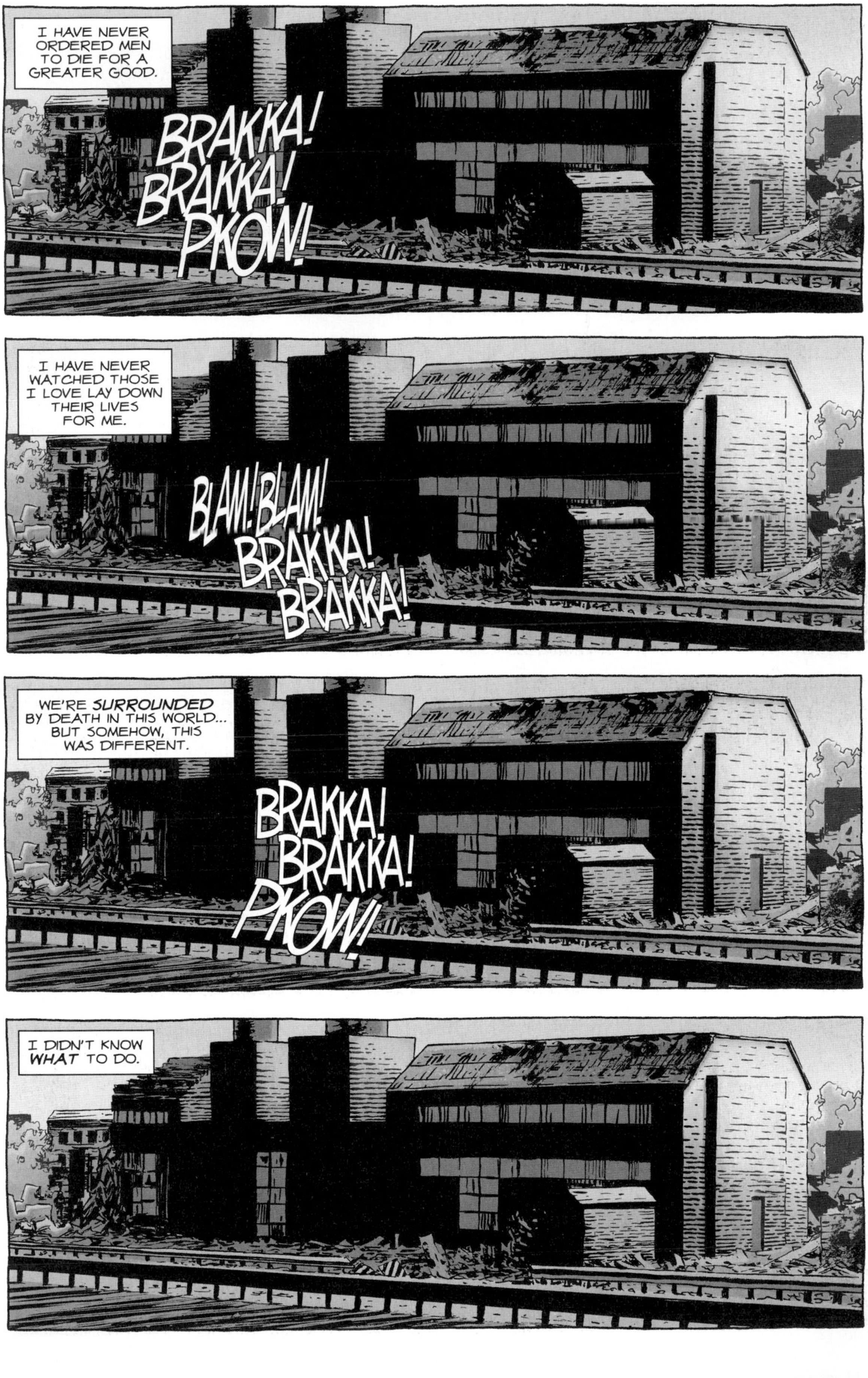
I HAVE NEVER ORDERED MEN TO DIE FOR A GREATER GOOD.
BRAKKA! BRAKKA! PKOW!
I HAVE NEVER WATCHED THOSE I LOVE LAY DOWN THEIR LIVES FOR ME.
BLAM! BLAM! BRAKKA! BRAKKA!
WE'RE *SURROUNDED* BY DEATH IN THIS WORLD... BUT SOMEHOW, THIS WAS DIFFERENT.
BRAKKA! BRAKKA! PKOW!
I DIDN'T KNOW ***WHAT*** TO DO.

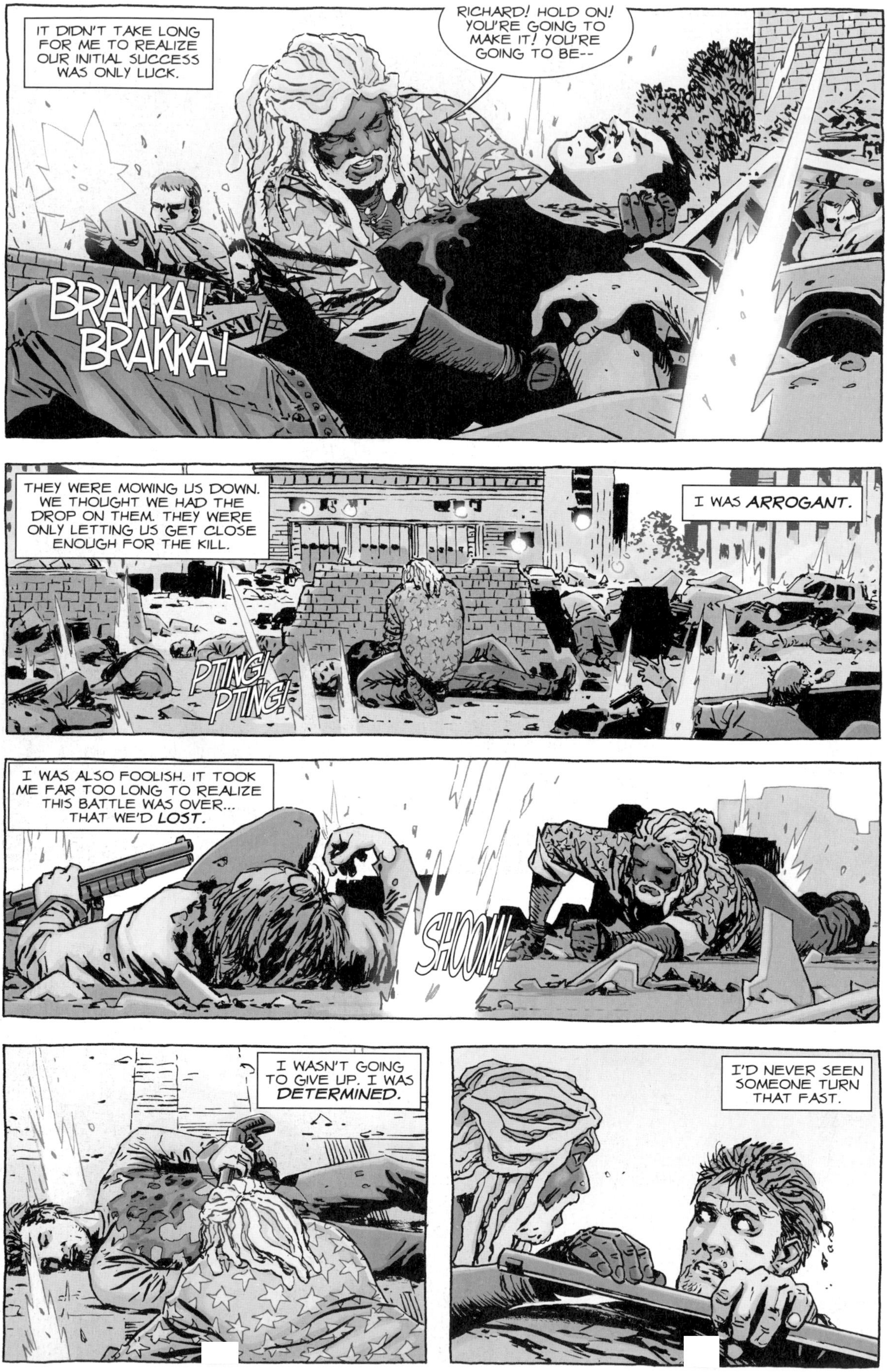
IT DIDN'T TAKE LONG FOR ME TO REALIZE OUR INITIAL SUCCESS WAS ONLY LUCK.
RICHARD! HOLD ON! YOU'RE GOING TO MAKE IT! YOU'RE GOING TO BE--
BRAKKA! BRAKKA!
THEY WERE MOWING US DOWN. WE THOUGHT WE HAD THE DROP ON THEM. THEY WERE ONLY LETTING US GET CLOSE ENOUGH FOR THE KILL.
I WAS ARROGANT.
PTING! PTING!
I WAS ALSO FOOLISH. IT TOOK ME FAR TOO LONG TO REALIZE THIS BATTLE WAS OVER... THAT WE'D LOST.
SHOOM!
I WASN'T GOING TO GIVE UP. I WAS DETERMINED.
I'D NEVER SEEN SOMEONE TURN THAT FAST.

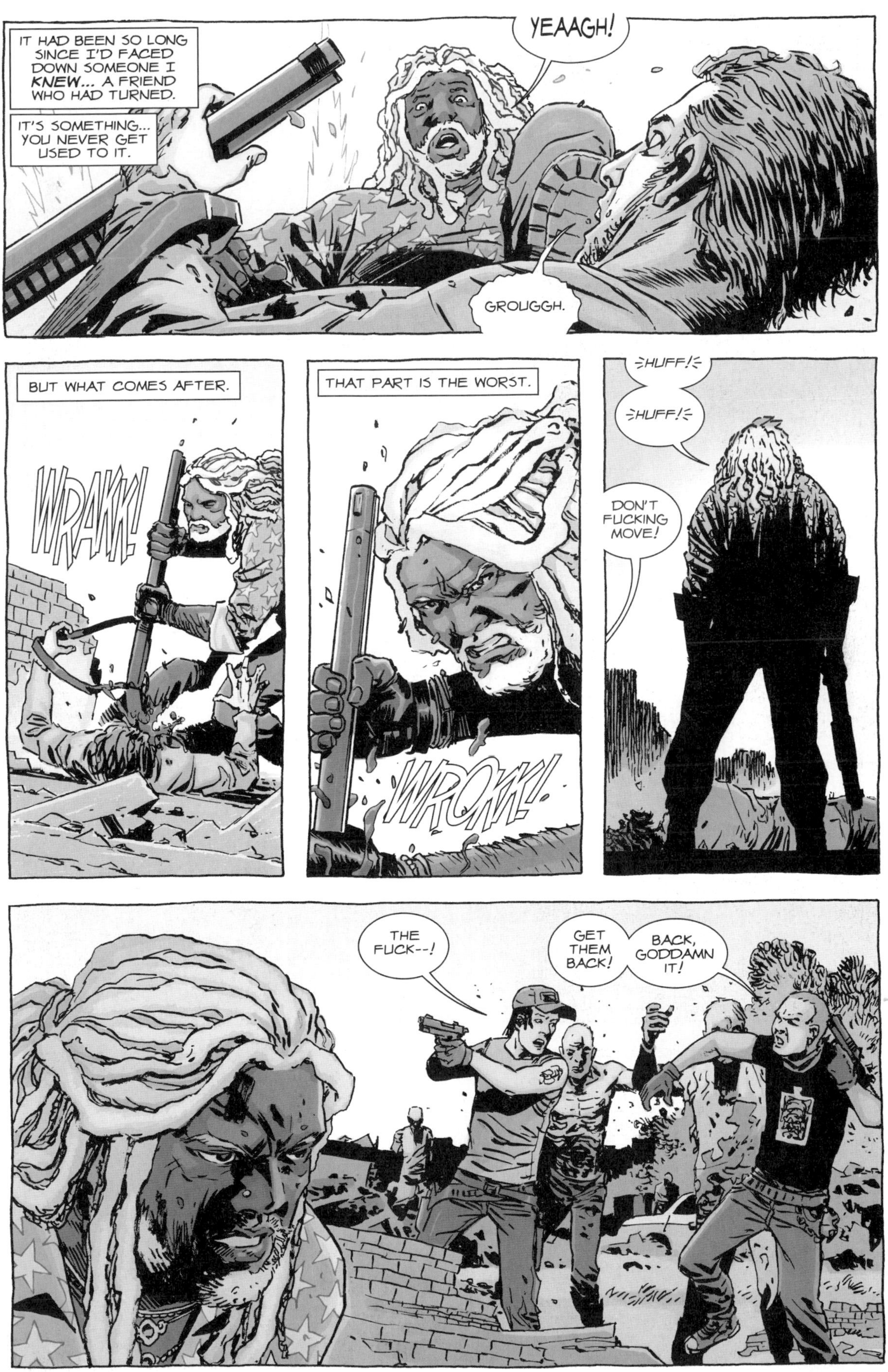
IT HAD BEEN SO LONG SINCE I'D FACED DOWN SOMEONE I **KNEW...** A FRIEND WHO HAD TURNED.
IT'S SOMETHING... YOU NEVER GET USED TO IT.
YEAAAGH!
GROUGGH.
BUT WHAT COMES AFTER.
WRAKK!
THAT PART IS THE WORST.
WROKK!
HUFF!
HUFF!
DON'T FUCKING MOVE!
THE FUCK--!
GET THEM BACK!
BACK, GODDAMN IT!

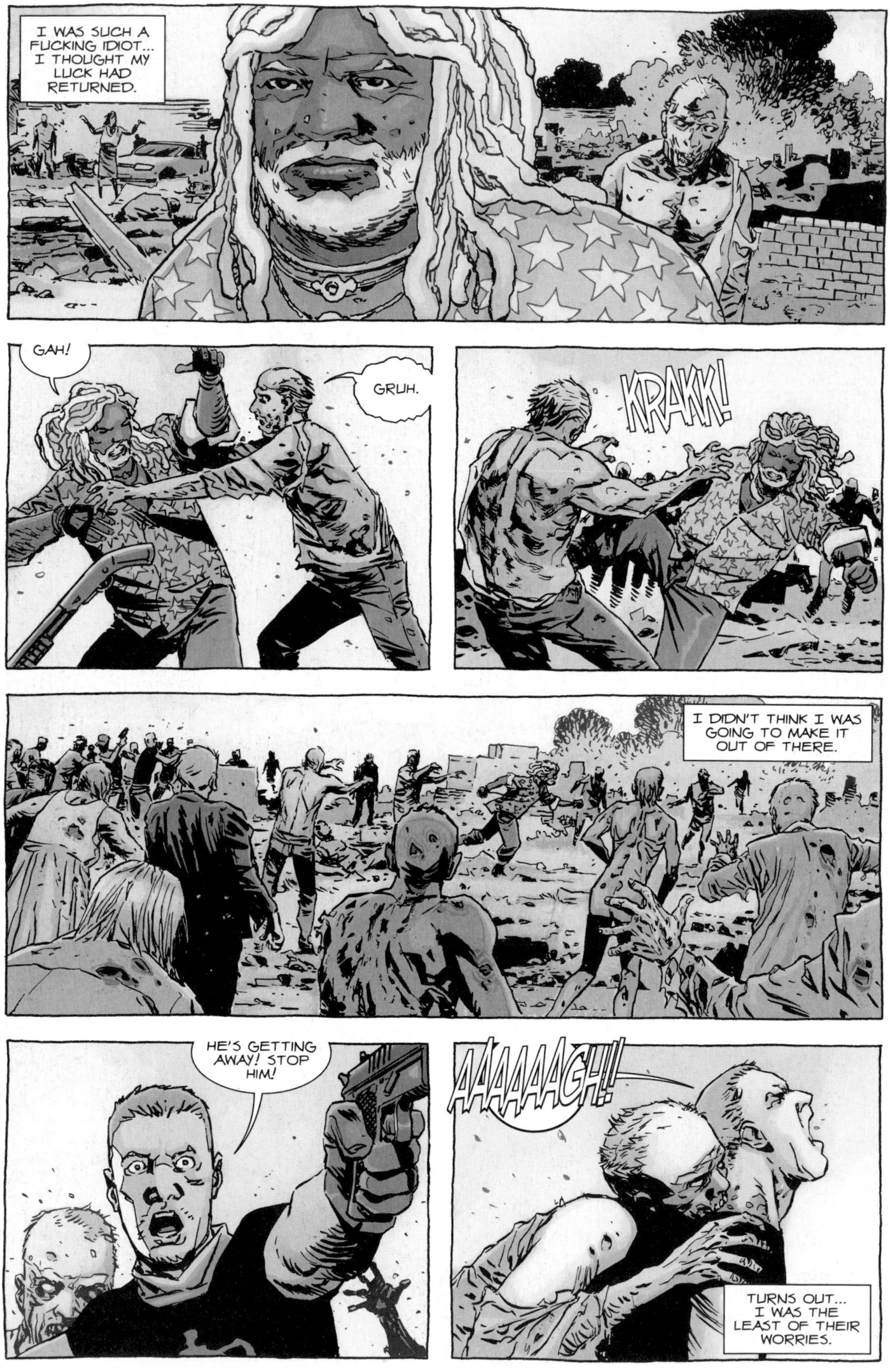
I WAS SUCH A FUCKING IDIOT... I THOUGHT MY LUCK HAD RETURNED.
GAH!
GRUH.
KRAKK!
I DIDN'T THINK I WAS GOING TO MAKE IT OUT OF THERE.
HE'S GETTING AWAY! STOP HIM!
AAAAAAGH!!
TURNS OUT... I WAS THE LEAST OF THEIR WORRIES.

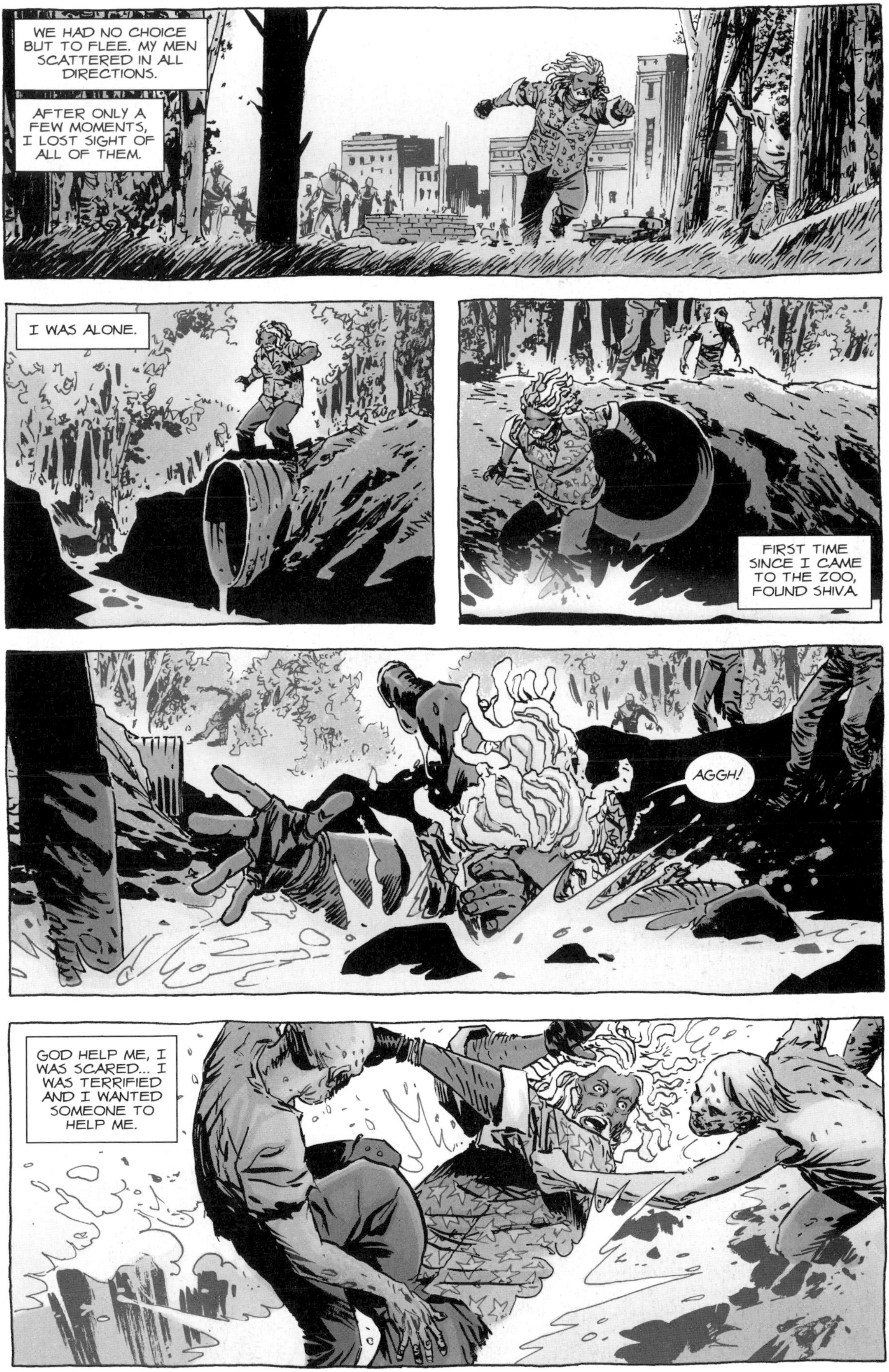
WE HAD NO CHOICE BUT TO FLEE. MY MEN SCATTERED IN ALL DIRECTIONS.
AFTER ONLY A FEW MOMENTS, I LOST SIGHT OF ALL OF THEM.
I WAS ALONE.
FIRST TIME SINCE I CAME TO THE ZOO, FOUND SHIVA.
AGGH!
GOD HELP ME, I WAS SCARED... I WAS TERRIFIED AND I WANTED SOMEONE TO HELP ME.

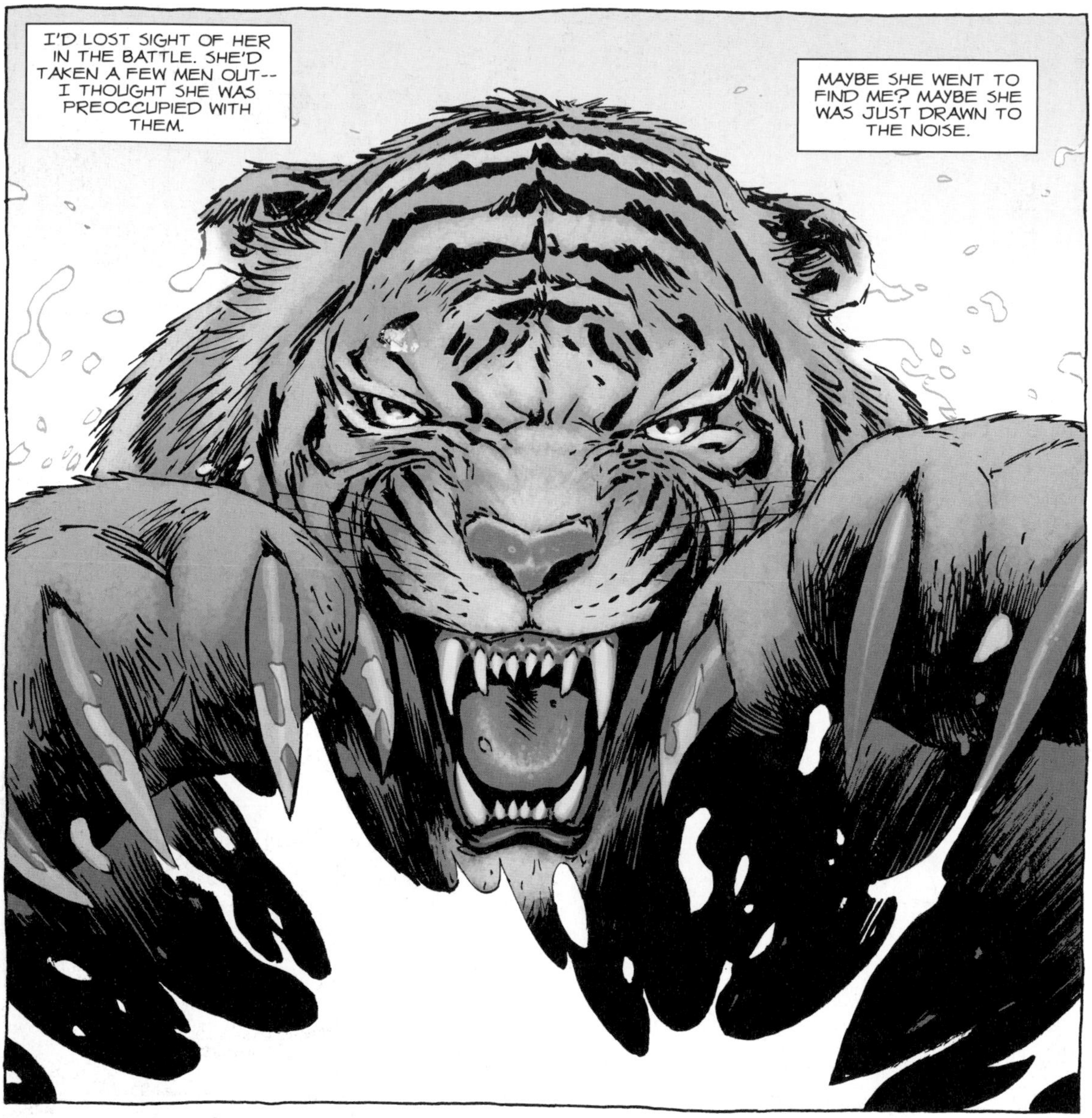
I'D LOST SIGHT OF HER IN THE BATTLE. SHE'D TAKEN A FEW MEN OUT-- I THOUGHT SHE WAS PREOCCUPIED WITH THEM.
MAYBE SHE WENT TO FIND ME? MAYBE SHE WAS JUST DRAWN TO THE NOISE.

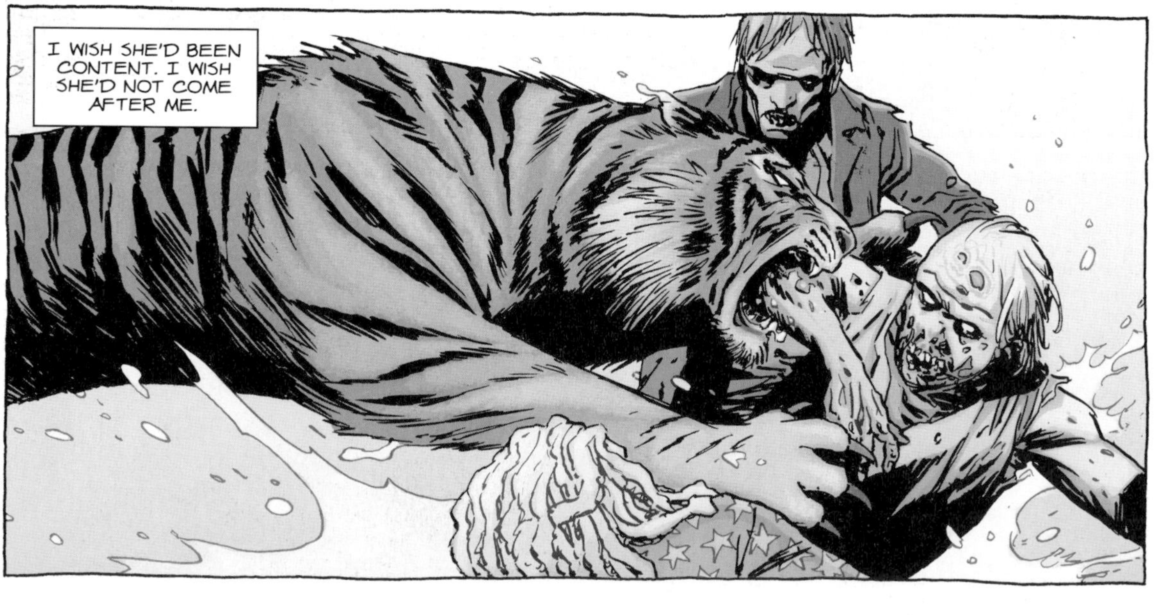
I WISH SHE'D BEEN CONTENT. I WISH SHE'D NOT COME AFTER ME.

THERE WERE SO MANY OF THEM.

WE WERE SURROUNDED-- BUT I WAS ABLE TO GET AWAY.

I TURNED TO CALL HER TO ME... SO WE COULD LEAVE... GET AWAY BEFORE SHE WAS SWARMED.

SHE KNEW THERE WERE TOO MANY, SHE KNEW I'D NEVER GET AWAY OTHERWISE.

THERE WAS NO OTHER WAY.

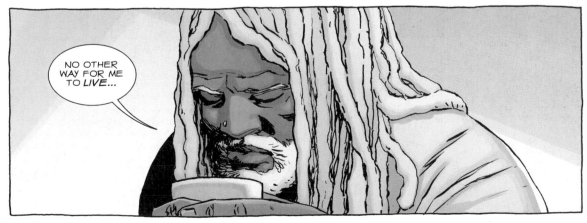

NO OTHER WAY FOR ME TO LIVE...

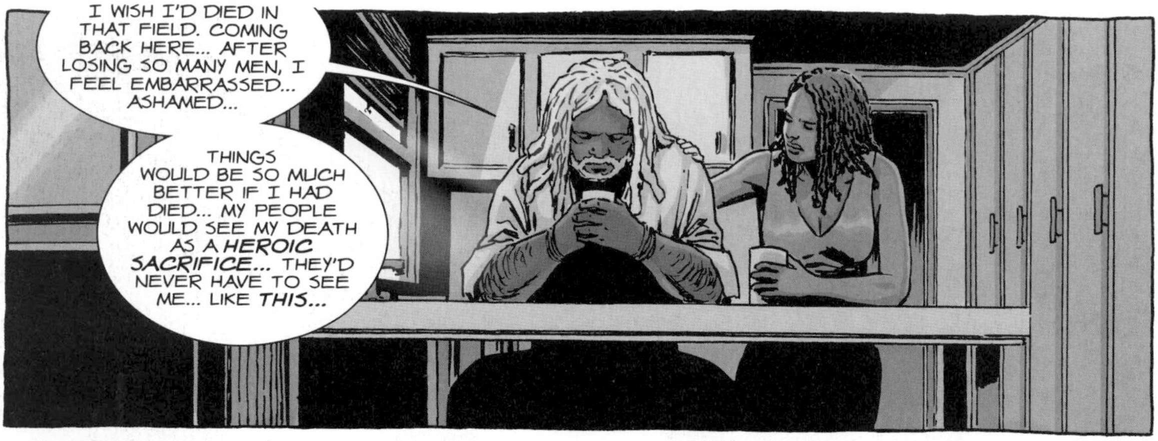
I WISH I'D DIED IN THAT FIELD. COMING BACK HERE... AFTER LOSING SO MANY MEN, I FEEL EMBARRASSED... ASHAMED...
THINGS WOULD BE SO MUCH BETTER IF I HAD DIED... MY PEOPLE WOULD SEE MY DEATH AS A HEROIC SACRIFICE... THEY'D NEVER HAVE TO SEE ME... LIKE THIS...

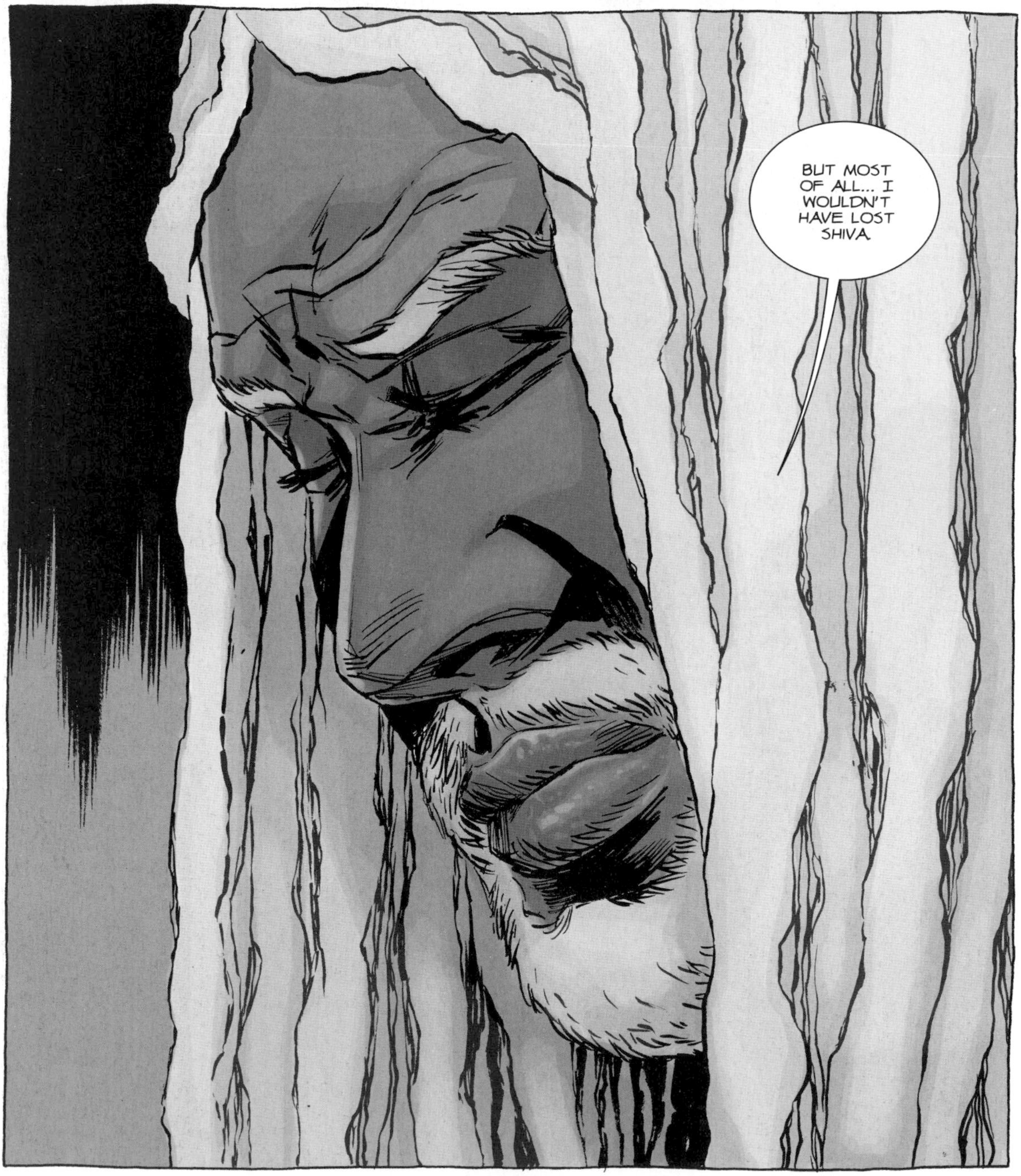
BUT MOST OF ALL... I WOULDN'T HAVE LOST SHIVA.

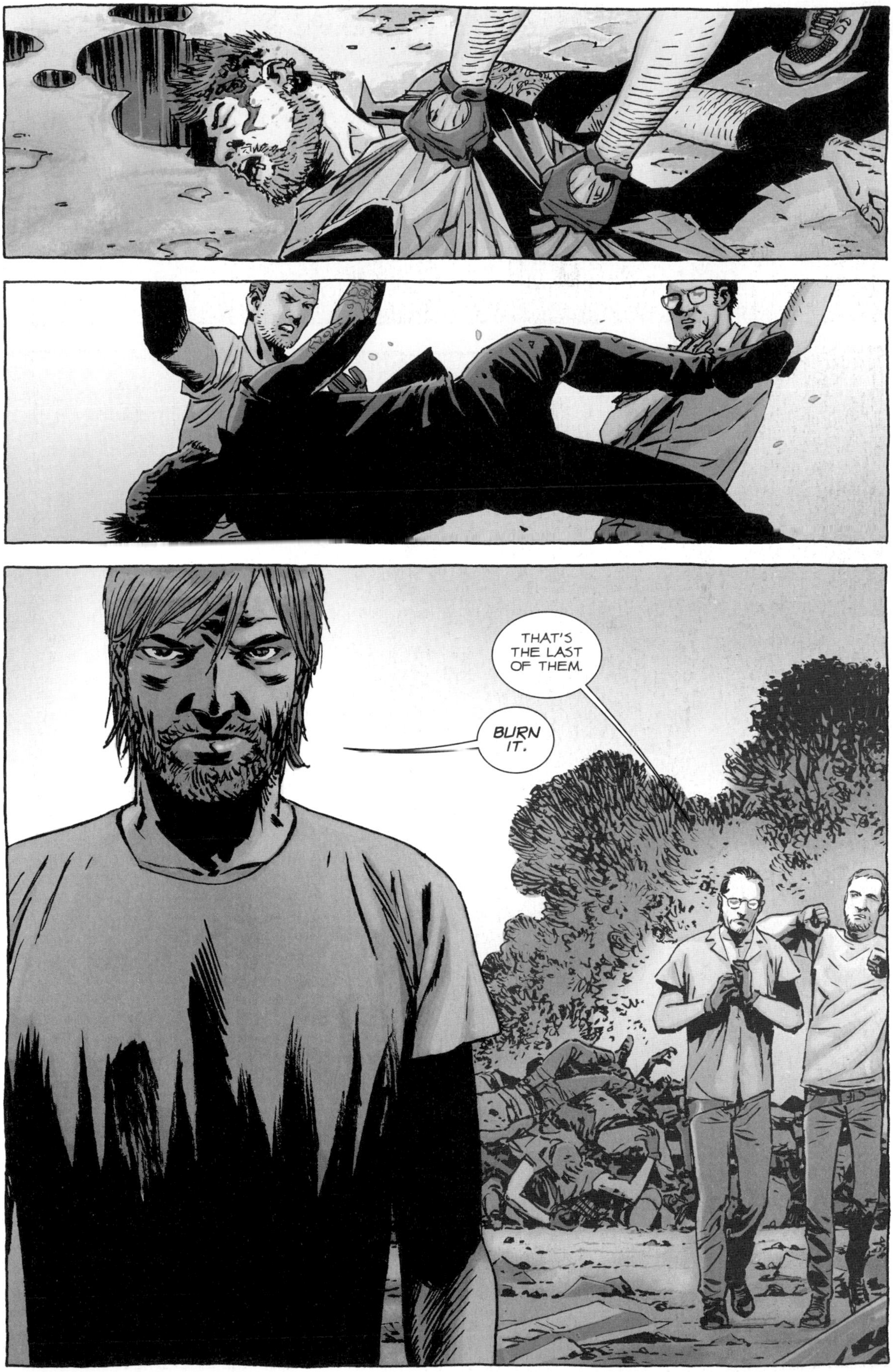
THAT'S THE LAST OF THEM.
BURN IT.

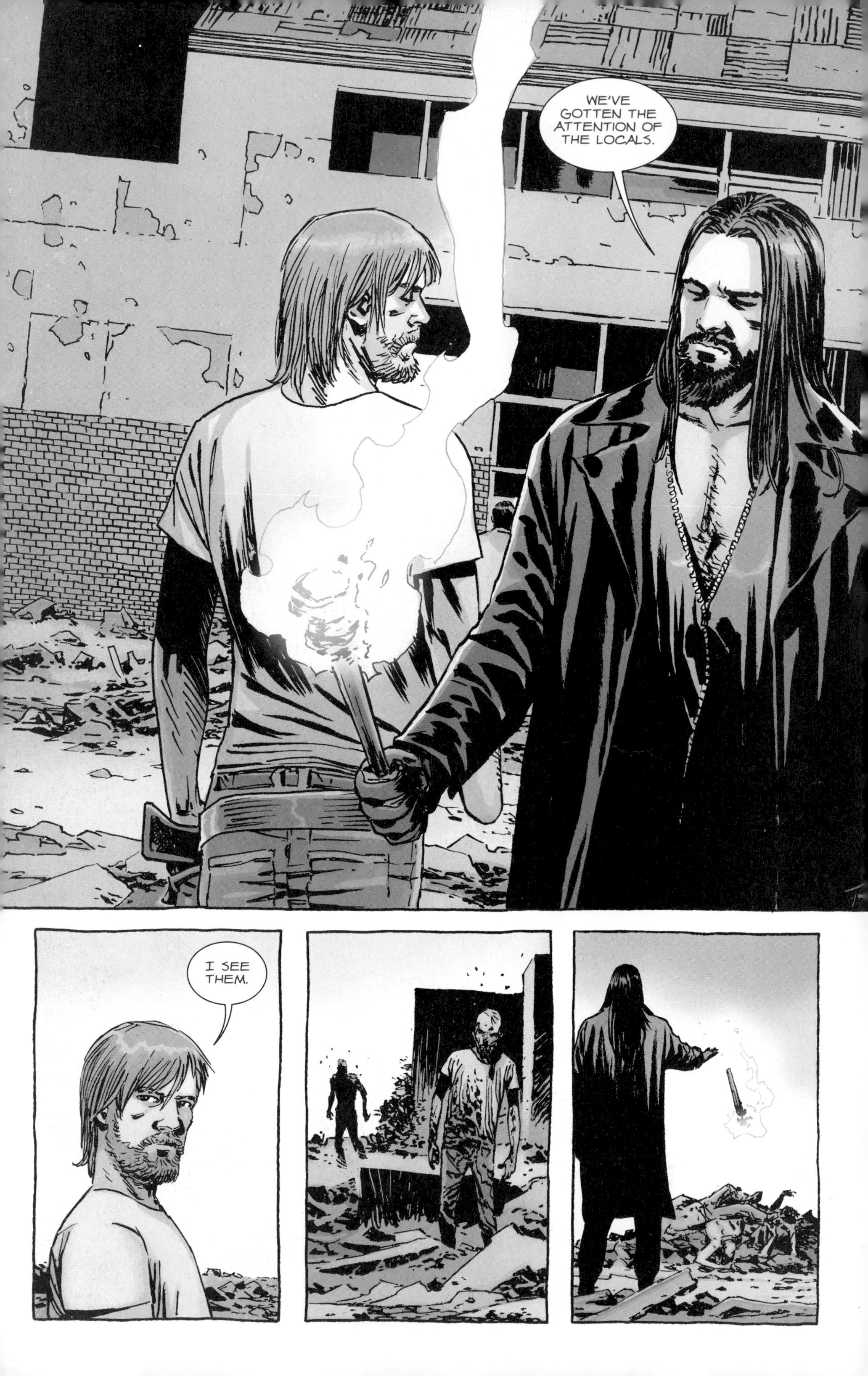
WE'VE GOTTEN THE ATTENTION OF THE LOCALS.
I SEE THEM.

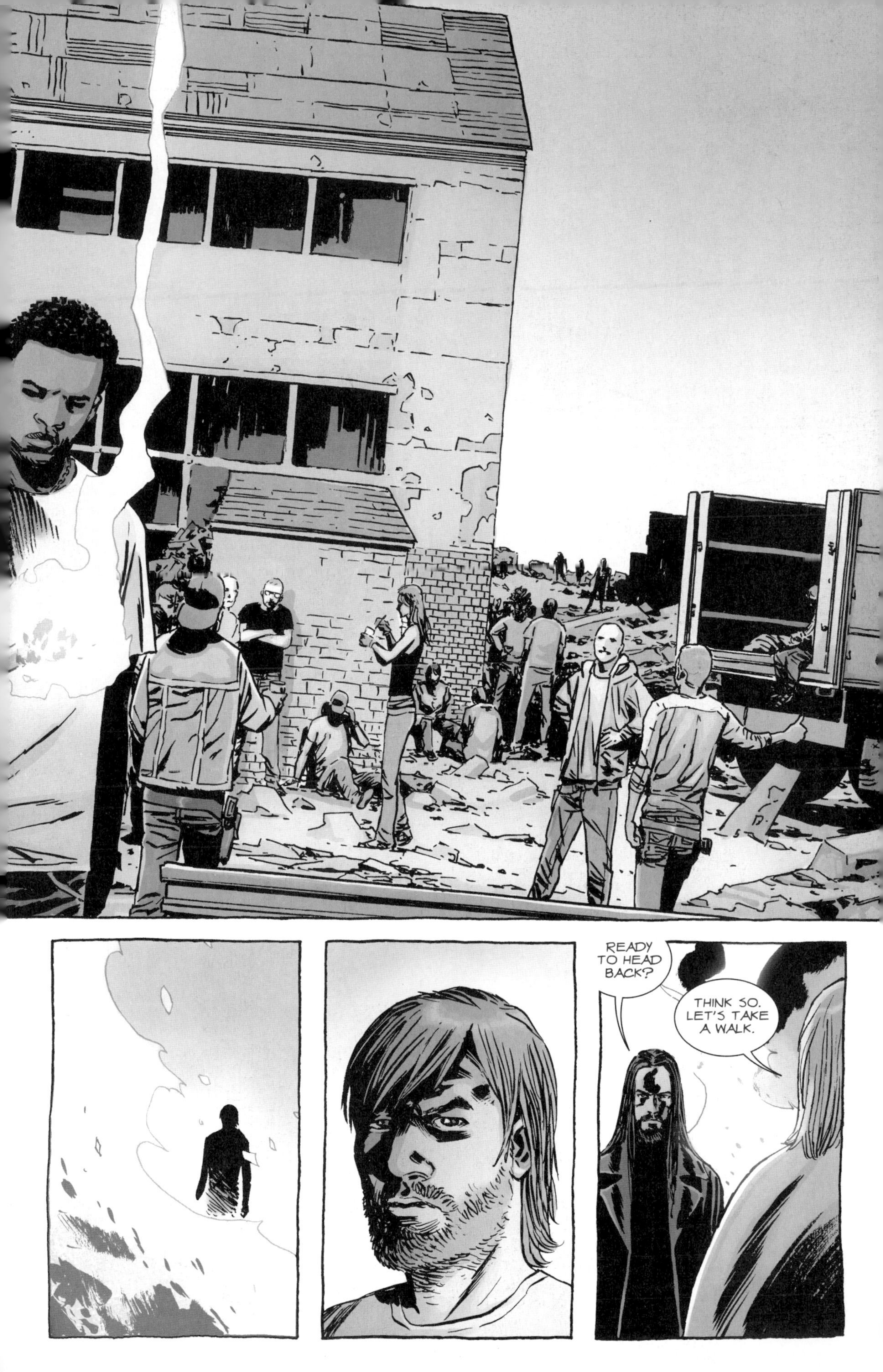
READY TO HEAD BACK?
THINK SO. LET'S TAKE A WALK.

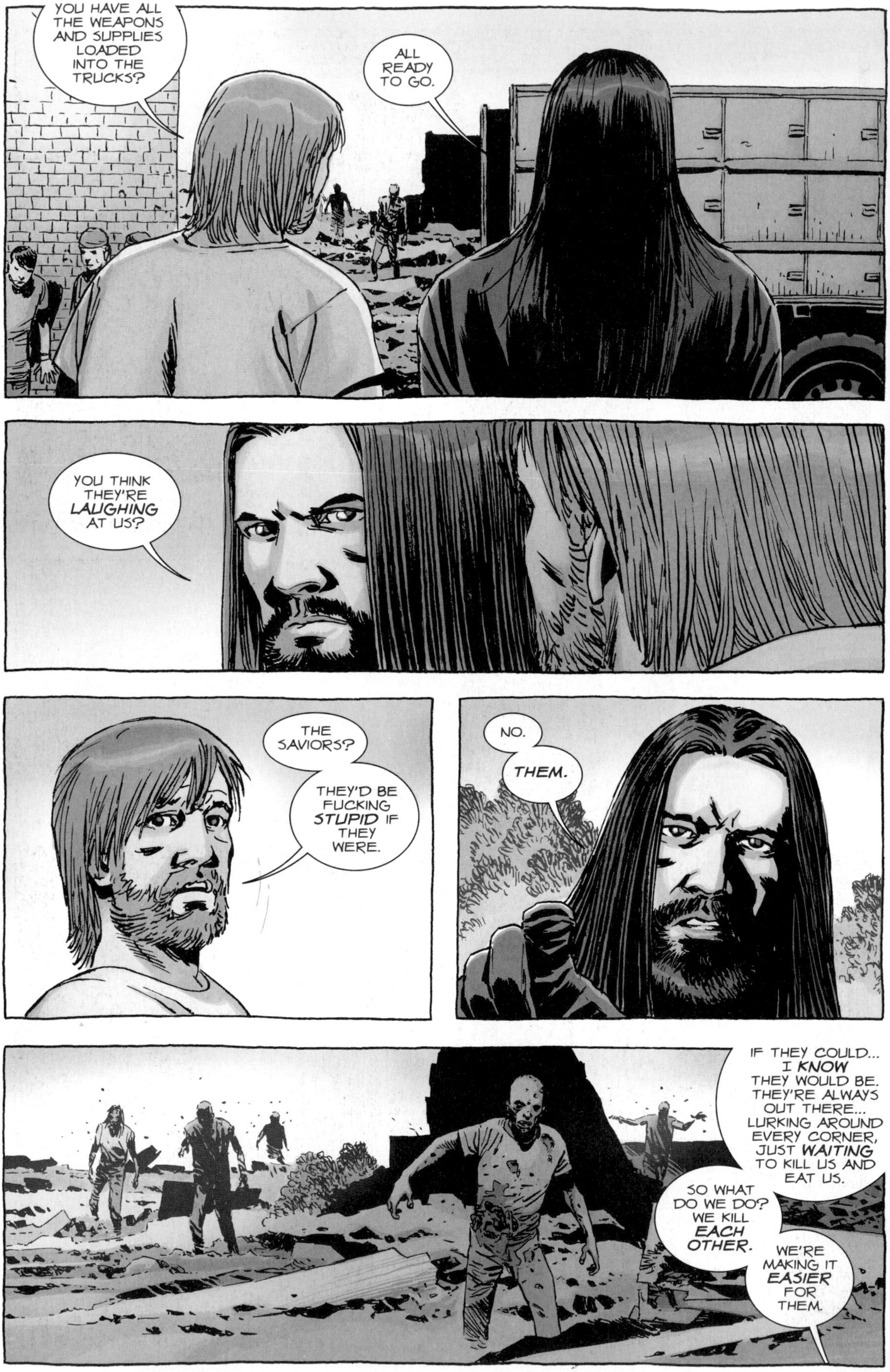
YOU HAVE ALL THE WEAPONS AND SUPPLIES LOADED INTO THE TRUCKS?
ALL READY TO GO.
YOU THINK THEY'RE LAUGHING AT US?
THE SAVIORS?
THEY'D BE FUCKING STUPID IF THEY WERE.
NO.
THEM.
IF THEY COULD... I KNOW THEY WOULD BE. THEY'RE ALWAYS OUT THERE... LURKING AROUND EVERY CORNER, JUST WAITING TO KILL US AND EAT US.
SO WHAT DO WE DO? WE KILL EACH OTHER.
WE'RE MAKING IT EASIER FOR THEM.

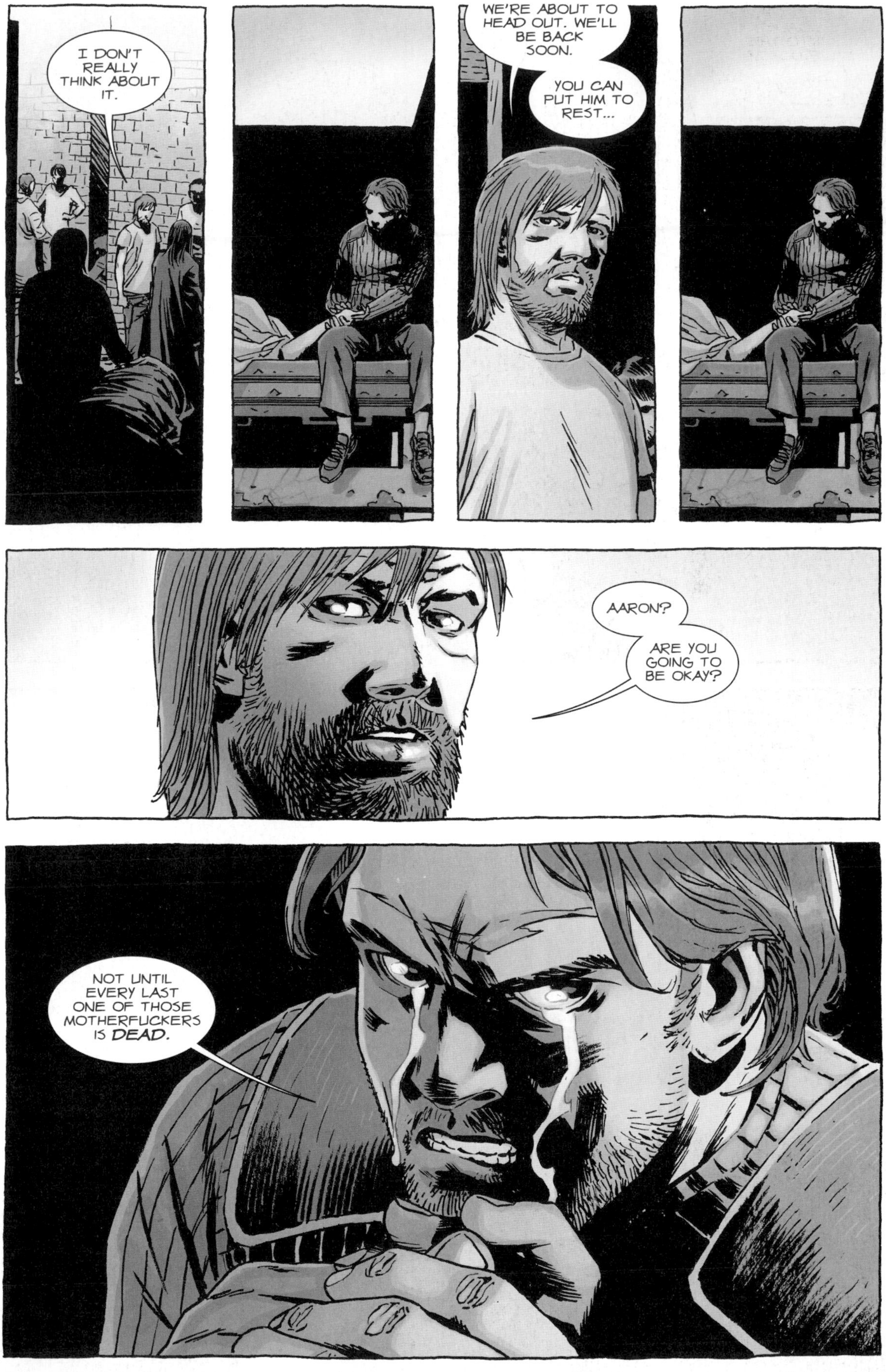
I DON'T REALLY THINK ABOUT IT.
WE'RE ABOUT TO HEAD OUT. WE'LL BE BACK SOON.
YOU CAN PUT HIM TO REST...
AARON?
ARE YOU GOING TO BE OKAY?
NOT UNTIL EVERY LAST ONE OF THOSE MOTHERFUCKERS IS DEAD.

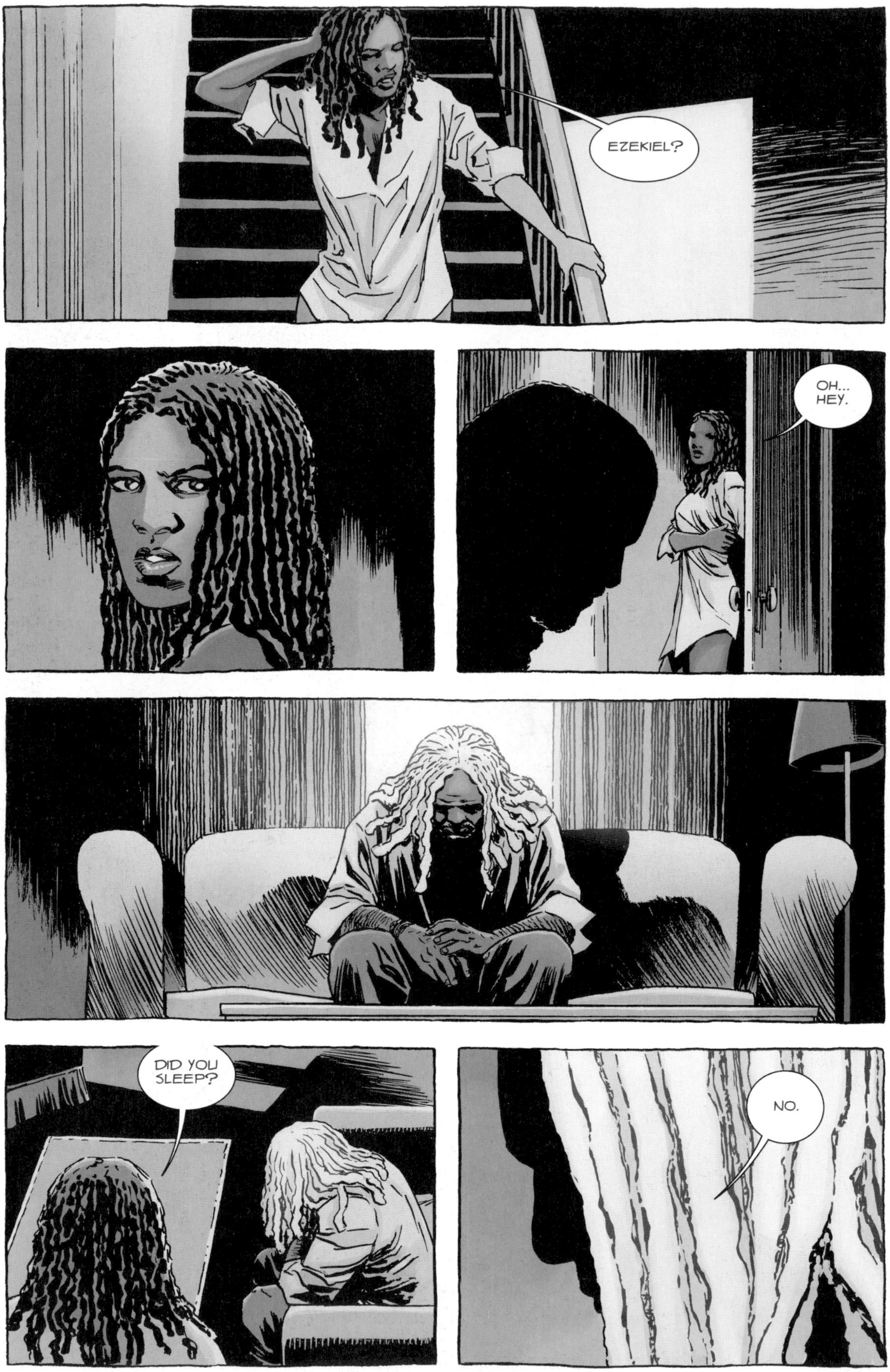
EZEKIEL?
OH... HEY.
DID YOU SLEEP?
NO.

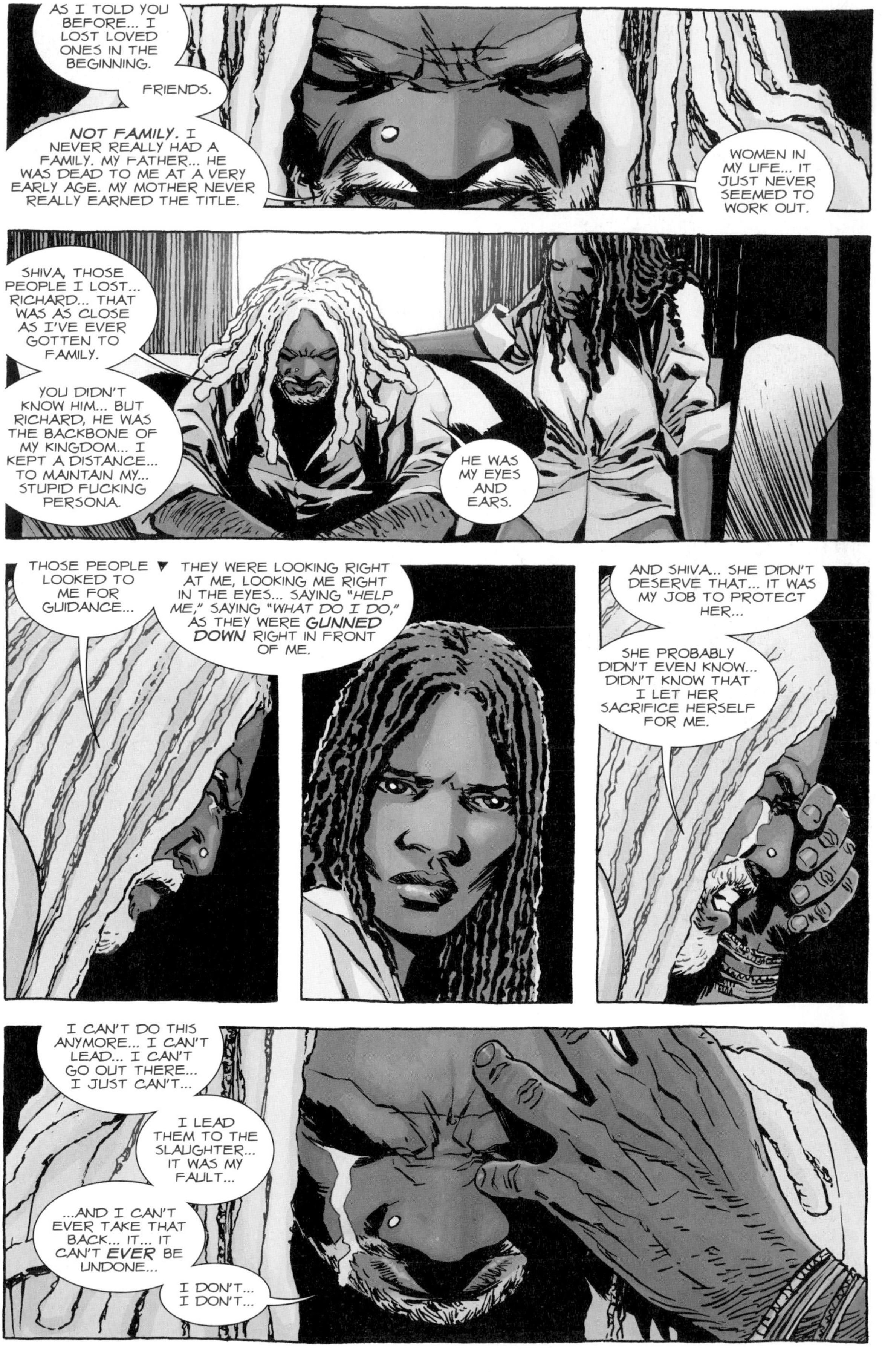

AS I TOLD YOU BEFORE... I LOST LOVED ONES IN THE BEGINNING.
FRIENDS.
NOT FAMILY. I NEVER REALLY HAD A FAMILY. MY FATHER... HE WAS DEAD TO ME AT A VERY EARLY AGE. MY MOTHER NEVER REALLY EARNED THE TITLE.
WOMEN IN MY LIFE... IT JUST NEVER SEEMED TO WORK OUT.
SHIVA, THOSE PEOPLE I LOST... RICHARD... THAT WAS AS CLOSE AS I'VE EVER GOTTEN TO FAMILY.
YOU DIDN'T KNOW HIM... BUT RICHARD, HE WAS THE BACKBONE OF MY KINGDOM... I KEPT A DISTANCE... TO MAINTAIN MY... STUPID FUCKING PERSONA.
HE WAS MY EYES AND EARS.
THOSE PEOPLE LOOKED TO ME FOR GUIDANCE...
THEY WERE LOOKING RIGHT AT ME, LOOKING ME RIGHT IN THE EYES... SAYING "*HELP ME,*" SAYING "*WHAT DO I DO,*" AS THEY WERE ***GUNNED DOWN*** RIGHT IN FRONT OF ME.
AND SHIVA... SHE DIDN'T DESERVE THAT... IT WAS MY JOB TO PROTECT HER...
SHE PROBABLY DIDN'T EVEN KNOW... DIDN'T KNOW THAT I LET HER SACRIFICE HERSELF FOR ME.
I CAN'T DO THIS ANYMORE... I CAN'T LEAD... I CAN'T GO OUT THERE... I JUST CAN'T...
I LEAD THEM TO THE SLAUGHTER... IT WAS MY FAULT...
...AND I CAN'T EVER TAKE THAT BACK... IT... IT CAN'T ***EVER*** BE UNDONE...
I DON'T... I DON'T...

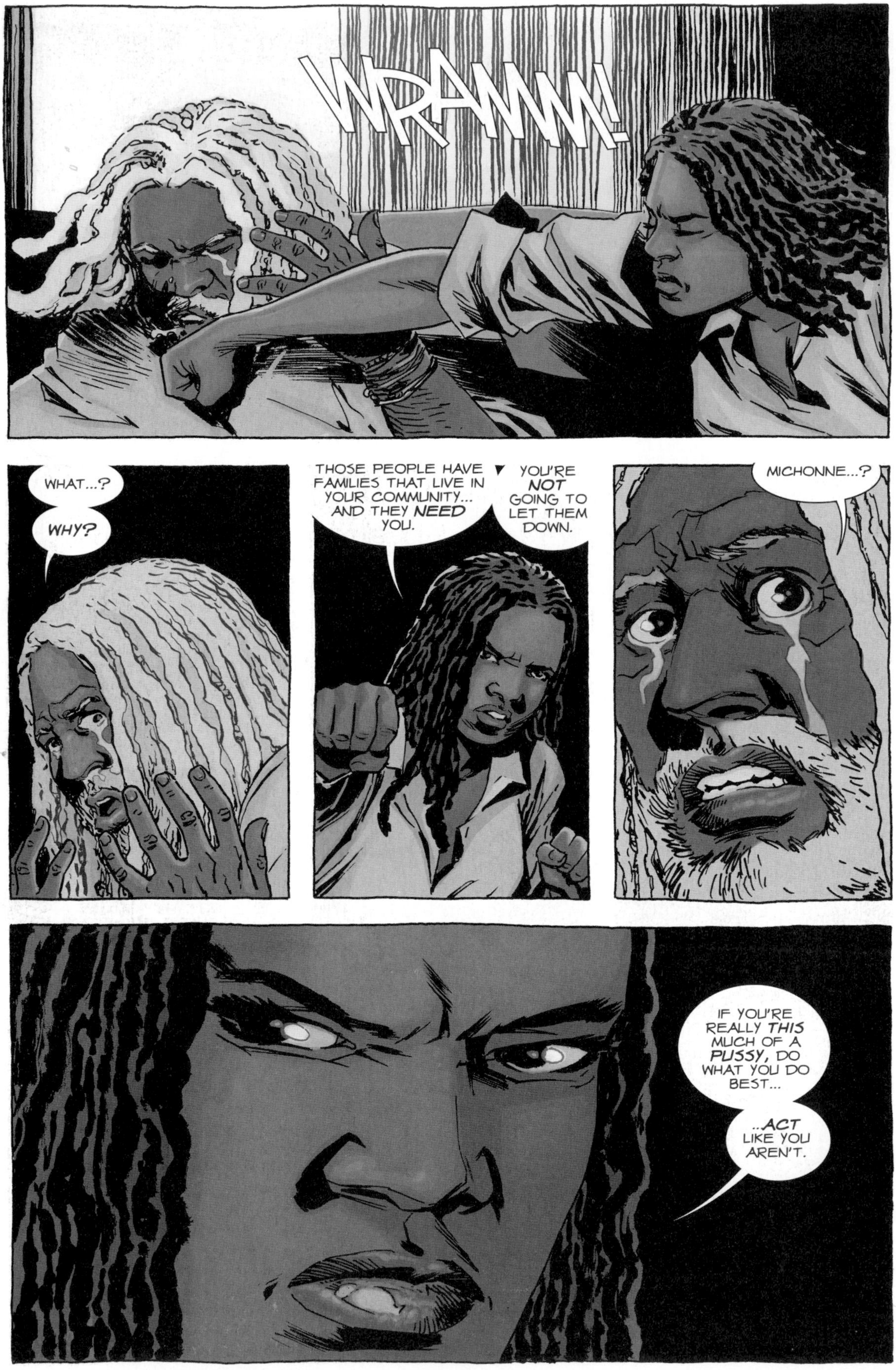
WRAMM!
WHAT...?
WHY?
THOSE PEOPLE HAVE FAMILIES THAT LIVE IN YOUR COMMUNITY... AND THEY NEED YOU.
YOU'RE NOT GOING TO LET THEM DOWN.
MICHONNE...?
IF YOU'RE REALLY THIS MUCH OF A PUSSY, DO WHAT YOU DO BEST...
..ACT LIKE YOU AREN'T.

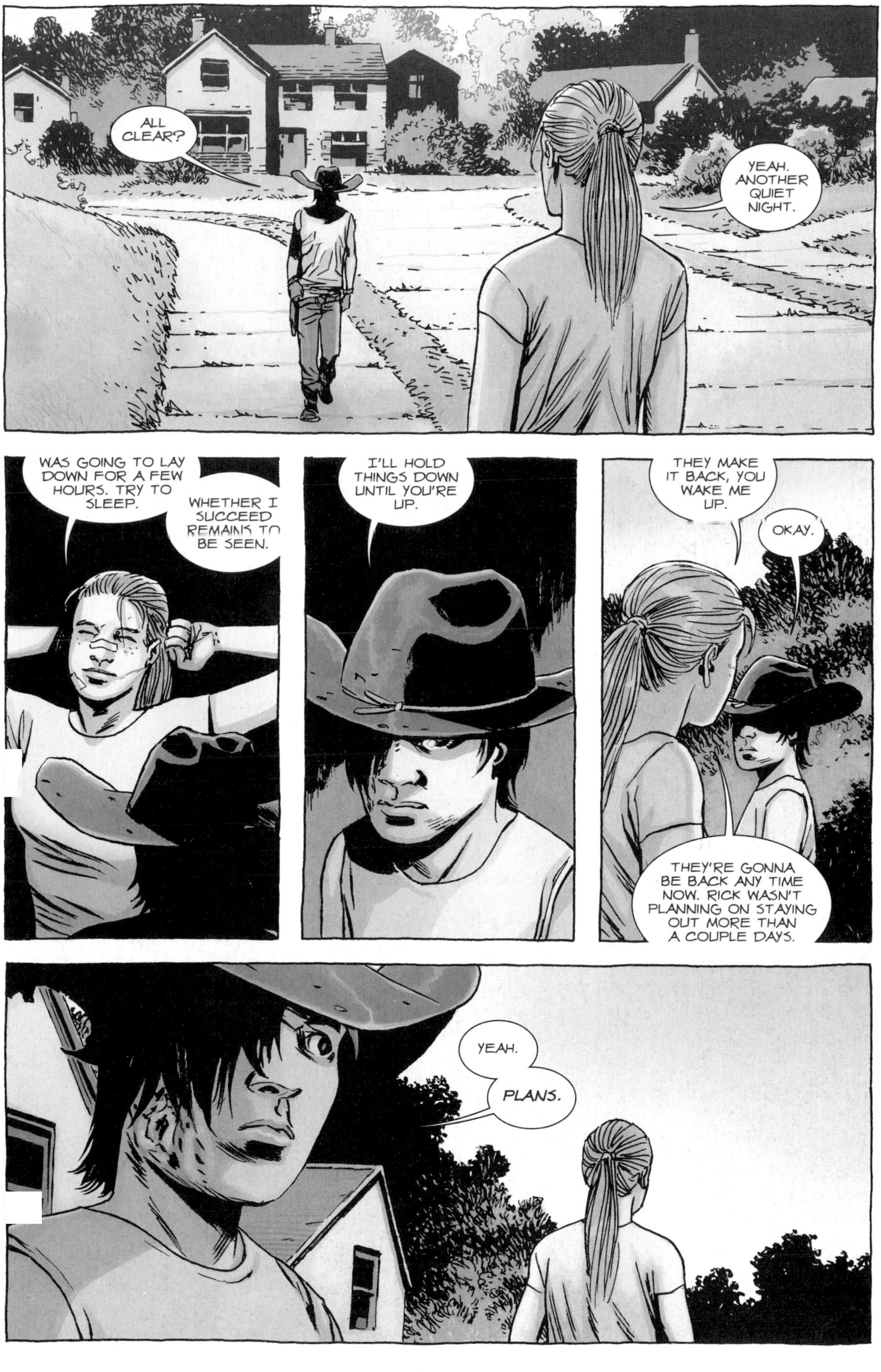
ALL CLEAR?
YEAH. ANOTHER QUIET NIGHT.
WAS GOING TO LAY DOWN FOR A FEW HOURS. TRY TO SLEEP.
WHETHER I SUCCEED REMAINS TO BE SEEN.
I'LL HOLD THINGS DOWN UNTIL YOU'RE UP.
THEY MAKE IT BACK, YOU WAKE ME UP.
OKAY.
THEY'RE GONNA BE BACK ANY TIME NOW. RICK WASN'T PLANNING ON STAYING OUT MORE THAN A COUPLE DAYS.
YEAH.
PLANS.

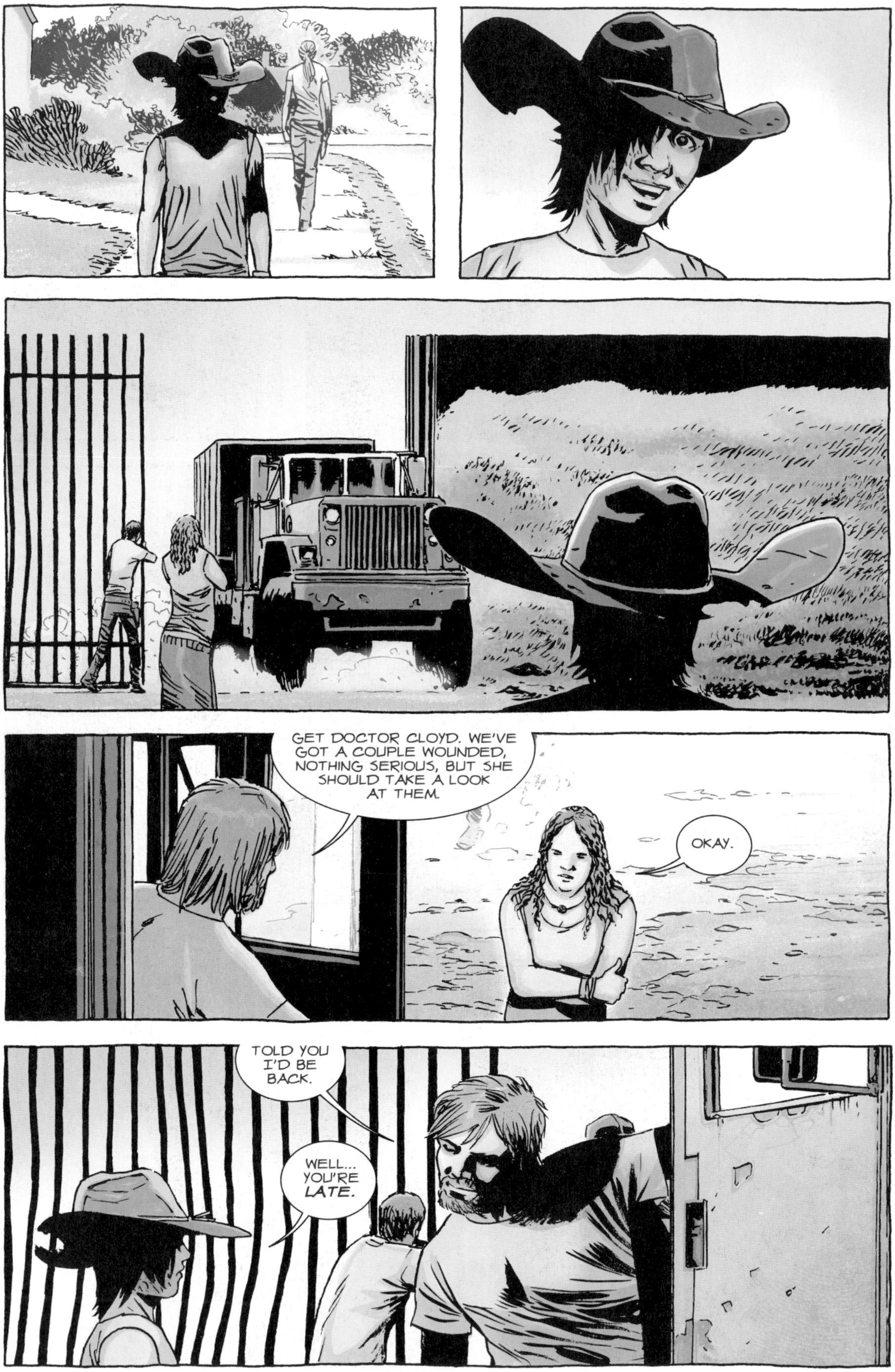
GET DOCTOR CLOYD. WE'VE GOT A COUPLE WOUNDED, NOTHING SERIOUS, BUT SHE SHOULD TAKE A LOOK AT THEM.
OKAY.
TOLD YOU I'D BE BACK.
WELL... YOU'RE *LATE*.

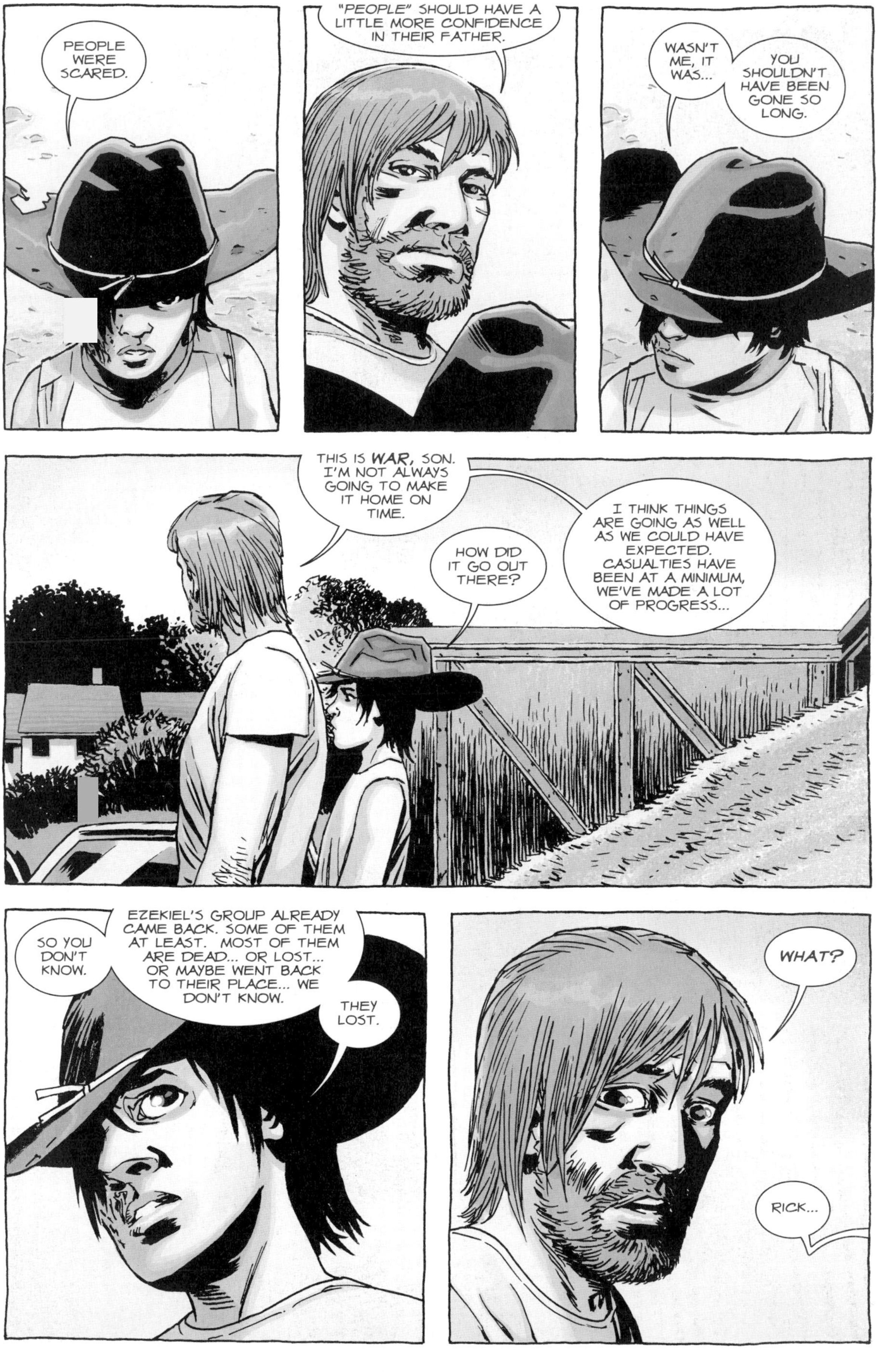
PEOPLE WERE SCARED.
"PEOPLE" SHOULD HAVE A LITTLE MORE CONFIDENCE IN THEIR FATHER.
WASN'T ME, IT WAS...
YOU SHOULDN'T HAVE BEEN GONE SO LONG.
THIS IS WAR, SON. I'M NOT ALWAYS GOING TO MAKE IT HOME ON TIME.
HOW DID IT GO OUT THERE?
I THINK THINGS ARE GOING AS WELL AS WE COULD HAVE EXPECTED. CASUALTIES HAVE BEEN AT A MINIMUM, WE'VE MADE A LOT OF PROGRESS...
SO YOU DON'T KNOW.
EZEKIEL'S GROUP ALREADY CAME BACK. SOME OF THEM AT LEAST. MOST OF THEM ARE DEAD... OR LOST... OR MAYBE WENT BACK TO THEIR PLACE... WE DON'T KNOW.
THEY LOST.
WHAT?
RICK...

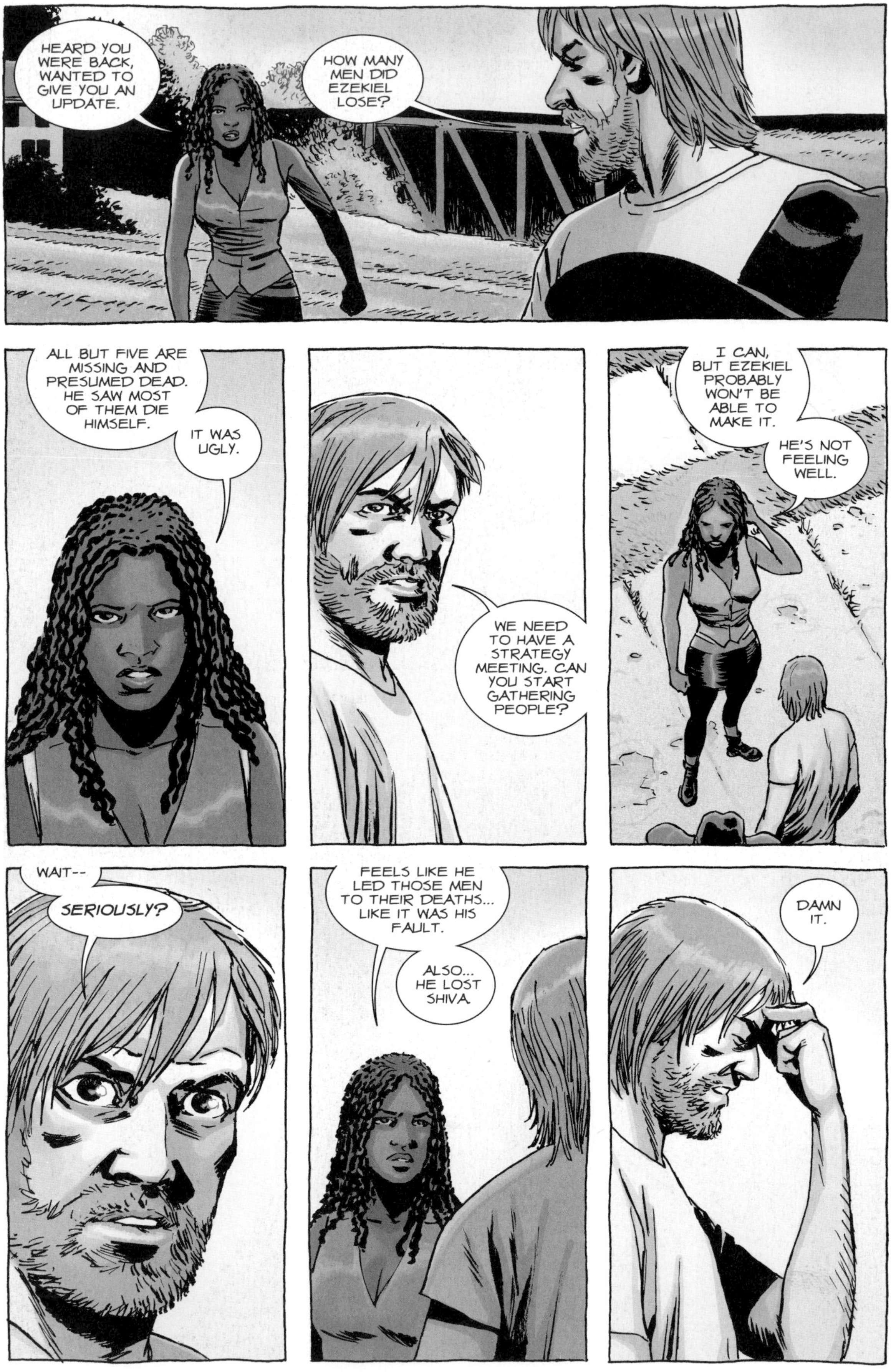
HEARD YOU WERE BACK, WANTED TO GIVE YOU AN UPDATE.
HOW MANY MEN DID EZEKIEL LOSE?
ALL BUT FIVE ARE MISSING AND PRESUMED DEAD. HE SAW MOST OF THEM DIE HIMSELF.
IT WAS UGLY.
WE NEED TO HAVE A STRATEGY MEETING. CAN YOU START GATHERING PEOPLE?
I CAN, BUT EZEKIEL PROBABLY WON'T BE ABLE TO MAKE IT.
HE'S NOT FEELING WELL.
WAIT--
SERIOUSLY?
FEELS LIKE HE LED THOSE MEN TO THEIR DEATHS... LIKE IT WAS HIS FAULT.
ALSO... HE LOST SHIVA.
DAMN IT.

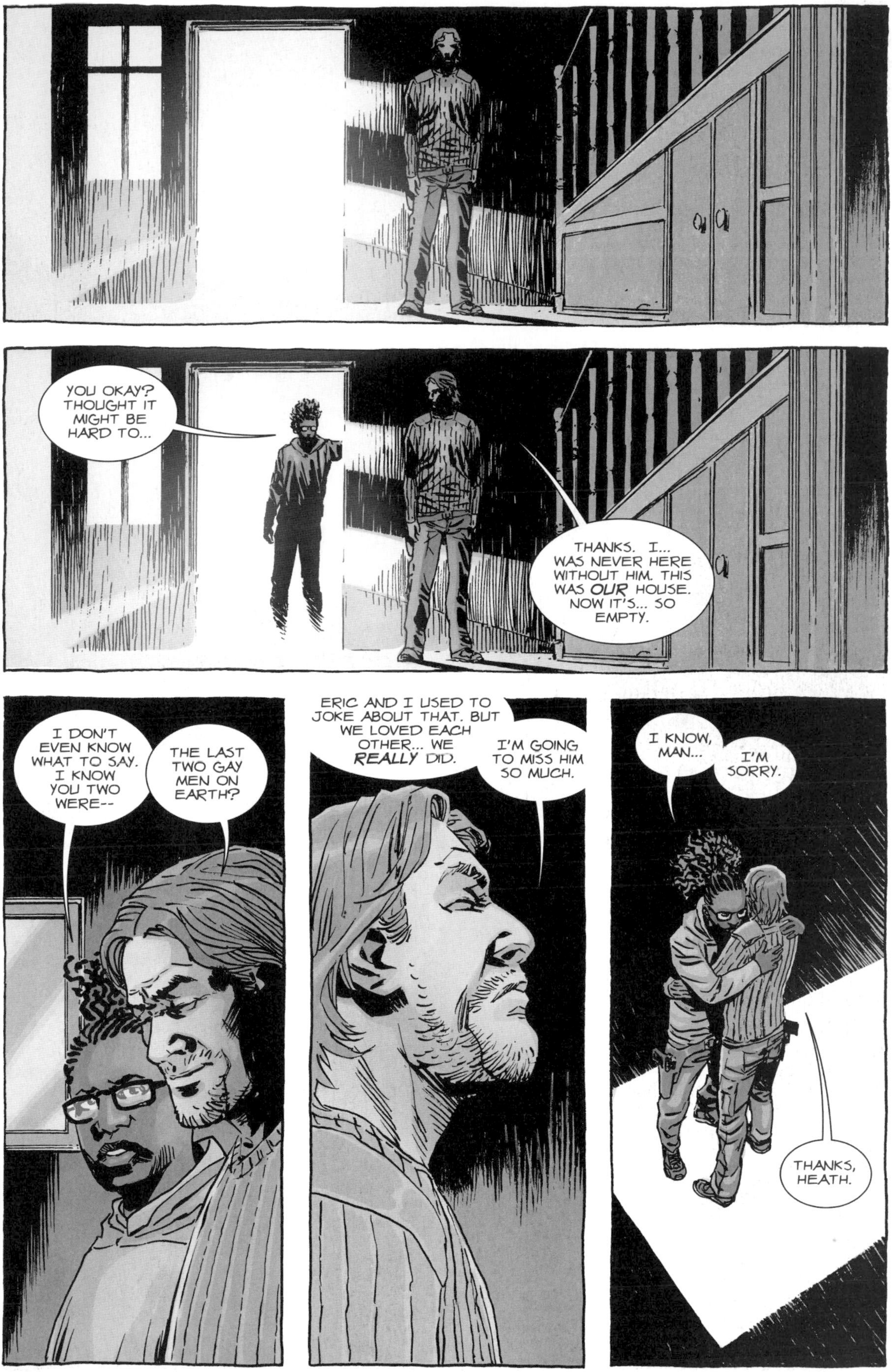
YOU OKAY? THOUGHT IT MIGHT BE HARD TO...
THANKS. I... WAS NEVER HERE WITHOUT HIM. THIS WAS OUR HOUSE. NOW IT'S... SO EMPTY.
I DON'T EVEN KNOW WHAT TO SAY. I KNOW YOU TWO WERE--
THE LAST TWO GAY MEN ON EARTH?
ERIC AND I USED TO JOKE ABOUT THAT. BUT WE LOVED EACH OTHER... WE REALLY DID.
I'M GOING TO MISS HIM SO MUCH.
I KNOW, MAN...
I'M SORRY.
THANKS, HEATH.

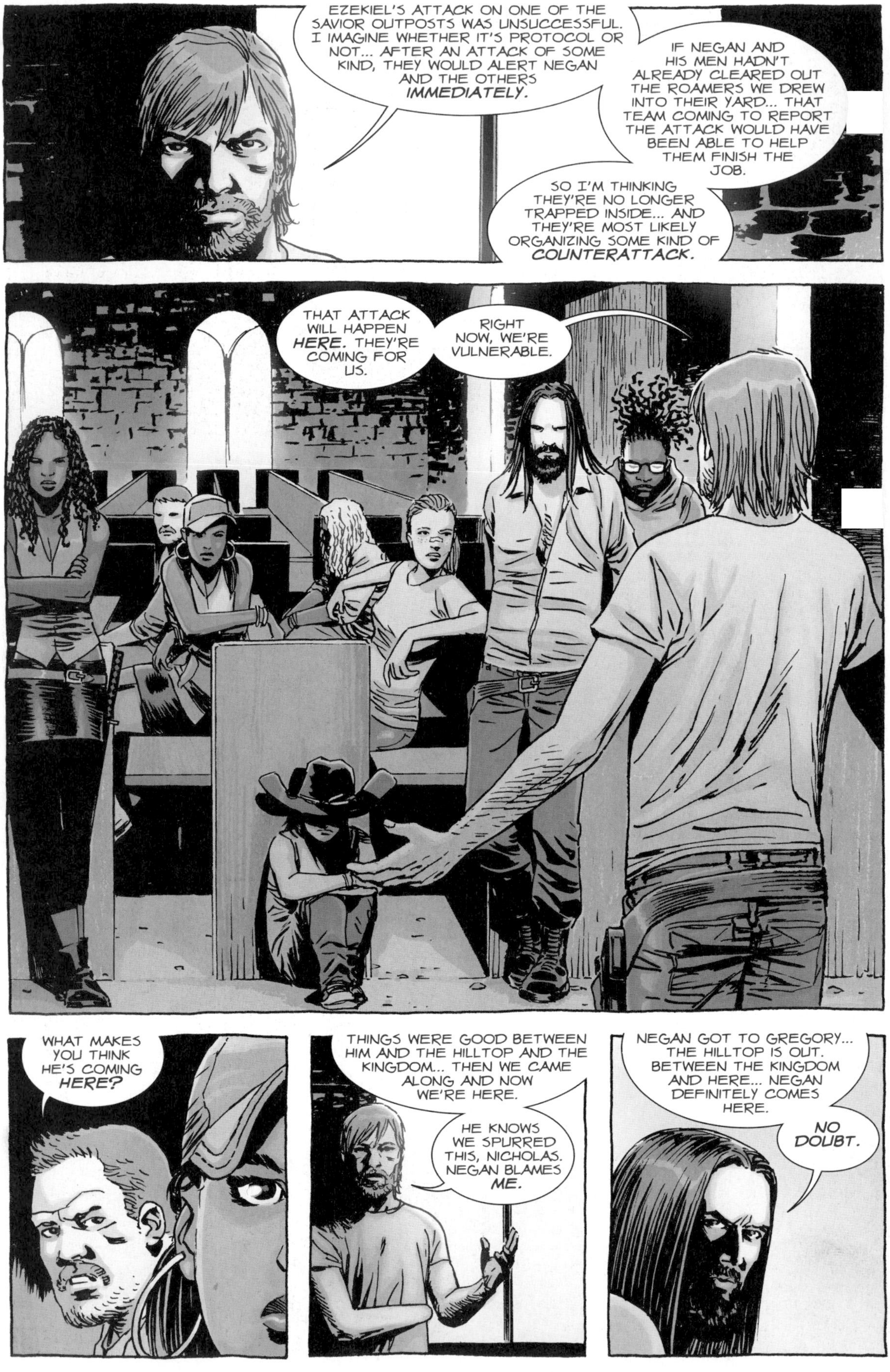
EZEKIEL'S ATTACK ON ONE OF THE SAVIOR OUTPOSTS WAS UNSUCCESSFUL. I IMAGINE WHETHER IT'S PROTOCOL OR NOT... AFTER AN ATTACK OF SOME KIND, THEY WOULD ALERT NEGAN AND THE OTHERS *IMMEDIATELY.*
IF NEGAN AND HIS MEN HADN'T ALREADY CLEARED OUT THE ROAMERS WE DREW INTO THEIR YARD... THAT TEAM COMING TO REPORT THE ATTACK WOULD HAVE BEEN ABLE TO HELP THEM FINISH THE JOB.
SO I'M THINKING THEY'RE NO LONGER TRAPPED INSIDE... AND THEY'RE MOST LIKELY ORGANIZING SOME KIND OF *COUNTERATTACK.*
THAT ATTACK WILL HAPPEN *HERE.* THEY'RE COMING FOR US.
RIGHT NOW, WE'RE VULNERABLE.
WHAT MAKES YOU THINK HE'S COMING *HERE?*
THINGS WERE GOOD BETWEEN HIM AND THE HILLTOP AND THE KINGDOM... THEN WE CAME ALONG AND NOW WE'RE HERE.
HE KNOWS WE SPURRED THIS, NICHOLAS. NEGAN BLAMES *ME.*
NEGAN GOT TO GREGORY... THE HILLTOP IS OUT. BETWEEN THE KINGDOM AND HERE... NEGAN DEFINITELY COMES HERE.
NO DOUBT.

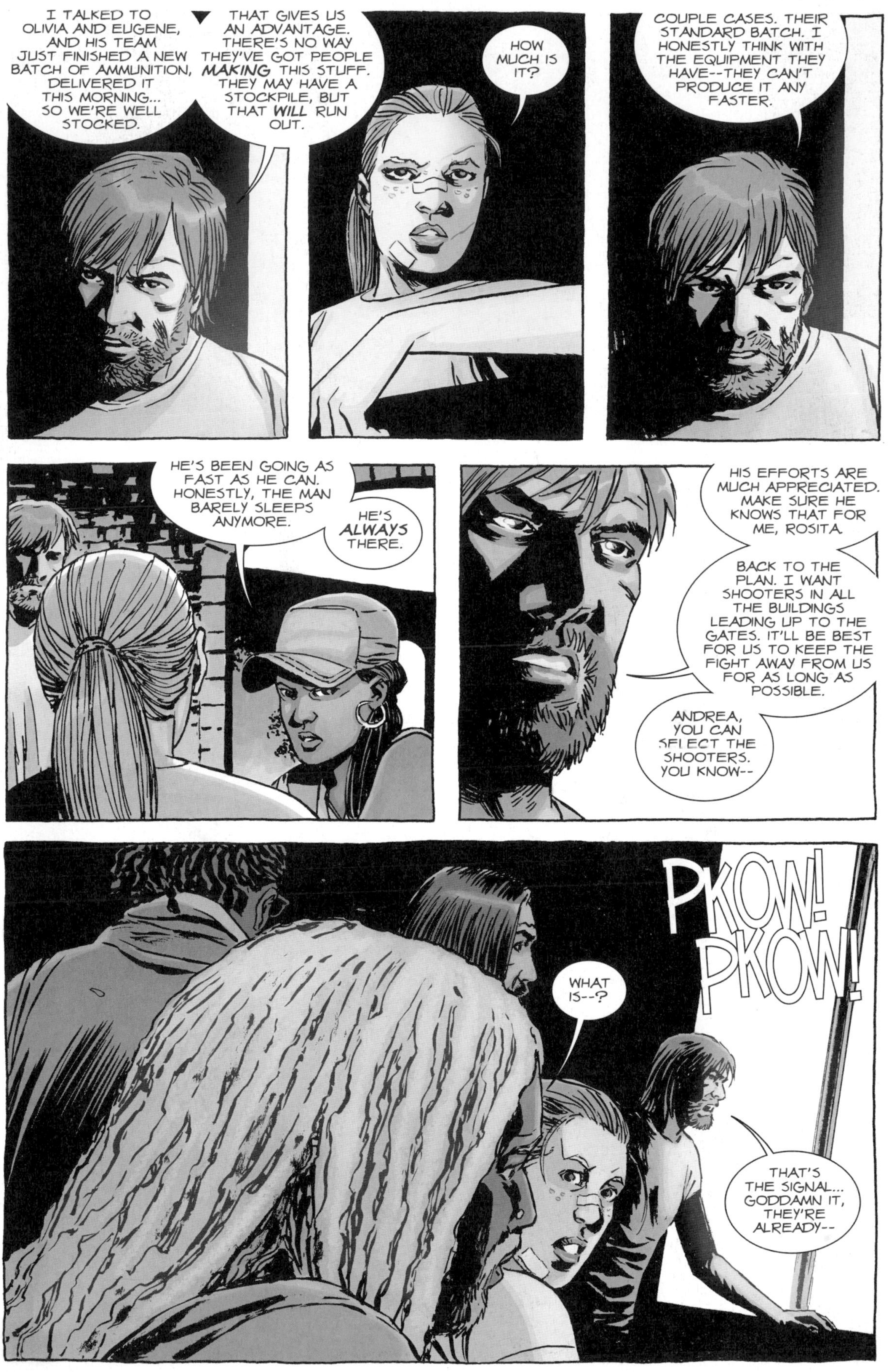
I TALKED TO OLIVIA AND EUGENE, AND HIS TEAM JUST FINISHED A NEW BATCH OF AMMUNITION, DELIVERED IT THIS MORNING... SO WE'RE WELL STOCKED.
THAT GIVES US AN ADVANTAGE. THERE'S NO WAY THEY'VE GOT PEOPLE MAKING THIS STUFF. THEY MAY HAVE A STOCKPILE, BUT THAT WILL RUN OUT.
HOW MUCH IS IT?
COUPLE CASES. THEIR STANDARD BATCH. I HONESTLY THINK WITH THE EQUIPMENT THEY HAVE--THEY CAN'T PRODUCE IT ANY FASTER.
HE'S BEEN GOING AS FAST AS HE CAN. HONESTLY, THE MAN BARELY SLEEPS ANYMORE.
HE'S ALWAYS THERE.
HIS EFFORTS ARE MUCH APPRECIATED. MAKE SURE HE KNOWS THAT FOR ME, ROSITA.
BACK TO THE PLAN. I WANT SHOOTERS IN ALL THE BUILDINGS LEADING UP TO THE GATES. IT'LL BE BEST FOR US TO KEEP THE FIGHT AWAY FROM US FOR AS LONG AS POSSIBLE.
ANDREA, YOU CAN SELECT THE SHOOTERS. YOU KNOW--
PKOW! PKOW!
WHAT IS--?
THAT'S THE SIGNAL... GODDAMN IT, THEY'RE ALREADY--

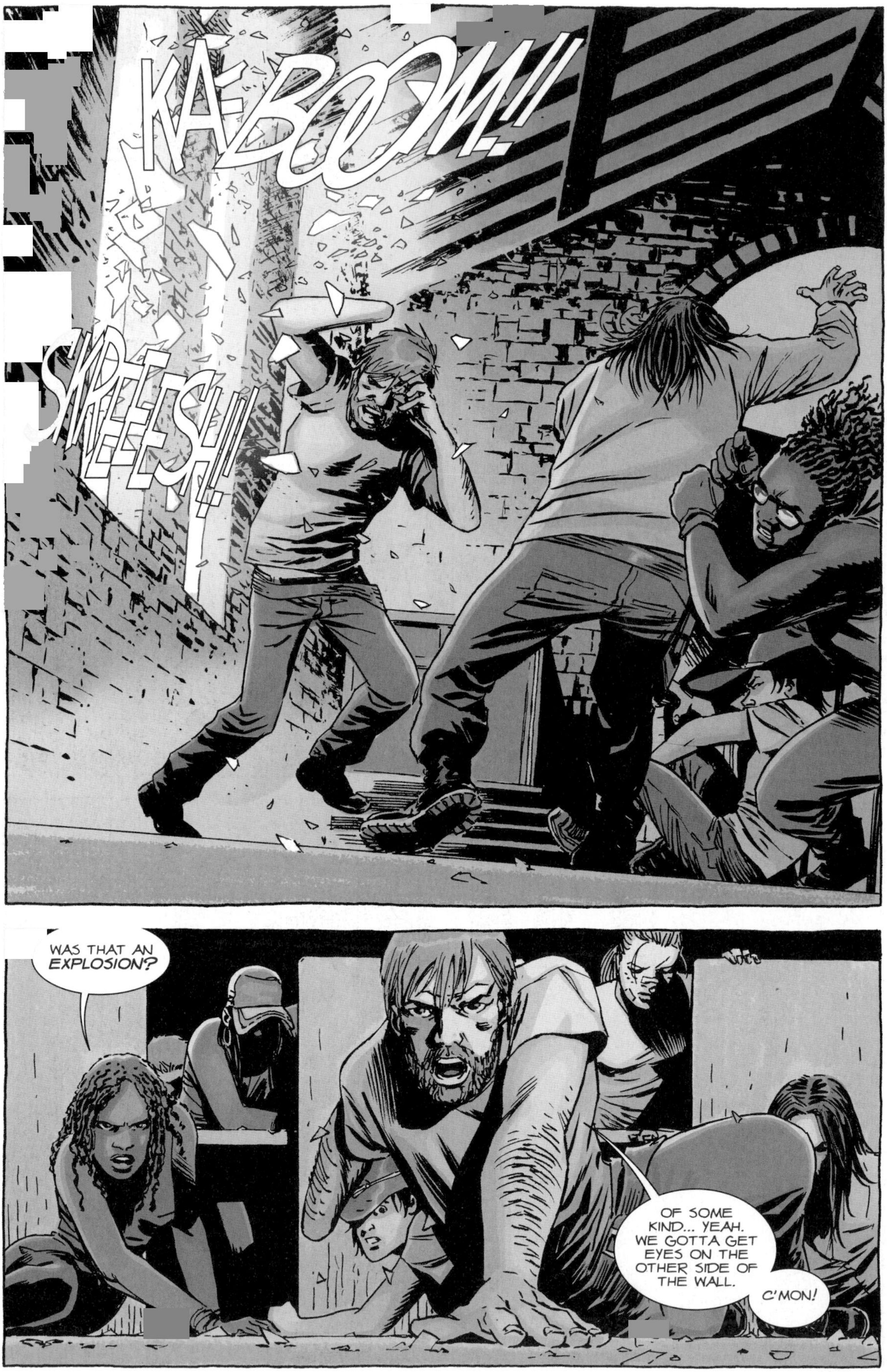
KA-BOOM!!
SKREEESH!!
WAS THAT AN *EXPLOSION?*
OF SOME KIND... YEAH. WE GOTTA GET EYES ON THE OTHER SIDE OF THE WALL.
C'MON!

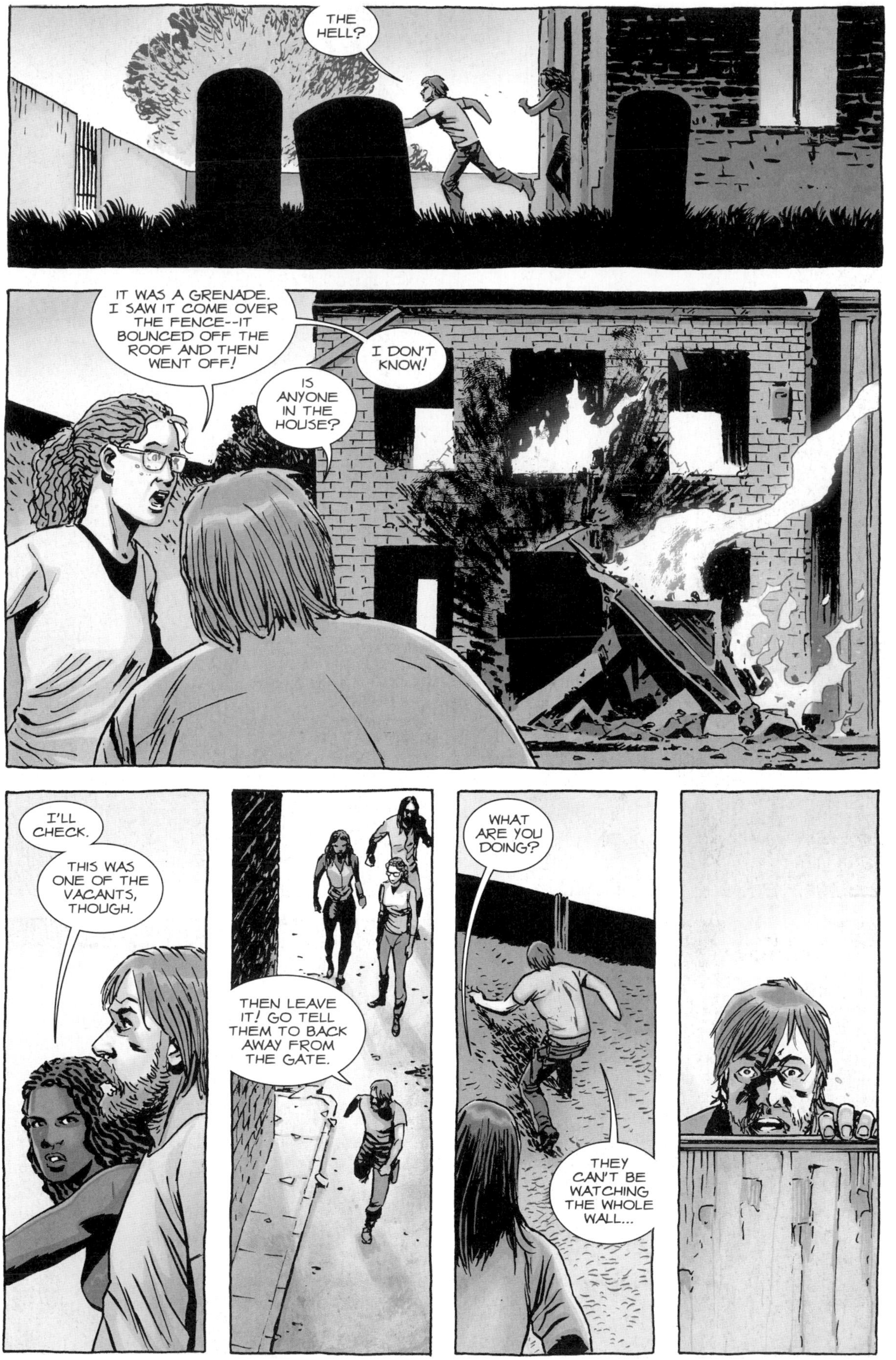
THE HELL?
IT WAS A GRENADE. I SAW IT COME OVER THE FENCE--IT BOUNCED OFF THE ROOF AND THEN WENT OFF!
I DON'T KNOW!
IS ANYONE IN THE HOUSE?
I'LL CHECK.
THIS WAS ONE OF THE VACANTS, THOUGH.
THEN LEAVE IT! GO TELL THEM TO BACK AWAY FROM THE GATE.
WHAT ARE YOU DOING?
THEY CAN'T BE WATCHING THE WHOLE WALL...

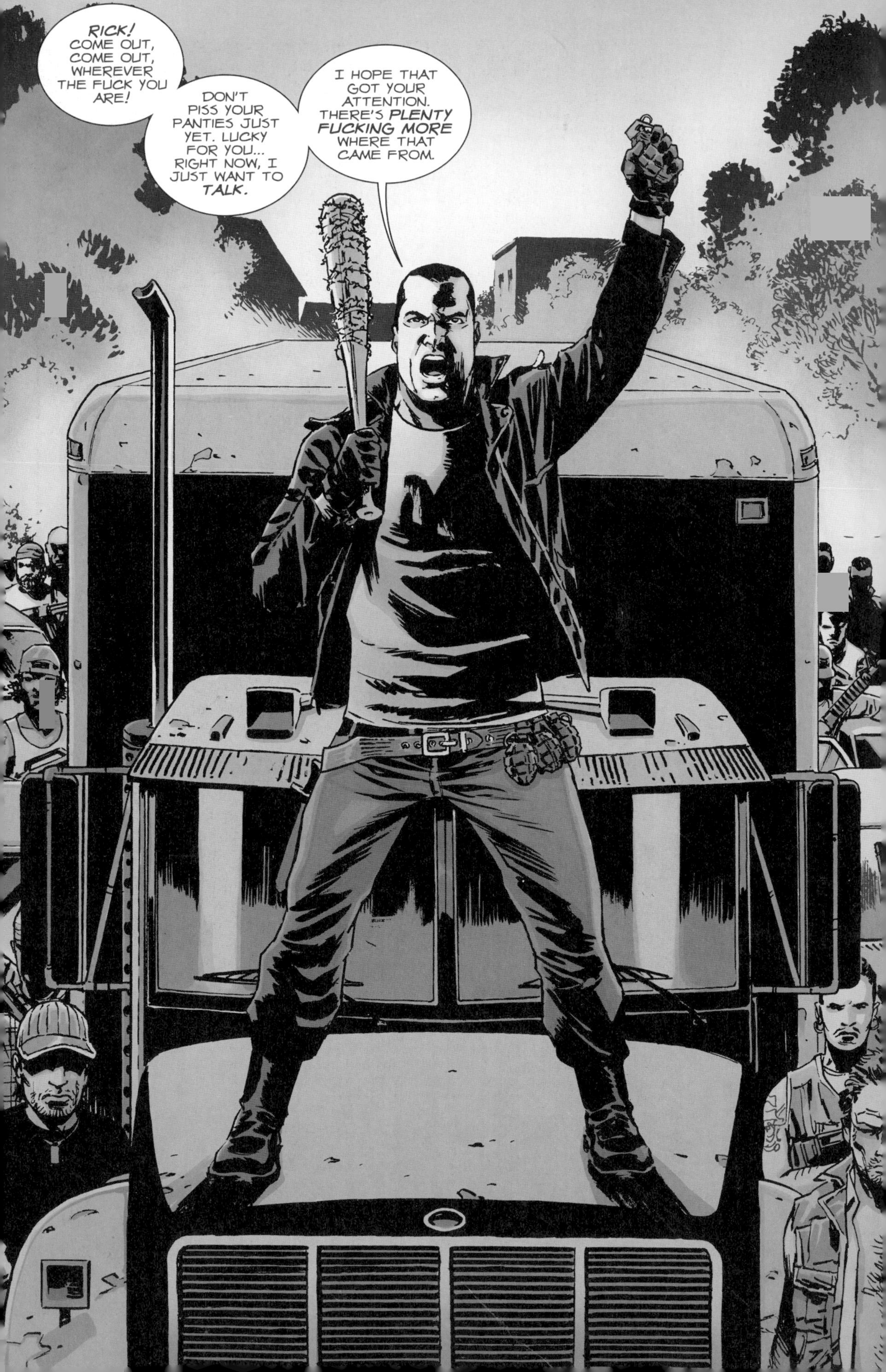
RICK! COME OUT, COME OUT, WHEREVER THE FUCK YOU ARE!
DON'T PISS YOUR PANTIES JUST YET. LUCKY FOR YOU... RIGHT NOW, I JUST WANT TO TALK.
I HOPE THAT GOT YOUR ATTENTION. THERE'S PLENTY FUCKING MORE WHERE THAT CAME FROM.

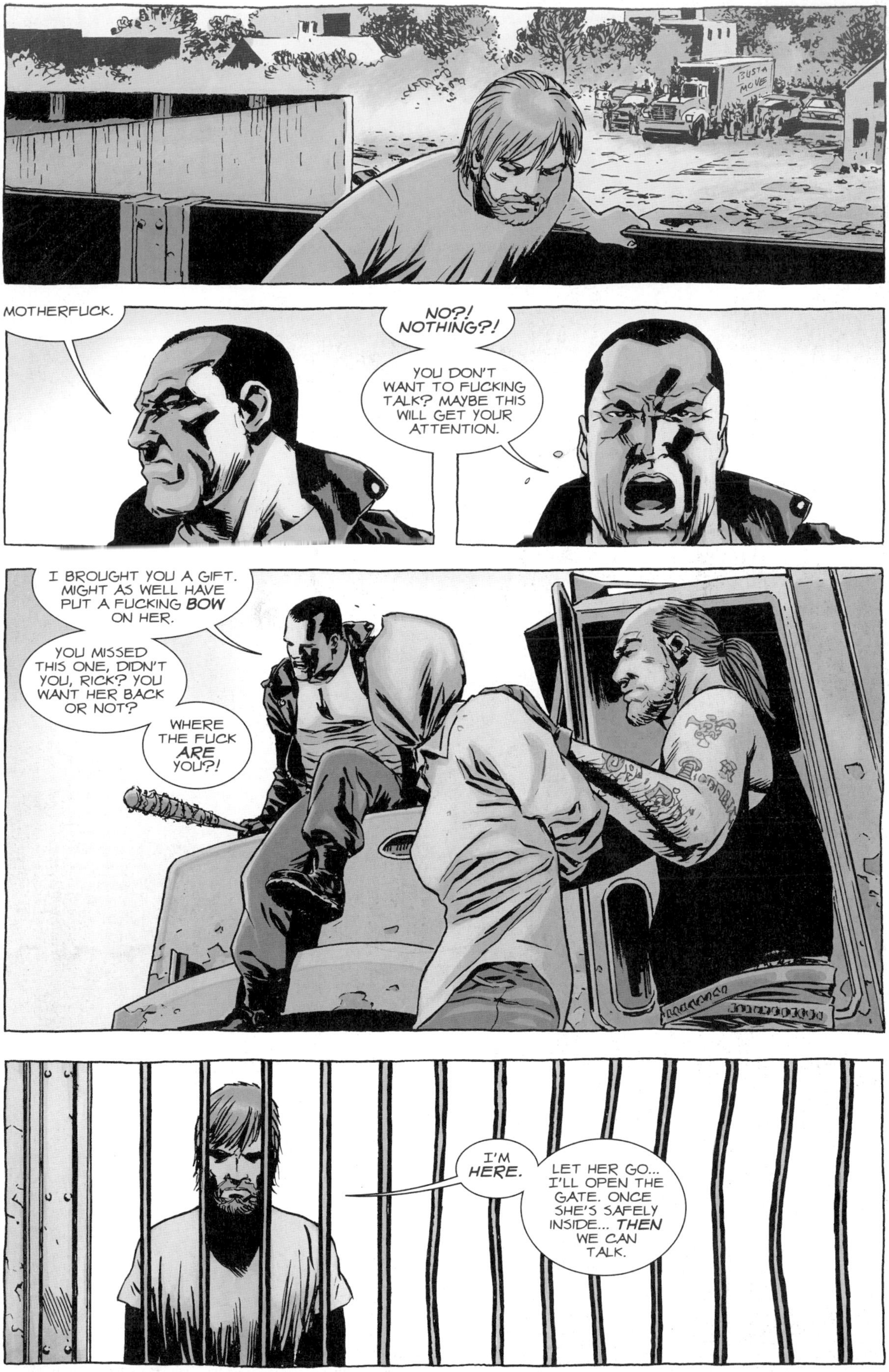

MOTHERFUCK.
NO?! NOTHING?!
YOU DON'T WANT TO FUCKING TALK? MAYBE THIS WILL GET YOUR ATTENTION.
I BROUGHT YOU A GIFT. MIGHT AS WELL HAVE PUT A FUCKING BOW ON HER.
YOU MISSED THIS ONE, DIDN'T YOU, RICK? YOU WANT HER BACK OR NOT?
WHERE THE FUCK ARE YOU?!
I'M HERE.
LET HER GO... I'LL OPEN THE GATE. ONCE SHE'S SAFELY INSIDE... THEN WE CAN TALK.

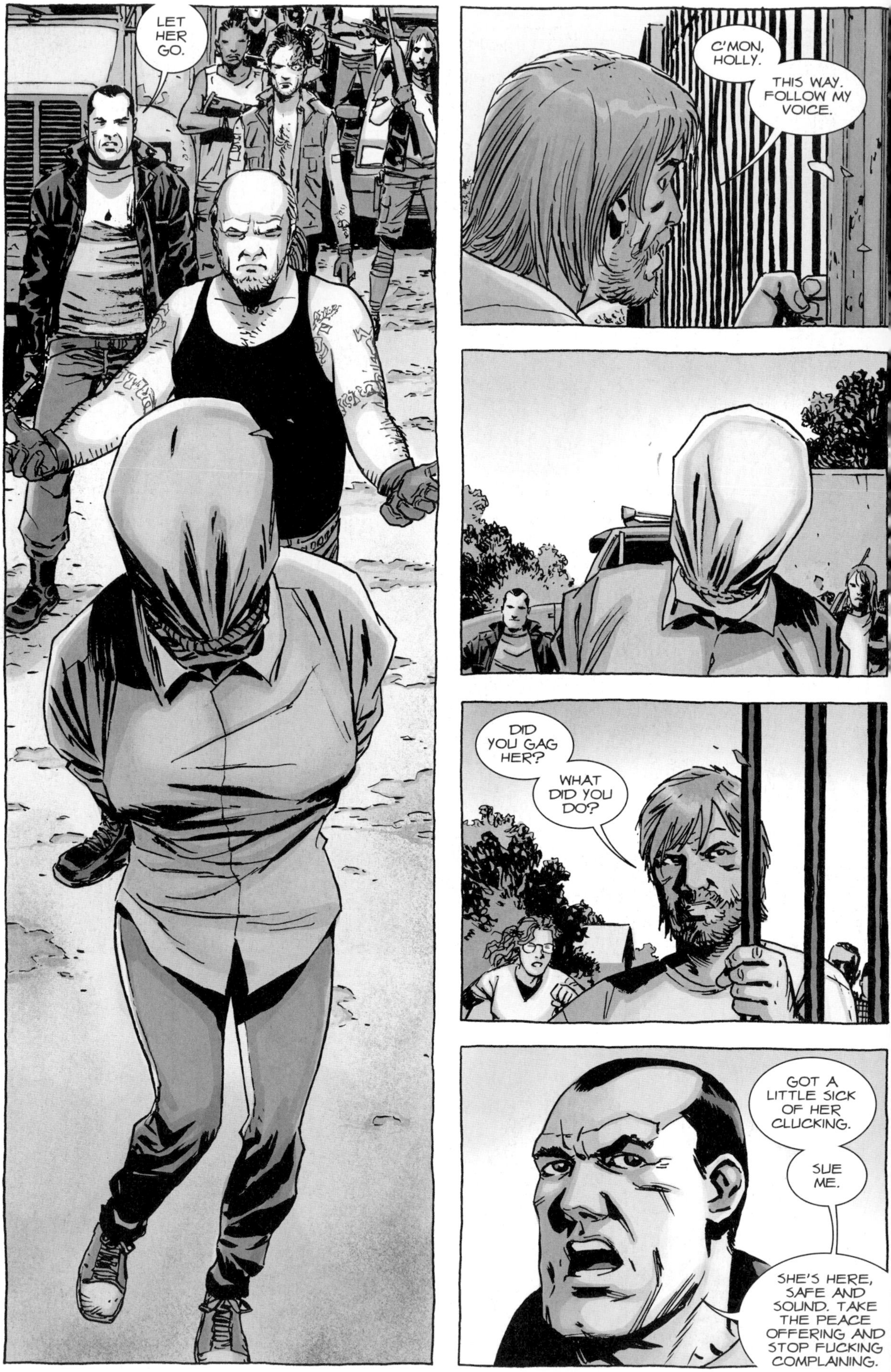
LET HER GO.
C'MON, HOLLY.
THIS WAY. FOLLOW MY VOICE.
DID YOU GAG HER?
WHAT DID YOU DO?
GOT A LITTLE SICK OF HER CLUCKING.
SUE ME.
SHE'S HERE, SAFE AND SOUND. TAKE THE PEACE OFFERING AND STOP FUCKING COMPLAINING.

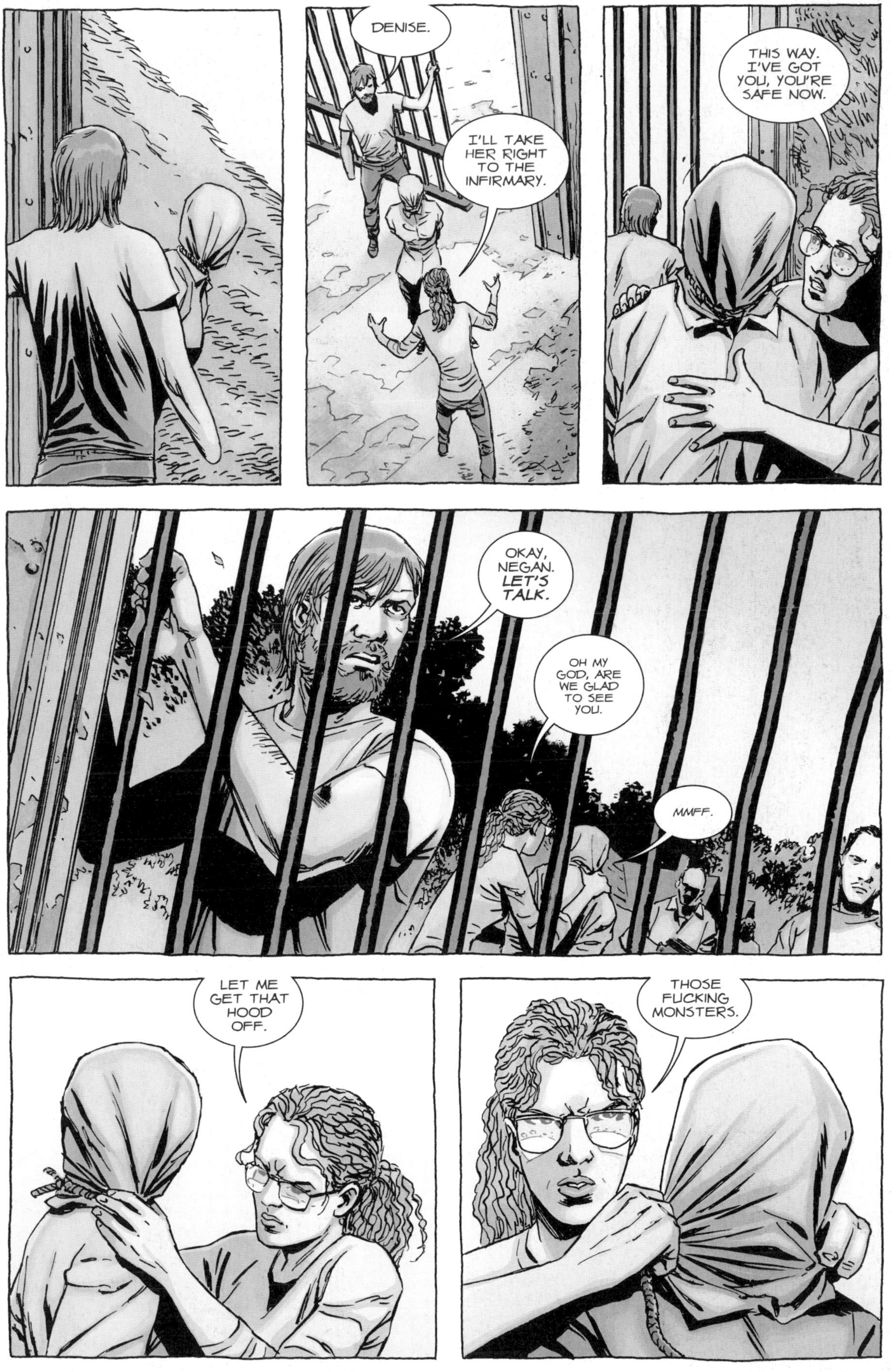
DENISE.
I'LL TAKE HER RIGHT TO THE INFIRMARY.
THIS WAY. I'VE GOT YOU, YOU'RE SAFE NOW.
OKAY, NEGAN. LET'S TALK.
OH MY GOD, ARE WE GLAD TO SEE YOU.
MMFF.
LET ME GET THAT HOOD OFF.
THOSE FUCKING MONSTERS.

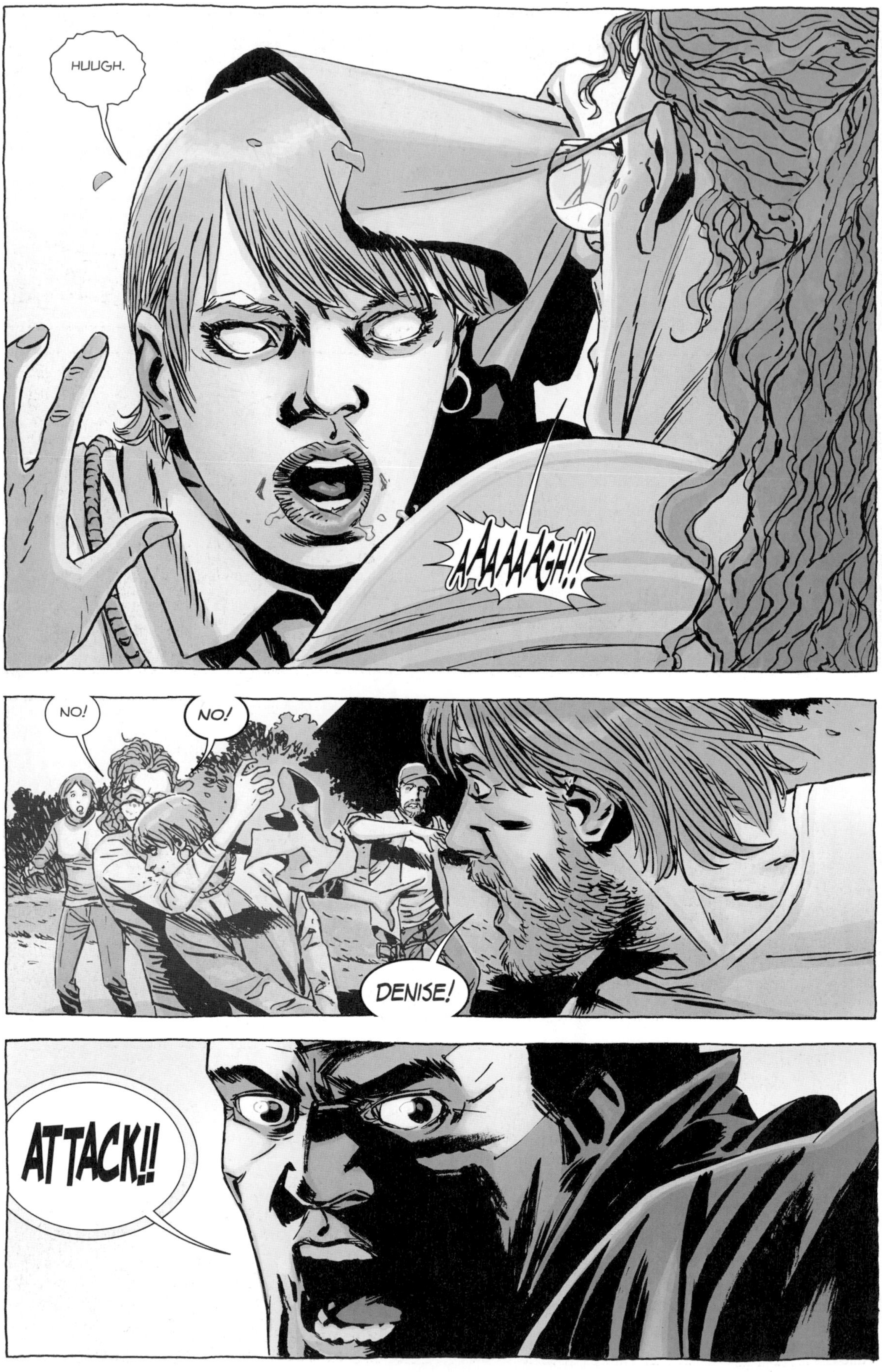
HUUGH.
AAAAAAGH!!
NO!
NO!
DENISE!
ATTACK!!

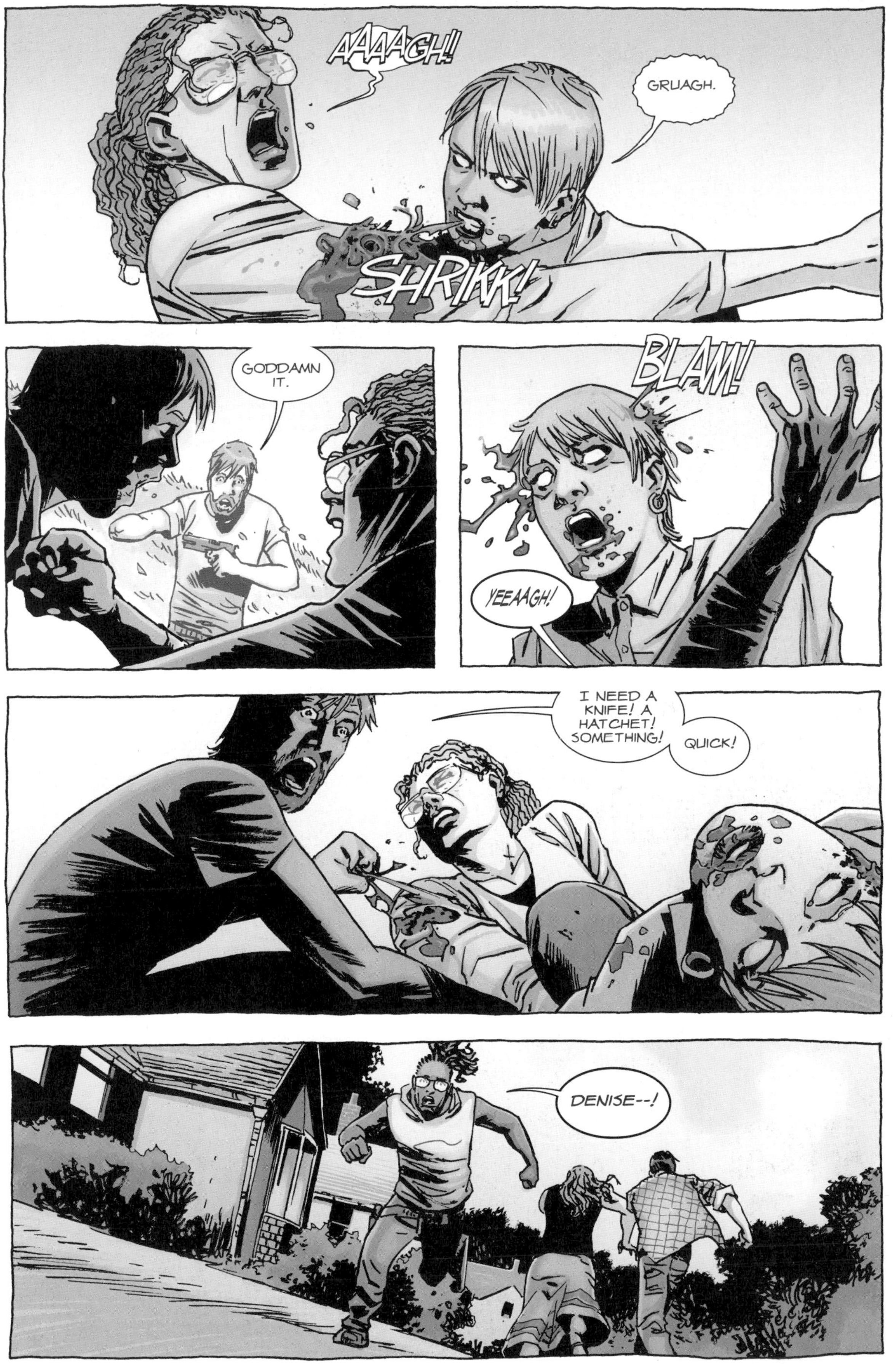
AAAAGH!
GRUAGH.
SHRIKK!
GODDAMN IT.
BLAM!
YEEAAGH!
I NEED A KNIFE! A HATCHET! SOMETHING!
QUICK!
DENISE--!

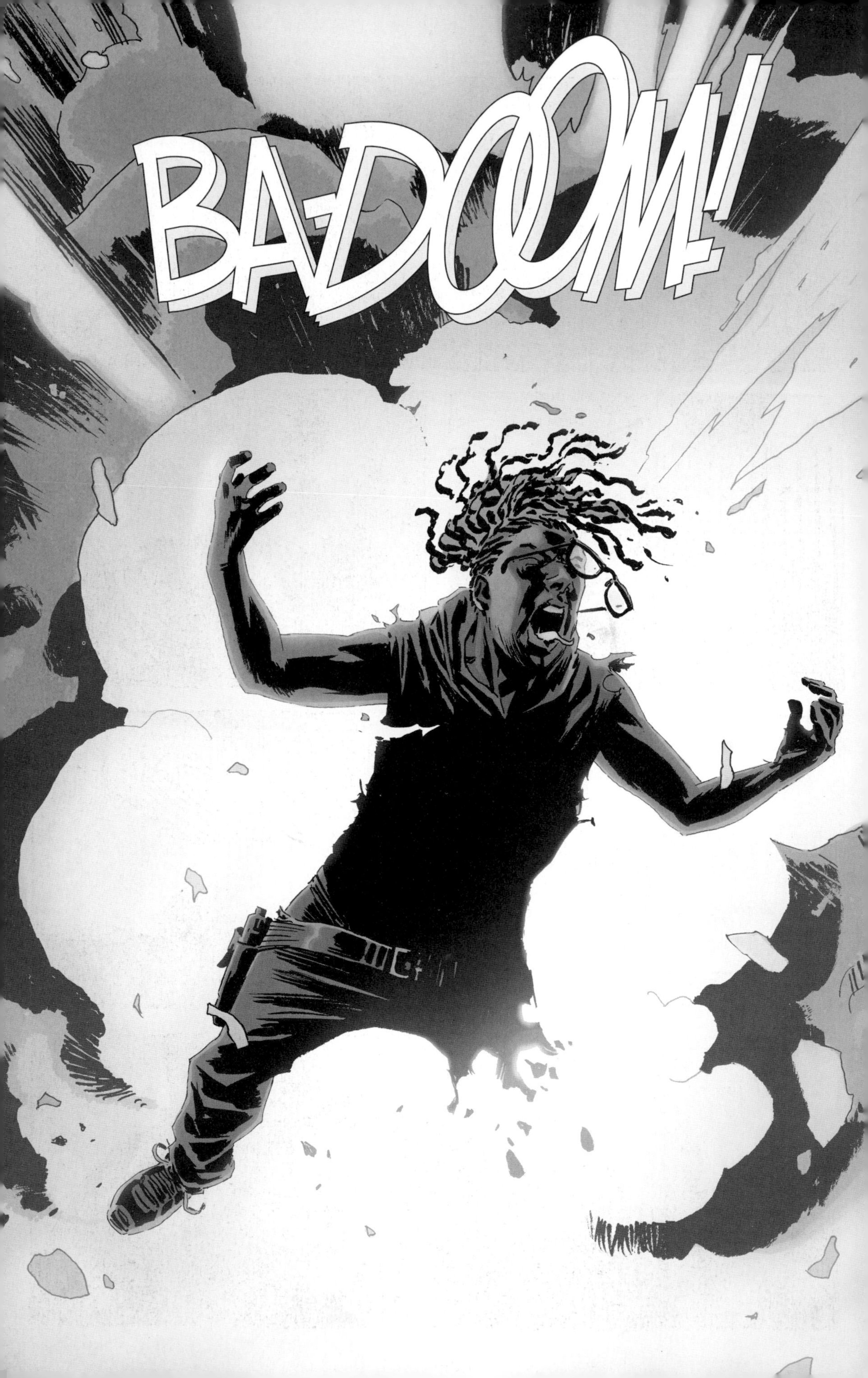
BA-DOOM!

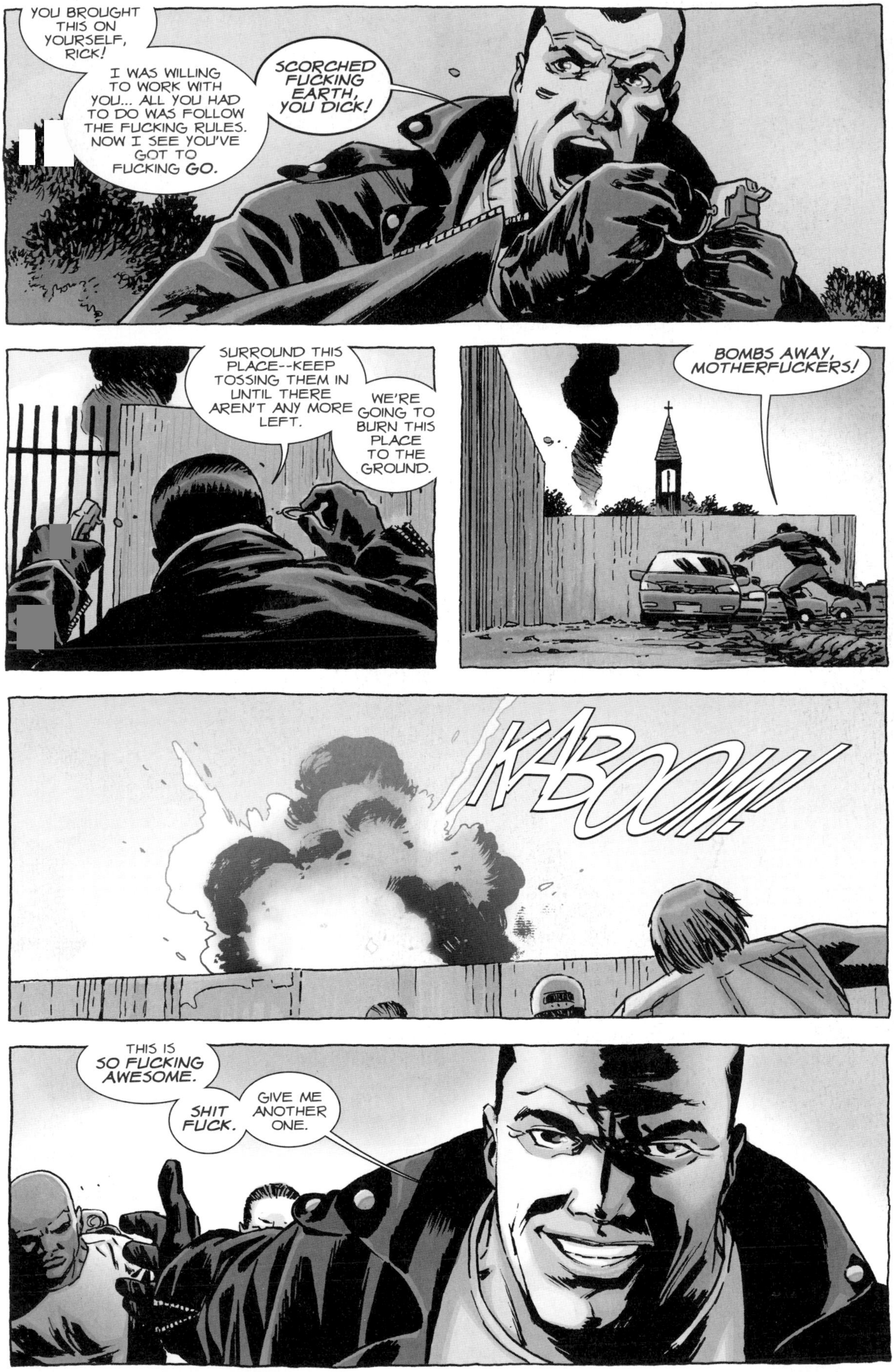
YOU BROUGHT THIS ON YOURSELF, RICK!
I WAS WILLING TO WORK WITH YOU... ALL YOU HAD TO DO WAS FOLLOW THE FUCKING RULES. NOW I SEE YOU'VE GOT TO FUCKING GO.
SCORCHED FUCKING EARTH, YOU DICK!
SURROUND THIS PLACE--KEEP TOSSING THEM IN UNTIL THERE AREN'T ANY MORE LEFT.
WE'RE GOING TO BURN THIS PLACE TO THE GROUND.
BOMBS AWAY, MOTHERFUCKERS!
KABOOM!
THIS IS SO FUCKING AWESOME.
SHIT FUCK.
GIVE ME ANOTHER ONE.

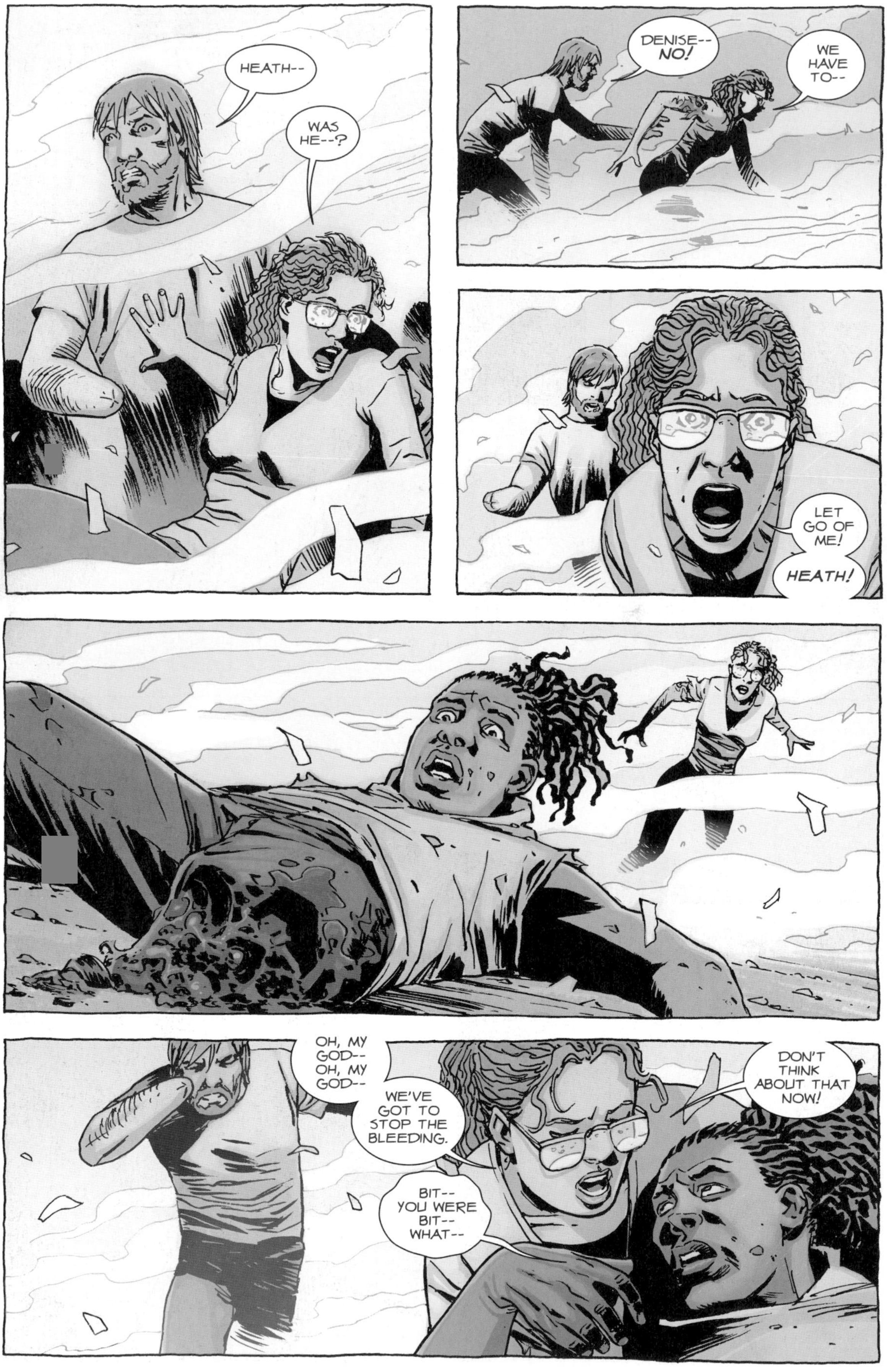
HEATH--
WAS HE--?
DENISE-- NO!
WE HAVE TO--
LET GO OF ME!
HEATH!
OH, MY GOD-- OH, MY GOD--
WE'VE GOT TO STOP THE BLEEDING.
DON'T THINK ABOUT THAT NOW!
BIT-- YOU WERE BIT-- WHAT--

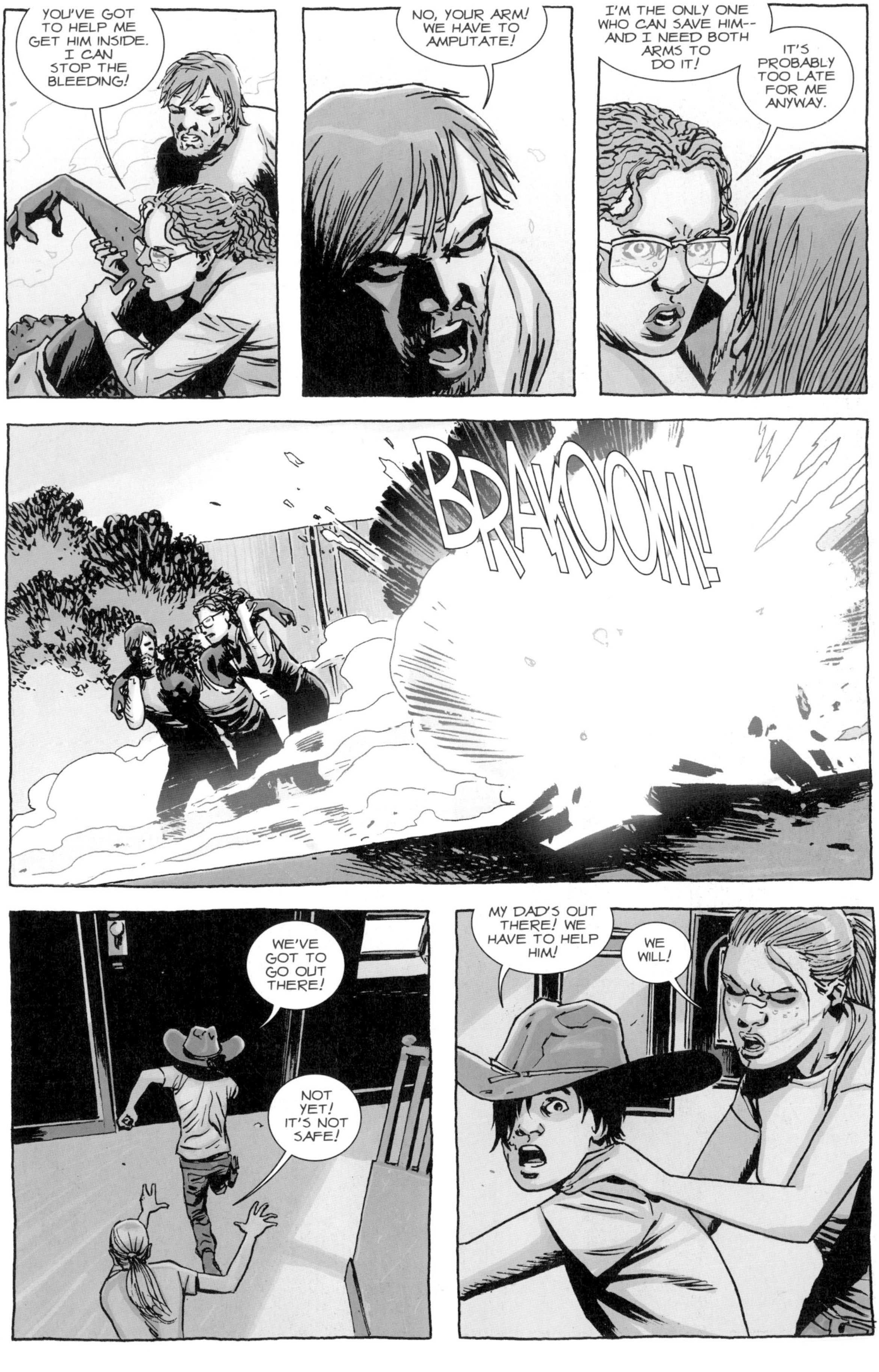

YOU'VE GOT TO HELP ME GET HIM INSIDE. I CAN STOP THE BLEEDING!
NO, YOUR ARM! WE HAVE TO AMPUTATE!
I'M THE ONLY ONE WHO CAN SAVE HIM-- AND I NEED BOTH ARMS TO DO IT!
IT'S PROBABLY TOO LATE FOR ME ANYWAY.
BRAKOOM!
WE'VE GOT TO GO OUT THERE!
NOT YET! IT'S NOT SAFE!
MY DAD'S OUT THERE! WE HAVE TO HELP HIM!
WE WILL!

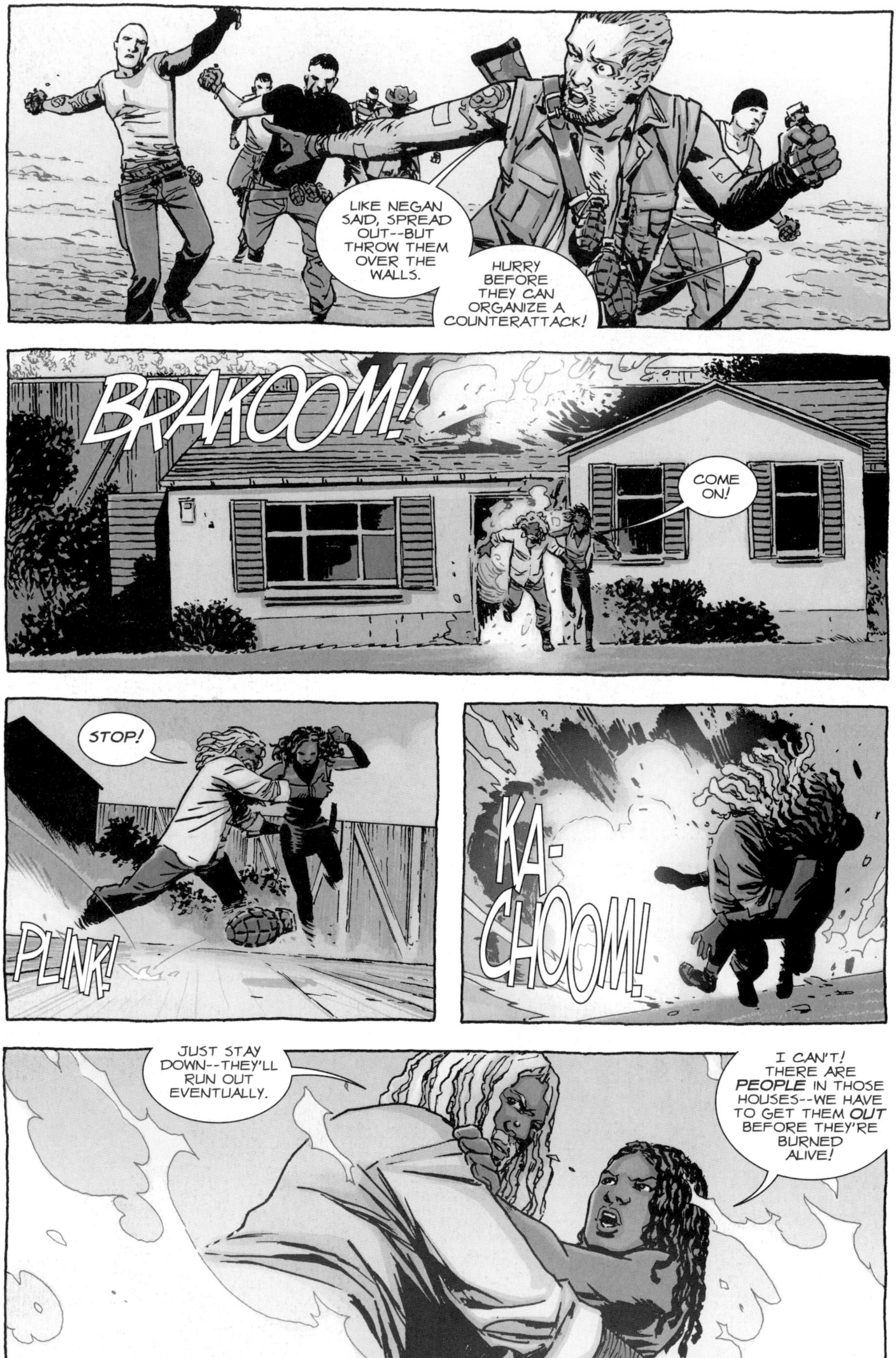
LIKE NEGAN SAID, SPREAD OUT--BUT THROW THEM OVER THE WALLS.
HURRY BEFORE THEY CAN ORGANIZE A COUNTERATTACK!
BRAKOOM!
COME ON!
STOP!
PLINK!
KA-CHOOM!
JUST STAY DOWN--THEY'LL RUN OUT EVENTUALLY.
I CAN'T! THERE ARE *PEOPLE* IN THOSE HOUSES--WE HAVE TO GET THEM *OUT* BEFORE THEY'RE BURNED ALIVE!

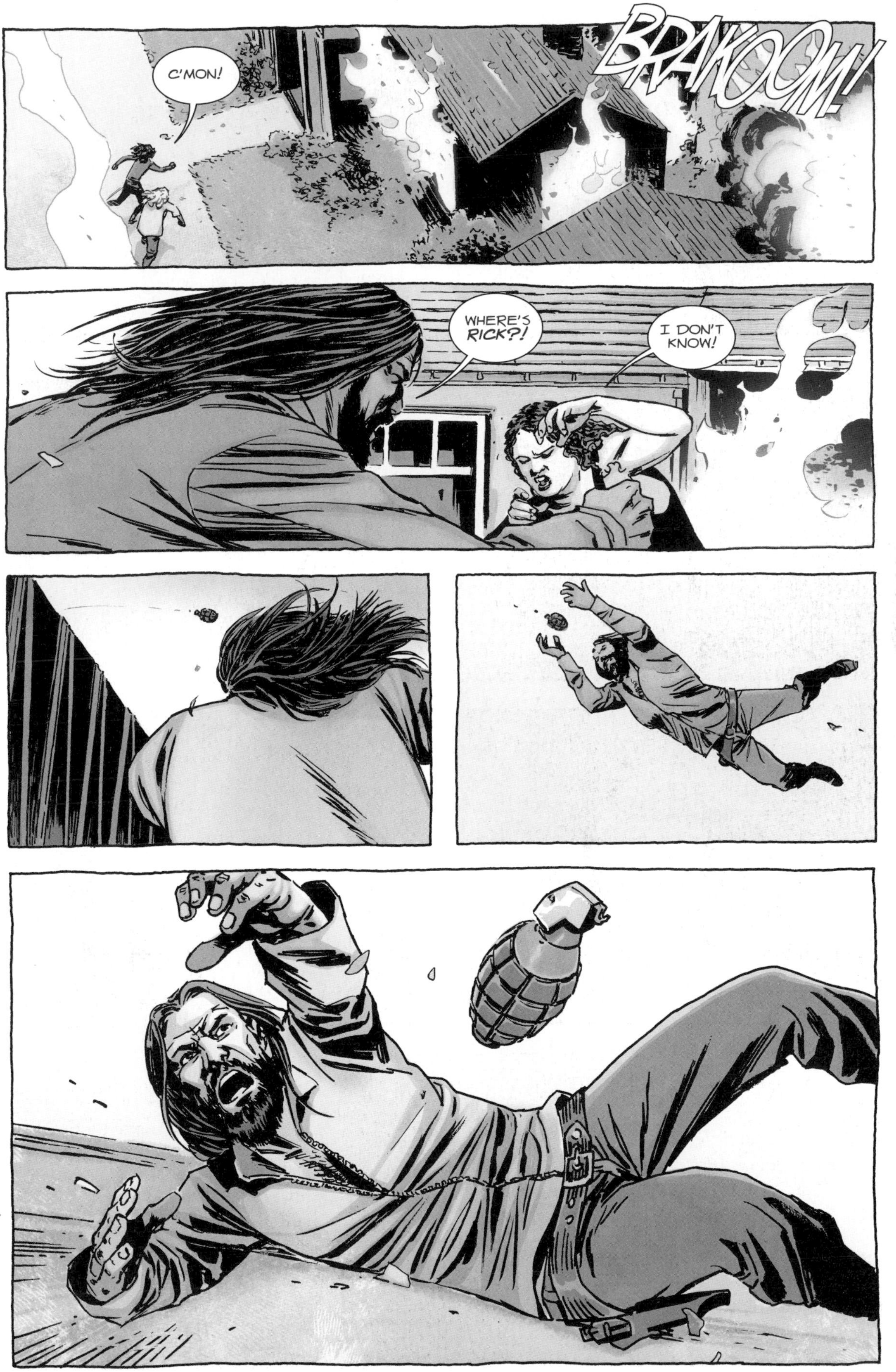
BRAKOOM!
C'MON!
WHERE'S RICK?!
I DON'T KNOW!

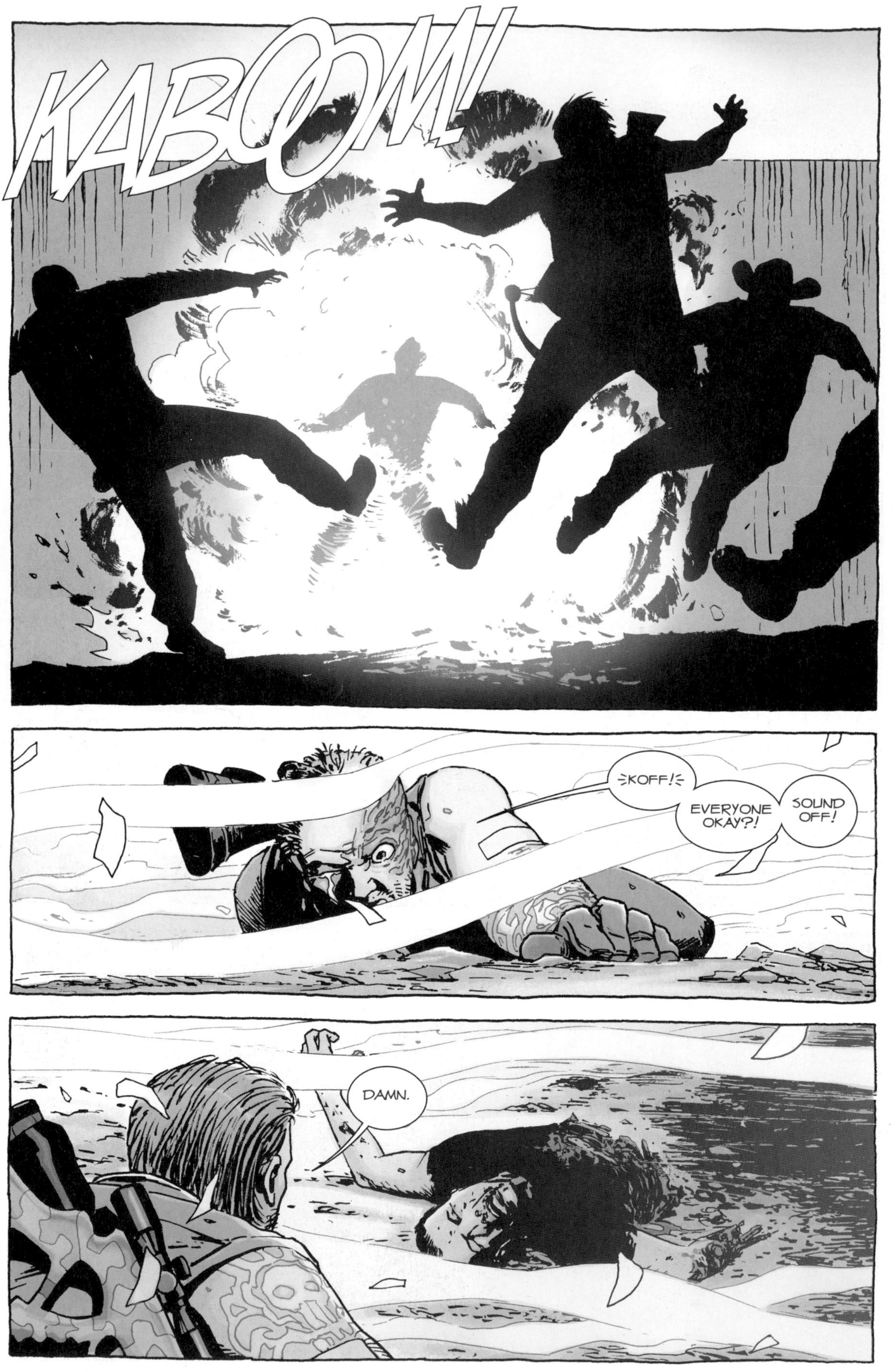
KABOOM!
=KOFF!=
EVERYONE OKAY?!
SOUND OFF!
DAMN.

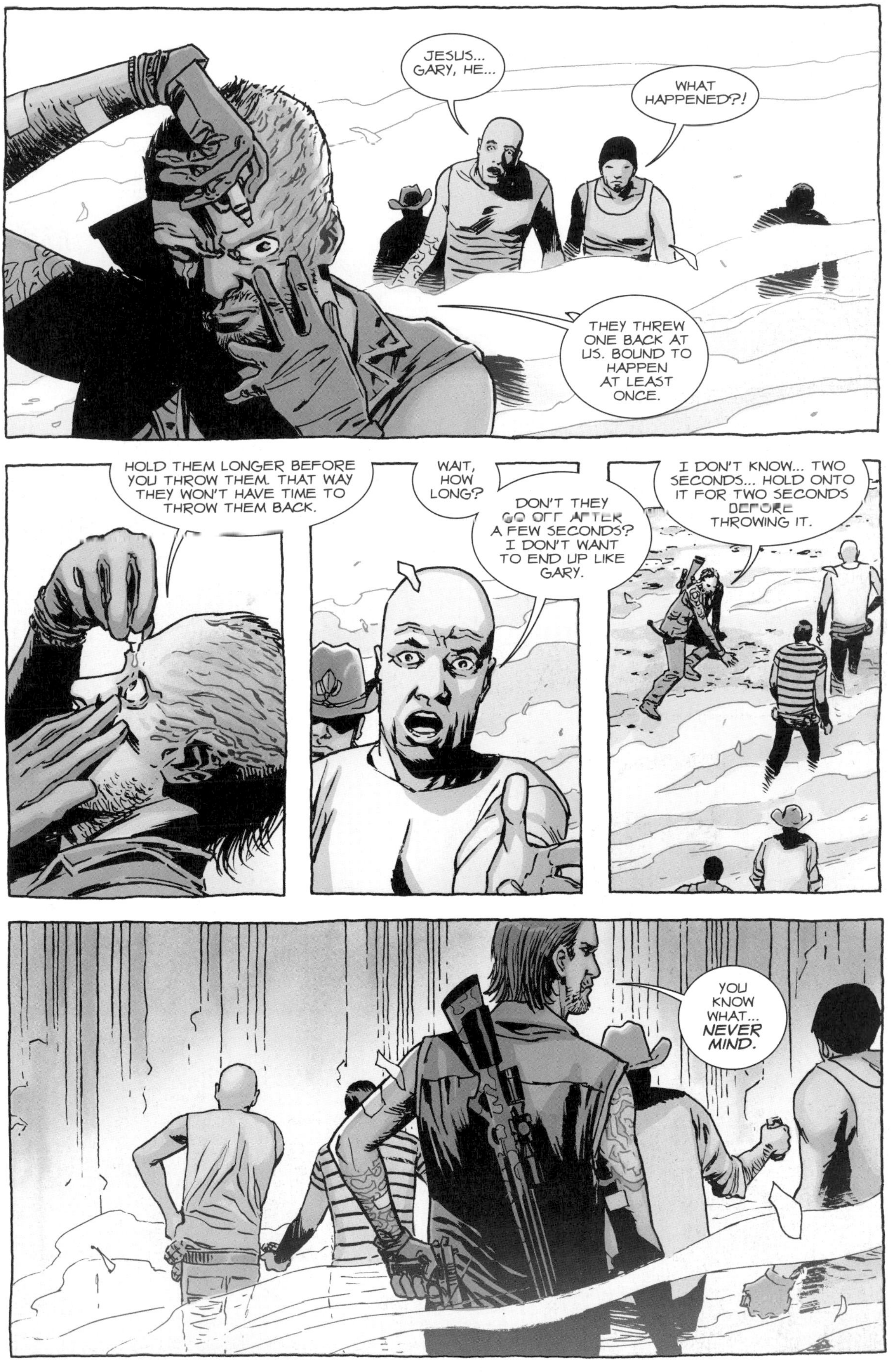
JESUS... GARY, HE...
WHAT HAPPENED?!
THEY THREW ONE BACK AT US. BOUND TO HAPPEN AT LEAST ONCE.
HOLD THEM LONGER BEFORE YOU THROW THEM. THAT WAY THEY WON'T HAVE TIME TO THROW THEM BACK.
WAIT, HOW LONG?
DON'T THEY GO OFF AFTER A FEW SECONDS? I DON'T WANT TO END UP LIKE GARY.
I DON'T KNOW... TWO SECONDS... HOLD ONTO IT FOR TWO SECONDS BEFORE THROWING IT.
YOU KNOW WHAT... NEVER MIND.

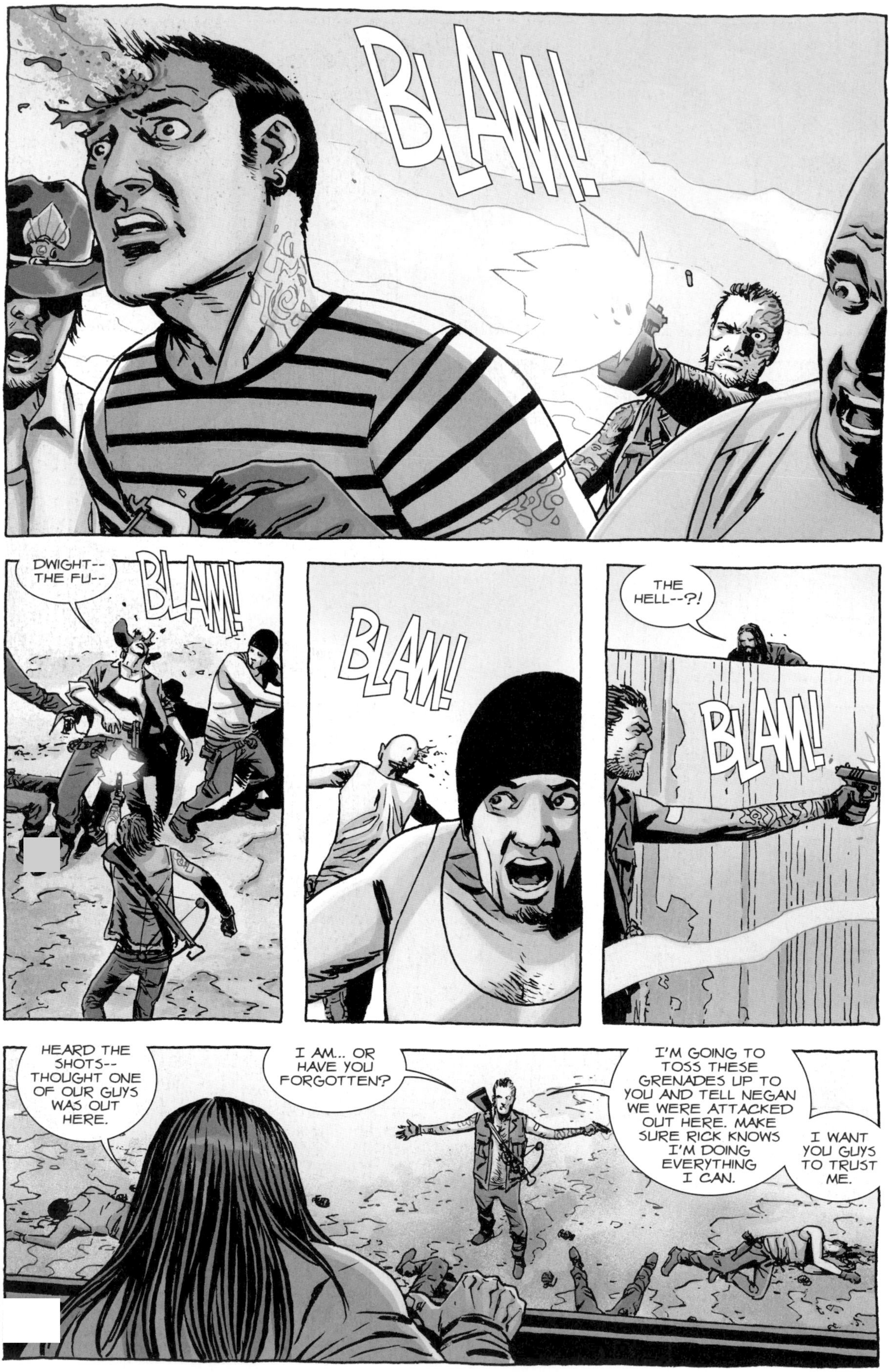
BLAM!
DWIGHT-- THE FU--
BLAM!
BLAM!
THE HELL--?!
BLAM!
HEARD THE SHOTS-- THOUGHT ONE OF OUR GUYS WAS OUT HERE.
I AM... OR HAVE YOU FORGOTTEN?
I'M GOING TO TOSS THESE GRENADES UP TO YOU AND TELL NEGAN WE WERE ATTACKED OUT HERE. MAKE SURE RICK KNOWS I'M DOING EVERYTHING I CAN.
I WANT YOU GUYS TO TRUST ME.

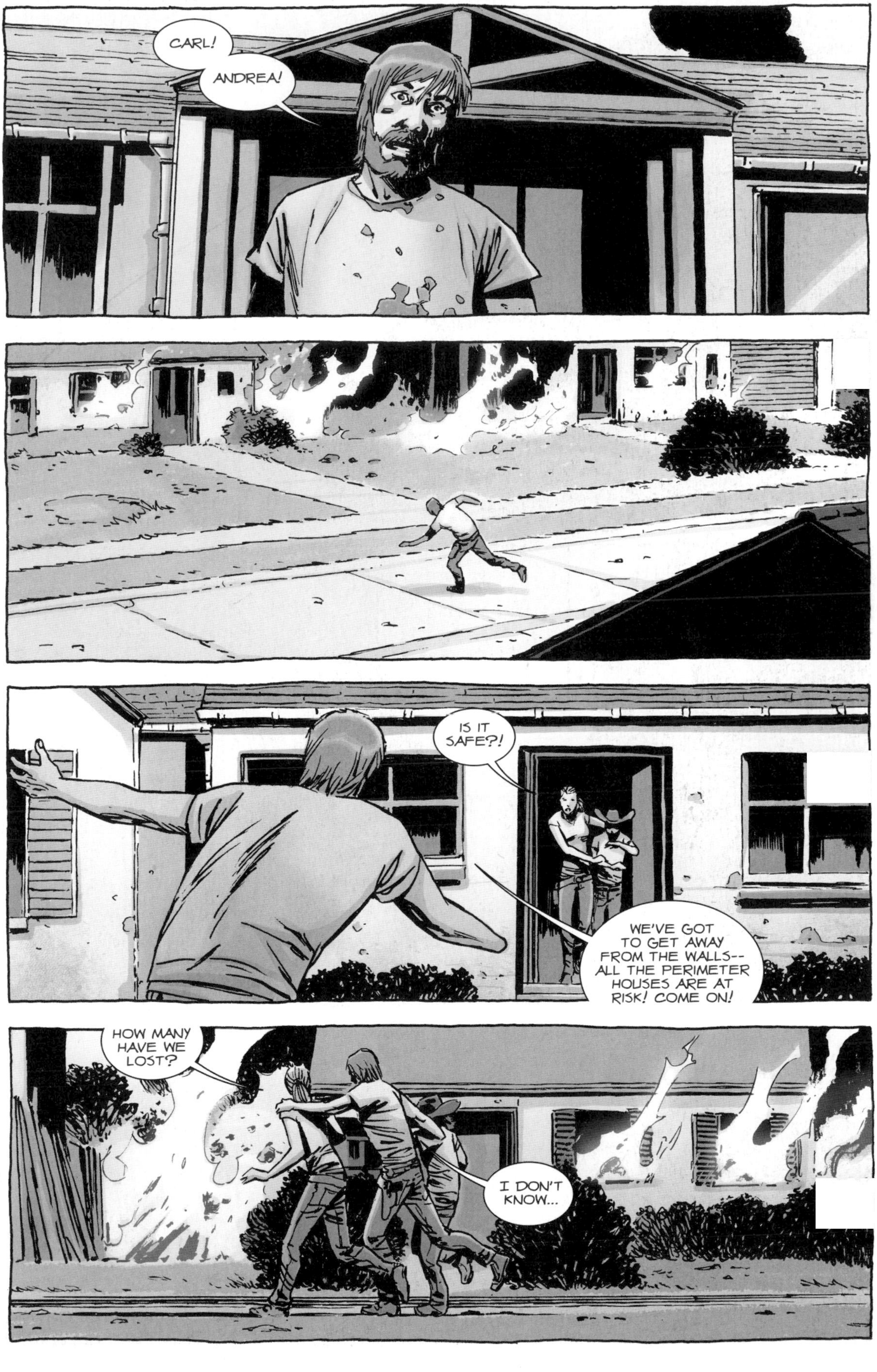
CARL!
ANDREA!
IS IT SAFE?!
WE'VE GOT TO GET AWAY FROM THE WALLS-- ALL THE PERIMETER HOUSES ARE AT RISK! COME ON!
HOW MANY HAVE WE LOST?
I DON'T KNOW...

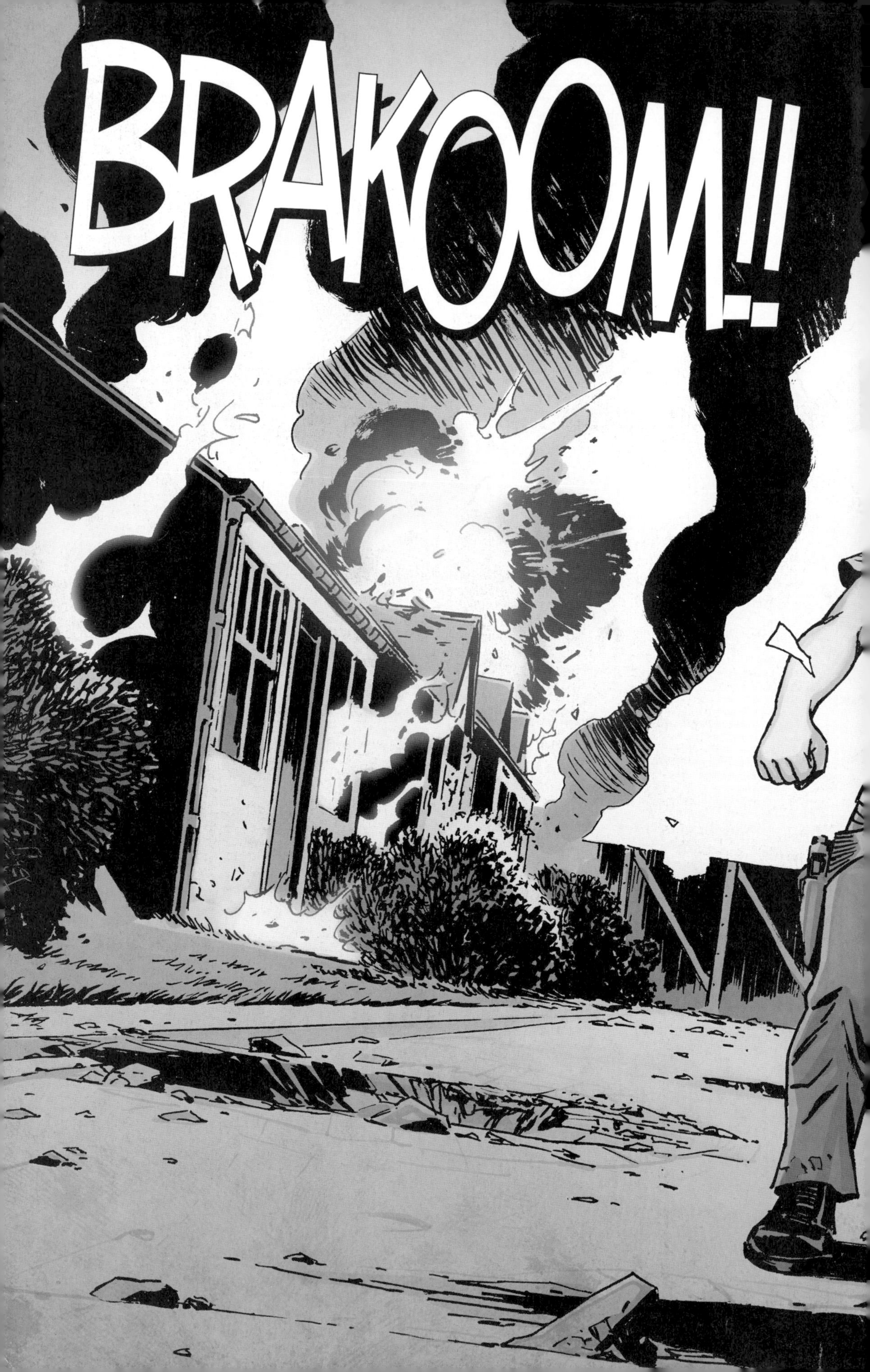
BRAKOOM!!

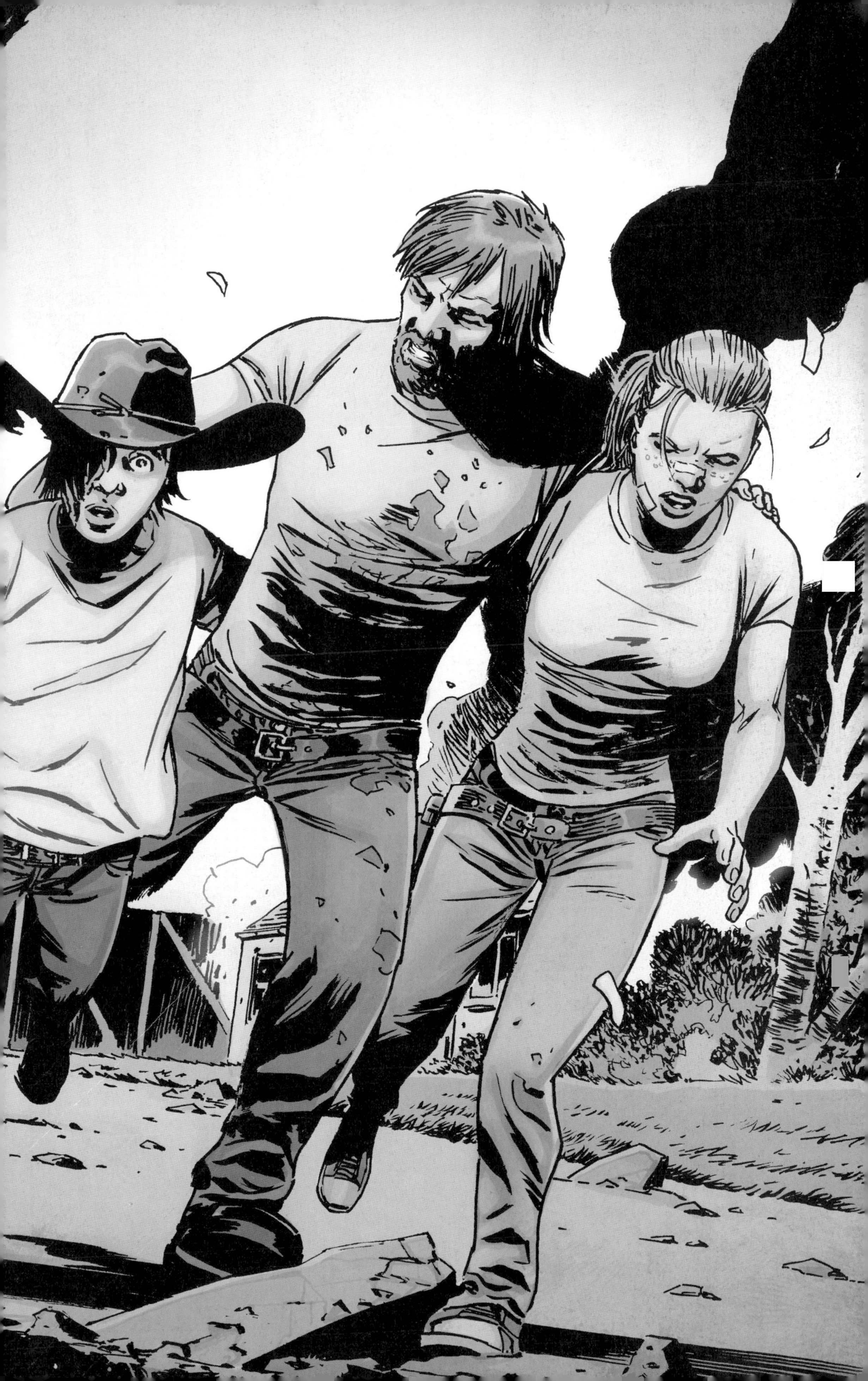

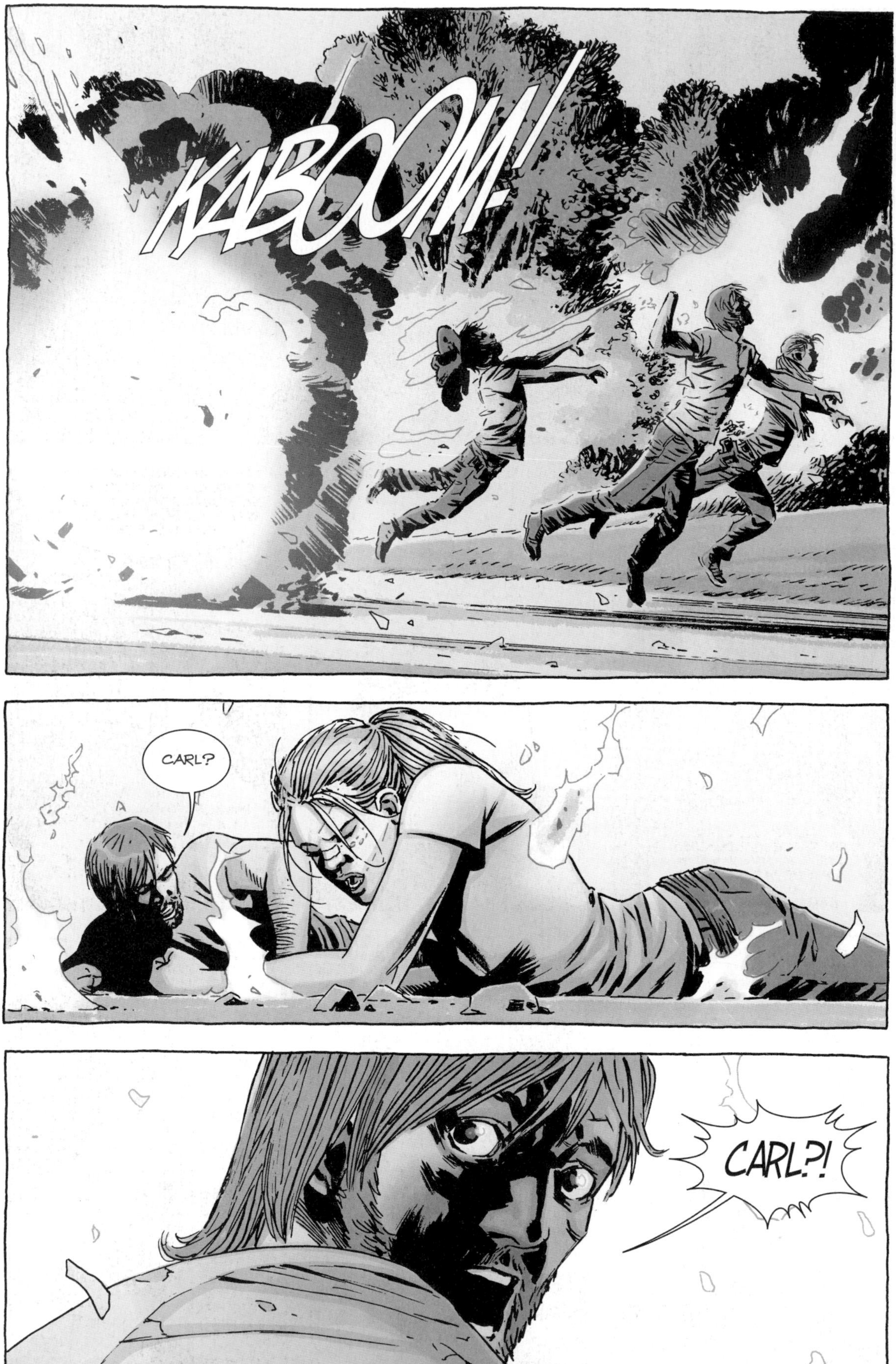
KABOOM!
CARL?
CARL?!

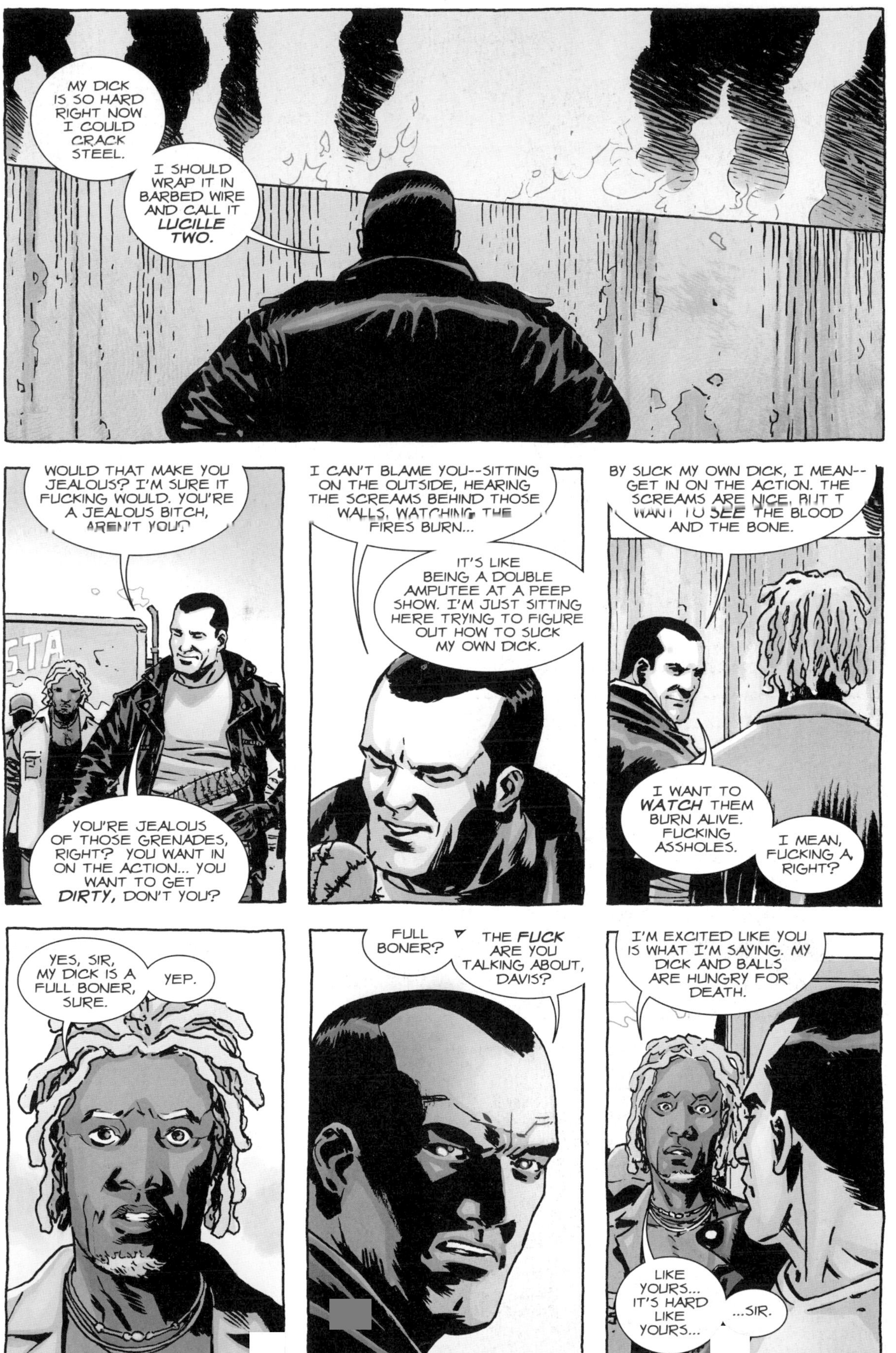
MY DICK IS SO HARD RIGHT NOW I COULD CRACK STEEL.
I SHOULD WRAP IT IN BARBED WIRE AND CALL IT LUCILLE TWO.
WOULD THAT MAKE YOU JEALOUS? I'M SURE IT FUCKING WOULD. YOU'RE A JEALOUS BITCH, AREN'T YOU?
YOU'RE JEALOUS OF THOSE GRENADES, RIGHT? YOU WANT IN ON THE ACTION... YOU WANT TO GET DIRTY, DON'T YOU?
I CAN'T BLAME YOU--SITTING ON THE OUTSIDE, HEARING THE SCREAMS BEHIND THOSE WALLS, WATCHING THE FIRES BURN...
IT'S LIKE BEING A DOUBLE AMPUTEE AT A PEEP SHOW. I'M JUST SITTING HERE TRYING TO FIGURE OUT HOW TO SUCK MY OWN DICK.
BY SUCK MY OWN DICK, I MEAN--GET IN ON THE ACTION. THE SCREAMS ARE NICE, BUT I WANT TO SEE THE BLOOD AND THE BONE.
I WANT TO WATCH THEM BURN ALIVE. FUCKING ASSHOLES.
I MEAN, FUCKING A, RIGHT?
YES, SIR, MY DICK IS A FULL BONER, SURE.
YEP.
FULL BONER?
THE FUCK ARE YOU TALKING ABOUT, DAVIS?
I'M EXCITED LIKE YOU IS WHAT I'M SAYING. MY DICK AND BALLS ARE HUNGRY FOR DEATH.
LIKE YOURS... IT'S HARD LIKE YOURS...
...SIR.

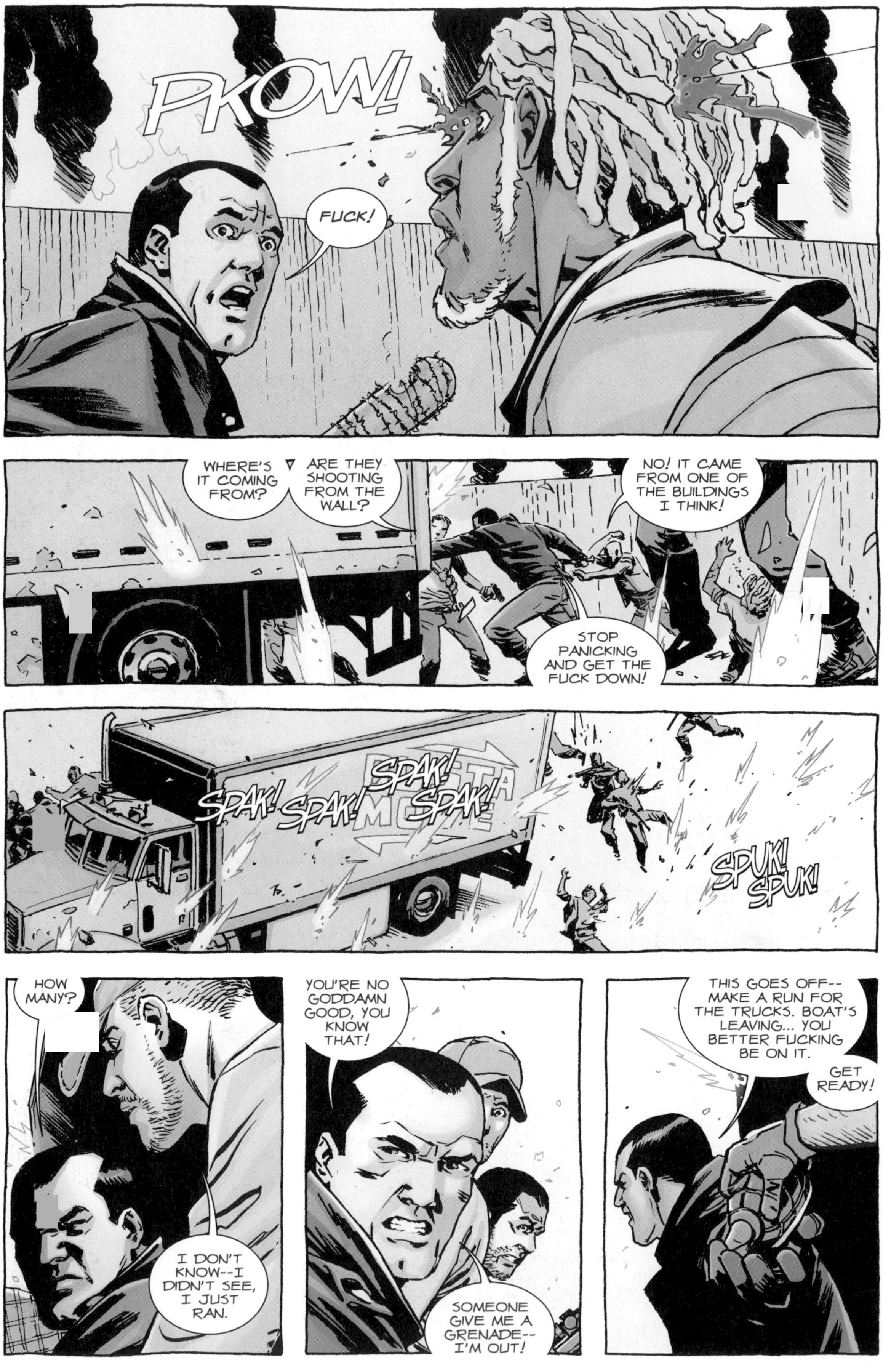
PKOW!
FUCK!
WHERE'S IT COMING FROM?
ARE THEY SHOOTING FROM THE WALL?
NO! IT CAME FROM ONE OF THE BUILDINGS I THINK!
STOP PANICKING AND GET THE FUCK DOWN!
SPAK! SPAK! SPAK! SPAK!
SPUK! SPUK!
HOW MANY?
I DON'T KNOW--I DIDN'T SEE, I JUST RAN.
YOU'RE NO GODDAMN GOOD, YOU KNOW THAT!
SOMEONE GIVE ME A GRENADE--I'M OUT!
THIS GOES OFF--MAKE A RUN FOR THE TRUCKS. BOAT'S LEAVING... YOU BETTER FUCKING BE ON IT.
GET READY!

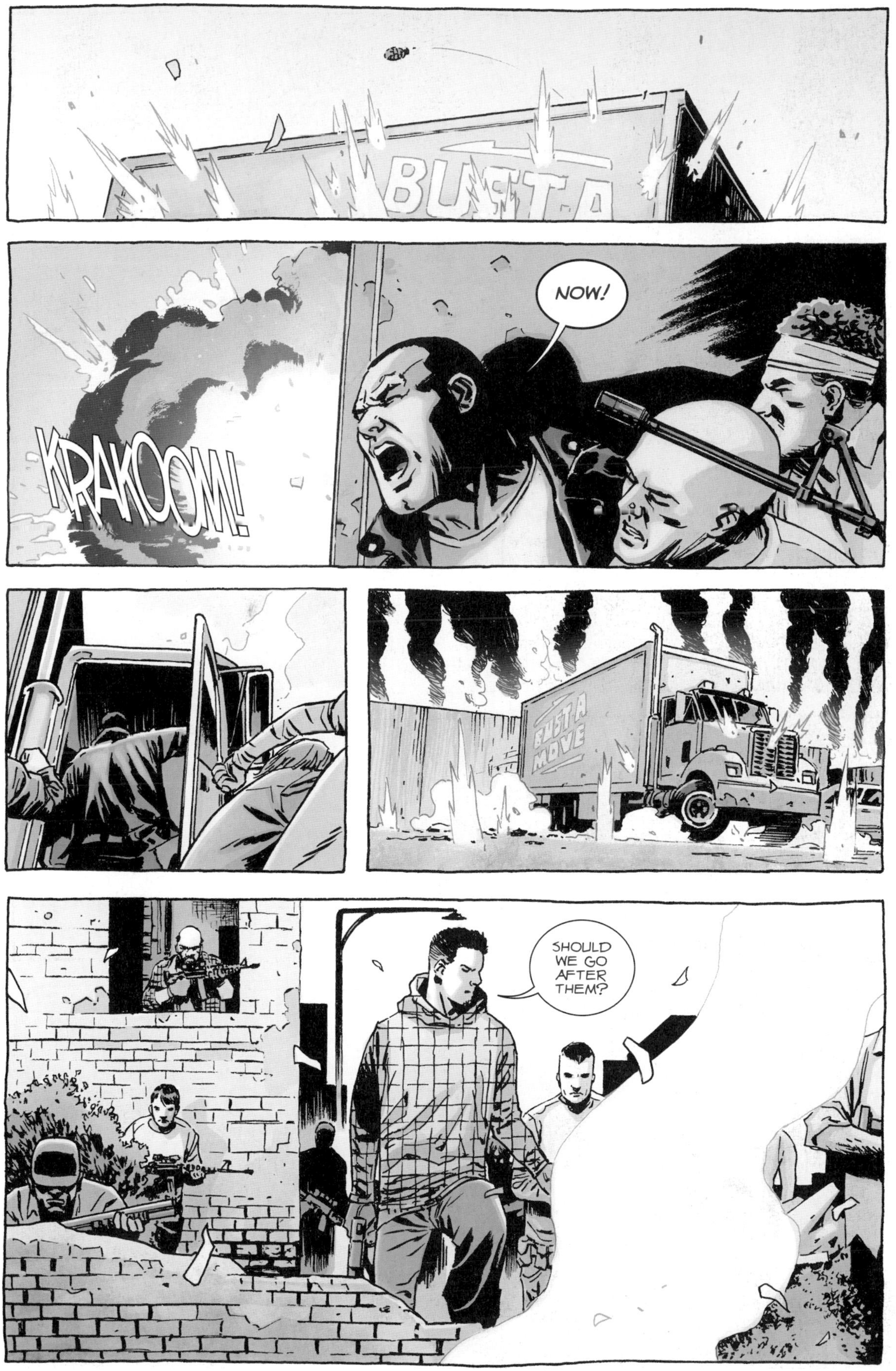
BUST-A
NOW!
KRAKOOM!
BUST-A MOVE
SHOULD WE GO AFTER THEM?

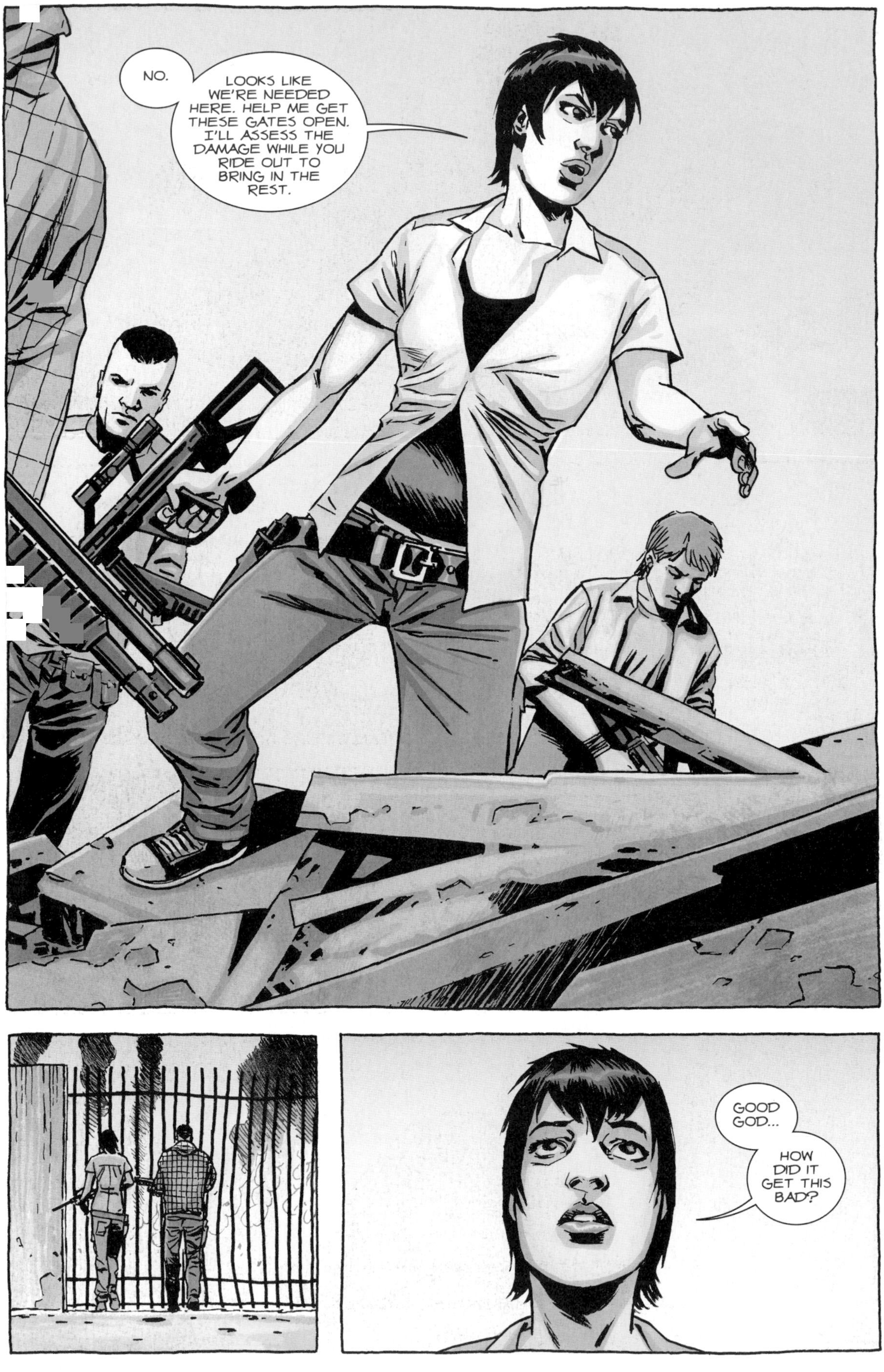
NO.
LOOKS LIKE WE'RE NEEDED HERE. HELP ME GET THESE GATES OPEN. I'LL ASSESS THE DAMAGE WHILE YOU RIDE OUT TO BRING IN THE REST.
GOOD GOD...
HOW DID IT GET THIS BAD?

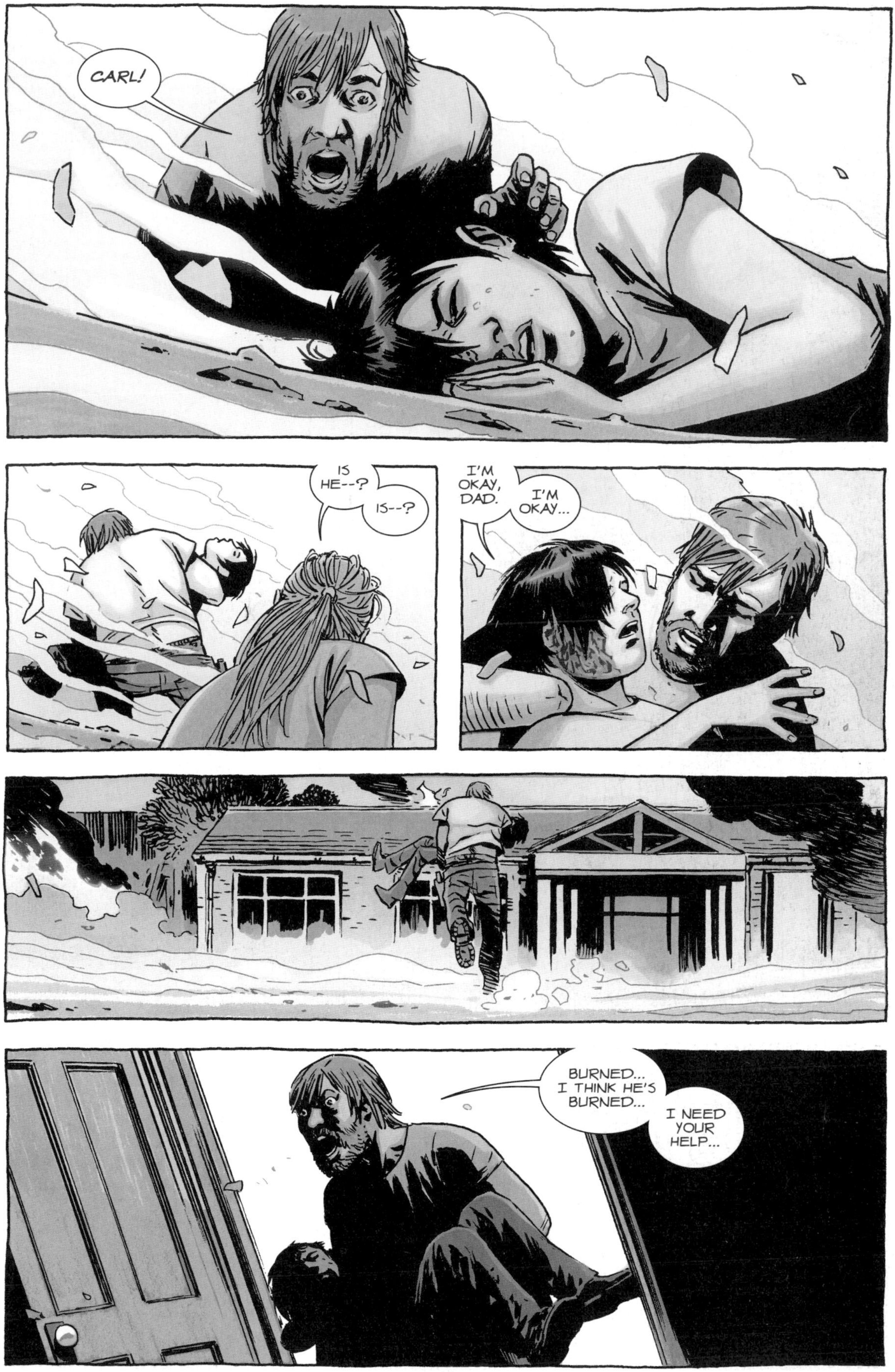
CARL!
IS HE--?
IS--?
I'M OKAY, DAD.
I'M OKAY...
BURNED... I THINK HE'S BURNED...
I NEED YOUR HELP...

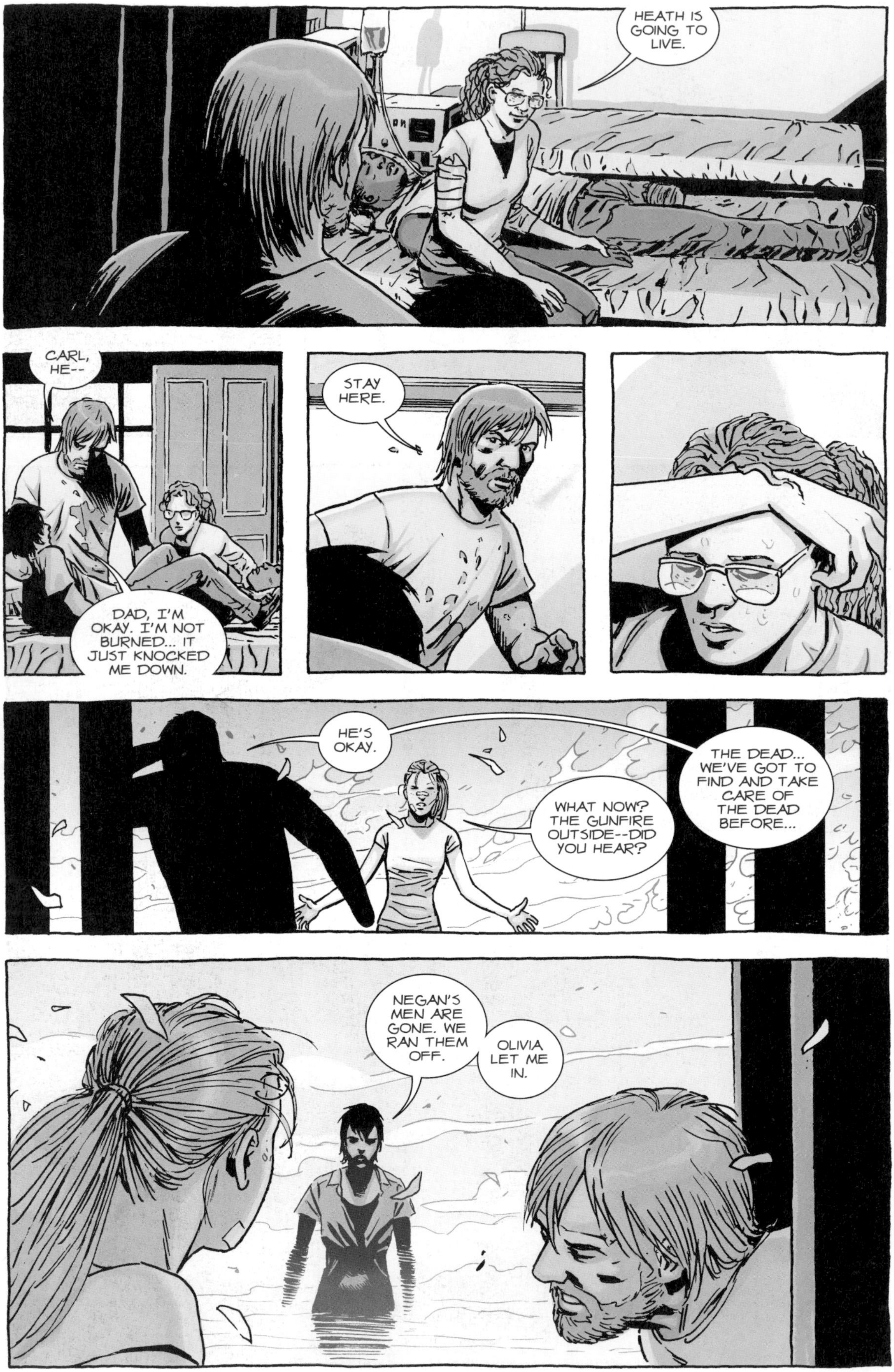
HEATH IS GOING TO LIVE.
CARL, HE--
DAD, I'M OKAY. I'M NOT BURNED... IT JUST KNOCKED ME DOWN.
STAY HERE.
HE'S OKAY.
THE DEAD... WE'VE GOT TO FIND AND TAKE CARE OF THE DEAD BEFORE...
WHAT NOW? THE GUNFIRE OUTSIDE--DID YOU HEAR?
NEGAN'S MEN ARE GONE. WE RAN THEM OFF.
OLIVIA LET ME IN.

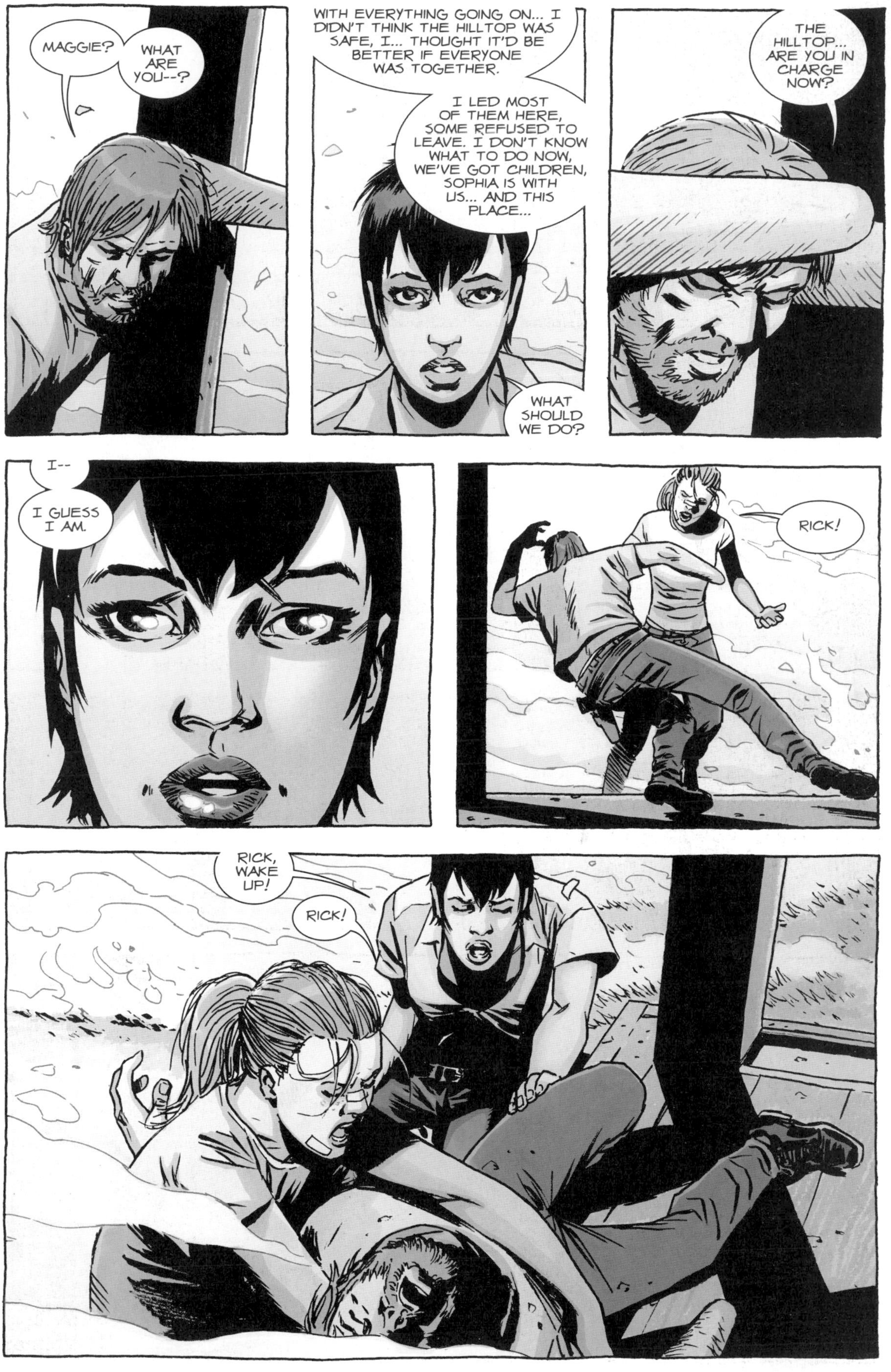
MAGGIE?
WHAT ARE YOU--?
WITH EVERYTHING GOING ON... I DIDN'T THINK THE HILLTOP WAS SAFE, I... THOUGHT IT'D BE BETTER IF EVERYONE WAS TOGETHER.
I LED MOST OF THEM HERE, SOME REFUSED TO LEAVE. I DON'T KNOW WHAT TO DO NOW, WE'VE GOT CHILDREN, SOPHIA IS WITH US... AND THIS PLACE...
WHAT SHOULD WE DO?
THE HILLTOP... ARE YOU IN CHARGE NOW?
I--
I GUESS I AM.
RICK!
RICK, WAKE UP!
RICK!

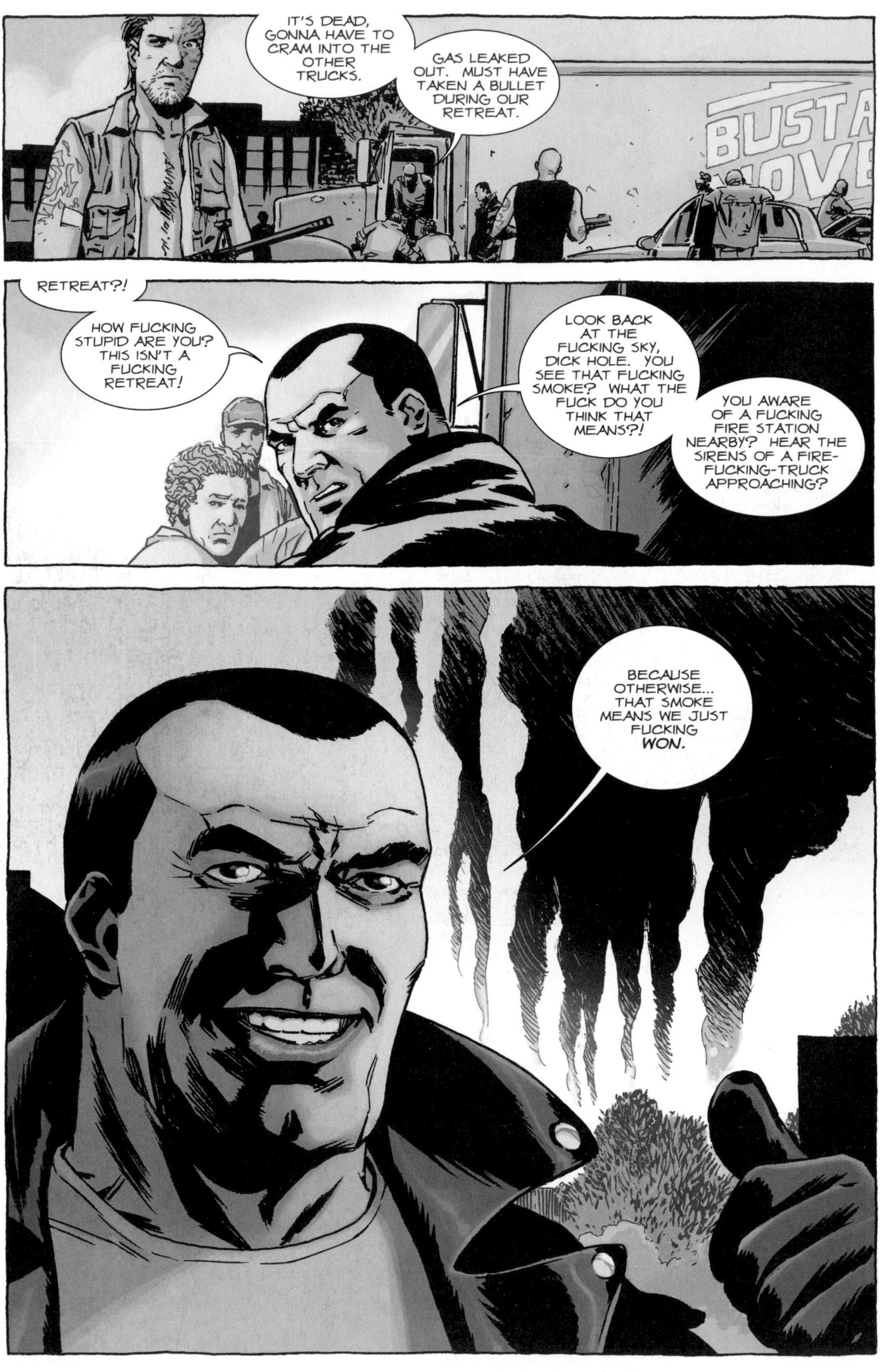
IT'S DEAD, GONNA HAVE TO CRAM INTO THE OTHER TRUCKS.
GAS LEAKED OUT. MUST HAVE TAKEN A BULLET DURING OUR RETREAT.
RETREAT?!
HOW FUCKING STUPID ARE YOU? THIS ISN'T A FUCKING RETREAT!
LOOK BACK AT THE FUCKING SKY, DICK HOLE. YOU SEE THAT FUCKING SMOKE? WHAT THE FUCK DO YOU THINK THAT MEANS?!
YOU AWARE OF A FUCKING FIRE STATION NEARBY? HEAR THE SIRENS OF A FIRE-FUCKING-TRUCK APPROACHING?
BECAUSE OTHERWISE... THAT SMOKE MEANS WE JUST FUCKING **WON.**

TO BE CONTINUED...

FOR MORE OF THE WALKING DEAD

TRADEPAPERBACKS

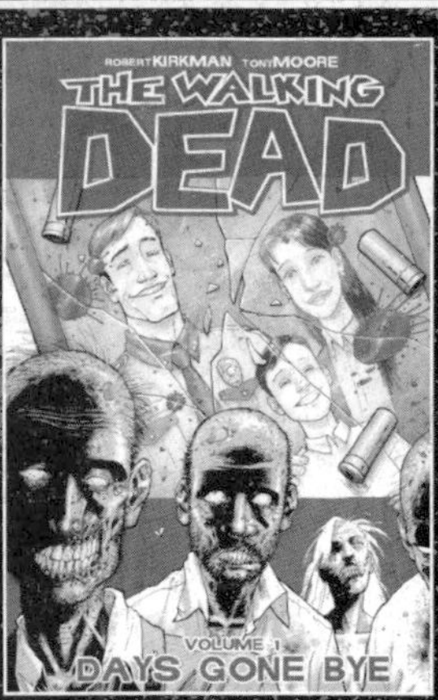
ROBERT KIRKMAN TONY MOORE
THE WALKING DEAD
VOLUME 1
DAYS GONE BYE

VOL. 1: DAYS GONE BYE TP
ISBN: 978-1-58240-672-5
$14.99

VOL. 2: MILES BEHIND US TP
ISBN: 978-1-58240-775-3
$14.99

VOL. 3: SAFETY BEHIND BARS TP
ISBN: 978-1-58240-805-7
$14.99

VOL. 4: THE HEART'S DESIRE TP
ISBN: 978-1-58240-530-8
$14.99

VOL. 5: THE BEST DEFENSE TP
ISBN: 978-1-58240-612-1
$14.99

VOL. 6: THIS SORROWFUL LIFE TP
ISBN: 978-1-58240-684-8
$14.99

VOL. 7: THE CALM BEFORE TP
ISBN: 978-1-58240-828-6
$14.99

VOL. 8: MADE TO SUFFER TP
ISBN: 978-1-58240-883-5
$14.99

VOL. 9: HERE WE REMAIN TP
ISBN: 978-1-60706-022-2
$14.99

VOL. 10: WHAT WE BECOME TP
ISBN: 978-1-60706-075-8
$14.99

VOL. 11: FEAR THE HUNTERS TP
ISBN: 978-1-60706-181-6
$14.99

VOL. 12: LIFE AMONG THEM TP
ISBN: 978-1-60706-254-7
$14.99

VOL. 13: TOO FAR GONE TP
ISBN: 978-1-60706-329-2
$14.99

VOL. 14: NO WAY OUT TP
ISBN: 978-1-60706-392-6
$14.99

VOL. 15: WE FIND OURSELVES TP
ISBN: 978-1-60706-440-4
$14.99

VOL. 16: A LARGER WORLD TP
ISBN: 978-1-60706-559-3
$14.99

VOL. 17: SOMETHING TO FEAR TP
ISBN: 978-1-60706-615-6
$14.99

VOL. 18: WHAT COMES AFTER TP
ISBN: 978-1-60706-687-3
$14.99

VOL. 19: MARCH TO WAR TP
ISBN: 978-1-60706-818-1
$14.99

VOL. 12: ALL OUT WAR TP
ISBN: 978-1-60706-882-2
$14.99

VOL. 1: SPANISH EDITION TP
ISBN: 978-1-60706-797-9
$14.99

VOL. 2: SPANISH EDITION TP
ISBN: 978-1-60706-845-7
$14.99

HARDCOVERS

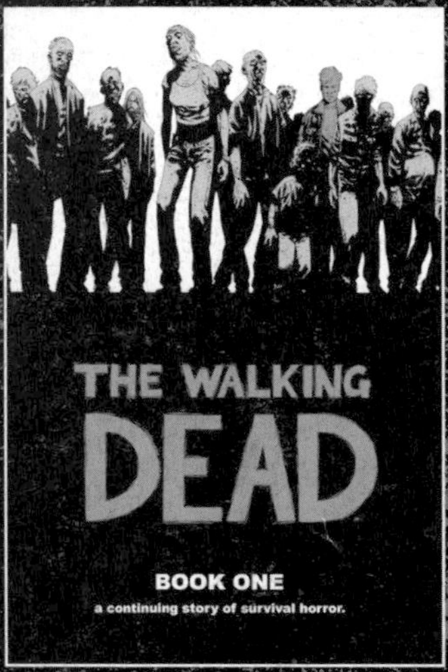
THE WALKING DEAD
BOOK ONE
a continuing story of survival horror.

BOOK ONE HC
ISBN: 978-1-58240-619-0
$34.99

BOOK TWO HC
ISBN: 978-1-58240-698-5
$34.99

BOOK THREE HC
ISBN: 978-1-58240-825-5
$34.99

BOOK FOUR HC
ISBN: 978-1-60706-000-0
$34.99

BOOK FIVE HC
ISBN: 978-1-60706-171-7
$34.99

BOOK SIX HC
ISBN: 978-1-60706-327-8
$34.99

BOOK SEVEN HC
ISBN: 978-1-60706-439-8
$34.99

BOOK EIGHT HC
ISBN: 978-1-60706-593-7
$34.99

BOOK NINE HC
ISBN: 978-1-60706-798-6
$34.99

COMPENDIUMS

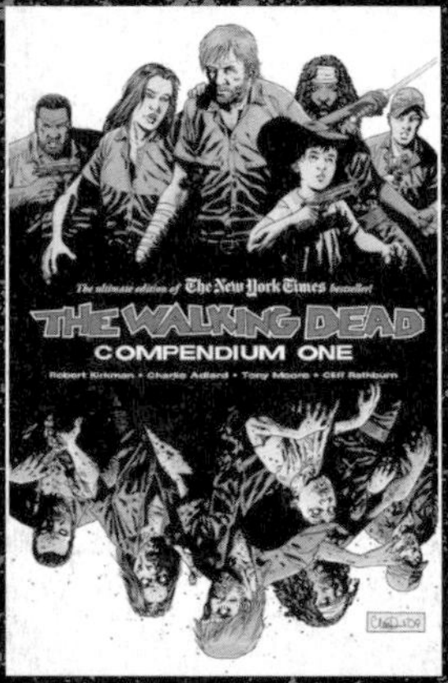
THE WALKING DEAD
COMPENDIUM ONE

COMPENDIUM TP, VOL. 1
ISBN: 978-1-60706-076-5
$59.99

COMPENDIUM TP, VOL. 2
ISBN: 978-1-60706-596-8
$59.99

SPECIALTY BOOKS

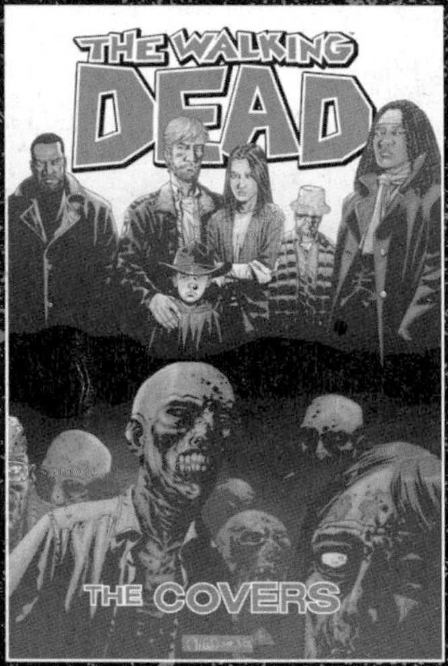
THE WALKING DEAD
THE COVERS

THE WALKING DEAD: THE COVERS, VOL. 1 HC
ISBN: 978-1-60706-002-4
$24.99

THE WALKING DEAD SURVIVORS' GUIDE
ISBN: 978-1-60706-458-9
$12.99

OMNIBUS

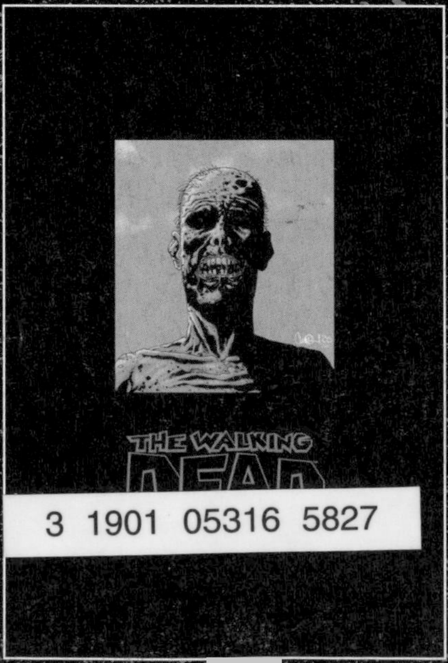
THE WALKING DEAD

OMNIBUS, VOL. 1
ISBN: 978-1-60706-503-6
$100.00

OMNIBUS, VOL. 2
ISBN: 978-1-60706-515-9
$100.00

OMNIBUS, VOL. 3
ISBN: 978-1-60706-330-8
$100.00

OMNIBUS, VOL. 4
ISBN: 978-1-60706-616-3
$100.00